THE Devil's Voyage

Books by Jack L. Chalker

THE DEVIL'S VOYAGE
AN INFORMAL BIOGRAPHY OF SCROOGE MC DUCK
A JUNGLE OF STARS
DANCERS IN THE AFTERGLOW
THE WEB OF CHOZEN
MIDNIGHT AT THE WELL OF SOULS
EXILE AT THE WELL OF SOULS
& others

THE Devil's Voyage

JACK L. CHALKER

A Critic's Choice paperback
from Lorevan Publishing, Inc.
New York, New York

Reprinted by arrangement with Doubleday & Company

ISBN: 0-931773-38-5

First Critic's Choice edition: 1985

From LOREVAN PUBLISHING, INC.

Critic's Choice Paperbacks
Lorevan Publishing, Inc.
31 E. 28th Street
New York, New York 10016

Manufactured in the United States of America

Kaiten: A miniature submarine with an explosive warhead as its bow intended to be guided to its target by a human operator sealed within, employed by the Imperial Japanese Navy in the last year of World War II. In essence, a *kamakazie* torpedo.

"For U.S. submarines, fifteen hundred yards range, sixty degrees on the target's bow, is an ideal firing position. U.S. or Japanese torpedoes would strike home so quickly—within about forty seconds—that there would be no time to swing to a course parallel with the enemy, nor any inclination to do so. Were a torpedo run of several minutes to be accepted, then Kaitens are positively indicated. Despite Hashimoto's unequivocal assertion to the contrary, only *kaitens* could fulfill the conditions of attack as he gave them. All doubts in my mind, therefore, are far from resolved. Maybe he did use *kaitens*, but, if so, why deny the fact in 1954?"

Captain Edward L. Beach, U.S.N., from his Introduction to the U.S. edition of *Sunk*, the memoirs of Mochitsura Hashimoto.

Monday,
February 28, 1944

This is a story about intelligence, and the lack of same; of The Bomb, and the bottom line of human courage and endurance; of the two sides of responsibility, the appetite of sharks, and the sharks who are human. Most of all, it's a tale about how a few hundred brave men might have been blown up, drowned, or eaten alive because Wernher Von Braun read science fiction.

February 1944 is a cold month in New York; still, on the last Monday of the month there was heavy cloudiness and a bitter-cold misty rain in the air above Floyd Bennett Field. The military officer got out of the airplane and, huddling against the elements, into a waiting staff car.

The car, too, was cold and drafty, although the heater was going full blast. It was simply too old and undermaintained; it protested loudly the attempts by the driver to put it in the proper gear.

The officer just grumbled and looked miserable in the back seat as the clutch finally engaged and they started away from the small Army airfield toward the high-rises in the distance. The driver, a lowly corporal, seemed to take things all in stride, if for no other reason than that the heater *did* have just enough output to reach *him*. To the officer it was all a part of some cosmic plot against him. In Washington the cars were fancy and dry and warm; in Washington any motor pool that allowed such conditions would find itself in Italy. In Washington they could get the parts.

There had been no need to instruct the driver as to the destination; Colonel Houlton Withers never did things unexpectedly or things that weren't completely thought out. Instead, he grumbled to himself, I spend most of my time straightening out the sloppy thinking of assholes who should be given a rifle and used as decoys in a combat area.

He clutched his briefcase in his lap as if at any moment some German or Japanese spy might jump out from beneath the rear seat and try to snatch it. The driver, noticing misery on his passenger's face, allowed himself a slight smile as he took the Brooklyn Bridge and crossed the East River into Manhattan. Small victories, but life was a series of small victories. You savored whatever came your way.

The mist was turning to a combination of rain and snow. The noises of the blower fan and the windshield wipers were the only sounds inside the car as they rode. Some were talkative, some were not; it didn't matter to the driver at all. Some were over there, in the thick of fighting, while others were here, chauffeuring around nervous somebodies in a less dangerous atmosphere. The driver had no more desire to be over there, storming some beach, than Houlton Withers wanted to be General Patton.

It didn't take long to get to their destination. New York's traffic was still a traffic horror, but far less so than in peacetime, when people could get things like gas and tires.

The Federal Building was one of several in the Wall Street

area that had been used since the dawning of the Republic. This particular subbuilding was a catch-all, used by a number of agencies from the Coast Guard to the Park service. It was old and slightly run down. But what isn't these days? Withers thought gloomily.

He didn't wait for the driver to run around and open the door. Withers was eager to get inside. He opened the door and, climbing out, said, "Wait for me."

The driver looked at his watch. "Sir, I can't stand here, Army vehicle or not. I can cruise around the block if you're going to be a real short time or I can come back at any time you say."

Withers scowled. He disliked it when the world didn't operate strictly according to his rules. "A half hour, then. And don't be late," he told the corporal.

Withers slammed the door behind him, making the doorway and getting inside with his precious briefcase before the driver had even shifted back into gear and pulled away.

The inside hall was dark and dingy. The flooring was coming up and the ceiling tiles looked like they might fall with the least provocation. He sniffed at the conditions and the dank smell in the hall and sought out the directory on a nearby pillar. He ignored the standard guard at the small desk near the elevators; Withers didn't trust anybody.

Finding the listings for the Federal Bureau of Investigation, he scanned the subdepartments until he came to the heading, "FBI Liaison, Manhattan District—4-C," nodded, and proceeded back to the elevators. The elderly guard offered him a small register to sign and he transferred his briefcase to his left hand while doing so.

Another elderly man peered out of an open elevator and Withers got in, instructing the man tersely. "Four," he said. The door closed and they rose rapidly, bringing him to his destination. He was getting himself up, now, thinking about the contents of his briefcase, thinking about how to tell the story.

Another dingy corridor. Room 4-C turned out to be a small

complex with a reception secretary. "I wish to speak to the liaison for the Manhattan District," he told her. "Colonel Houlton Withers."

She nodded, punched a button on her phone, and reported
his arrival, then nodded and hung up, turning back to him. "If
you'll just take a seat there, Colonel, Mr. Cameron will be
right with you."

Withers sighed and sat down, still clutching the briefcase.
He was used to this sort of indignity—a colonel had very little
pull at the Pentagon.

Harvey Cameron was prompt. He was a slightly built man
of medium height, balding, with a cherubic face that was
deeply lined. He looked more like a minor bookkeeper than
what he was. He extended his hand, and Withers stood and
took it.

Cameron pegged Withers quite rightly as a career Army
officer in his midforties, a man who looked like an overage
West Point cadet. *The very model,* Cameron thought sourly. *I
bet he even starches his shorts. And he has a handshake like a
wet fish.*

Outwardly, Cameron smiled broadly. "Come into my office,
Colonel, and relax," he invited. "I must say we've been curious
as to what this is all about."

As Withers followed him back to a small suboffice in the
rear of the complex his eyebrows rose in anxious surprise.
" 'We'?"

Cameron laughed. "Oh, come, come, Colonel!" Cameron
chided. "We are, after all, the FBI, not the Gestapo or Kai-
tempei." He took a seat in the padded chair behind his desk
and motioned for Withers to take the comfortable-looking
chair in front of it. Withers closed the door carefully and sat,
facing FBI Inspector Harvey Cameron.

"I'll come right to the point," Withers began, unlatching his
briefcase and rummaging through it until he came up with
what he was after—a small, digest-sized magazine. He slid it

over to Cameron, who picked it up and looked at it in sheer bewilderment.

"*Astounding Science Fiction?*" he managed.

Withers nodded. "The damn thing got through censors and everything. We should have enough personnel to clear *everything*, damn it! The only reason we even found out about it was that it has some readers among the scientists at Oak Ridge. Came in only yesterday and it was all the talk down there. One of my people noticed it and called me."

"Looks pretty harmless to me," Cameron remarked casually. "This sort of pulp stuff's been going on for years now. I'm a *Shadow* fan myself."

"This isn't a joke," Withers said coldly. "I did not come all the way up here for a joke, sir."

Cameron picked it up and idly flipped through the pages. "So? What is the big deal here, then, Colonel?"

"The lead story 'Deadline,' by a fellow named Cleve Cartmill. It's about a future war in which the government undertakes a crash secret project to build an atomic bomb through nuclear fission using uranium 235."

Cameron dropped the magazine and sat up straight. "*What?*"

Withers nodded. "We looked up this fellow Cartmill. Can't find anything on him except that he's 4-F, thirty-six years of age, and"—he paused and his face grew even more serious—"he lives in Manhattan Beach."

Cameron suppressed a snort at that one and substituted a look to heaven, but this *was* serious. "And you think there's been a leak?"

Withers nodded. "How else could this sort of thing come out? Hell, he talks of things like reaching critical mass and shit like that even *I* don't understand. It's a perfect transmitting vehicle, too. Found on any newsstand and with overseas sales including places like Switzerland and Sweden. Even if a spy here didn't get the message it'll turn up sooner or later in the hands of the Germans. We know they've been working along these lines for years—now here's our whole thing, thinly disguised and served up on a platter to them!"

Cameron sighed, seeing a fine career coming to a less than idyllic end. "Well, what do you expect me to do about it? This is the March issue—it's on sale now. Subscription copies are out, they're probably in every station and newsstand in the country by now."

"My own people will see Cartmill this afternoon," Withers told him. "Your office should deal with the magazine. Find out if we can stop it from further distribution, at least make sure the foreign copies don't get anywhere. And see if it's just this Cartmill fellow alone or whether anybody on the magazine staff is also a spy."

Cameron sighed. "I'll go over this afternoon myself," he assured Withers. "This is a matter to be handled discreetly if at all possible. I'd like to get there before your men go to Cartmill so there'll be complete surprise."

Withers nodded and stood up. "As quietly as possible," he warned the FBI man, "that magazine must be suppressed!"

The editor of the magazine, it turned out, wasn't due in that day. So Cameron got his phone number in New Jersey, called him, identified himself, and asked to see him on a matter of grave importance in his office, please, this afternoon.

The editor, a fellow named John W. Campbell, Jr., seemed puzzled but agreeable and they set the meeting for two in the afternoon. In the meantime Cameron was on a secured line to Washington getting as much as he could on Street & Smith Publications, Inc., and the people on the *Astounding Science Fiction* masthead. There was astonishingly little. Campbell was known to be right-wing politically and had supported some causes to that end, particularly in the late thirties, but he was considered loyal. On the others there was even less. Essentially nothing at all.

Cameron resolved to tell Campbell as little about what was going on as possible. Cameron doubted there was a spy ring going on in the pulp magazine industry, but there had been a breach somewhere, whether Campbell realized it or not.

Skimming the story over a hurried corned beef sandwich, the FBI agent felt a bit better. It wasn't very close to the truth, really, and its futuristic setting and purple prose tended to magnify the differences more than the similarities. One thing seemed certain, though—Cartmill knew all of the theory behind building an atomic weapon, from the ingredients needed and requirements for detonation down to its operating principles. It wasn't much of a story, really; a typical piece of pulp action writing, of special interest only to those of the Manhattan Engineering District, the most massive and top-secret project ever undertaken by the United States or any other government. And those who might want to penetrate that secret.

Street & Smith Publications, Inc., occupied a square block over on Seventh Avenue; it didn't look like much—a dingy sort of warehouse, perhaps, with some offices. There was a receptionist who directed him to a creaky old elevator and an operator who knew where to take him.

The third floor was a mess, littered with rolls of pulp paper, stacks of covers and cover stock—a true warehouse appearance. You almost walked a maze to get back to Campbell's small office.

Campbell himself was a man of medium height, stocky but not in any way fat, a sharp nose set between two bluish eyes that seemed to be looking through you with amusement at some private sort of joke. He was young, the youth accented by his military-style haircut, yet he puffed on a cigarette like he was attacking it, using a long FDR-type cigarette holder.

They shook hands. "Come in, by all means," Campbell invited, and they went into the inner office. It was even more cluttered by books, stacks of magazines, and general clutter than the rest of the building.

In some ways Campbell reminded the FBI man of Colonel Withers; a civilian version, perhaps, but still absolutely sure of himself. There wasn't an ounce of insecurity in the man, he thought. Campbell sat back in his chair, seemingly relaxed, and fixed a curious gaze at Cameron. Campbell was certainly not the way the agent had pictured a pulp magazine editor.

"Now, what the hell is this all about?" Campbell wanted to know.

Cameron had been considering all day how to say what he had to say. "There's a—ah—security problem in your March issue," he tried delicately. "Some information got past the censors somehow, and, well, it might cause great harm if it goes too far, if you know what I mean."

Campbell frowned. "Security problem? What the hell's that? You mean something's leaked? In *my* magazine?"

The FBI man nodded. "A leak, yes. One of your writers knows things that he shouldn't, and things that shouldn't be published."

The editor jumped forward in his chair with such force that Cameron jumped a bit. "Which one? There isn't much in the issue except . . . hmmm . . . the Cartmill, maybe?"

Cameron's heart seemed to skip a beat and his face clouded with suspicion. "Yes, as a matter of fact. It contains—certain material—we'd rather not have distributed right now. Particularly not to, shall we say, certain overseas readers."

Campbell relaxed. "Overseas readers? I doubt if the Gestapo could even read the magazine. Maybe a few science types . . . Say, that's it, isn't it?" Campbell's mind seemed hyperactive. "You mean the United States is currently building an atomic bomb using uranium or plutonium and Cartmill found it out?"

Cameron sighed and sank back a bit in his chair. "You know I can't tell you that," he told the other man. "Even if it were true I couldn't."

Campbell grinned. "You don't have to." He reached for the phone. "Let me call Cleve and we'll get this straightened out right away."

Cameron was on his feet. "Don't! Please! You can't get

through to him now, anyway. I—I'm afraid he's in the hands of military intelligence right now."

The editor's grin faded and he replaced the receiver and sat back down in his chair, looking squarely at the diminutive FBI man. "That's the most asinine thing I ever heard of. Hell, I've known that boy for years. He's no spy."

"Nevertheless, he somehow gained access to highly classified material and he published it in the one medium we'd be sure not to catch it in," Cameron pointed out. "After all . . . *pulps?* Next it'll be *Donald Duck!"*

"Classified hell," Campbell spat. "I remember when we tossed that idea around. Hell, man, there hasn't been a year since I took over this job when we haven't done an atomics story. It's one of the standard types, like robot stories and space exploration stories and time travel and all that. The word 'atomic' was in every good and bad science fiction story of the thirties, including mine. Atomic blasters, atomic power, atomic toilet paper—you name it. Atomic bombs have wiped out many a planet. I thought it would be interesting to our science-oriented readership to see how you might go about one."

"Then you suggested the story?"

"More or less," Campbell agreed. "I do that a lot with the local writers. They drop by and we bullshit ideas. I know I challenged Cleve on a couple of scientific facts in the story— we have enough scientists as readers that if we make any errors we get deluged with mail about it. Most of the stuff is right out of *Scientific American.* It's published. Public. Everybody who'd know what he was talking about already knows the facts."

Cameron nodded dully, thinking of all that information just lying around. The tip of the iceberg, he thought sourly. And we'd been so proud of our security up to now!

Aloud, he said, "Well, be that as it may, this sort of thing must stop for the duration."

Campbell shook his head, an expression of disbelief mixed

with contempt on his face. "Look," he responded, "let's grant you're right on the follow-up. Let's say that the German scientists get *Astounding*. Let's say they've been getting it all along, since before the war, even."

"Fair enough," Cameron allowed.

"Now, what happens if they notice that there are no more atomics stories? Up to now, as I said, they've been common. If you put a censor in here and he starts getting rid of what they think of as normal, somebody's bound to get suspicious fast, right? It's the absence, not the presence, that'll be noticed. As for 'Deadline'—what were you thinking of doing?"

"Confiscation," came the reply. "Get back as many copies as possible, block the ones still unsold."

Campbell laughed drily, not believing what he was hearing. "And what do you do? So you go into the New York Public Library and yank the March *Astounding*. And all the newsstands just in the New York area. You *might*, with sufficient manpower, get away with it. But we're national. Do you have any idea of the number of libraries and train stations, newsstands, and drugstores that carry the magazine? Thousands nationwide. Any spy worth worrying about is bound to spot it. And if your supposition is right about the Germans getting all the issues, then what will it say to them when the March 1944 issue—and *only* the March issue—doesn't show up? No, Mr. Cameron, you're in the position of the bank manager who comes in the next morning and sees that he forgot to close the safe the night before. You want to call the cops, put up signs that the safe's unlocked, then sit back and wait to be robbed. If I were you, I'd just close the damned safe door before anybody else showed up and not mention it to anybody."

"I'm not sure whether that's possible," Cameron told him. "I'm on the horns of a dilemma here—and you don't know what kind of people military intelligence are."

"Up to you," Campbell said calmly. "But consider my argument, too. Consider that you have committed a far more serious security breach by simply coming here—and certainly by picking up Cartmill—than you ever would have by ignoring that story. Now two men outside of government, outside your project, outside everything, in very public jobs, know that the U. S. Government has a major project to create an atomic bomb using U 235. With that knowledge alone, were I a disloyal American, I could probably, with a little help from the library, figure out who was working on it—and, if I were a spy, I could then find at least one, maybe more of those men. Blow your whole cover. You think about *that*, Mr. Cameron. You tell your intelligence people that. Tell 'em they better lay off me, Cartmill, *Astounding*, and everything else."

Cameron sighed. "I'm afraid you're right, but, as I say, it's not up to me. The FBI is not even in complete charge of security—the Army is, and they tend to think a little differently."

"You spell it out for 'em," Campbell urged. "Somewhere in military intelligence is a jerk who has some."

"I'll think about it, but no promises," Cameron responded. "What I need from you is help. If you have back issues of any other atomics stories, as you call them, that will help—particularly if they're prewar. I also would like a list of your staff—people likely to have had immediate access to the story before its publication. It's purely routine, you understand, but it's better to have me handle it than someone else."

Campbell nodded. "I think we can handle that—although it's a *lot* of people, you understand. And it's wasted motion, anyway—when you can buy the damned thing on any newsstand."

"I know, I know," Cameron conceded, "but it has to be done." He got up and so did Campbell. "I think I can be assured of your complete cooperation and discretion?"

Campbell grinned. "Why not? You'll have people on me anyway." He put out his hand across the desk and Cameron took it. They shook, and the FBI man turned to go.

Just at that moment the windows started rattling like mad and the whole world seemed to shake. Odd noises and vibrations were everywhere. It felt like an earthquake. "What the hell—?" Cameron managed.

Campbell laughed. "They're just running the presses," he assured the startled agent. "Happens every time. One good reason why I wasn't coming in today."

Cameron just shook his head, muttered incomprehensibly to himself, and walked out, barely glancing at a small woman carrying some ad paste-ups who at that moment seemed to be trying to keep things from falling off shelves from the vibration.

Anna Kaminski was a second-generation American without a disloyal bone in her body. She worked as a clerk at Street & Smith mostly as a glorified messenger, carrying paste-ups of ads from the big make-up room to the presses. She hadn't meant to be there just after Cameron entered Campbell's office, hadn't really meant to do more than kill time until the editor was free. She was going to burst in on them—there was always some writer or other in the office when he was there—but heard the magical phrase "security problem" and decided to wait. Quite by accident, Anna Kaminski heard the whole conversation.

She knew, of course, that she shouldn't say anything about it to anybody. She'd seen the "Loose lips sink ships" posters in the subway and she wouldn't betray her country for the world, no, sir. But, of course, she had to tell *somebody*. . . .

Before quitting time at Street & Smith most of the lower-echelon office staff knew it. They blew it up and distorted it, of course. But none of them were disloyal, they all swore their friends to secrecy, yes, sir.

And, of course, those people had husbands, wives, and lovers and a very dull and boring existence, what with the war so far away and even the lights of Broadway blacked out.

Eventually, of course, it reached the ears of someone who found it of more than ordinary interest. He was not a great secret agent or a man on the lookout for enemy information but he was associated with agents who he knew would find such information useful. They might even pay for it.

Even this man wasn't truly disloyal. Under no circumstances, except maybe for a price a lot higher than he could expect, would he tell a Kraut or a Nip agent anything, knowingly or unknowingly. He was a loyal American, yes, sir.

But the Russians, now, that was different. . . . They were our Allies.

Wednesday,
March 1, 1944

Viktor Lemotov was a survivor. At the age of fifty he'd survived the Czar, the Russian Revolution, the terrible years of the twenties, and the forced-labor programs and purges of the thirties. He'd risen steadily, a man who had shown himself capable and useful. Instead of being arrested in Stalin's purges he was in OGPU, the state security committee, doing the arresting. He was good at it. He arrested all the people on his list and got them all to confess. He arrested people *not* on his list and got them to confess, too. Occasionally he found total unknowns and accused them of being traitors when he couldn't find the real traitors. Even they had confessed.

Yet his most valuable trait was his ability to hide his intelligence from his superiors. He made the right friends in the Party. He socialized and held his liquor remarkably well. He passed all the advancement tests with just enough and no more.

The system amused him, really. Little bureaucrats with littler minds, so shallow they seemed almost hollow to him. Yet they were the people with the power. What foolish little people they were! And when something went wrong, well, hold a purge, blame the other guy. He wondered, idly but often, who would pay when the war was over for allowing Germany to attack his country. Certainly not the head of state who ignored the warnings or the sycophants on the Presidium who were there because they agreed with whatever the deadly little Georgian thought.

He felt himself well out of it; he was in America now, in Washington, D.C., as the agricultural adviser. He often chuckled at that. He had a real nightmare that, sometime after the war, they'd be inviting him to Kansas or Iowa or someplace like that for a series of better-yield-through-efficient-farming demonstrations.

He didn't know much about farming. People were his crop. His country required a strong set of agents deeply hidden within the U.S.A. for the postwar period when old alliances might falter. For now that alliance made everything much simpler; the stupid Americans treated the U.S.S.R. as just another major ally, certainly not a country to be feared or spied on. At least he hoped so. Paranoia came with the job, too.

Thousands of reports came across his desk each week from the active agents already in place. The Americans were incredibly free with their information, even in a wartime situation; a whole subdepartment gathered incredible amounts of intelligence simply by reading through the nation's newspapers and magazines.

In general he could dismiss most of the reports out of hand with a simple glance; most repeated old information or had very little new to add. Now, though, sifting through the huge piles, tossing a lot of them into the red can marked "burn" or occasionally into a follow-up basket, he noted one his assistants had "red tagged" a new bit of information. He read this more closely.

According to the report federal agents had swooped down on a pulp magazine and investigated everybody because they had printed something that was a state secret. Not much, he told himself. Follow-up reports as to what the "state secret" might be ranged from the wild to the impossible. Still, it was plausible. He leaned over his desk and lifted the intra-embassy phone.

"Sarachevko, will you come in a moment?" he asked pleasantly. Within thirty seconds a younger man who reminded him far too much of himself at that age rushed in. "Sir?"

He tossed the report over to the assistant, who picked it up and glanced at it, then shrugged. "So? Like a hundred others," he commented, tossing it back to his boss.

"And the odds are that there's nothing to it," Lemotov admitted. "Still, check it out. Have our people in New York see if such an investigation was actually carried out. If so, put more people on it, find out the reason for that investigation. It shouldn't be hard—just plug into the inevitable rumor mill and —hell, I shouldn't tell you how to do it. If you weren't competent you wouldn't *be* here."

The aide leaned over and picked up the file once more. "It will be done, sir." He turned to go.

"Sarachevko?"

"Sir?"

"Quickly. By the end of the week, if possible?"

"I'll try, sir," the aide replied and left.

It took eleven careful days, but Sarachevko walked into Lemotov's office in the Soviet Embassy looking pretty pleased with himself. Sarachevko bowed slightly, then threw a copy of a digest-sized magazine on the spy master's desk. Lemotov picked it up and looked at it curiously.

"Astounding Science Fiction?" was all he could manage, reading the title.

His aide nodded. "That's what it's all about. The security-leak business up in New York. You remember. It was easy to narrow it down to the magazine from the employee gossip; finding the story with the leak was a bit harder—we tried to track down every writer in the issue. Quietly, of course. We needn't have bothered. A fellow who lives out in Long Island and wrote the lead story there is the man. Army Intelligence just oozes around his house—he's a virtual prisoner."

Lemotov looked suddenly very interested. "And the story?"

"A project," Sarachevko said quietly, "to manufacture an atomic bomb. The kind of bomb that works like the sun and wipes out whole cities in one flash."

Lemotov's mouth pursed and he let out a low whistle. "An atomic bomb. The Germans have been working on it for some time but came up a failure. Of course, we knocked out a lot of their research facilities on it. So, what do we know that we didn't know before?"

"The Americans are trying to build an atom bomb in total secrecy," Sarachevko responded, citing the obvious.

His boss nodded. "Just so, just so. You know we have such a project ourselves?"

The aide was startled. "We do?"

The older man nodded. "Yes, been on it for some time—but we just lack the specialized scientists needed in this area."

"But the mere fact that they have a project for it doesn't mean the Americans have the bomb," Sarachevko pointed out. "After all, bombings or not, the Germans have managed to come up with every feasible technological advance they set out to get. If *they* couldn't do it then it might just be, well, science fiction."

"I agree, it may well be that way," his superior admitted, "but we don't dare take the chance. Suppose the Americans come up with it in the latter stages of the war? Suppose the Germans invent it next week? A bomb that could turn Moscow or Leningrad into a tiny sun—from one bomb, Sarachevko! From one plane! We have to *know*. You realize that." He suddenly grew calm and very businesslike. "Which Army group is handling this?"

"We followed them at change of shift, photographed them, tracked them all over," the aide told him. "They are very good, but they *do* seem to report to, of all things, the Army Corps of Engineers, Manhattan Engineering District."

Lemotov sighed. "A local New York outfit, then. Not what we're after."

Sarachevko allowed himself a proud smile. "No, not New York. Very little in New York. The intelligence group works right out of the Pentagon. Run by a Colonel Houlton Withers of Fairfax, Virginia."

The spy chief grew thoughtful. "A Manhattan Engineering District located in Washington—in headquarters, yet, right in the War Department. This is getting interesting, most interesting. And who does this Withers report to? Colonels are only leg men here."

"A Major General Groves, about whom we've been able to learn almost nothing," the aide told him. "But you're right. It's Withers who is on the move. Groves we can't locate but Withers is right here. He used to be a supply officer, so maybe Groves was, too."

"I want Withers shadowed day and night," Lemotov ordered. "I want to know how many times he brushes his teeth and why. I know we're helpless within the Pentagon but sooner or later our colonel will lead us to the atomic-bomb project."

Sarachevko nodded philosophically. "And, of course, he's all we've got."

"No he isn't," the spy chief responded. "We have other names. If it's atomics they're after then Einstein is probably involved, but indirectly. They have a lot of other good scientists courtesy of Herr Hitler, though. Fermi, Bohr—many more. They'll be shadowed, of course. Well covered by Army and FBI. I want to know where all the men likely to be working on this are now. Companies likely to be involved. That sort of thing. A project this big can't be hidden—that was the Germans' problem. It exists only in complete anonymity. Well, it doesn't have it anymore. We'll find it. We'll find it and we'll find out if they have actually built the bomb. Put everybody we can spare on this, Sarachevko. Everybody. I want to know as much about this project as Franklin Roosevelt. Move!"

Washington, D.C. Wednesday, August 16, 1944

"Harvey! Harvey Cameron!"

The FBI man stopped in the parking lot of the Pentagon and turned in puzzlement to see who on earth could be calling him.

"Over here!" he heard a deep, pleasant voice approaching him and finally he spotted the man running through the tangle of parked cars.

"Jim?" Cameron called back hesitantly, then, seeing the other man clearly, breaking into a broad grin. "Jimmy boy! How the hell are you?"

The two men shook hands warmly. The newcomer was a tall young man, the sort of person they used for Marine public-relations posters. A shade over six feet, muscular, with short-cropped sandy brown hair and eyes of the deepest blue. Thirtyish at best, he had the look and bearing of a movie star.

James Tyler Fargo laughed and put his arm around the

older man. "So they've got you in on this too, huh? I should've guessed."

It was Cameron's turn to be surprised once more. "You're going to the staff meeting?" He could hardly believe that anyone under the rank of chief inspector would be involved.

Fargo nodded. "I've been working around the outsides of this thing the past year and a half," he told him. "Mostly security screenings, the usual routine. Shocked the hell out of me when I got the call to come here."

Cameron was puzzled yet pleased to find a familiar face. This was the military's preserve and the military's game. The FBI was just providing some support services—at the "request" of the President, he knew, and against the wishes of Army Intelligence.

"Come on, let's get inside," Cameron suggested. "It's hot as hell out here and I hear those generals have refrigerated offices."

The younger agent nodded and they walked together up to the side entrance of the Pentagon they'd been instructed to use.

Fargo was equally relieved to see Cameron. Back when Fargo had just graduated from FBI school and was on his first assignment Harvey Cameron had been his supervisor. The older man had already become something of a living legend by the end of the thirties, rising quickly as the assistant to the godlike Melvin Purvis. Together Purvis and Cameron had tracked down the most notorious gangsters of the thirties. There was a widely held belief in the minds of the young men who worked for Cameron that he fired the fatal shot that felled John Dillinger. Cameron always shrugged it off with the comment that everybody present shot the man.

Cameron had all of Purvis' determined detective skill and a love of the game but none of his mentor's flair for publicity. In fact, Cameron had shunned it, allowing his boss to take all the glory and get his picture in all the papers.

Cameron had taken a liking to young Jim Fargo, seeing in

him some of the same qualities he had at that age. They had worked together for more than three years, and developed an almost father-son relationship. Cameron had no children and Fargo had lost his father at a very early age, factors that had accelerated the friendship. Even after Cameron had been transferred they'd kept in touch through correspondence and an occasional phone call.

"Who'd ever thought we'd wind up together here, of all places?" Fargo said unbelievingly.

"Well, we always said we were going to get together and talk old times," Cameron laughed. "Seems somebody was listening."

They were inside now, facing a reception desk. A gruff-looking Marine sergeant whose face and bearing said that he'd rather be in the war than at a desk looked up at them. "Yes, sirs?"

Cameron and Fargo each produced special orders and their FBI identification. The sergeant inspected them closely, as if he expected to detect some sort of forgeries. Finally he handed them back and said, "You'll have to be escorted." He twisted around in his chair, and seeing a sentry barked, "Meyers!"

The sentry approached on the double. "Yes, Sergeant?" He was as stiff and upright as a cartoon soldier.

"Take these men to Taft 416 in the blue," the sergeant ordered. "Then report back to me."

The young Marine nodded and turned to the two FBI agents. "Follow me, gentlemen," he said and set a brisk pace down one of the corridors.

They were stopped a number of times, their papers and IDs checked and rechecked as they went along. Some of the corridors in the labyrinth of the Pentagon were actually blocked with prison-style gates that had to be operated from inside.

"I feel like I've been sentenced to Alcatraz," Cameron muttered sourly. Fargo just chuckled under his breath and whispered, "It's just as bad as where I came from."

Cameron raised an eyebrow. "And where's that? All your

letters have been postmarked Albuquerque. I kind of figured you were in Siberia."

Fargo shook his head as they continued to walk, following their guide. "No, nothing like that. I was down at Site Y. You —you *were* in New York, weren't you?"

Cameron nodded. "Damn! I'm getting out of condition for this sort of thing. You'd think in a building this big they'd have trains or moving walkways or something. I don't understand how some of those fat generals make it to work every day."

Fargo noted the change of subject and accepted it without comment. "They have their own private entrances," he told the older man. "Probably have privates to push 'em to their offices in rickshaws or something."

They both chuckled at that and Cameron didn't fail to notice that their young Marine guide was suppressing a smile.

"You have any trouble working with the Army?" Cameron asked him.

"Not much," Fargo replied. "They're mostly pretty good Joes. They're more than happy to have somebody else do the work and take the responsibility from them. The only problem I've had is with their operations boss. He works out of here so I don't see much of the officious little fart but one time is too many."

Cameron played a hunch. "He wouldn't be a bird colonel named Withers, would he?"

Fargo almost stopped in his tracks. "Yeah, that's him," he replied, a little amazed. "You know him?"

"Only briefly. He mucked up a minor matter in New York last winter and I had to move heaven and earth to cover it. I tell you, Jimmy, I don't like his type much. The Constitution is a minor inconvenience to men like that."

Fargo nodded but didn't press the matter. Such talk in the lair of the enemy was better backed away from. Cameron could be in hot water if their young Marine were in Withers' employ, cross-services or not.

"How much farther is it, son?" Cameron asked their guide. "My legs are giving out."

"Almost there, sir," the sentry assured them. "See the elevator ahead? We take it and once you're downstairs you're about where you want to be."

At the desk outside the elevator their IDs were checked again and this time their thumbprints were, too. Fargo looked at Cameron and silently mouthed, "Withers." The older man nodded and smiled wanly.

Another sergeant took over now, first unlocking the desk and removing a large ring with a lot of keys on it, then finding one and putting it in a slot next to the elevator. A small light went on, and a few moments later the door slid open. Inside was a civilian operator and another Marine, this one armed.

They dropped what seemed to be at least six floors, then stopped. The Marine with the keys pushed back the metal gate and fitted another key into the door. A latch gave and it now slid back revealing another long corridor filled with servicemen and servicewomen of various branches going this way and that. Waiting to greet Cameron and Fargo was a youngish-looking major. They stepped out and the elevator closed behind them. Cameron at least felt like the gates of hell had just slammed shut behind him, trapping him forever. He'd never felt so claustrophobic before. It was the atmosphere of the place, he decided.

"I'm Major Conklin, gentlemen," he introduced himself. "May I see your orders, please?" They handed them over for his inspection.

The major gave them only a quick glance and handed them back. "Sorry. Security and all that," he apologized. It was the first human gesture either man had encountered since entering the Pentagon and they were grateful for it. The major looked with concern at Cameron. "You look tired. Rough trip?"

"Only once I got inside this rabbit warren," Cameron managed. "I think we've been walking for the last three days."

The officer looked surprised. "Why didn't you park in Lot

B? The entrance is only a couple hundred feet from the elevator."

Fargo looked knowingly at Cameron. "The orders said Lot N," he pointed out.

Major Conklin sighed. "It figures. 'B' and 'N' are next to each other on the typewriter." He shrugged. "Well, you're here —and a little early, too. Come on down to the conference room and relax. I have some coffee and doughnuts there. You can relax until the others get here."

"We're the first?" Fargo asked unbelievingly.

"Well, most of the others are already here, work in the building. So they'll come in just before time."

They nodded and followed their new guide to a set of imposing double doors that said only "Conference Room 287" and had the insignia of the Corps of Engineers on it. Fargo and Cameron entered and stopped, aghast. It was a *huge* hall, complete with movie screen, stage, podium, all flag-bedecked, with a long semicircular table around the raised platform large enough to accommodate several dozen people with no trouble. In a pinch you could put a couple hundred folding chairs in back of the conference table, Fargo thought.

Cameron seemed to read his mind. "Consider the implications that this is Conference Room 287," he muttered.

There were small nameplates in front of each seat—the seats, they saw, were swivel chairs of pure brown leather—and in front of each, aides were scurrying around putting packets of papers all stamped "Top Secret" in bold letters at top and bottom.

Majors, they understood, were errand boys in the Pentagon. Conklin pointed out their seats to Fargo and Cameron and left them, probably to receive the next dignitaries.

Fargo and Cameron made for the large silvery coffee urn and the boxes of glazed doughnuts next to it. Fargo poured a cupful of coffee for himself and Cameron and took a sip, then made a face. "Well, it's good to know that even the generals get bad coffee in the Army," he commented.

Cameron chuckled and gestured with his head back toward the conference table. "Did you notice the nameplate over there, third from the left?"

Fargo shook his head from side to side. "Uh-uh."

"Withers."

"Oh."

Cameron looked up at the younger agent a little nervously. "And I don't suppose you noticed the nameplate next to yours?"

Fargo was genuinely interested. "No, who?" he said, looking over.

"It says 'Mr. Hoover,' Jimmy. Just Mr. Hoover."

Fargo almost choked on his doughnut.

Major General Leslie R. Groves, commander of the Manhattan Engineering District, entered with an entourage of other high-ranking brass and several officious-looking civilians, all of whom took their seats quickly. Next to the distinguished-looking general was Colonel Frank McCarthy, Secretary to the General Staff, and next to him was Brigadier General Anthony Bruse, chief of security for the Manhattan District, and his chief aide, Colonel Houlton Withers. Fargo and Cameron looked at Withers with a dispassion they didn't feel and Cameron leaned over and whispered, "Well, with a boss who looks like that it's more understandable." Fargo just chuckled and nodded. Bruse looked like a heavyweight boxer who'd had one too many fights, the kind of man you were always afraid you'd meet in a dark alley.

To Groves' left sat Dr. Robert Oppenheimer, the civilian head of the project, and a number of distinguished aides from his far-flung yet hidden scientific and industrial empire.

Mr. Hoover's seat remained empty, somewhat to the relief of the two agents. Finally a large, hawk-faced man entered, looked around somewhat apologetically, and made for the director's seat. He nodded to Groves, who was staring at him.

"Deputy Director Moulton, sir," he introduced himself.

"The director extends his regrets but he was summoned to the White House this morning on a different matter, and you can understand which call takes precedence."

Groves gave a hint of smile and nodded.

"I've been in charge of this section anyway, so I guess I'm the logical man to be here," Moulton concluded.

General Groves took in a breath, reached down and picked up his attaché case, opened it, and pulled out a sheaf of file folders. "Very well, then. I think we're ready to begin," he said quietly. "Dr. Oppenheimer? You want to begin?"

The man in the gray ill-fitting suit looked up at them through thick glasses. "All of you here have had the maximum security check and have been involved in one aspect of this project or another almost since the start," he began. "Most of you have been involved with the remarkable security we have achieved, and that is the basis of this particular meeting. Gentlemen, what I am about to tell you is something that must never leave this room. Once I tell you there is no turning back." He leaned back a moment and studied their faces. Just a brief glance said who was hearing all this for the first time.

"As you know," he continued, "we launched this Manhattan Project over two years ago as part of an ongoing project that started long before. You know that we have been engaged in trying to harness the very power of the sun, to create a weapon so terrible that, many of us hope, it will end not only this war but also all wars in the future. It depended on us being able to take the atom, the basic building block of all matter, and break it up—break it with such force that it will create a chain reaction, breaking up other atoms with which it comes in contact, in effect nullifying matter. Such a bomb would be impossibly powerful. A single bomb could conceivably destroy an entire city. No enemy could withstand it. It would make Dresden look like child's play. The nation that develops this bomb will win the war—and, we hope, insure peace in the future. We are not alone in this quest, you understand. The Germans have been working on it for a great many years and it has taken a lot of brave men's lives to slow them down. We got a lucky break there in any event—they took a wrong path. What is lesser known is that Dr. Yoshiro Nishina has been working along the *right* track for the Japanese. Although intelligence indicates he is being slowed down by troubles getting certain materials, we are in a race with him. The good news is that we are about a year and a half ahead of him." He paused, took a deep breath, and looked at them gravely. "We believe that we can now build the bomb. We have, in fact, started building the bombs. The first of these will be ready, we hope, by the spring of next year."

"We are already starting to train bomber crews on how to use it," Groves added. "By the time the bombs are ready we'll have an experienced flight team ready and able to deliver it, providing, of course, our boys can secure—and I mean *secure* —a landing strip close enough in to use it."

One of the operational military men, Army Air Force from his wings, looked surprised. "I assume by that you mean the assumed target is Japan. I'd think Berlin would be more likely."

Colonel McCarthy took that as his own cue. "While it's true that Berlin would be the ideal place, remember the time scale," he reminded the others. "The Normandy landings have been secured. Our boys are pushing into France right now. We can't stop them even if we wanted to—remember, just because we're on the Continent in two places doesn't mean that the Germans are finished. If they get the momentum, the offensive, they could still push us right back to the Channel. We're talking about the spring of 1945 at the earliest. By that time we'll either be kicked out or we'll be driving into Germany itself. If the former, then our special bomb group will, of course, be located in England or Scotland. If the latter, it would be foolish to bomb them that way. Japan is a different story. We're lagging behind there because of the European effort. It's going well, but even if we take everything we're going to face a massive invasion of the Japanese home islands. We need bases for our boys in *both* theaters."

"I hope the bombs do not have to be used at all," Oppenheimer put in. "I hope that, by the time we are operational, there will be no war and no reason to use them. Still, this conference has been called because we can't assume that."

Groves nodded. "Current events, the military situation at the time, and, of course, the President's decision about whether to use the bomb all could make our efforts needless," he admitted. "However, we can't assume that. We must be prepared. This preliminary conference is being held because we must assume the worst. If that is the case, it is now time to think about our two basic security problems." He looked over at General Bruse, who rose stiffly and spoke.

"We have two operational security problems," he said crisply. "First, the bomb, when operational, will have to be tested. If the scientists are right it's going to be a hell of a bang, impossible to keep totally secret. We can only minimize it—which is why Site Y was established. It's desert, a proving ground, and sparsely inhabited. Only two small towns are within the estimated visual range. Many of the people in the towns work for us, of course, but the FBI has been checking everyone, including the regular inhabitants." He glanced, not a little disdainfully, at Fargo, who felt suddenly uncomfortable. The spotlight had shifted to him along with their gaze. He hadn't been told in advance he'd be expected to report.

"My team has done a thorough check on the people involved," he assured them with more confidence than he felt. "We know those people better than they know themselves. All lines of communication have been monitored and will continue to be. Anyone who reacts in any uncharacteristic or unusual ways will be known, I assure you. Also, the mountain and desert landscape is ideal for securing from outsiders. Any new people, even casual passers-by, are carefully checked out. We feel we can monitor, halt, or do whatever we want with anyone who comes near the area, all so quietly I doubt if they'll even know it was done. This is an ongoing process. There are over three hundred agents, both from the Bureau and on loan from Army Intelligence, involved. Nothing can ever be said to be a hundred percent secure, but I think this is as close as human beings can come." He sat back down, feeling fairly well satisfied with himself and relieved it was over.

Withers made some sort of grumbling sound. Bruse turned to him. "You don't agree, Colonel?" he prompted.

"No I don't," Withers growled, not getting up. "I think it's almost a miracle it's gone this far. This security should have been exclusively in the hands of the military right along. Breaches have occurred and been laxly sealed." He looked straight at Cameron. "It's only dumb luck we haven't been compromised. It's my feeling that if this bomb's all you say it is then it'll be compromised the moment it's tested despite all the precautions."

Groves' eyebrows rose slightly. "And what would you propose if you had a free hand there?"

"Move 'em out," Withers responded unhesitatingly. "Clear the area entirely of everybody not connected with the project."

Deputy FBI Director Moulton, who to this point had said nothing beyond his self-introduction, leaned over and whispered into Cameron's ear, "You're an expert on the dangers of overkill, aren't you, Harvey?"

Cameron started, then suddenly realized why Moulton had him be here. The chief inspector's report on the fiction-magazine business had been most scathing of Withers and the dangers of drawing attention by overreaction.

Fargo was there first, though. He was feeling particularly pissed off. "Wait a minute. Dr. Oppenheimer: How far could this blast be detected?"

Oppenheimer shrugged. "Nobody knows. Conceivably it could be seen and felt for hundreds of miles."

Fargo smiled slightly and turned back to Withers. "Would you clear Albuquerque, then? They might see something they shouldn't. We can't secure a city of that size."

Withers was too intent to recognize that as a taunt. "Damn right," he came back. "The whole goddamned state of New Mexico. My boys could do it in a matter of a week or two."

Cameron saw his opening. "And in so doing you would put up a neon sign visible in Tokyo and Berlin for all to see," he said sharply. "Such a move could not be hidden. The cover stories will attract more attention than they cover up. You'll tell not only everybody in New Mexico something's up, but also every foreign agent within thousands of miles. It's easier, cheaper, and much better from a security point of view to invent a cover story for a big blast than for moving out the population of an entire state."

"But you can't be *sure*. . . ." Withers objected, voice trailing off weakly as he became aware he was losing the debate.

"Nor can you," Cameron retorted. "Until this moment I had no idea that it was New Mexico we were talking about but let's consider it. Not a large population, but large enough and scattered as well. There will be those in the back country who'll be missed, Indians on large reservations, prospectors, maybe. Spies, maybe—who, alerted that something's up, will take extra precautions to see that they have ringside seats. I think there's less security your way than there is now."

Withers started to protest but Groves cut him off as McCarthy scribbled furiously. "I have to agree with the FBI here, Houlton," the project chief told him. "Not only for security, either. This isn't Germany and it doesn't have to be. Perhaps if we'd had to make this decision in 1942 or even last year it might be different, but we're talking about a war we're winning. At least we were still winning in this morning's Washington *Post*. Have you heard anything differently, Colonel?" He looked straight at Withers.

They could see Withers' fury boiling inside him; hands clenched and unclenched and he seemed to be having trouble with a little facial twitch—but there was nothing wrong with his survival instincts. Two stars far outranked one silver eagle. He swallowed hard and managed, "No, sir."

Groves nodded and turned back to the others. "All right, then. We will depend on our colleagues in the FBI for external security as usual, and will lend them any personnel or other assistance they require for their jobs. Mr. Fargo assures us that Site Y is under control and can be secured at any time. Internally, though, things are different. That is an Army matter. For the military portion of this the tables must be reversed, and there, I trust, we can leave things in the hands of General Bruse and the colonel, here."

There was no dissent, although Oppenheimer cast a less than pleasant look in Withers' direction.

"The second problem is moving the bomb," Groves continued. "At this point we don't know in which direction the bomb will have to be moved—Atlantic or Pacific. Doctor? How would you suggest a move?"

Oppenheimer cleared his throat. "My staff is working in the dark, you understand, General," he said apologetically. "No matter what, though, we are talking of taking the bomb thousands of miles from here. I'm not really concerned with the bomb casings or arming mechanisms—those we can turn out rather easily. But it takes tons and tons of uranium ore to produce just the thimbleful we require for the bomb itself. That and the complex triggering mechanism that must be integrated with the material is large, complex, and with our current technology virtually irreplaceable. The bomb casings can be flown, but I would prefer the fissionable materials to go by a separate and, perhaps, more gentle means."

"The guts of the bomb, then, by ship," Groves interpreted.

Oppenheimer nodded.

"An all-services proposition, then," the general summed up. "FBI and Army Intelligence to provide security at both points, the Navy to carry the guts of the bomb, the Army Air Force to drop it." He sat back, thinking for a moment. "We'll leave the actual ship until the last moment. It should be a large, fast ship, of course—but I can hardly ask for one to be diverted now. We'll have to leave that until the last minute, which we don't even know yet. When we're set to move I'll want Intelligence on that convoy so thick nothing can get at it, and I want FBI support at all vulnerable points along the route. Whichever ship we use should also have some people on it. I want no chance of slipups. In addition to the usual security I want men we can trust on that ship. The Navy need not know about them."

Withers nodded intently, looking over some papers. "How many, sir?" he asked, not looking up.

"Up to you," Groves told him. "Could be up to a couple thousand men on a battlewagon, though. At least half that on a heavy cruiser. We have to have enough to be able to mix with the various elements of the crew and just look and listen. They have to be good, though—so unobtrusive nobody will suspect them. That means a very small number, since any large force will tip things off. We have to add them as just regular replacements."

"Sir, if I may?" Jim Fargo intruded.

"Yes?"

"I was in the Naval Reserve—still am, technically. A capital ship is like a small town, sir, not New York City. Our purpose is information gathering for security, not a huge guard force. The ship's personnel can do that. And if any of our people uncovers anything the ship's a closed prison, with lots of men aboard to help. Like all small towns, particularly out in the middle of an ocean with no place to go, there's gossip, talk, you name it. Scuttlebutt. It runs up and down the ship from the lowest deck-swabber to the captain. If you have just one man in each key section they'll know anything that's going on by the second day out even if they're new."

Groves nodded thoughtfully. "All right, then. How many people do you think we need?"

Fargo shrugged. "Four or five ought to do it, sir, I'd think. A small enough number. Any ship putting into, say, Norfolk or San Diego would take on more men than that. I'm sure they could be easily hidden. And they'd be enough to get what was going on. A mixture of the high and the low, enlisted and officer. If it's a capital ship, maybe add a Marine."

Groves turned back to Withers. "Colonel?"

"For once I have to agree," Withers admitted. "I'll have to check with ONI—hopefully you could ease that—but I'm sure we could come up with five excellent choices."

Colonel McCarthy looked up from his steno pad for the first time. "I'll make certain you have no trouble with interservice rivalries, Colonel," he said flatly. "Any problems and they'll explain to General Marshall himself. You'll have no problems."

Groves seemed satisfied. "All right, gentlemen. I think that's it for now although I expect we shall meet again once or twice before we are ready to go and we'll certainly keep in contact. Mr. Cameron, would it be a hardship if you were to join Mr. Fargo at Site Y? I'd like an old hand there—no offense, Mr. Fargo, this is more for internal harmony's sake."

Fargo shrugged. "There's nobody I'd like more to work with—or for—than Harvey," he assured the general.

Cameron looked resigned. "About the only problem I can think of is Mrs. Cameron. Moving from New York to Dustville, New Mexico, or wherever isn't going to thrill her all that much, particularly now, in the summertime."

Groves chuckled. "We all have to make sacrifices, Mr. Cameron. There's a war on, you know. I'm sure she'll understand if you put it like that."

"You don't know my wife, sir," Cameron responded glumly.

Groves got up from his chair and packed his material back into his briefcase. Some of the others did the same. "All right, then, gentlemen, until we meet again, that's all."

They all got up to go without much conversation. A few stretched, and Harvey Cameron started groaning a bit about the long walk back to the car.

General Bruse and Colonel Withers walked down a different corridor to the general's office. Once inside his inner sanctum, both men took off their formal uniform coats and relaxed. Withers went over to a small private bar and poured them both a Bourbon on the rocks, bringing one to the general.

Bruse sipped his, sighed, and leaned back in his chair. "Well, Holly? What do you think?"

Withers shrugged philosophically. "I'll get the job done. If there are any breaches it won't be from our department."

"It better hadn't be," Bruse warned him. The tone was friendly but the threat was real. "I want you to pick those men personally, Holly. I want every one of them checked top to bottom, interviewed by you, certified by you, responsible to you. I want no slipups."

Withers nodded somberly. "I know what you want. Give me a few weeks with ONI files to pick my people, then I'll be able to assemble the team."

"Get it out of the way," Bruse urged. "After all, we still have the proving grounds to do, you and I."

Withers drained his drink. "A lot of shitwork," he said morosely.

"We all fight the war in different ways," Bruse soothed.

The Soviet Embassy
Thursday,
August 17, 1944

Vasily Sarachevko was cautious but pleased. "There's been a meeting," he told his superior.

Viktor Lemotov was interested. "Where? And how did you hear of it?"

Sarachevko chuckled. "We've had Withers under surveillance since February. He's a hard man to keep track of. At least three times he's boarded private courier airplanes for place or places unknown. His superior, General Bruse, works out of the Pentagon and rarely leaves it, but *his* superior, General Groves, is almost never there. Where he is we don't know —yet. Still, we have people trying to keep them in view where possible. We also put people on some of the peripheral men involved, FBI included. Yesterday, our people tell us, a large number of the principals, including all I have just named, met in a two-hour or so meeting at the Pentagon. Something's

definitely up. For one thing, the FBI man who handled the
New York thing is being transferred out West."

"West?" Lemotov's interest perked up even more. "Where
'out West'?"

"Don't know—yet. But he is highly regarded in his department and we can take it that such a move coming only a day
after a meeting here is significant. Almost as interesting is that
he stayed a bit yesterday, actually changing to a later train, so
he could have dinner and socialize with a younger agent he
apparently knew. That agent is due to fly at least as far as
Albuquerque, New Mexico, today according to United Air
Lines, the first of the companies he's using. I have people on
him and on the transferee, Cameron. Between the two we'll get
a pretty good idea of what the final destination is."

"It's remarkable," Lemotov mused, shaking his head. "I
was about to call this whole thing off. Eight months with nothing from that improbable lead!" He smiled sardonically. "Patience, Vasily Ivanovich. The greatest virtue in our line of
work. Second is tenacity." He suddenly looked straight into the
eyes of his assistant. "Did you know that at one time or another most of the major physicists in this country, most particularly the refugees from Herr Hitler's *pogroms,* have worked
together? No? A bit *too* together, it appears. Some would cross
normally, of course, but everywhere there seems to be a link
with the code word 'Manhattan.' Manhattan Engineering District, Manhattan Project, and so forth—yet the city of New
York is barely touched by these."

Sarachevko was impressed. "So *that's* why you kept me on
this other thing."

"Once things started coming in they fit together fairly
nicely," the spy boss told him. "I'm still impressed. They have
managed to keep a huge project such as this involving thousands—perhaps many, many thousands—under an effective
cloak. But now, I think, we *know*. Not all of it, certainly, but
enough. It is serious business, my young friend. Grave for our
country—a threat in its own way worse than the Germans."

"The thought of a General Patton with such a terrible weapon is grave indeed," the other agreed. "I do not forget Churchill's views on our future, nor the fact that there were American troops in our homeland at one time, too, during the Civil War."

"It's more immediate than that, I fear. That is the long-term view, one that I cannot appreciate while the short-term problems are upon us. After all, we are currently allies. The world is war-weary. Too many young people of all our countries will never grow up."

"I'm from Stalingrad," Sarachevko reminded him somberly. "My family was there."

There was no adequate response to that except to nod gravely and go on. "It's not Patton and Churchill I fear right now—it's MacArthur with this bomb."

The aide was startled. "Huh?"

"Germany is losing," Lemotov explained, "but she is losing slowly. There is a lot of fight left in her, a lot of potential for grave destruction. Her defeat is, I think, inevitable now—but in how long? Months? A year? Two? And look at our poor country, Vasily Ivanovich. Devastated. Ravaged. We can do nothing until Germany is disposed of. Nothing else, that is. Then we will need a period of time to regroup. To pick up the pieces, as it were. It is certain that, with the American attack so consistent, Germany will fall before Japan—but once Germany falls, America will turn its fighting machine on Japan. If America can turn and conquer Japan before our own country is ready and able to enter that war, well, then, we shall have no say in the peace. No say in what happens to Manchuria, Korea, the Kuriles—or Japan itself. It would be the Americans pretty much all alone. Add this superbomb and you see where we stand. Nowhere."

"Surely our own government is aware of this," Sarachevko argued. "Obviously we declare war on the Japanese the moment the Germans surrender."

"I wish it were that simple, but it is not," his boss replied.

"You ignore the realities, including the reality that our army is six thousand or more miles from where it will be needed. In addition, it is dependent on a single-track railway. We'll need time, my young friend. Time to assess the situation in an unsettled Europe. Suppose they have this bomb now? At least, suppose they have this bomb before Germany goes under? Ten such bombs and you destroy the major cities, the population, the industry, the government. The war is abruptly over by default. But if they had to invade the home islands—invade with a huge force and fight for every inch of ground—*that* takes time and effort and the same kind of shift *we* require. We must make sure that that bomb is not dropped. For the sake of our future."

Sarachevko sat back, slightly dazed by all this. "You have reported home on this, surely?"

Lemotov nodded sourly and gestured at a small stack of diplomatic cables. "Oh yes. There's agreement on this every place except where it counts." He sighed and gave the cables a nasty look. "We are allies, you see. Uncle Joe may have some reservations about Churchill but he *trusts* Franklin Roosevelt. Dear old FDR. So open, so free with information, so trusting. Stalin just won't believe that kindly, idealistic FDR would hold out on him. He is convinced that, were the Americans making an atom bomb, he would have been told of it."

"It's Germany all over again," Sarachevko said unbelievingly.

Lemotov's eyebrows rose. "You could get shot by sentiments such as those," he warned but his tone was mocking, not threatening.

The younger man wasn't upset by that idea. "We could get shot for not finding this out and doing our best to counter it, too," he pointed out.

"Exactly my idea," his superior agreed. "Now you see the bind we are in, my friend. Our continued welfare and well-being depend on us making certain that this bomb is not used against Japan."

Sarachevko sighed in resignation and got up.

"Where are you going now?" Lemotov asked.

"First I am going to sample some excellent vodka in my office," the aide replied. "Then I am going to pull out every stop, put every available agent on this. Finally, I might stop by a good metal shop and see if I can be fitted for a bulletproof suit."

Lemotov did not laugh. Such thoughts were too close to his own.

Sunday
October 29, 1944

Houlton Withers had reason to be pleased with himself. Out of the hundreds of names the sorting machine had provided him for his so-called Covert Security Team he believed he'd chosen three men who'd provide excellent backup—a physicist with the Navy's research and development wing; a senior-grade chief who was expert in damage control and dangerous-weapons disposal; and a Marine sergeant with the Bronze Star, every combat citation in the book, and a burning ambition to avoid returning to the war, an ambition Withers would gladly help him realize. Withers liked men with solid records, men you could depend on, and, of course, men who would be willing to do something for him if he in turn would turn a favor their way.

But the fourth and last man, Lieutenant John Coringa, was not merely Withers' man but also his property. Everybody had something you could use as leverage. Find a man's weakness and you could make him jump through hoops for you, Houlton Withers believed—and why not? It had always been so for him. Coringa was perfect. The sure thing, the ultimate operative. With Coringa aboard, Withers knew, it would be as if he himself were accompanying the precious packages.

John Coringa was the kind of officer everyone instinctively hates. NROTC, so he didn't rise through the ranks or come out of Annapolis, he entered the service with the absolute conviction that his education and his commission made him truly a superior form of human being to the "EMs," the enlisted personnel he would boss and whom he considered less than human.

Coringa had an attitude that to be an officer was to have power and command respect automatically; he gloried in it, reveled in it. He hadn't been much before—a social wallflower, only child of a protective, moderately well-off family. His father had done pretty well in real estate in Racine, Wisconsin.

Coringa had been an ugly, ungainly youth, short, thin, pushed around by the big guys. Generally he identified as a youth with the "before" examples in the Charles Atlas ads in the pulps.

Coringa discovered early on, though, that there were other ways of gaining mastery over people. If you wanted to quarterback football, first own the ball and second have your father own the lot you played on. It made things simple. His father didn't own the candy store, but he did own the mortgage on it.

The University of Wisconsin had made Coringa an accountant, and his ownership of a car along with a suspiciously endless supply of ration coupons to feed it gave him a social life he otherwise would have lacked. Still, it always seemed like somebody else wound up in the back seat with the girl, while he was relegated to driving.

He knew he'd have to go into the service. His draft notice would beat his diploma, most likely, and there were a lot of men better educated than he sloshing through Europe's mud with a rifle and a pack. It was the social appeal of the uniform more than anything else that made him choose NROTC—also a guarantee that he'd be allowed to graduate before they gave him that gun.

When they'd pinned those two little gold bars on him he knew his future was made; an officer, an accountant—he'd be a purchasing officer somewhere, he knew. Somewhere safe and comfortable.

Safe and comfortable it was, but there were a lot of accountants in uniform and the service really didn't need any more right then. So they sent him to school for a few weeks and put him in charge of an SP unit in San Diego.

It took a little while before the men working under him discovered that it wasn't just an NROTC punk but an all-around skunk they'd drawn. He was the sort of fellow who'd come in and tell an off-color joke expecting a laugh, yet when you relaxed around him he'd freeze and accuse you of a lack of respect. He was so disarming that you were constantly surprised when he shafted you.

There were plots, of course. Lots of them. In the Army such men generally learned quickly in combat or they died. On ship they might find themselves in the middle of an ocean on a dark night. In San Diego they talked about bribing some unsavory Tijuana types to mug him or spirit him away but, like most such plans, it never really came to anything. He was a rotten guy to work for but not the kind you'd want to get angry.

If Coringa was nasty with his own men he was a terror with those they brought in. Those arrested for even the most minor infractions had the book thrown at them. Nobody got a break in the 3341st, nobody. And if they were particularly lowly, common seamen, he was almost sadistic. He baited them, he played with them like a child with new toys.

As unpopular as he was with the enlisted men, though, he was very popular with the officers whom he considered his social equals. He was the life of the Officers' Club parties, ready with the joke, and absolutely gushing with flattery for higher-

ranking officers and their wives. Far from being a tough war
he was having the time of his life—and, thanks to his uncanny
ability to say just the right thing to his superiors at just the
right time and to the terror he placed in his enlisted personnel,
he was promoted fairly quickly, too. Every promotion gave
him more status, more power, more men to bully. Here he
was, only two years in, with two shiny silver bars for each
shoulder and looking for the big one, the jump to a gold leaf,
as soon as regulations permitted.

That was, until that one evening late in 1944 when they'd
brought in two very drunk Marines, both mere privates, who'd
gone a bit too far in town that evening and had started busting
up the furniture. They didn't like getting picked up very much
—it'd taken four men to subdue each of them—and they didn't
like getting cussed and threatened by a snotty little Navy bastard, either. They were drunk enough to tell him so, too.

"What the hell do you think you were doing, you lousy
creeps!" he screamed at them as they stood there, handcuffed,
being booked. The CQ, a youngish chief, just looked briefly in
embarrassment to heaven and continued writing.

"Ain't no goddamned fuckin' Navy desk jockey kin talk
t'me or m'friend like that," one of the Marines snapped back,
drunken but angrily. "We jes' took 'part a dozen better'n you."

Coringa stared at them, speechless, his face glowing a deep
red. "How *dare* you talk to an officer like that!" he fumed. "I'll
lock you away forever, you mindless substitute for a human
being! That's not drunk—that's insubordination!"

The talkative Marine staggered a little, then smiled with
yellowed teeth at the smaller officer. "No, sir! That ain't in-
suborginashun," he tried. "*This* is."

And with that he spit foully into Lieutenant John Coringa's
face.

For a moment Coringa just stood there, looking incredu-
lous, as if he simply couldn't believe what had happened. All
he could think about was his nice clean uniform and how this
must look to the nine enlisted men on his own staff who looked

on. He thought he could hear some of them snickering, and that was intolerable.

Something snapped.

Without even realizing what he was doing, without thinking about it a single instant, he attacked the Marine, shoving him against the wall and beating him. The Marine, drunk and shackled, tried to defend himself by bringing up his knee and pushed Coringa away with enough force that he was flung back against the CQ's desk. The lieutenant roared; none on his staff had ever seen him like this, almost an animal himself. He grabbed a billy club that was on the desk and flung himself back onto the Marine, who was still struggling to get back up, and he started beating the man with the club over and over and over again, again, again! It felt good to do it, satisfying, his rage seemed to concentrate into his right hand and into that club.

Fear of their officer and absolute shock at what they were seeing rooted the other SPs in the office for a moment, then, as they realized what was going on, they leaped on him, pulling him off the Marine, trying to pry the club from his hands. Such was his fury that he knocked one in the mouth and it took the same four who'd subdued the Marine earlier to force him to the floor and hold him there until the rage subsided.

As they held him they thought him wild, insane, like nobody they'd ever seen before. His eyes were wild, he seemed almost to be foaming at the mouth, and he kept screaming threats at them if they didn't let him go. It took almost ten minutes for him to calm down and the light of reason to creep back into his dark brown eyes.

He seemed to snap out of it as suddenly as it had overtaken him and looked around a little puzzled. One of the SPs went over to the Marine bleeding on the floor and examined him hesitantly, then raising the man's head and looking into staring, unseeing eyes.

"Jesus Christ, sir! I think you killed him!" he breathed.

They'd covered it up, of course. Officers just don't do that sort of thing. Somebody had to take the fall, naturally, since the dead man had parents, a commander of his own, and an outfit of his own. Fortunately, the other Marine was too drunk to give very much testimony. The others could be blackmailed into a better story—a most unfortunate incident, that poor drunk attacking the officer like that. They'd pounced on him because the Marine was berserk and, in the scuffle, a few too many hits, a little too hard. So sorry. Reprimands all around, including for Coringa, but nobody served any time for it. Involuntary manslaughter. Like accidentally hitting somebody with your car. And everybody was transferred not only to different bases but also to different parts of the world.

As for Coringa, he was in charge of Records in the main SP unit in Norfolk now—three thousand miles from it all and out of any contact with prisoners and the seamier side of life. It wasn't the same, though. They'd cover up, yes, but they'd never forgive. They *knew*. Everybody knew. And even if they didn't, *he* thought they knew.

It took the edge off the sure and certain knowledge that he'd gotten away with murder, the ultimate in power and position. He felt no remorse, though, only an odd fury when he thought of the Marine—the man who'd spoiled his good life. No gold leaf now, that was for sure. Counting paperclips until the war was over, that was all that was left for him now. No more life of the party—he was shunned by his fellow officers, imagined every whispered conversation was about him, every group at a table that suddenly broke into laughter was laughing at him.

They didn't know, of course. Few did, for all the difference it made. You'd never have convinced Coringa otherwise.

One who did know was sitting now in Coringa's office in Little Creek, a prefab Navy community halfway between the base and the city, looking at him with complete satisfaction.

Quickly and matter-of-factly Colonel Houlton Withers gave the same explanation to Coringa as he had to the other men on his security team, heard the same questions and objections, and answered them in much the same way.

But this one, he was different.

"Look, Coringa, let's be frank. You have a blot on your record and you're in a dead-end job," Withers told him. "You know it and I know it. But I'm giving you a way out. Nobody on this ship will have any information on your real past or background. You'll be just another officer to them, just one more new man. You won't be working for the SPs, either— you'll be working for me, through ONI. These others—they're good men, but they're not *my* men. They're guesses on my part and on the part of Naval Intelligence. You're my backup—*my* man on that ship. In addition to watching the crew you'll be watching the watchers—and the whole operation. There can be no screwups on this. None."

Coringa just stared at him and said nothing.

"Pull this thing off flawlessly, without a hitch, and you'll find yourself in a whole different Navy—a bright future, status, good job, maybe even a lieutenant commander's stripes. The past all washed away. Fuck this up even one little bit, and I mean one teensy bit, and there'll be no cover-up. I swear to you that you'll be the goat. You'll take the fall, no cover-ups this time. They've all got their jobs and I have mine. Some of them outrank you, others don't. Makes no difference. I have you in my hands, Coringa, and you are responsible. You. You alone. You understand me?"

Coringa nodded expressionlessly. He didn't like the tone of this conversation or this strange Army man one bit. Yet it was the chance for redemption, for a clean slate.

Withers relaxed and took on a more kindly, fatherly look and tone. "Now, son, you can refuse this. Tell me no and I'll walk out of here—several men already have. I'll walk out, all you do is forget we ever had this little chat, and that's that. Everything's the same as before."

He knew what the answer would be. There was really no choice. "I'll do it, sir."

The colonel nodded in satisfaction. "Sorry to be so hard on you, son, but you have to go into this thing with no illusions. This thing's so big that it will cream *me* if it goes bad—so you can see where that would leave you."

Coringa just nodded.

Withers got up and gave him a big smile. "But I know you'll come through. Good luck, son. You'll hear from me in the spring."

Long after the colonel had left, Coringa just sat there, mostly not even thinking. He felt strange, disassociated from his mind and body. Finally he sighed and got up. Nothing would louse up his new friend, his guardian angel. Nothing. By God, this one would be flawless! No slipups. None. He'd see to it.

"You are responsible," Withers had said.

Coringa had been crucified and he was damn well not going to let anything or anybody get in the way of his resurrection.

Anybody.

Thursday,
November 2, 1944

"There's your list," Sarachevko told his superior, tossing a small, neatly typed sheet on Viktor Lemotov's desk.

The older man picked it up and looked idly at the names. "So few? How can you be so certain?" he asked skeptically. "There are barely twenty names here."

"And yet, that's the sum total of personnel outside his normal duties that our Colonel Withers has seen in the past few months. And, fortunately, he spends most of his time on his fat hindquarters right here in Washington. You note the similarity between the names?"

Lemotov nodded. "All Navy personnel. Not an Army man among them. No naval aviation, either. So it's to travel by ship."

"Probably as soon as they test a prototype," the younger man agreed. "If, in fact, they intend to do so. I would say they would, considering the nature of the beast. We *did* lose track of our colonel twice in the past three months. Where could he have gone but to where they are building it or where they will test it? I am satisfied that among the names on that list are men who will help transport the superweapon to the Pacific Front. We're keeping a close eye on all of them, naturally, from now on."

"Anybody there we can use?" Lemotov wondered. "It would be most convenient to have our own man aboard."

"There are some indications that one or two might be reachable—but we don't know how much time we have. A week? A month? A year? And what if we choose wrong? All they have to do is get any notion whatsoever that we're on to their secret and any chance we have will go out the window. No, I think that would be a last-resort strategy. We have a good idea it's going by ship. It's almost certain to be a major ship leaving from one of the Pacific ports, and we have those very well covered as you know."

Lemotov sighed, wishing there were some surer way of doing it. Since there wasn't, and since he was feeling more insecure than ever with each passing week of inaction, he shifted the subject. "Any progress on where the thing is being made and where it will be tested?"

Sarachevko smiled confidently. "The scientists were mostly grouped in the Chicago area, and from what we can tell the big work is being done in southeastern Tennessee. We think, however, that it will be tested in neither of those places, but rather in the deserts of the West. I don't have that site nailed down as yet, but it's only a matter of a few more days. There were a *lot* of Party members among the top of their classes in the past decade, and many of those are now in high places as you well know. The problem hasn't been getting the information—the problem has been sorting through the tons of it we are getting, looking for materiel and manpower orders that fit what we are looking for."

"Take whatever staff you need," Lemotov told him sharply. "I want the where if not the when as soon as possible. I want it yesterday. Our lives and our country's future may depend upon it."

Okinawa
Saturday,
March 31, 1945

Captain Charles Butler McVay III walked to the edge of the
bridge of his huge vessel and looked at the panoramic view
from in front of the armored plates. It was cloudy and dank
and extremely misty but visibility was still more than a mile.
In front and behind him he could see the massive naval firepower in strict formation as it had been the past week. It was
impressive. The ships were large, their massive guns, all five-
inchers or more, all trained upon the island that could be
clearly seen to port. Almost sixty miles long, the island was
less than two miles wide in the middle—narrow enough for his
own ship, the U.S. heavy cruiser *Indianapolis*, to have fired
upon an enemy force on the opposite shore of the island.

For seven days now they'd bombarded key points on the island with regularity; by the end of the day they would have
carpeted the key landing beaches on the island with over
twenty-seven thousand rounds of heavy shells. They were now
off the once-beautiful, now pockmarked Hagushi beaches,

the places where, tomorrow, thousands of Army and Marine troops would land and move inland against stiff Japanese opposition. The *Indianapolis* had participated in the bombardment of many islands in the long Pacific campaign and acted in support of carriers in many key naval battles. It was also the flagship for Admiral Spruance, the man in charge out here. This battle would be different. Okinawa was less than eight hundred miles from Japan; her two airfields would allow routine bombing of the Japanese home islands with the same ease that England had been used to bomb Germany in the later stages of the war. More, this island was part of Japan—it was one of Japan's forty-seven prefectures, with a seat in the Japanese Diet. Its fall would mean a great deal psychologically both to the United States and Japan.

It was, McVay thought, what Hawaii was to the United States. The mental blow would be just that severe.

Flags went up all along the line; the order to come to a full stop was given although some adjustment was needed to maintain exact space and interval between the shelling vessels. They faced no danger from shore batteries, not now, nor were the airfields much help, but from elsewhere in the Ryukyus and perhaps as far away as Japan herself had come planes, bombers, fighters, and most especially *kamikazes*. The last in particular had taken a toll on the naval bombardment force. At L-Hour tomorrow morning, Easter Sunday, the total landing and support force would be over thirteen hundred ships, the biggest operation since D-Day.

"Commence firing!" came the order throughout the ship, and almost as one the various ships in the line opened up on the beaches. This was particularly important today. After the initial bombardment Navy frogmen would go in to clear the landing area of mines, debris, and anything else that might impede the landing force.

McVay hadn't been captain of the *Indianapolis* long but he loved the ship and the command. His father had been a great man in the Navy. The elder McVay, now a retired admiral, had started with the invasion fleet at Santiago in the Spanish-American War, had gone on to command the *Saratoga*, the *New Jersey*, and the *Oklahoma* in the First World War, then commanded the Washington Navy Yard, the Bureau of Ordnance, and had retired as commander in chief of the U. S. Asiatic Fleet. McVay's grandfather was a banker who had rescued the Naval Academy from its near collapse during the Civil War and helped build it into the finest institution of its type in the world.

There was a sense of tradition in the youngest McVay and a total love for the Navy. He simply could not remember wanting to do anything else or be anywhere else.

What he'd always wanted was command of a cruiser, the kind of huge floating city that was almost a battleship yet had the speed and maneuverability to do a multitude of jobs. *Indianapolis* herself was an old cruiser, built in 1932, more than 610 feet long—more than two football fields—and over 66 feet wide at her extreme beam.

She was an odd-looking craft, too, almost like two ships on a single hull linked by a single seaplane catapult and hangar in the middle dividing the superstructure neatly into two sections with a stack rising from each section. She bristled with 20mm and 40mm guns that were equipped with the latest in electronic and radar guidance and had shot down six planes during the bombardment. Crews stood ready at the guns now, watching the skies for the inevitable Japanese attacks. It was the two forward batteries and one rear battery of huge eight-inch guns that shelled the beach.

All those not directly involved with the bombardment or air defense watched the show as usual. Everyone was at battle stations just in case, although there was a general feeling among the crew that their ship was charmed, that even if hit, as it had been before, nothing could sink it. The watchers' thoughts were all the same as they watched the beaches become a massive blur of smoke and flame.

No living thing could possibly live through something like that.

And yet they knew that it was not so. Though it might move them back temporarily, few enemy were ever killed in such a bombardment. Mainly it knocked out shore-gun emplacements and detonated mines. It set up the enemy for the soldiers.

CPO John Coyle felt the ship shudder every time it let loose its terrible volleys. He checked out his gun emplacement, nervously looking at the gray skies. Although it was March, it was hot as hell and the air was thick with humidity. The only thing he could tell his complaining gun crew was that it was even warmer in the hot boxes of those eight-inch guns.

"Fresh air," he told one complaining seaman with a light chuckle. "Best thing in a bombardment. Just sit back and try and keep from going deaf."

The seaman relaxed slightly, then looked covetously at the big gun forward. "Yeah, but ain't no machine-gun bullets gonna get to 'em, Chief."

The NCO feigned a laugh at the little joke and looked back up at the low ceiling. It was *always* a low ceiling around here, damn it, he thought worriedly. You could have a dozen squadrons of Japs coming in on you and never know it. You'd never hear them over the tremendous thunder and vibrations of the bombardment.

Almost on cue he heard the alarms sound, creating an eerie modern symphony with the sounds of the big guns and he raised his binoculars to his eyes and searched the sky.

Ships more than a half mile down the line started opening up and gun crews on *Indianapolis* and several companion ships turned and angled to get in shots at the attackers. There were dozens of them, tiny specks like distant birds circling over some dead carcass. It was a familiar sight by now but each day it had seemed there were more of them.

The ship itself came to life now as they made ready for a mobile defense. The bombardment was lessened until the interlopers were dispatched.

The small guns of the cruisers and destroyers joined in trying for the planes. Like the ground bombardment it seemed to everyone that nobody could possibly fly through that. Still, for every plane that came down with a crash in the sea there were tremendous plumes of water where bombs struck and on the decks of some of those ships men were dying in machine-gun blasts.

It wasn't the bombers or standard Zero fighters they all feared, though, and as a new flight came through the clouds their greatest nightmare was realized. They watched as unbelieving now as the first time they'd seen it, small planes with huge bombs strapped to their underbellies disregarding all incoming fire and steering toward the biggest ship they could, deliberately, methodically.

Kamikaze!

Even now they just couldn't grasp what drove those men to do it. To die in battle was one thing; even to fight to the death, as most of the Japs had, was in some ways acceptable. They could understand that. But to climb into a plane for a flight you *knew* would be one-way was inconceivable. Scuttlebutt said they were hypnotized, or brainwashed, that their planes' landing gear fell off on takeoff and their bombs were automatically armed, but nobody really knew and nobody could really understand.

Of course their single-minded suicidal charge from the air made them easy targets. Most were shot down in huge balls of flame but some got through, crashing into the ships. Occasionally Coyle's battery and a number of others on the ship, which was now under full steam, took their shots at the attacking planes but this time they never came close enough to *Indianapolis* to be direct threats.

And now, as quickly as they'd come, all was over. There was a lot of burning oil on the waters, and a couple of ships far up the line had taken some hits but it was nothing serious. They moved on up the coast now, reforming their bombardment group, as a new cast of ships recommenced the shelling of Hagushi beaches. They would continue north to bombard a few other, smaller beaches just on the off chance that they might mislead some Jap commander into diverting forces there. There was even to be a diversionary landing on beaches far to the south of Hagushi for that purpose but nobody in higher command thought anybody would be fooled. It was just something you did because there was that one chance you might save a life by it.

After the last feint the group would disperse and reform for the trip back down, hopefully timing it so the frogmen could go in between volleys. Then they would relax, regroup, and form a protective picket that evening for the massive number of troop transports that were even now approaching the island. A huge number had already arrived.

There were no other air attacks near *Indianapolis* the rest of the day although some of the staging-area ships got hit hard.

McVay brought the ship around and headed out to his assigned night position. It would be a busy night and an even busier morning; they would have to help cover the transports from air attack until 0800 hours, then provide cover and support for the landing. One last bombardment and it was the groundhogs' show.

Even the perpetually nervous Coyle felt relaxed; all was going very nicely now and he felt confident not only of *Indianapolis*' survival but also of the fact that this was the last hard duty he'd see for some time. Unless they invented some new islands or something really funny happened, they would spend a good deal of time ferrying Admiral Spruance around and eventually get back home before the big one, the invasion of Japan itself, got rolling. The men liked Spruance, a cruiser man himself who seemed to share their love and affection for the *Indianapolis* and who, when aboard, was never so high and mighty that he wouldn't visit and talk with the lowliest of seamen in the lowest of jobs. But the main thing was that the admiral could have had a big, fancy new carrier or a massive battlewagon for his flag but he'd chosen *Indianapolis*. They knew it and loved him for it.

McVay, too, was well liked. He seemed to be everywhere and know everybody, no mean feat for a command that had twelve hundred men in it. He was strict and kept a spit-and-polish sheen on the old girl, but that was natural for a flagship. The crew knew he expected them to be the best and look the part, too, but, like Spruance, he was no snob or distant ruler. He shared their love for the ship and told them often that they were partners in the entire enterprise, with the ship their boss and mistress. He had a way of making even the lowliest deckhand feel an essential part of the ship's operation.

They believed in themselves, their commanders, and their ship and took tremendous pride in her. It was an odd, almost textbook love affair between twelve hundred men and one mighty woman.

The nervous seaman cocked his head. "Hey! Chief! You hear something?"

Coyle frowned and turned, listening hard. The ship was knifing through the water now toward its rendezvous point; the sun was partially out reflecting on the Pacific's blue water, giving it a beautiful color but also a blind spot on Coyle's side.

He listened. For a moment he could hear nothing except the thrumming of the ship's mighty engines and the sound of water being parted by her knifelike bow. Then, over the sounds he knew so well, he heard it. A tiny buzzing, like a far-off insect, somewhere off to his left. He looked but could see nothing; still, he knew better than to take such things for granted. He grabbed his intercom phone.

"This is Coyle in number six," he reported. "We hear an airplane."

He waited a moment, then somebody said, "Yeah, I think we have him. One blip north-northeast about two miles."

Coyle frowned. *One* plane? A half dozen or more he could see, but a single plane might be friendly. He decided to leave the decision to higher-ups but he ordered his men to put on

their helmets and prepare for action, then leaned over the rail
and saw Morley staring back at him. "You hear it?" he yelled.
Morley nodded. His men already were in position. Coyle
turned back to the rapidly increasing sound of the approaching plane. Damn! This morning he'd have given money for
that sunshine; now he wished it would vanish.

The phone rang on the bridge and McVay answered it. He'd
tried to get a little sleep in his tiny cabin behind the bridge but
it wouldn't come and he was, as usual, back on the bridge with
the fidgets.

"One plane, sir," radar reported to him. "Approaching
fast."

"Absolutely alone?" McVay, too, was surprised.

"Yes, sir. Still above the clouds as far as we can tell, too."

He didn't hesitate. Better safe than sorry. "Sound general
quarters," he ordered.

He walked briskly over to the bridge radar, then looked out
and up at the sky. What the hell was a lone plane doing there?

"He's dropping low through the clouds!" radar reported and
McVay and several others on the bridge strained to see the in-
terloper.

"Begin evasive maneuvers!" McVay ordered. The helms-
man brought the great ship around sharply as the engine room
was told to increase speed.

"Damn!" swore Johnny Coyle. "I wish that sun would go
away!"

As if on cue the clouds rolled over and swallowed the glowing orb; for a second their eyes had to adjust but then they saw
it, bearing down sharply on them.

"It's a Jap!" Coyle yelled. "Give it to him!"

All starboard batteries opened up immediately; it was an
easy target, a bomber by the looks of it, heading straight for
them. They all had it in their radar guidance and on visual.
Streams of bullets tore through the sky, many of them ripping
into the plane. Smoke appeared, but still it came on like some
large *kamikaze*. It was like something ghostlike and evil, bear-

ing down relentlessly on them no matter what they could put against it. It didn't even have a reason for being there, all alone, and a bomber, yet!

So many 20mm and 40mm shells tore into its vitals that finally it had to give. But even after it swerved it still was coming at them at full speed. There was no question in anyone's mind that it would hit the ship.

The plane's pilot also realized this and yet had little control over his plane at this point. Still alive, though, he decided he could do one last thing no matter what and just moments before the plane struck the after main deck he released his bomb. The plane struck, tumbled across the afterdeck like a child's toy spewing bits and pieces of itself all over, then toppled harmlessly into the sea. It caused little damage and no loss of life. The men of the batteries started to cheer as they realized this but few had seen the bomb.

The bomb had a determination of its own; it penetrated the deck armor on the port quarter, continued down through the crew's mess, a lower berthing compartment, the main fuel tanks, and right on through the bottom of the hull, exploding finally under the hull with tremendous force. Coyle and the others on the afterdeck felt the whole rear of the ship seem to rise up in the water and come back down again with a wallop that sent gun and deck crews sprawling.

On the bridge a startled McVay, who could see little of what was going on but had also been knocked down by the force of the explosion and the massive vibration that followed, was on his feet in an instant and grabbing for the red phone.

"Damage control!" he called. "What's the situation?"

Unable to get a coherent answer from the still shaken-up damage-control office he ran from the bridge and around to the rear side of the deck housing to get a better look.

Men were yelling and screaming and there was a lot of torn metal on the port side of the afterdeck but he couldn't tell much more. It would be several minutes before full damage could be assessed although the watertight compartments had done their duty and damage control was efficient and accurate.

In the barely fifteen seconds that seemed to all of them to be fifteen minutes since they'd confirmed the Jap plane heading down to attack them they'd suffered tremendous damage. Fortunately, she was afloat, although her great speed was much reduced. Because of the general alarm in overall effect for the Okinawa operation few were below decks in the stricken area. Nine had died, a number more were injured.

McVay listened impassively to the damage-control reports, then sighed. Despite it all they'd been very lucky. The old girl had beaten the odds again and they with her. Nine were dead, but 1,191, give or take a few, were alive. She could operate and, with some refueling help, get back for repairs.

"Notify Admiral Blandy that they will have to invade Okinawa without us," McVay said wearily. "Give the gun crews a 'well done' and tell them they did the best they could," he added, "and particularly commend the damage-control sections."

That done, he turned to Commander Joseph Flynn, his exec, who was standing behind him. "Joe, fill out all the forms and do what we have to do. Then tell Janney to get us out of here."

They headed toward home.

Monday,
April 9, 1945

Alamogordo, New Mexico, was not exactly the garden spot of the universe. Nestled in a desert valley near the white-gypsum sands that had been a prewar tourist attraction, it was within a couple of hours' drive of the mountains and the scenic Lincoln National Forest.

The country was crawling with history. Just to the north, in Lincoln County, there had been the fierce and legendary range wars. The specters of Pat Garrett, Billy the Kid, and John Chisholm haunted the landscape.

The recreational trade and the more commercial gypsum mining had been supplanted by the government, which had appropriated an enormous tract of desert land to the north and west of the town for its own mysterious purposes. It had built large tracts of "temporary" prefabricated housing for the increasing personnel.

Maintaining was not difficult. The town was quite small and

delighted to have the government's business. Nobody but the government could get the gas and tires to reach there. A few salesmen and a few truck drivers, were the only folks to pass through Alamogordo.

"This place is so dry and so dead even the Indians left it alone," Harvey Cameron remarked upon seeing the place for the first time. "Jesus! At least I expected Albuquerque or Santa Fe!"

Jim Fargo laughed and waved a hand. "Welcome to my domain, Harvey! It's not so bad once you get used to it. Hell, the movie shows a new feature every Friday night and there's three Coke machines in town to watch when things get dull."

Cameron coughed. "How do you stand it? There's nothing in the air at all. No fumes, no smoke, none of the crud civilized man has learned how to breathe. This kind of stuff could kill you." He took out a handkerchief and wiped his brow. "Hot as hell, too."

"This is winter," Fargo reminded him. "Wait until you're here through a summer."

"I won't survive spring," Cameron said with more sincerity than sarcasm. He looked off across the sandy flats toward the mountains. "Lots of snow up there, though, looks like. Kind of weird, boiling here in sight of that."

Fargo nodded. "Any climate you want. There's some good stream fishing up there when the thaw comes—not bad hunting, either, on the edge of the national forest."

Cameron just looked back at the dusty streets and drab housing and shook his head. "Somehow this is exactly the way I envisioned Site Y."

"Oh, this isn't Site Y," the younger agent told him. "That's up north near Santa Fe. You couldn't get all those brains and bigwigs to live in a hole like this. No, this is the place closest to the proving grounds. Harry Donaldson has Site Y. And Withers, of course." He made a face.

Cameron laughed. "Yeah, Withers, Withers, Withers. Makes you wonder, really, about this whole project. I mean,

Bruse seems to be on the ball and Groves could play his own life story in the movies. So why is it always Withers?"

"Hatchet man," Fargo replied casually. "He's ambitious so he'll toadie up to all the higher-ups. He'd slit his grandmother's throat if ordered by a superior officer who could do him some good. There are guys like him in every organization, every business—even ours. You should know that."

The older agent nodded. "They do the dirty work so the muckety-mucks seem like Joe Friendly. If they do well they get to be a higher-up; if not, they get the blame. Yeah, I know. It doesn't make me like them, though."

"Withers is a bit worse than most," Fargo agreed. "Come on—let's get your stuff in the trunk and I'll run you over to your luxurious new quarters."

As they drove they continued the conversation.

"You're right. Withers is worse than most," Cameron commented. "Maybe that's what's getting to me. I can't put my finger on it but there's something downright *slimy* about him. We deal with his type every day. Everybody has them, even Lockheed and Coca-Cola. But underneath, they're mostly normal guys with a taste for nasty jobs. Responsible, though. Maybe it's our old snooping sense or something, but I keep having a wrong feeling about the man."

"You think he's dishonest?"

"Rotten to the core," Cameron replied unhesitatingly. "He's loyal only to himself and I bet he has a spy shadowing him. He's wrong for this one, that's for sure. Even his record's slimy."

Fargo's eyebrows went up. "You ran a check on him?"

Cameron nodded. "His entire field experience was infiltrating the Bonus Marchers. He bragged about his reports on them, even boasted that he'd directed setting fire to the whole encampment. I know a few Army men who were in on that. They're all convinced they did their duty—but none of them is proud of it. Withers is."

"Well, here we are!" They pulled up in front of a prefab

shack sitting on a slab. It looked like the kind of cabin you might go to on a mountain vacation, only a little dilapidated. It was sparsely furnished in a combination of Army green and cheap hotel modern and was neither roomy nor comfortable. Its smell was less than mountain fresh.

"Well," Cameron said glumly, "I warned Mary we'd be roughing it for a while. She insisted it couldn't be that bad. Now, at least, she can't claim I didn't warn her. I wouldn't blame her if she turns around and goes back to New York. This place isn't fit for human habitation."

Fargo chuckled. "You get used to it after a while. A little creativity is what's needed. We've made ours downright homey."

"We—oh yeah, Jim! I forgot you were a married man now. When do I get to meet her?"

"Soon, I hope. You look all in now, so shake some of the topsoil from the blankets and get some rest. Cut through Hap Arnold Lane over there for a shortcut to the main drag when you're hungry. I'll pick you up bright and early tomorrow and break you in."

Cameron nodded, sighed wearily, and flopped on the bed. "I *am* kind of tired. It's a long ride. O.K., my boy, take off early and kiss her for me."

Fargo grinned. "I'll do that," he assured his old friend, but the grin faded as he stepped outside once more. The truth was, he was anything but eager to get home. He hadn't been truthful with his old friend or with anybody else.

Still, he told himself as he drove off, maybe this time it'll be different. Maybe this time things will go back to the way they used to be, the way they were back before they'd come to this damn place.

That had been part of it, of course. This was a lonely place, busy for him and deadly dull for her. He *wanted* to be home more, to be with her more, but this was a huge area and he was in full charge.

It was early yet, barely four-thirty in the afternoon. There would be plenty of time in the next few days to get Harvey fitted into the new routine. He was confident of the security screen he'd established here and Harvey Cameron had confidence in Jim Fargo. There'd be no problems—he really *could* take the rest of the day off, maybe surprise Carol, take her out to a big sit-down dinner, then maybe a movie or a show at the base. Make it a real occasion this time.

But when he pulled up to the house he found it closed and locked, the drapes drawn. The old hurt started within him as he sighed and put the key in the lock, then opened the door.

It was junky, messy, smelly, and hot inside, as if it had been shut up for some time. He threw his bag on the bed, opened the drapes and the windows, airing the place out, then looked around the small bungalow.

No notes, so she was coming back, at least, he told himself. He snapped on the radio and fiddled with it as he decided he really couldn't care less about what happened on "One Man's Family." You didn't get much here; just the one local station and the armed forces feed. Throwing off his coat and tie and kicking off his shoes, he flopped into a chair and waited with Tommy Dorsey.

James Tyler Fargo was thirty-five. He'd never married, never had any intention of marrying despite his parents' hope for grandchildren. He was handsome, he was ambitious, and he'd had no trouble finding women or sex when he wanted them. It had always come easy for him, right from junior high school. The All-American Boy, they teased enviously. Marriage was a trap, he'd always believed. Marriage was unfair to the woman if you were an FBI agent on the way up. And marriage was expensive. As the Phil Harris song put it, two could live as cheaply as one provided one of you doesn't eat. Of course, all that had gone right out the window when he'd met Carol.

She was only twenty, so there was quite a gap in their ages, but it hadn't mattered much at the start. The handsome, athletic Jim Fargo looked, felt, and acted closer to her age than his own; he still had all his hair and there was nary a wrinkle or trace of gray in sight. They'd been a handsome, picture-book couple.

She was incredibly beautiful; in fact, she'd just barely missed going to the Miss America pageant. He'd never been able to imagine a more attractive woman than she and had often wondered what the girl who beat her out for the Miss Connecticut title looked like. Carol was the All-American Girl for the All-American Boy, fascinated by older men, especially the big, handsome FBI man whose job had that hint of romance and danger.

And their first year had been a good one, everything both had expected from such a union. He'd been a big-city agent with routine hours, and the social whirl of the city was a delight to them both. Then, just a little more than a year after their marriage, he'd been transferred to Alamogordo. Neither of them were in love with the town but they made do, and got involved as much as possible with the local government and military families who were in the same fix. It was a bad but temporary situation.

But the security perimeter was hundreds of miles long, and his job kept him away quite a bit, more and more as the test date grew closer. While he was in the field supervising his own agents, coordinating things with Army security, or up in Albuquerque running checks on locals and making use of the Bureau office there, or over at Los Alamos—Site Y in Manhattan Projectese—she was spending lonely nights in this hole. He felt guilty about it—and a little worried that the combination of boredom and temptation would eventually get to her. It was tough on *him*, and at least *he* had his job to occupy him. Still, he was faithful to her, spending the nights alone in lonely hotel rooms in dry, dusty New Mexico towns. He expected the same from her.

He knew better now. Alamogordo was too small a town for anyone to keep secrets. He'd been shocked, and terribly hurt at first but he'd kept it to himself, hoping she'd bring it up, get it out in the open and over with. If she had, he told himself, he would understand and forgive her.

But finally, *he* had brought it up, when the hurt just couldn't be contained anymore. She had been contrite, and begged his forgiveness, and told him that it was only the loneliness and pressure and that it was all over now, she'd never do it again. She'd told him with utter sincerity, with feeling, and he'd believed her and forgiven her.

Now, as darkness engulfed the house, and the silence of the desert was broken only by the sound of the radio, he wondered how he could have been such a fool.

It wasn't even the fact that she'd done it again, he reflected morosely. It was the fact that she'd done nothing to disguise it or hide it, almost as if she *wanted* him to know, wanted to hurt him. Time passed, the radio played on, and he dozed almost without realizing it. The sound of a key in the latch woke him with a start, and before he could get his bearings, let alone move, the door opened and the light was switched on.

Carol stopped and stared at him, frowning. "What the hell are you doing sitting here in the dark?" she snapped.

He gave a low, humorless chuckle. "So the loving wife greets her returning husband," he grumbled. He yawned, then reached over and grabbed the alarm clock. "Jesus! Eleven-thirty!"

She walked over, snapped off the radio, and put her purse on the dresser. "You hungry?" she asked. "Want me to fix you something?"

He shook his head slowly, both in answer to the question and in reaction to her casual attitude. "Who was it tonight?"

She stopped and just stared at him for a moment. He could see her mind working, arguing with itself, trying to decide if she should lie, get angry, be defensive, or maybe throw herself on the mercy of the court.

"Oh, come off it!" she said sharply. "What's gotten into you, anyway?" She paused, making it look good. "You don't think I . . ." she added, letting it trail off into an expression of indignant amazement.

He felt the anger welling up in him, yet he didn't move from the chair. It was no good, he realized. No matter what, he couldn't belt her, couldn't bring himself to harm her. Not even now. Instead he just said, "You gave me your word. You promised me."

She grew agitated and nervous. "I—I didn't. A group of us—Army wives—we went to the movies, that's all. A Kay Kaiser comedy. I swear it, Jimmy!"

He sighed sadly. "Carol," he bluffed, "I'm a detective and this is a very small place."

She swallowed it, and her innocent demeanor was suddenly gone, replaced with an angry and determined look. "All right, all right. I tried, Jimmy. I really tried. But you don't know what it's like here. How could you? You're never here! Jimmy, I need somebody or I'd go nuts. I need *you*—but you might as well be in the Army someplace overseas yourself. While you're off all over the whole goddamned country I'm stuck with a bunch of matronly old officers' wives with their teas and bridge parties. I need *you*."

"You knew I had this job when you married me," he responded, feeling empty somehow, his voice wooden in his ears, without a trace of the emotion she was exuding.

"Sure! In New York or Chicago or L.A., fine. But in Alamogordo? Hell, I came here with you like a good wife. I've *been* a good wife. I was a good wife for a godawful long time. But while I was married to you, *you* were married to J. Edgar Hoover!" She paused, and some of the anger and frustration softened. "I still love you, damn it! All the others, they were just pale substitutes, people I could pretend were you. My God! It's just that I'm so cut off here I actually dream of Albuquerque!"

He sighed and got up, walking past her to the bed, picking up his coat and tie and still unpacked bag. She turned and watched him, puzzled. "What are you doing?" she wanted to know.

"Leaving," he told her. "It doesn't work. Not anymore. I hurt too much, Carol. I can't stand it. I can't kiss and make up and pretend it's all over again. I just couldn't live with that. I give up. I just can't take it anymore—it's eating me alive."

"But—where are you going?" she asked, nervous and apprehensive now.

"I'm going to drop by Alvarez's bar and get a fifth of something, then I'm going to check into the hotel and get drunker'n hell," he responded.

"And what about me?" she pressed. "Jim—I'm sorry. I wanted to hurt you and I feel bad about that. It was cheap and childish."

He reached the door and opened it.

"Jim—*please!*"

"Go home, Carol," he said wearily. "Go back where you can be happy. Go back where you won't kill me." He walked out and slammed the door behind him.

She didn't try to follow him, didn't try calling him back. He walked to the car, got in, and drove down to Alvarez's, then to the hotel.

He spent the next few hours just lying there on the motheaten bed in the run-down hotel room, drinking. Occasionally, he looked at the pistol in his shoulder holster. But he didn't go near it, just stared at it and cried until he couldn't cry any more.

"I hear Carol's gone back East," Harvey Cameron remarked casually. He knew more of the story than he let on, but after three days of waiting for Fargo to bring it up he'd finally decided to take the plunge and do it himself. The change in Fargo had been incredible. He looked tired, haggard, suddenly older than his real age. His concentration was poor and he seemed to have no more interest in anything.

"We split up," Fargo responded. "It was coming for a long

time, Harvey. I'm just sorry it came at this time. I know I haven't been the best of company since you got here."

Cameron had known Fargo for years and liked him a great deal. Cameron was concerned personally as well as professionally for his old pupil, and he decided to take advantage of their old father-son relationship.

"Is it your pride, Jim, or do you still love her?" he asked as gently as he could.

Fargo chuckled. "Pride. Love. I dunno. A little of both, I guess. Disappointment too, I guess. The whole world isn't like it should be, not for anybody, not for me, either. People are very different on the inside than they are on the outside. I—oh hell! Yeah, I still love her. Still want her a lot."

"Why not give it another go—if she's willing?" Cameron suggested. "It might never happen again."

"Don't you think I'm tempted?" the younger agent asked. "Hell, it's the most tempting thing I can think of. But I can't, Harvey. I'd never know for sure. It'd be a living hell. It'd eat me alive. And suppose she got pregnant? Would I—could I—be fair to the kid? I'd always wonder whose it was. No, I couldn't live like that, Harvey." He paused a moment, then added, "You know I've been thinking of quitting the Bureau."

Cameron was shocked. All his life, he knew, Jim Fargo had never wanted to do anything but be an agent. "That's nonsense. There's no other job for you—and you'd just get drafted immediately anyway."

"I was thinking of volunteering," Fargo responded. "Remember, I still have that Naval Reserve commission. I've had a pretty easy war, Harvey. All those young kids have been getting killed. . . ."

"That's bullshit and you know it," Cameron snapped. "You know just how important all this work has been, how close we are to turning this whole thing around and ending the war. Somebody had to do this job. Damn it, Jim, you've contributed a hell of a lot to the war effort.

Jim Fargo nodded and grinned sheepishly, but he said, "I still want to get into the war before it's over."

"Get yourself bored to death on some leaky tub, you mean," Cameron responded in what he hoped was a deflating tone. "Or maybe killed."

"Even that would have some meaning," Fargo replied. "All those boys who got killed—their deaths meant something I think, I *know*. My mind's made up, Harvey. As soon as you get completely oriented here and take over the system I'm leaving. That's that."

"That'll be a while yet, Jim. Relax and don't think about it until the time comes," the older man said.

"We'll see," was all Fargo could manage.

"Jim? You remember George Moulton? The deputy director at that Pentagon meeting?" Harvey Cameron asked one morning. It had been four weeks since their conversation on Fargo quitting, and the younger man hadn't changed his mind but the system of security was complex and Harvey Cameron was suspiciously slow in grasping all of it.

Fargo nodded. "Yeah. What about him?"

"Well, you know those men Withers has recruited to slip into the crew of the ship that takes the bang box. Moulton's worried about them. He doesn't trust the kind of men Withers might pick and he's afraid they might queer the deal. He wants us to add a Bureau man to the team, somebody from Manhattan Liaison, just to make sure they don't screw things up and the Bureau somehow get the blame."

Fargo was interested. "When's this supposed to be?"

Cameron shrugged. "All I know is that the box will leave Site Y so we have a bomb on the way the day we test the baby."

"I thought it was going by air now," Fargo said curiously. "Back to square one again?"

"Uh-uh. Fat man goes by sea. Another goes by air. The

third stays here. That way we have one to test and two alternate ways of guaranteeing at least one bomb gets there."

Fargo was interested. "Any idea who he wants?"

"Well, do you know an agent with Manhattan who's had naval experience and would be willing to undertake a covert assignment in a combat zone?" Cameron asked sardonically.

Fargo grinned. "I can think of at least one."

"So did Moulton. Your work here has made a big impression on him, my boy. There's only one hitch."

"Huh?"

"Withers will have to know. Even if we didn't tell him he'd know your name and face."

The grin widened. "Oh my. I know he'll just *love* this!"

It was the brightest and most eager spark Harvey Cameron had seen in Jim Fargo for a month.

The Pentagon
Thursday,
July 5, 1945

They sat in the lighted conference room uncomfortably. All of them knew why this meeting had been called and who had called it. Almost all of the men from the earlier meeting were there, including Moulton and Harvey Cameron; Fargo was not. There were several additional men as well, representing the various services and units involved. It was the last in a series of meetings they had held in the past few weeks. It was for a final checkout.

General Groves rose and addressed them all. "Gentlemen, our time has come. Long years of hard work have borne fruit and we're now in a position to end this war in a hurry. Although the final decision on deploying the bomb will be made by President Truman after the test, we can't wait. Frank McCarthy is already cutting orders for the principals involved. There has also been a hell of a lot of debate on this the last two months, let me tell you. On the military front I have been fighting the Secretary of War over this. Secretary Stimson was appalled by the estimated damage our baby could cause and has tried everything in his power to persuade the President to keep us from finally using it. Failing that he wants us to notify the Japanese that we have the bomb and will drop it, even send them films of the test."

Some of them, the security staff in particular, were appalled at this and showed it. Colonel Withers was beside himself.

Groves took note of the consternation. "Calm yourselves, gentlemen. Our scientific colleagues agree with us in the main. Bush, Conant, and Compton, the Interim Committee, agree with us and we have the support of Dr. Oppenheimer. Dr. Franck saw fit to send an alternative to the President signed by seven of his colleagues in which he proposed we first set it off in an announced neutral area to demonstrate what we have. Of course, putting aside the idea that this would invite shooting down the plane or invite a charge of trickery—and as for film, Hollywood could probably do a pretty good atomic bomb."

There were some rumblings around the group and nodding heads. None of the men in the conference room had any doubts that the bomb should be used on the enemy.

Withers leaned over and whispered to General Bruse, "Franck's a damn Kraut. Trying to stop this thing now shows him for what he is."

Bruse smiled sardonically. "Maybe he's just a humanitarian," he whispered back.

"Humanitarian hell!" Withers hissed. "Fourth Reich is more like it. Why the hell did he work on the bomb if he didn't think it should be dropped?"

It was Colonel McCarthy's turn now. The GSC Secretary was the man with the ultimate operational responsibility.

"Fortunately, of course, General Marshall is all for using the bomb as soon as ready," he told them. "And the President is an old artilleryman from the First World War. He's gone alone with us one hundred percent so far. I think we can guess what his decision will be by the fact that he's approved our entire timetable so far."

Groves nodded. "Of course everything's up the creek if the thing doesn't go off but we have to assume it will. The final argument against Stimson and Franck is simple—the Japs have what they call their 'national essence.' By that they mean that the individual counts for nothing in their society as long as their culture survives. That's why they will fight suicidally to the death and why we see *kamikazes*—it's a holy war. If they die protecting their national essence then they'll go to a bigger and better reward in heaven. Gentlemen, the bottom line is that not even an invasion of the home islands can force a surrender without horrible cost. Okinawa showed us that—men, women, children all trying to kill everybody they could. The bomb—*our* bomb—changes all that, gentlemen. It says that we can eliminate their entire culture, their entire population, at no cost to ourselves and with them unable to do a damn thing about it. Faced with that they will give up, for the same reason they fight to the end now. To save their national essence from total destruction."

"We are currently proceeding with plans for the invasion," McCarthy took over again, "but the earliest it could be mounted is November 1, hopefully with the Russians in it by then. But if we can force a surrender before that time we'll not only save countless lives but also be in a politically advantageous position. Therefore, we want to go ahead as soon as we are able to do so. Drop one, announce it to the world, let the Japs stew, then drop a second with a warning that a major city will be destroyed every other day until they surrender."

Somebody, an admiral who was ONI liaison, asked, "How many bombs do we have, Frank?"

Groves interceded. "That's not necessary for you all to know," he said curtly. "Not enough. We'll be running a bluff, that's for sure. You wouldn't believe how many millions of tons of rock you have to crush to get a thimbleful of uranium.

What we're concerned with is getting just one to our drop group."

"Where's it going?" someone else asked.

Groves smiled. "That, too, is our little secret, General. But how we move on the first one is our job. Frank?"

"I've already cut orders and coordinated with Oppenheimer at Site Y," McCarthy told them. "The general will be meeting shortly with Major Robert Furman, who's been with this project since the beginning. Furman will leave here on the tenth for Los Alamos and there join with Captain James F. Nolan, who'll be radiological officer. George, inconspicuously shepherding him to Los Alamos will be your baby."

Deputy Director Moulton nodded. "Harvey and a couple of his agents will be with him all the way. Harry Donaldson will take it from there, with Harvey going south to handle Alamogordo and outside-perimeter security. Inspector Donaldson has coordinated with Army security. That's going to be the most covered convoy in military history."

Withers looked a little apprehensive. "The bomb won't be armed at this point, will it?"

Groves chuckled. "No, of course not. Can't you just see us rumbling into San Francisco and then *blooie!* The scientists assure us that this thing can't go off in its transport state."

"But then again, nobody's ever built one of these before," McCarthy added, which did nothing for their comfort. He turned to Bruse. "Your end?"

"We'll have Army, ONI, and FBI at all steps along the way and the convoy itself will be armed to the teeth and constantly monitored by air and radio. Colonel Withers will see to its dispatch and then proceed south to the test site to assume command of internal security for the test site. ONI and FBI are being added to the ship's company in routine jobs both to assure security on board and to judge leaks among the crew. To allay suspicion, they'll remain aboard until the ship starts its next mission, then be flown back here. Once delivered it's up to the flyboys."

McCarthy nodded, satisfied.

"Excuse me, but won't the added men be suspect just for being added?" Moulton asked them.

"Not at all," Withers assured him. "As you now know, as of this morning we are using the *Indianapolis*. She's been getting repaired and refitted since a *kamikaze* hit during the Okinawa bombardment and is in good shape but she's down something like two hundred and fifty crew members due to the long length of time she's been drydocked. It's a closed society with a good command—Captain McVay is as good a security risk as Eisenhower—and we don't expect them to actually have to subdue any spies or saboteurs. They're just to listen. If some real trouble came up most of the crew would be there to support them. We're using only five men, really. That's enough, since they're distributed throughout the ship. Five out of something like two-fifty is hardly conspicuous."

"Have these men already reported?" McCarthy asked him.

Withers shook his head. "No, sir. Just this morning I sent their orders. They will group in San Francisco day after tomorrow, when I'll brief them. Then I'll add them a day at a time to the ship's company. Their jobs have been kept open pending this, and there are still about forty other slots to fill that don't concern us. I don't think there will be any problem there."

"Why *Indianapolis*?" someone else asked.

"First, it's a capital ship and armed to the teeth," McCarthy told him. "After this latest refit it'll have the best and most modern gadgetry known to man. It's also fast, possibly the fastest cruiser in the fleet—it can do twenty-six, maybe twenty-seven knots, more like a destroyer than the small battlewagon she is. Finally, she's one of the only two of her class. She's got a low silhouette, which means she'll be hard to spot if she should get into an area with a Jap sub. And, finally, she's available right now and just where we need her."

The ONI admiral nodded. "I don't think we have to worry about subs much," he told them. "Latest intelligence estimates state that the Japs have no more than a half dozen left by now. Even if it's twice that, the odds of *Indianapolis* running into one in the Pacific Ocean are pretty high. Hell, the Pentagon parking lot's more dangerous. And even if she did—well, the *Indy* took a direct hit with a bomb that went completely through her and out the bottom of the hull and she steamed back to port."

"She's top-heavy, though," another Navy man pointed out. "She *could* capsize."

The admiral glared at the other man, a mere captain. "She could also run aground or sprout wings," he snapped. "It's about as likely."

Subdued, the captain retreated.

"We're set then," Groves concluded. "Gentlemen, it's been a pleasure working with you and I'll see some of you again shortly at the test. I've never had greater anticipation, worry, and excitement about a single date as I have about sixteen July next."

The youngish-looking crew-cut officer sat nervously in Leslie Groves' office and waited for his boss to give him his orders. He'd been back in Washington since early spring and knew this was coming. Now that it was here, however, he felt as nervous as a schoolboy in the Christmas play. He'd been a key man in Manhattan, not only in tracking down and recruiting key personnel, particularly among the refugees from the war in Europe, but also in monitoring Germany's atomic progress and engineering daring ways to slow it down or stop it. Barely thirty, he'd been the key security man for the scientists themselves and reported not to Withers or Bruse but directly to Groves.

Major Robert R. Furman, engineer, Princeton '37, was more scientist than Army.

"Bob, this is it. The big one," Groves told him. "Next Tuesday, the tenth, ATC will fly you to Santa Fe, where Dr. Oppenheimer will brief you on the science particulars. Then you'll go over to Los Alamos and meet your radiological officer, Dr. James F. Nolan, who'll accompany you and the package. You'll be on a small and security-tight convoy that will leave on the fourteenth for San Francisco. You and Nolan will board the U.S.S. *Indianapolis* posing as artillery officers. Buy some insignia to that effect somewhere along the way. Nobody—and I mean *nobody*—is to know what you're carrying, where, or on what. Not even the captain of the ship will know what you're carrying, although he'll know you're on special detail to get something secret there. He'll be under sealed orders so even he won't know he's going to Tinian until he's well out to sea."

Furman managed a worried smile. "I feel like I've just been transferred to the OSS," he said wryly.

Groves nodded seriously. "It's at least that bad. Pick up your cloak and dagger from supply." He looked at the young officer gravely. "Bob, you're to stick with that shipment no matter what. If the ship sinks you still sit on that box. Understand? And you and Nolan swim to Tinian with it. I don't want any accidents, any thefts, any leaks of any kind. We just don't have many of these to spare—Oak Ridge and Hanford are just getting cranked up. That bomb *will* get to Tinian."

"Something tells me I'd be better off in the OSS," Furman muttered glumly.

The Soviet Embassy
Friday,
July 6, 1945

"It strikes me, Sarachevko, that if I'd become a coal miner I'd probably be fat and married and have six grandchildren by now," Viktor Lemotov said sourly.

"Huh?" It was all his aide could manage beyond a puzzled expression on his pudgy face.

Lemotov pointed to a stack of reports. "There it is. The best-kept, biggest secret of the whole war. Thousands of hours of legwork operating from a chance discovery and we know now that the Americans are developing an atom bomb. The Manhattan Engineering District, Major General Leslie Groves, C.E., commander. And about the only scientist in physics in America who didn't work on it was Einstein. It is amazing, Sarachevko, amazing! Countless dollars, flawless organization, thousands of people working on it all along—and we knew nothing about it. Nothing!" He threw up his hands. "So much for theory." He sat up straight. "You know what they say back home? Beria, he's always fond of noting this. The Americans are rich and fat, he says, but basically weak because their system makes it impossible to keep secrets. Impossible to keep secrets, the man says!" He gestured at the stack. "Hanford! Oak Ridge! Los Alamos! Alamogordo! Even at a university in Chicago! It's amazing!"

"But we know it now," the aide pointed out.

Lemotov nodded. "Yes, we have it now. The question is what we are going to do with it."

Sarachevko's eyebrows went up. "I assume you let others make that decision. I assume all this has been transmitted home."

"To OGPU, yes," Lemotov affirmed, "but what do I get back? Wait, watch, get proof. Proof!" He sighed. "Oh, it was rather easy to get all the details once we knew what to look for. But what do we know? We know only that they have this great bomb. Nothing else. How many bombs? How does it work? What does it do? Bah! We know nothing that will not be on the front pages of all the newspapers in this country the day the bomb is dropped."

"You are convinced they will use it?"

He nodded. "My colleagues back home are convinced they won't. The Americans are too moral or something. I think they misunderstand that this country is closer to the cowboy than we, culturally, are to the cossack. To use it on Germany— they might have hesitated. But on the country that caused Pearl Harbor? Hah! They will use it in a moment when it is ready."

"Our information from the preparatory teams for the Potsdam Conference indicates that the Americans still will press for us to get into the war against Japan immediately," Sarachevko noted. "That says to me that they do not yet have the bomb or will not use it."

"Not yet *tested*," Lemotov retorted. "The American invasion is scheduled for November 1, plus or minus a few days.

We know that. That is what worries me. Our superiors are so convinced that they have until November that they discount the bomb."

"They may have a point," the aide argued. "We've had people on the New Mexico sites for some time with no result. There *has* been a lot of movement from Los Alamos down to the Alamogordo area in the last month but who knows what that means?"

"It means they are preparing to test the bomb," his boss said flatly. "Probably soon. Now, if you were General Groves, and you knew you had to produce this bomb and drop it before November, what would you do?"

"Step everything up, of course," Sarachevko responded. "If I could," he added, still skeptical.

Lemotov nodded. "I would say he would aim at Potsdam so he wouldn't have to bargain with us. Failing that, as soon afterward as possible—so that the war could be won before we could get involved."

"You really believe Japan would surrender based on this?"

"Yes I do. But the Japanese are already trying to make peace, with us as the intermediaries! Don't look so startled—we are the logical choice. Allies of their enemy and a nonaggression pact with them. They've been trying to pressure us into helping them get out of the war. Of course, we're not about to do it, but—consider. If they are trying to make a deal now, they already know they are beaten. They are trying to be like Germany in the last war—get out with a whole skin and their own nation not invaded. Assume that what some of the scientists say is true—that this bomb can turn a city into dust in a moment. How many cities in Japan would have to be destroyed before they made peace? They know history, those Japanese. Germany rose again because she had the sense to quit when she did the first time. It's close, Sarachevko, very close—and home will not act! They don't see things the way we do here." He shuffled some of the papers, took out a file folder, and opened it. "Those men Withers talked to last winter. Anything?"

The aide shrugged. "They are being covered, of course. Nothing yet, though. None of them have been transferred since Withers talked to them."

"Which is in itself significant," Lemotov pointed out. "In wartime such long assignments are rare." He tapped the folder. "Navy. Marines. We have to know the name of the ship they will use."

The aide nodded, then suddenly grew thoughtful. "These men will lead us to the ship. But what good will that do us? We don't know where it's going, and short of a miracle we won't know. And if we did? What could we do about it?"

"That's all I've been thinking about," Lemotov admitted candidly. "That is why I yearn for the simple life of a Siberian coal miner and a nice little pension to squander on my grandchildren. Moscow's unwillingness to make decisions on this matter or even to recognize its urgency is making this difficult. The easiest thing would be to do nothing—on the grounds that no one higher up handed me the responsibility. Into my hands has been dropped something that tells me that I must risk either my own safety, perhaps my life, or endanger our position in the world." He looked suddenly very tired. "When Japan surrenders we *must* be there."

"And what can you do?"

Lemotov sighed and tapped the files nervously. "I can notify our people in Japan. I can do my best to see that the ship, whatever it is and wherever it is bound, does not arrive."

The younger man was startled even though he'd suspected as much. "I should not want that responsibility," he said honestly. "Not without orders from home."

Lemotov nodded. "I know. Great men take great risks, Sarachevko. That is why I am here. If this works I will be a Hero of the Soviet Union, with a secure place on the Politburo and a future mostly of getting fat and enjoying life after all. If it doesn't—well, sending information to an enemy leading to the sinking of an ally's ship . . ." He let the thought trail off but the other man understood all the implications.

"Don't fail me, Sarachevko," the older man warned. *"Get me the name of that ship!"*

Wednesday,
July 11, 1945

Harvey Cameron felt stiff and achy; a long flight on a military plane was not an exercise in comfort and convenience. His ears seemed permanently stuffed up and he was certain he'd be hearing the roar of the propellers and feel the vibration from the engines for weeks.

He greeted his FBI counterparts at the air base with a nod, then ignored them. He was on his way south and home; Major Furman, now under a new set of eyes, was proceeding to Alamogordo by staff car. All aboard were sleepy. None of them had gotten much sleep.

Furman got in the staff car and it pulled out, an unmarked car in front and back. He was heading first into Santa Fe to meet with his immediate boss.

J. Robert Oppenheimer looked tired but he welcomed the major warmly in the small office and offered him a drink, which Furman declined. "On no sleep I don't dare," he explained.

Oppenheimer smiled knowingly and poured them both glasses of iced tea. Although the two knew each other by reputation, this was the first time they'd ever met and, in accordance with procedures, Furman handed over a letter to Oppenheimer, who glanced at it routinely.

TO WHOM IT MAY CONCERN:

This will introduce Major Robert R. Furman, C.E., ASN 0-350657, who is on a special mission of the utmost importance to the Secretary of War. All assistance should be given this officer as may be necessary to complete his mission.

By direction of the Chief of Staff.

Frank McCarthy
Colonel, GSC
Sec'y, General Staff

"That should do it," the scientist commented, handing the paper back. "At least it will remind the security boys who's the boss." He sat down and sipped his iced tea. "Major, do you know where I'm going from here?"

"No, sir," was all Furman could manage. He had the oddest feeling of being in the middle of an Alfred Hitchcock movie.

"Alamogordo, to the south of Albuquerque," Oppenheimer told him. "We are going to find out if this thing works—on the fifteenth or sixteenth, hopefully. The bomb's already in place."

The hairs on Furman's neck seemed to stiffen slightly. "Will I be accompanying the director?"

Oppenheimer shook his head. "No. We're pressed for time and we have our orders from the President. If it works we're to drop it on Japan at the first opportunity. Announcements and diplomatic-information packets are already being prepared. General Marshall decided to move the fissionable materials as soon as possible so that if the explosion should let the cat out of the bag, a bomb would already be on the way and not easily traceable. You'll go over to Los Alamos this afternoon and meet with Captain Nolan. He's a nice fellow—you'll get along fine. His wife's also an extremely good cook, I hear. He'll brief you on the specifics."

Furman could only nod, his sense of unreality returning.

"Major, I can only say again and again that you *must* deliver this material. You *must*. Should the package be lost it would mean we'd have a delay—too long a delay. Incredible tons of rock have been crushed and refined to get just the tiny bit of uranium we need for the bomb. The invasion date cannot be changed. If your shipment is lost it could mean a longer, bloodier war."

The major was surprised at this. "Surely, sir, there are other backups?"

"None!" Oppenheimer exclaimed, ramming his fist on the table for emphasis. "It'd take months to replace it. Our production facilities are terribly inefficient. If your shipment is lost then, I fear, the atomic bomb is lost as a weapon. If we invade we can hardly use it. The lives of tens of thousands of American boys are riding on you getting it there. I can't say that to you strongly enough. What there is you have. Bomb casings and mechanisms we can replace—but that uranium we cannot replace. It's so tight, Major, that the bomb we'll be using for our test isn't even the same as the ones we're sending. It uses plutonium, not uranium. We're sending the uranium with you because it's a surer bet—we're ninety-nine point nine percent certain that the bomb will work with uranium—but you'll have our entire supply. Don't fail me, son. Don't fail your country and those troops."

Furman's throat seemed dry despite the tea and he was perspiring from the responsibility as much as from the heat. He wondered idly what John Wayne would say to all this. "I'll do my best, sir," he decided on.

It was enough. "I've got to run. Good luck, Major—to you, to us, and to the country."

"Good luck to you, too, sir," he replied mechanically and they shook hands warmly.

The road to the Los Alamos Scientific Laboratory—or Site Y, as it had been referred to in the security codes—was winding, twisting, tortuous. Nobody was ever going to get on this road by mistake, Furman thought to himself. Nobody sane, anyway.

The complex of buildings that constituted Los Alamos was a pleasant surprise, though. Everything looked new and quite routine. Neat houses with well-laid-out streets flanked the large buildings that were the laboratory and support facilities. It looked like a newly built company town for some steel or power company.

And yet he knew in that building over there was a cyclotron that could split the basic building blocks of all matter and that those buildings housed some of the top scientific brains the world had ever seen.

He checked into the BOQ and found a message for him from Captain Nolan inviting him to cocktails at the doctor's home that afternoon. Tired and sleepy, Furman nonetheless was eager to meet his partner and get the rest of the story.

The Army staff was solicitous of his every wish. He began to know what it felt like to be a general. He simply had to notify the motor pool and in minutes a staff car complete with chauffeur pulled up in front. Less than an hour after getting to Los Alamos he was on his way to Captain Nolan.

Captain James F. Nolan, M.D., was young, warm, and friendly, much as Oppenheimer had assured Furman. They sat on a patio while Mrs. Nolan fussed with hors d'oeuvres and brought them drinks. Furman thought she looked particularly nervous. She dropped some of the bite-sized delicacies, spilled drinks, and seemed to be all thumbs. Finally the captain told her to sit down and relax.

"I'm sorry," she apologized. "I—well, it's been so nice and peaceful here. Now Jim's going God knows where except it's toward the Japanese. . . ." She trailed off, looking nervously at her husband.

Furman was surprised. "She knows?"

Nolan nodded. "I had special permission to tell her." He patted her hand tenderly. "She worries too much about me."

"Actually, it makes things more comfortable," the major replied. "Now I don't feel like we have to lock ourselves in an underground bunker to talk things over."

"Actually," Nolan commented, "I'm lucky to get this. Default, I suppose. This hospital is the only one in the Army that handles the sort of by-products we're experiencing with radioactive materials."

"Did you start as a diagnostician?" Furman asked curiously, thinking that X rays had been, up to now, the only real sources of radiation danger.

Nolan chuckled. "No. I suppose I was a case of arrested interest. I always wanted to be a doctor but not a G.P. I interned in surgery and did residencies in surgery and gynecology, of all things." He assumed a leering expression. "My wife didn't approve. Finally I got a fellowship at Memorial Hospital for Cancer and Allied Diseases in New York and that, I guess, finally hooked me. Everywhere else I was either bored or learning to do what everybody before me had already mastered. Cancer, now, and its relatives—that's new ground. When they drafted me and sent me here it was mostly because of my work there."

Furman nodded understandingly. "And this uranium produces cancer?" He couldn't help thinking about the package he and Nolan would carry.

Nolan saw where his partner was going. "Well, yes. And no. It produces a whole new set of diseases, of which cancer is only one. The hard radiation produced by these atomic products and by-products is hundreds of times more dangerous than X rays by far and seems to have lasting and long-term effects. Leukemia, sterility, just about everything known in the disease catalog and a lot of new stuff have shown up despite our best precautions." He smiled reassuringly. "Don't worry, though. The stuff we'll have will be so well shielded with lead and so compartmentalized that there's just about no chance of us even being aware that there's any radiation there. That's what I'm going along for. Remember, I'm going with you and I'll also be there to supervise when they put the bombs together. I have no desire for any ill effects."

Furman tried to look reassured but Mrs. Nolan was no help. She was obviously thinking the same dark thoughts as he. What if there were a leak? Would they ever know? Nothing was foolproof.

As the evening wore on, though, they managed to calm down a good deal as the drinks took their toll and soon they were all planning with more bravado just what they intended to do. There was a sense of excitement to this, and in all these years nothing really serious had actually gone wrong.

The next morning Nolan picked him up and they took that bouncing, winding road down to Santa Fe to Bruns General Hospital's PX and bought the artillery insignias they'd need for their disguises. Each man stood and pinned the tiny insignias on the other's uniform. Later that day a chance encounter with an administrative sergeant revealed that they had pinned on the things upside down.

They and the administrative staff at the laboratory spent the next couple of days checking on all arrangements with Army, Navy, and ATC authorities, going over plans, routes, every single detail of the mission. Withers was there and briefed them on the enormous security both Army security and the FBI would provide their swift convoy at all points until they were on the ship. "And even then," he assured them, "you'll seldom be out of sight of either my men or the FBI. We're thorough, gentlemen. Rest assured you'll have a safe and peaceful trip."

They hoped so.

On Friday the thirteenth they made a dry run down the mountain to Santa Fe for the benefit of security men and seemed satisfied. It was all set now; they were committed.

Neither man slept much that night.

On a bright, sunny morning, Saturday, July 14, 1945, they met outside the laboratory and stowed their gear in the trunk of a car. The convoy formed—a small, enclosed black truck, four unmarked cars in front, three behind. Furman and Nolan could hardly avoid noticing that while all of the other men in the cars were in civilian clothing, there was almost a superabundance of firepower, including submachine guns.

The guns made Nolan nervous. "I wish they'd just keep all that out of sight or put it away," he muttered uncomfortably. "The only people likely to get killed are the bunch of us shooting each other's feet off. This oversecurity is too dangerous."

Furman chuckled as he watched the combined efforts of many men lift a two-foot black cylinder about eighteen inches around and strapped onto a small pallet on the back of the small black truck.

"But you feel safe around *that*," the major noted glumly, gesturing toward the black cylinder with his head.

Nolan laughed. "There's no danger. It's subcritical. It can't explode on us—and I assure you that there're a few hundred pounds of lead and other shielding between it and the outside world, capped by a totally sealed airlock better than any used in a submarine—and that in turn has a cap of more lead. You're as safe around it as you are in your own bed," he assured his nervous partner.

Hordes of security men got into the cars and one huge, beefy individual came over to them. "Time to go, sirs," he said, looking at his watch. "We're right on schedule."

Both Nolan and Furman gave almost collective sighs as they felt the tension mounting. "Here we go," Furman muttered to himself. They got in and the car door was barely shut when the convoy roared off.

Roared was the word, too. The road was terrible and these men were taking it like madmen, at breakneck speeds. Furman looked worriedly out his window and saw what kind of a drop they faced. He could almost see the footnote in all the history books saying how the first atomic bomb had been born of blood when the whole security team went off a New Mexico cliff.

Furman also wasn't reassured by Nolan's glib assurance that the stuff couldn't explode. Little was known about this sort of thing, really. He was less worried about the speed and the possibility of going over the side than he was with the bouncing and pounding the road was giving the car and the black truck just ahead of them. He could almost see the truck sway one way, then the other, then almost bottom out on its shock absorbers. The security men also looked particularly tense and seemed to be thinking the same thing.

Suddenly there was an explosion and their car swerved, barely stopping from going straight over the edge. The two cars behind almost plowed into them and the whole convoy came to a sudden screeching halt.

Furman was almost in shock; he couldn't speak, couldn't move for a moment, fear paralyzing him. The only thing he could think of was that the "subcritical" mass had gone off and they were now being bathed in horrible, killing radiation. The driver of their car got out and walked back where he was met by others from the cars front and rear.

"A goddamned flat tire," somebody growled. It took a minute for the words to penetrate to the two scared men in the car.

It was quickly fixed, with most of them just standing there along the road, waiting. A number of security men deployed around the truck and took up vantage points in the nearby rocks and just below the edge of the mountain road just in case the flat was part of some prearranged plot but nothing showed up.

Furman admired their professionalism, though. They had

everything covered and had acted without panic from the moment of the flat.

"Look up there," Nolan whispered to him and pointed. He strained, shielding his eyes from the sun, and saw the figures of several men on the hilltop above them.

"Think they're somebody dangerous?" Furman asked nervously, a queasy feeling in his stomach. His hand fumbled for the pistol.

"Uh-uh," Nolan replied. "We're covered, all right. Every step of the way."

They roared through Santa Fe with no concern for police or speed limits. In fact, some local police blocked intersections for them. They passed the time to Albuquerque mostly in silence or exchanging small talk and beyond the city to Kirtland Field. They didn't even stop at operations but roared right onto the field and then and only then did the convoy slow to a halt in front of the base operations building. Nearby were three DC-3s already warming up, one with its cargo bay open. They were issued parachutes by a loadmaster and then made their way toward the plane, where the bomb was already being loaded. It had its own parachute, Furman noted.

They were barely buckled into their seats when the security men in the other two planes radioed signals and they taxied out in formation to the end of the runway. They were airborne so fast they were hardly aware of having been at the air base at all.

Shortly after takeoff the copilot, a first lieutenant, came back and greeted them. "We'll be there as quick as the old crate can get us there," he assured them.

Nolan looked out the window at the desolate desert landscapes of the Southwest. It looked like another planet. "What happens if something goes wrong with the plane, Lieutenant?" he asked nervously.

The second officer smiled. "Then our instructions are to forget the people, save the package at all costs." He tried to look a little more reassuring. "Don't worry. This is the safest and solidest plane ever built and this particular one's the best of the batch. We'll get you there, all right."

The land below lost its parched look and started turning green; they flew over the Sierra Nevadas and almost directly over Yosemite on a day so clear they could almost see the famous falls. It looked strange from the air—like an indentation made by a huge hand.

And now they touched down at Hamilton Field just outside of San Francisco, taxied up to the terminal, and the engines were cut. In seconds it looked like the whole place had erupted. Cars and Jeeps with security men popped out of every nook and cranny, surrounding the planes. The security men had spent weeks checking out everything from traffic patterns to stoplights. They knew their business.

An enclosed and reinforced Jeep was brought up and the bomb was lowered, unstrapped from its pallet, and several men managed to lift it and place it in a preprepared metal-reinforced berth in the back of the Jeep. Two Navy captains came out, both very obviously in charge of security procedures. They introduced themselves so fast that the two Army men barely caught their names. Then they all got in and they roared off in another convoy.

In less than an hour the bomb was safely in the commander's office at Hunter's Point Navy Yard, and Furman and Nolan found themselves signing an interminable number of forms—one of which said that they temporarily but completely released responsibility for the bomb to the Navy.

For the evening they were free.

"I'm still spinning around," Nolan grumped. "I feel like I've been on a roller coaster for the last twelve hours."

Furman nodded and stretched his tired muscles. "I don't know about you, but I need a drink," he said.

Alamogordo
and Elsewhere
Wednesday,
July 11, 1945

"I'm leaving, you know. Today. Just got my orders and my old uniform out of mothballs," Jim Fargo told Cameron. He sniffed and wrinkled his nose. "Damn. I'm safe from insects forever."

Cameron laughed. It was good to see his friend in a more cheerful mood and, in a way, he envied the younger man. Despite the momentous test that was coming up, most of the security work was routine. Out there, on a ship, racing for a front-line airbase, Fargo would be far away from the places that conjured up unhappy memories for him. Maybe out there he'd come to terms with himself, Cameron hoped. He wasn't worried about the mission—it was the kind of milk run the Navy didn't even think twice about. But Jim—Jim he was worried about.

"You know I heard from Carol Saturday," Fargo said quietly.

Cameron's eyebrows rose a trifle. "Oh?"

"She went back home to her parents," he said in a tone that showed some surprise. "I don't know what she told them but it wasn't the truth. She says she hasn't told anybody anything except that I'm on some kind of business and she had to move back." He paused a moment, then added, "She says she's pregnant."

"Oh." It was the only thing Cameron could think of to say.

"She claims it's mine for sure, since it's far enough along that it couldn't be anybody else's."

"What do *you* think?" Cameron asked.

Fargo sighed. "I don't know. The trouble is that I'd never be *sure*. And, of course, it doesn't change anything. Going back to her is out of the question now."

Cameron let it drop. "Well, there's nothing you can do for a few weeks anyway. Think about it. Now, I'm supposed to give you your final briefing from Moulton. Ready?"

The younger agent nodded.

"O.K. You already have your activation orders, which are your cover, and you are a graduate accountant and C.P.A. No mention of FBI service to anyone, not even any others in the security detail. Clear?"

Another nod.

"You'll get to Albuquerque tonight by bus, then take a train to San Francisco. Here are your tickets—it's commercial all the way. Once there report to the commander, Hunter's Point Navy Yard. He'll put you up. I want to warn you that you'll probably see Withers there."

"Withers?"

"Yeah. He's decided he wants you to know each other so you have somebody in the know to depend on in a pinch. He'll brief you there and you'll go aboard shortly thereafter. It's the heavy cruiser *Indianapolis,* by the way. You're not supposed to know that yet but I thought I'd let you know."

Fargo's expression seemed approving. "The *Indianapolis,*

huh? That means a lot of the comforts of home. That's a pretty famous ship."

"And an admiral's flagship—Spruance, in fact—although I understand he's not going to be aboard. The bomb travels first class, probably in the admiral's quarters. You're from supply and you're there TDY to check and see that everything's there and O.K. and shipshape after the refitting, the excuse being that they couldn't send anyone before and this is an unexpected trip. It sure is—they're just doing their first sea trials now and don't know themselves yet that they're going on a trip." He picked up a thick sheaf of Navy manuals that collectively weighed a ton. "Here are the regs for your job. Study them so you get the forms right. It's the perfect job, though—a supply auditor. You'll be able to go all over the ship, to practically every department, and talk with officers and men all over the place."

"Will they know what they're carrying?" Fargo asked.

"Nope. Just that it's some supersecret weapon, nothing more. They'll be under a total security blackout, though, and they'll know they're carrying something mighty important. Just make sure that's *all* they know. Because of the blackout you'll be well away from the drop-off before the ship resumes normal service. If there's nothing to report you'll probably be dropped off as soon as you complete your audit so learn those manuals well. Guam or someplace like that. As soon as you're off, drop the forms in the right place and then phone the resident agent. He'll take it from there."

"And if there's no resident agent?" Fargo asked.

"ONI—as high as you can get. Have them contact Moulton. You're to be debriefed in either Guam or Hawaii with the others—but we want you debriefed by Bureau personnel, not Withers."

Fargo looked at the stack of manuals and groaned slightly. Then, sighing, he got up. "I guess that's it, then," he said resignedly. "I guess I better go catch my bus."

Cameron got up and helped him with his things. "I'll make

sure the bulk of your belongings is looked after," he assured
the younger agent. They shook hands warmly. "Good luck,
Jim. Take care of yourself."

Fargo smiled wanly. "What could happen, Harv? A *kamikaze?*" He paused a moment, then added, reassuringly, "Don't
worry about old Jim. I'll be back."

"See that you are," Cameron responded sincerely.

Fargo shook his head. "Still, after all this craziness, I'd really love to know if the damned thing worked."

Bremerton, Washington, was a large naval base an hour's
ferry ride across Puget Sound from Seattle. Since the Aleutian
campaign, though, Bremerton had mostly been a backwater of
the war effort, the place for research and development, for
refitting some of the older and more damaged ships, and little
else. No one seriously feared a Japanese attack on the mainland anymore. They were too busy defending their own neighborhood.

In the code room, a pair of exceptional telegrams arrived
for two of the base personnel. The code clerks were amazed to
discover that the telegrams, using the most secure military
channels and in the most top-secret code then in use, were in
fact routine military orders for what appeared to be TDY. The
officer in charge looked at them, grumbled something about
overuse of secrecy, then ordered two clerks to take them to the
addressees. It was even more unusual to discover that one of
those getting the orders was an enlisted man.

The first clerk, grumbling about being turned into a post-
man, took a car over to the R&D developmental lab and, after
going through the bureaucracy, located and handed the sealed
envelope to Lieutenant Commander Ronald Allan Sarbic,
U.S.N.R., Deputy Director of the Ordnance wing. The tall,
gaunt man looked surprised and, when he opened it, seemed
even more so. Still, he sighed and walked down the hall to his
commander to tell him the news.

The second clerk, thankful to be out of the office for a

while, walked the half mile or so to the Damage-Control Research section and found the office of CPO Donald Sobel, a beefy block of a man in his early fifties who looked like the fellow Hollywood always cast as a Navy chief in John Wayne movies. Sobel, too, read the orders through unbelievingly, then went out to tell his men that he'd be leaving them. He was surprised, but not particularly unhappy. Like Sarbic, of whom he knew nothing and who he'd never met even though they worked on the same base, he'd just about given up on this mysterious project that Army colonel had talked him into so long ago. He'd figured he'd been passed over for the job or the thing fell through.

Both men left the base after their commanding officers verified the orders with Washington and went to their quarters. Within a few hours both were on the same train south, wondering just what the hell was going on.

And, unknown to both of them, from the moment each man had been handed the orders they were never out of sight of observers who notified their own boss in Washington of the two men's progress. And their boss was in the Soviet Embassy.

The Soviet Embassy
Saturday,
July 14, 1945

"You're certain that it is the *Indianapolis?*" Viktor Lemotov gave a look that said he wanted no hedging.

"Ninety-nine percent," Sarachevko hedged anyway. "It's big, it's fast, it's a veteran under an able skipper, and, most of all, it's there. I'd stake my reputation on it."

"You may be staking more than that," his boss grumbled ominously. "Now, I think we can assume that they won't set sail until there is a successful test. Since Withers has activated his team and is in San Francisco himself at the moment we can assume that the test is imminent. I'll wager that our little colonel will be in New Mexico by tomorrow night at the latest. However," Lemotov continued, "once the test is done they'll get the bomb on the way as soon as possible. As soon as a message could be gotten to San Francisco, in fact. The same day. That leaves the one question we cannot answer, and that is, Where is it going?"

"Okinawa, most likely," Sarachevko guessed. "It's the closest to Japan."

"The closest, true," his boss agreed, "but that also means it's the most vulnerable to enemy reconnaissance and even bombing. I don't think they'll risk such a thing."

"Guam, then," Sarachevko suggested.

"No, I think not." Lemotov shook his head and looked over a map of the Pacific. "Too many people for an operation of this kind. They've put too much into security on this end to expose it all at Guam."

"One of the small islands, then," the aide suggested, feeling like the fool in a puppet show.

"Hmmm . . . perhaps. I would think, though, that they would still need major support facilities. This thing would have to be assembled. The Ryukyus are too exposed, the Marianas too busy as a naval control center. It's an Army mission, basically; the air force will drop the thing, of that we can be certain. I'd say . . . here." He pointed to the map.

"Clark Field in the Philippines?" Sarachevko was clearly surprised. "But isn't that even more crowded than Guam?"

"It's a bigger place. Good position, lots of B-29s for cover, easily secured, and strictly under Army control. My guess would be a route from San Francisco to Hawaii, then to Guam, finally to Manila Bay. It has to be there. MacArthur would never stand for it to be left to Nimitz."

"A lot of guesses," his aide said dubiously.

"It's a game of guesses."

Sarachevko had to admit that his boss had him there. "So what will you do?"

Lemotov chuckled sourly. "First I shall compose all this into a coherent dispatch listing my reasons and send it home with a recommendation that we do something. They'll have to make the decision now!"

"But what if they do?" Sarachevko asked him, playing devil's advocate. "Nothing, I mean."

"Then, my dear Sarachevko, I shall use my own initiative. I shall arrange for our friends in our embassy in Tokyo to know what I have known. They will whisper it to the Imperial Navy."

"And if you're wrong about the route?"

Lemotov smiled. "But that is the beauty of it, you see! First, the Japanese could not really hit anything beyond the Philippine Sea. Their sea power's crippled. They will take the information and act on it because they cannot afford to do otherwise. They will send a submarine out between Guam and the Philippines and try to sink the *Indianapolis*. If it appears and they sink it, the Russians are big heroes to the Japanese. If it appears and they do not sink it, or if it does not appear, then we have lost our clever game, Sarachevko, but who will ever know?"

The aide sat there but couldn't think of a negative answer to that one. It sounded pretty solid to him.

"Shall I arrange for it?" he asked the spy chief.

"Patience, Sarachevko! Patience!" the other urged. "First we give Moscow the chance to make the decision. Then, even if we hear nothing, we will know when our ship sails, yes? Four days to Honolulu, another three to Guam, another three to the Philippines making flank speed. Plenty of time to decide, don't you think?"

"If you say so," the aide grumped. "At any rate we'll have people in the Alamogordo area. We'll know if this superbomb goes off—and if it is powerful enough to have warranted all this planning and risk."

"We'd better," Viktor Lemotov growled.

"Maybe the bomb won't go off," Sarachevko said hopefully.

"Our own people say it will," Lemotov replied. "The odds of it not working are about the same as the other odds that have also been calculated."

"Huh?"

"That it will produce an uncontrollable chain reaction

which will ignite the atmosphere and destroy all life on Earth."
He grinned at the aide's shocked expression. "Don't worry so
much, Sarachevko! If it happens we'll not have to worry about
making the right choice, will we?"

San Francisco Thursday, July 12, 1945

Jim Fargo had tried to keep his mind on the upcoming assignment but his thoughts kept going back to Carol. That's the trouble with long trips, he decided. Too much time to think, too little else to do. The manuals, while essential, didn't really help matters much. There is nothing so boring as the *U. S. Naval Auditor's Manual*. This was made even worse by the fact that his work was more than a cover; he was actually expected to do the job. Somehow he saw Harvey Cameron's subtle hand in all this. After completing a basic audit of every department of a heavy cruiser at sea, if he really wanted to go with the Navy instead of returning to the Bureau he'd know the worst of it.

It wouldn't be that bad, he told himself. He'd have a chief and a bunch of supply clerks to do most of the real work—his sleeve held too many stripes for him to be anything more than a supervisor.

At least he'd gotten practice from the trip in saluting, something he hadn't done since almost before the war. The entire world seemed to be in uniform and traveling, he thought, and all of them were enlisted.

He'd been in the Navy since college, when he'd graduated as an Ensign, U.S.N.R., but also had been recruited for the Bureau. He'd been on active duty very little. Theoretically he owed them two years at some point, but mostly it'd been going to meetings and playing sailor a few times a year. He felt guilty about being a lieutenant; it'd been more or less automatic bumps, particularly when the whole world had been activated early in '42. Almost everybody—but not he. The Bureau considered him vital and protected him. There would be combat-hardened officers on this ship that, after several years of active duty, would still be j.g.s, he knew. He decided that if they ever learned how he'd gotten this big he'd probably be tossed to the sharks.

And, of course, he wasn't *really* in the Navy even now. It was a cover only for a Bureau assignment. At least he'd be in the war, he told himself.

San Francisco was a beautiful city undimmed by wartime problems; everybody fell in love with its picture-postcard appearance and, in July, coming from scorching-hot Alamogordo, the coolness of the area felt almost like winter. Only the palm trees convinced him that snow was not imminent.

At Hunter's Point he showed his orders at headquarters and was told that he would be expected at a meeting at 1900 hours in such-and-so building and until then he was free. He got the distinct impression that Hunter's Point was not to be his final destination.

He ate at the Officers' Club, discovering just how out of it he was by his inability to understand most of the in-talk and initialese the other officers used routinely in talking to one another, and also discovering that, even at service prices, the food was overrated and he didn't dare drink at this stage of the game.

Nineteen hundred hours—seven o'clock, he kept reminding himself—came slowly and he wandered over a few minutes before to the featureless gray wooden building he'd been directed to and, after a moment's hesitation, walked in.

A nasty-looking Marine sat inside at a desk and looked at him suspiciously. "Can I help you, sir?" he asked in a tone that said he really didn't want to help at all.

"Lieutenant Fargo," he introduced himself. "I was told to report here."

"Orders, please," the Marine responded quickly. The sergeant took them, looked at them, then said, "ID card, please, sir." Fargo fumbled with his wallet and finally pulled out the photo ID after first reflexively reaching for the FBI identification he no longer carried. The sergeant matched photo with man and orders and decided he passed.

"Second door on the left, room 2-A," he was informed and his material handed back. Fargo shrugged and walked in the indicated direction. Suddenly his sixth sense was alerted by such treatment; he *knew* who was in that room, knew with utter certainty, long before he reached the door and went in.

Houlton Withers looked up and even gave him a slight smile and nod. A good sign, Fargo decided, since Withers really didn't want him and couldn't control him.

He looked at the others in the room. A high-ranking Marine NCO, a big, burly, white-haired senior CPO with hashmarks on his hashmarks, an eager-looking Navy lieutenant, and a bookish lieutenant commander. They were all just sitting there, looking mostly bored, not talking to each other.

As the only man who knew Withers before and also the only one not there by Withers' fiat Fargo felt no need to stand on ceremony. He offered his hand to the colonel who took it, looking a bit surprised at the action.

"Good to have you aboard, Fargo," he rasped.

Fargo turned and looked at the others. "This the lot?"

Withers nodded. "Enough."

"I'd think a warrant and maybe a common seaman," he commented.

Withers shrugged. "We were going to use another enlisted man but then they added you and he got dropped. I doubt if it'll make much difference." He gestured. "Have a seat and we'll get this over with fast. I have to catch a plane for your old stamping grounds in less than three hours. This won't take long, though."

Fargo did and sat back, relaxed, studying the others. He guessed that the reason for this group was more likely that Withers distrusted the lower ranks completely.

"Good to see you men again," Withers began, sounding as friendly as possible. "We considered not having any of you know who the others were but finally decided that, in a pinch or if a real problem comes up, you'd better know who else could substantiate your stories to the captain. That, and a final briefing, are what this meeting is all about."

Withers turned and looked at their faces, looking thoughtful. Finally he said, "All of you were hand-selected by Army, ONI, and FBI intelligence because of your excellent records, your peculiar background qualifications, and your availability. Some of you know why we are doing all this, others of you do not. I'd just as soon keep it that way. For those who don't know, we are shepherding a shipment of a precious and irreplaceable revolutionary weapon—or the key element in it, anyway—for use against Japan. I can only say that if this gets where it is supposed to and there are no security breaches it might end the war when used, saving countless lives and perhaps making an invasion unnecessary."

Fargo looked over the others' faces, found Sarbic doing the same thing. Fargo thought he knew now just who knew and who didn't.

"The U.S.S. *Indianapolis,* a superb ship newly renovated and outfitted, has been chosen for this task. Right now it is up San Francisco Bay at Mare Island Shipyard and that is where you will board her even though she will be coming down here

for the shipment. All of you have elaborate cover stories for
being on board. You all know them. Although none of you are
permanently assigned and will not even be listed on the official
roster you should be aware that between twenty and thirty percent of the *Indianapolis* crew is new. And I mean *new*. Ensigns fresh out of OCS, seamen who've never been to sea, that
sort of thing. I can only say that the senior staff, both officers
and NCOs, is established and competent. I'm not as worried
about them as I am about the new people, who are tradi-
tionally the loosest lips."

He paused for a moment as if to let this sink in, then continued.

"Now, on the way out there will be a large number of passengers, some military but also a lot of civilians. Most of these
men are new to ships and the Navy and almost all of them
know what's going on. I will be concerned if they should have
more than normal contact with the crew since they are also
likely leaks and open to pressure. Most open are two Army
officers, Captain Nolan and Major Furman, who are in charge
of the shipment and responsible for it. They are masquerading
as artillery officers but I doubt if they can even spell it. If they
get into any real trouble I hope one of you can cover for them.
They are the two most important men on the ship. Any questions on these generalities so far?"

Chief Sobel raised his hand. "Colonel, who among the
ship's company will know everything? Anybody other than the
captain?"

"Not even the captain," Withers told him. "I have just come
from Admiral Purnell and we decided that there was no need
to know. The less who know the better."

"But Colonel," the Marine, Sergeant Glass, put in, "if *we*
don't know then how'll we know what's true and what's a wild
guess?"

"You don't have to," he replied. "At debriefing you'll be
asked to report on all such rumors and suspicions and we'll
make the determination while the ship's still at sea in a combat

zone. Plans now call for the ship to drop off some of the passengers at Pearl Harbor but most of them, including the Army men and the package, will be dropped at their final destination farther on. Orders will then take you to Guam, where you'll be able to let us know if there's a major breach, and then to Leyte, PSF headquarters, where you'll all disembark and be interrogated in full by a debriefing team that will probably include me. From there we'll get you home or to other assignments with the exception of Chief Sobel, who's indicated a desire to be added to the ship's permanent company. CINC-PAC has no objections and so that's the way it'll be. Captain McVay is going to be pretty pissed off about this mission as it is—he's top-heavy with officers and light on seamen and has had only a few days to get this new crew in shape. He'll be breaking in on the go and then after in the Leyte area."

"What about the passengers, Colonel?" Fargo asked. "Do they know about us?"

"Nolan and Furman know you're around but not who you are," he was told. "I'd like to keep it that way unless absolutely necessary. Fargo, you have the most routine mobility aboard ship and you know the full score, so I'll leave the panic button to you. Check with these men from time to time but press it only if you hear the magic word."

Fargo nodded, surprised, flattered, but a little suspicious. It sounded too much like an effort to placate. He wondered which of the others was the inevitable man Withers assigned to keep watch on all of them. Especially him.

"When do we leave, sir?" Coringa asked.

"You'll start boarding the ship in the next few hours through Saturday morning, not all at the same time. Pick up your specific orders from the sergeant at the desk outside. As to when you sail—well, if you don't know you can't betray the fact to anybody else. Let's just say that if I were to go to the movies I would not pick a double feature and let it go at that." They chuckled appreciatively, which pleased Withers.

"Anything else? I've individually briefed all of you except

Commander Fargo here and he was briefed by his department." Nicely subtle, Fargo thought. "No?" Withers continued. "Well, good luck, then. And, gentlemen—I remind you of
this one fact and it's no joke. You, the ship, everybody is one
hundred percent expendable. Only the cargo is not. It *must* be
delivered. Too much, perhaps the whole war, depends on that.
I know that sounds trite but in this case it's true. If it's a choice
between saving the ship or that cargo you save that cargo.
Clear?"

It was an uncomfortable thought for all of them but they
remained silent.

"All right, then," Withers concluded. "Good-bye, good
luck, and I'll see you in a couple of weeks on Leyte." With that
he picked up his ever-present briefcase and walked out.

They got up and started for the exit and one of them, the
lieutenant, came up to Fargo. "You know what this is all
about, then, huh?" Coringa prompted.

"I have a fair idea," he admitted. "Why?"

"C'mon. I just gotta know," the other prompted. "Please?
Hell, I wouldn't be here if I wasn't trustworthy but I like to
know what it is I'm being asked to stick my neck out for."

He thought about it a moment, then pulled him to one side
farther down the hall as the others walked out. "O.K., I'll tell
you," he whispered. "It's a gigantic purple death ray that only
kills Japs. Turns 'em to stone. Something in their skin. It'll
make the invasion a piece of cake."

"Wow!" Coringa breathed. "Thanks a lot!" and he was
gone.

Fargo stared after him a moment unbelievingly and chuckled at the man's gullibility. Well, at least he knew now who
Withers' man was. He was just what was to be expected.

San Francisco
Sunday,
July 15, 1945

Captain Charles Butler McVay III was both puzzled and slightly annoyed as he left the *Indianapolis* for a waiting staff car. Only last Thursday he'd been told to make ready for sea, this after repeated assurances that he'd have another month or more to shake this green crew into shape.

It didn't make any sense. Spruance was in Guam plotting the invasion of Japan, which wouldn't be before the end of October or early November. Everybody, even the Japanese, knew that. There were no other islands that would require the kind of bombardment the *Indy* had been used for, and the Jap Navy was a pitiful remnant of what it once was. He was realistic enough to know that his ship was a venerable old lady past her thirteenth birthday and had long ago been superseded by more modern designs. As part of a bombardment group or a flagship she was just fine, but for anything else she would be marginal.

He'd also, indirectly, been feeling the complaints of his crew. He liked his men and depended on them and understood them. A couple of them had asked him for advice on whether they should get married and he'd told them to go ahead if they wanted to, that it was a good bet they'd do nothing but sea trials and a good painting and housecleaning into September. They would never say a word, but he could already hear in his mind what they'd be thinking about *this*.

Worse, he told himself, a single day of sea trials just wasn't enough to work the bugs out and get used to the new stuff they'd crammed on board at Mare Island while repairing the bomb damage. Somebody, he thought, was a little crazy.

There had been consternation the last few days as wives and sweethearts were suddenly wrenched as the men were ordered to report. A number of the new men were still in service schools and now wouldn't graduate. Others were having monkey wrenches thrown in their roads to promotion. It was not, he told himself, going to be a happy ship.

About the only things he felt good about were the life jackets. With a make ready for sea order he hadn't a single life jacket aboard and had wasted a considerable amount of time Thursday and Friday trying to get some, going all the way to the office of the commander, Western Sea Frontier, before he was through. The obstinacy of supply officers and petty bureaucrats was a constant source of amazement to him. He suspected that they would refuse a ship permission to sink in enemy action until the proper forms were filled out and signed by the appropriate officers. He remembered the little memo from the Naval Aviation section that had been sent by routine channels to his reconnaissance pilots and maintenance crews on what forms to fill out if your parachute failed to open.

The car sped across the bay from Oakland to San Francisco and over to naval headquarters, where McVay was quickly ushered upstairs to Rear Admiral William R. Purnell's office. The admiral and his exec, Captain William Parsons, greeted him cordially.

"How'd the old girl shape up, Cherub?" Purnell asked, using the appropriate nickname that described McVay's careful appearance and that was permitted only from superior officers and family.

"What can you say about one day?" he complained. "She's afloat, she seems sound, but her crew needs weeks, not hours, to get itself and her into shape. The place is a mess. Tools and remains of shipyard work all over, fresh paint on some areas, and no paint at all on others."

"The bottom line, Charlie," Parsons put in. "Could you take her out and clean up the mess along the way or not?"

McVay looked at the other two. "Yes, of course. Provided we didn't have any hostile action during that period. I wouldn't like to take anything nasty on without whipping this crew into a lot better shape."

"You get your life jackets?" Purnell asked.

McVay nodded. "Yeah. Finally." He decided not to mention that, by pulling out all the stops, they'd somehow received twenty-five hundred life jackets from two different sources and were now being smothered by them. He was afraid they'd take them all back.

"All right, then," Purnell continued. "So you proved yesterday your boys can sail her and that she's shipshape. Everything else will have to be done on the run, at least until this is over. This afternoon you'll bring her down to Hunter's Point and take on a small top-secret cargo and a couple of passengers. You'll sail tomorrow morning at 0300 making top speed —the best you can do, flat out!—making Pearl Harbor, where you'll stay only long enough to drop most of your passengers and refuel. Get away as soon as possible and, still at top speed, get to Tinian and turn your cargo over to others as specified in your sealed orders."

McVay said, "*Hmph.* Sounds very mysterious. Am I to be told what we're carrying?"

The other officers looked a little embarrassed. McVay understood the meaning immediately and dropped the subject.

He'd heard rumors of work on a lot of nasty weapons and knew that Japan itself would be no picnic. A small top-secret cargo meant that somebody had come up with a germ to soften up, maybe decimate, Japan before it was invaded, he decided. It made sense to him although he didn't like it.

"Charlie, this cargo is *vital*. One of a kind," the admiral emphasized. "We can't replace it, we can't afford not to have it in Tinian as soon as possible. It's so important it's to be guarded over your own ship. Even if she goes down, stick it in a lifeboat and plop your Marines on top of it if you have to. Two Army officers will accompany it but your own Marines will handle security aboard. Nobody else is even to go near it, not even you. Clear?"

McVay nodded soberly. If a plague could be dropped on Japan well in advance of invasion, and our soldiers were immunized, it could save tens of thousands of American lives. He wasn't too worried about the delivery, though, just the package itself. Green crew or not, he was confident that any ship that could take the kind of hit his had at Okinawa and still sail back to port would have no problems with a milk run like this. His suspicions as to the cargo were confirmed by Parsons' next statement.

"One small part of the cargo will be kept apart from the rest," the captain said. "It should be as far from the crew as possible, maybe in officers' country, with a guard on the door at all times, the Army men near it, and absolutely no other human being is even to approach it. I have your sailing orders here." He fumbled on the desk, found a manila envelope with wax seal and nothing at all written on the outside, then handed it to McVay. "You wouldn't believe the security they had even on *that*," Parsons told him. "I had to unhandcuff the courier personally with a key that came from a bank vault somewhere."

McVay sighed and got up. "I guess I'd better get moving, then." Purnell and Parsons also stood. "I'll get you a good movie tonight to occupy everybody's mind," the admiral added lightly. "An Esther Williams maybe, to get your new boys used to the water."

They laughed and shook hands and Purnell walked McVay to the door. "This is serious, Charlie, but not too hard. Do it good. Every hour sooner you get this stuff to Tinian is an hour shorter the war will be. Believe it when I say that. I promise that when it's used you'll be the first to know. O.K.?"

McVay just nodded. "All right, Admiral. We'll do our job."

"I know you will," Purnell replied confidently.

Major Furman and Captain Nolan had spent an enjoyable night in town but now they were at the Presidio for final preparations and check-out. There were so many overseas shots that even Dr. Nolan complained, then duplicate sets of orders that made references to oddly encoded island names and such but that clearly assigned them to the 509th Composite Group, 313th Wing, 21st Bombing Command, Twentieth Air Force. For an engineer and a doctor it was quite a mouthful and Furman complained that he'd never remember all the stuff he was attached to. Nolan suggested it be tattooed on their chests. By this stage of the war the Air Force was to the Army what the Marines were to the Navy—the same department but still a whole different world.

Finally they each were issued, and signed for one .45 caliber revolver and one box of .45 caliber bullets. Furman just stowed his with his regular gear but noted with amusement that Nolan packed the bullets in one bag and the revolver in the other so that under no circumstances could they come together.

By the time they returned to Hunter's Point late that afternoon they saw that a huge ship was now docked there. It looked more like a floating city than a mere warship, almost dwarfing nearby buildings. Nolan whistled. "If that's a cruiser then imagine what battleship or carrier size must be!" Neither man had ever been on anything like this before.

"Wonder why it's kind of broken in the middle, like two ships on one body?" Furman mused aloud.

"See those catapults?" Nolan pointed. "I think the damn thing's got airplanes on it, too!"

Furman was unconvinced. "Taking off I could see, maybe, but I wonder how they land?"

"In the water," he was told. "Those cranes come over and lift them back up. I'll make you a bet on it."

"Uh-uh. You probably read up on it or something."

Nolan grinned. "Saw it in *Movietone News* a few months back."

Now they were rolling right up the dock to the ship, and sailors seemed to spring out of nowhere to unload and take their bags aboard. One opened their door, saluted, then directed them to a gangplank nearby. There was a guard or something posted and for a moment they were unsure what to do. Furman took out a copy of his orders and handed them over. The guard took them briefly, gave a cursory glance, then handed them back and stood there seemingly waiting for something. Finally he said, out of the side of his mouth and in a very low tone, "You're supposed to ask me for permission to come aboard, sirs."

Nolan coughed slightly in embarrassment. "Major Furman and Captain Nolan requesting permission to come aboard."

"Permission granted, sirs, proceed," the guard responded, visibly relieved. They made their way up the gangplank and neither saw the roll of eyes and disgusted look to heaven behind them.

A commander was at the other end and offered his hand as they stepped aboard. "Commander Joe Flynn," he introduced himself. "I'm the exec. Welcome aboard the *Indianapolis,* gentlemen." They shook hands warmly. Flynn was easy to like and had the knack of putting people at ease quickly. "I'll take you to the captain."

They followed him past a huge number of men and

threaded their way past equipment stacked all over the place. The ship was a huge madhouse, the Army men decided.

Captain McVay welcomed them warmly. "None of the crew knows this," he told them, "but we'll spend a relaxed night, put everybody to bed, then about 0300 take your cargo aboard. Most of the crew and all of the passengers will be asleep and we can do it with a minimum of fuss. We'll sail at 0800."

"Ah, Captain, it's the small cargo that we're most concerned about," Furman said hesitantly. "Where will we put it?"

"I've already gotten the dimensions and given them to the metal shop," the captain told them. "The most secure area aboard is Admiral Spruance's cabin below the bridge. He's not home and not likely to be, so I'd say that's probably the best place on the whole ship. We're ready for it."

Flynn took them down to the cabin and they examined the area and the fittings furnished by the Navy Yard and the ship's own shops and decided it would do. One thing bothered Furman, though.

"There seem to be a lot of civilians around," he said, a little puzzled. "Or is it just me?"

"No, it's highly unusual," Flynn admitted, "but we have to live with it, at least to Pearl. They've been coming aboard and getting in the way for the past week and they're driving all of us up the wall. It's the old story—they're needed somewhere and we're going to be going that way so they hitch." He went over to a bulletin board and took a memo off it and handed it to them. "I made this thing up in self-defense a couple of days ago."

It was an open letter to the passengers that said, in part, "This ship has twenty more officers than called for, and, on the other hand, only 84 percent of the steward's mates allowed for its normal complement. It follows, then, that our messing and berthing facilities are taxed to the limit. With all hands cooperating and showing consideration for others, there is no reason why we cannot be comfortable—at least more comfortable than many of our service mates on the beaches in the Forward Area. A large percentage of the crew is new to the ship and some are new to ships, period, and they have allowed us no training at all so we're going to have to teach them as we go along. You will assist greatly by remaining clear of the activities. With services taxed to the limit we cannot do your laundry. However, we have just purchased a large supply of games from our wardroom funds. You are welcome to use them in the wardroom. Lights go out in the wardroom at 10:00 P.M. Ain't war hell? We thank you for your understanding and cooperation."

There was more, such as blackout regulations and information on smoking and such, but it was clear that the ship wasn't 100 percent prepared to do all the Navy demanded of it.

"Are you sure you can handle this job?" Nolan asked, worried.

Flynn smiled and retacked the memo on the bulletin board. "Sure. As I said there, it's the fact that we're inconvenienced. We could be on some shitty little tropical island flushing Japs out of caves, too. When you think of that I think we can all stand a little inconvenience." He looked thoughtful. "Oh, since you're in a special category we'll do *your* laundry," he added almost playfully.

They walked back to the gangplank and Flynn gave them another Irish grin. "Come back again real soon, won't you?"

The Army men laughed. "We'll try and work it in," Nolan assured him and they walked off. About halfway down Furman whispered, "Do you have to ask permission to leave, too?"

"Let's just walk past and find out," Nolan suggested and they did.

Next they were taken over to the headquarters building, where they met with Captain Parsons.

"I'm going to be leaving soon for Trinity," he told them.

"By that time we'll know. If you suddenly find out you're not sailing you'll know that all was quiet over there."

"It'll work," Furman assured him confidently. "This project is the result of the most geniuses ever assembled with all the money and facilities they wanted. If this doesn't work it'll collapse every physics department in the world."

They got down to cases. "Very few on the ship know what it's carrying. Not even the captain knows." Again Parsons outlined the procedures just in case—of anything. Again he suggested the lifeboat idea.

"I don't remember seeing any lifeboats," Nolan remarked nervously.

"Whatever," Parsons said, dismissing the thought. "Anything that'll float. And Captain Nolan—I'd suggest you use your own judgment on this, of course, but you might tell the captain you're a doctor and reassure him that there's nothing that'll harm him or the crew. It would ease his mind. I have a feeling he has a totally wrong but equally dangerous idea of what might be on there."

"I'll do that, sir," Nolan assured him.

"Get a few hours' sleep," Parsons suggested. "It's been arranged that you'll be called for about 0130 and taken to the ship. Loading's at three and then you can relax and enjoy a balmy ocean cruise."

"I hope so, sir," Furman replied nervously.

A young couple, looking like young couples everywhere, stood in the parking area near the Golden Gate Bridge taking pictures of each other against the skyline and looking through a big, long telescope they had. They even used the telescope to take some pictures of the classic San Francisco skyline in the distance and helped a few other tourists, mostly servicemen and elderly couples, to do the same. They were a handsome pair; he looked like he was on leave from the Army or perhaps the Marines, she like the perfect newlywed.

An elderly man who'd just driven in walked over to them

slowly, taking in the view. San Francisco's famous fog was already rolling in. It was late afternoon and in another hour the view would be completely obscured.

The newcomer smiled and nodded to the young couple and they did the same. Finally he opened a conversation about the telescope and even asked for a look, which was proudly offered. As he peered in he said, very low, out of the corner of his mouth, "Teams two and six confirm it's at the Point and they moved a big ship down from Mare Island this afternoon."

The young woman nodded. "We saw it. Earlier surveys at Mare Island say it's the *Indianapolis*. We saw her go out into the ocean yesterday and come back."

The elderly man nodded, fumbling with the scope as if trying to see something better. He appeared to be looking at Alcatraz. "Damn this fog!" he muttered. "They could be loading now and out after dark and you'd never see 'em."

"Still, I think you should make your call," the young man said enigmatically.

The older man nodded. "I agree. I'll do it within the hour. You two pack up when the fog socks the city in and get back to your hotel. Our part's over now." With that he thanked the couple loudly for the use of the telescope and walked back to his waiting old car.

Viktor Lemotov studied the reports. "It fits," he sighed. "Our targets are there, we know from the convoys that the bomb is there, and now a ship just made for transporting it is there. They wouldn't have the ship down at the Navy Yard, particularly on such short notice, without a decision already made. They will load tonight and sail with the tide, I'd bet on it."

Sarachevko nodded. "Any word from Moscow yet?"

Lemotov scowled. "Nothing. You'd think I was sending in blank reports. I'll wager they haven't even told the Secretary yet—they're letting me take the responsibility. If I'm right, they'll take the credit—if not, I will burn."

"You're going to do it on your own, then," Sarachevko said more than asked.

His boss nodded. "Life is a series of gambles," he said philosophically. "I'm going to gamble on this one. Send the following in High Code to Kransky in Tokyo: Superbomb being shipped aboard U.S.S. *Indianapolis* this A.M. for Forward Area, probably via Tolosa, Philippines. Weapon could force end to war disadvantageous to us. Recommend leak to Japanese Admiralty for intercept in our best interest. Ship leaving San Francisco probably via Honolulu and Guam. Time accordingly." He grinned evilly. "Sign it Beria," he ordered.

Sarachevko's eyebrows rose. "That's taking on a bit *too* much, isn't it?"

Lemotov shrugged. "If I'm wrong it's my neck, and if I'm right the son-of-a-bitch will take the credit anyway. They wouldn't act on my say-so alone."

His aide sighed and stared at the message, his head shaking slowly from side to side. Suddenly he looked up into Lemotov's steely eyes. "After I send this could I get a transfer approved? Say, Mongolia, China, someplace safe like that?"

"Quit worrying so much," Lemotov chided. "Siberia is beautiful in winter."

Hiroshima, Japan
Monday,
July 16, 1945

They stood in a line, four dragons of the sea, larger, fiercer, more deadly than any denizen placed there by nature. Once they had been there in almost countless number, back in the old days, the very old days, when their sisters had gone out with the great Imperial fleet from this same port to attack a different base, so far away, at Pearl Harbor on a December day that seemed ten thousand lifetimes ago.

Now they were four, perhaps destined like the great predators of long-past prehistoric seas to extinction, yet they sat there, proudly, in the early-morning light.

Now, slowly, with whatever fanfare could be mustered in these dark days, one rumbles and shivers into life, then, slowly, deliberately, it slides out into the blue picture-book harbor and takes a slow turn to the south.

It is July 16 in Hiroshima; hours later it is July 16 in far-off

New Mexico, where other men, too, take actions as the dawn that began near Hiroshima reaches them, actions that will link the great predator, her place of origin, and history together.

And reaching out to both is a ship preparing to sail from San Francisco, also on this very morning.

It has begun.

Site "Trinity" North of Alamogordo Monday, July 16, 1945

A hot July wind was blowing the gypsum-topped sands of New Mexico. It was a dry, lonesome desert wind that sandblasted rock and carved weird formations out of rock. The wind had worried the project controllers a great deal but now it seemed to be dying down and forecasters were confident that, by dawn, it would vanish as such winds often do.

About thirty miles from Trinity, along a high set of mountains that seemed to jut out of the desert floor just south of Bingham, two tiny figures against the darkened landscape made their way on horseback to their now-accustomed hiding place. Their vigil had been discouraging. The two, a man and a woman, had been coming for almost two weeks now hoping to see something that was supposed to have been a secret.

The first fence lay just beyond the mountains. It was an easy one of low barbed wire and they and their horses managed to jump it with no problems. The second was worse—it was perhaps seven feet high, topped with nasty barbed wire and spikes, and was electrified, as warnings every few hundred feet attested. Frequently the dead body of a coyote or jackrabbit heaped against the fence left no doubt about the truth of the warning.

The height was much too great for the horses and the sinister humming sound the fence gave off was enough deterrent.

But the pair on horseback were not stupid. They'd picked this spot because it had several advantages. It was far from any roads, shielded by natural barriers, and the hard-packed gypsum here was like concrete and would not leave signs of unauthorized entry.

The fence that guarded the proving ground was manned by regular Jeep patrols.

Now the man removed elaborate equipment from a large saddlepack on the back of his horse and donned thick, insulated gloves. The hard work had been done two weeks before; he had only to find the correct section of fence that had been invisibly cut and spliced. He unwrapped his own section of fence from his roll with the woman's help and carefully attached it to predetermined points at the main fence, securing it in place with electrical tape. Once he'd almost botched it when the temporary electrical bridge had come loose. Another time the woman had almost touched a horse while gripping the fence.

The temporary link was attached and carefully unrolled around them and the horses and then back to another section of fence about ten feet farther on. Only after it was firmly attached at both ends and hummed with voltage itself did he carefully undo the main-fence section and lower it carefully to the ground so it was flat and not touching the other sections. The woman, holding the horses still, nervously glanced at her watch. Patrols were due in a very few minutes.

With the current unbroken but bypassed around them, she

led the horses through the gap and breathed a sigh of relief when they were clear.

Now came the trickiest part; the man walked back through and carefully pulled his bypass section back toward the hole in the fence. If his temporary connections broke during this the voltage would be interrupted and the place would quickly be alive with sentries.

On taped-together spring joints, the section was brought through and over the cut section of original fence. The cut section was lifted and restored, and the taped sections dabbed with rust-colored paint once more. Only after he was certain that all was secure did he remove and reroll his bypass section of fence and affix it to his horse's pack.

It was a good job but only an expert could have managed it.

"Listen!" the woman hissed. He froze for an instant, cocking an ear expectantly. To the north along the fence came the unmistakable sound of a Jeep.

"They're early," he said worriedly. "Let's get out of here fast. We have to be set up by dawn."

She nodded and they both mounted, took another quick, nervous look around to make certain they'd left no telltale signs, then rode off just as a pair of headlights appeared and came slowly toward the invisibly breached section.

The terrain was as rugged inside the fence as out and they took temporary shelter behind a large rock outcrop and watched anxiously to see if they had fooled the sentries.

The Jeep pulled up near the breach and dropped a sentry off, then roared on. They saw he had a flashlight and was starting to walk slowly.

"Dimitri! You don't suppose . . . ?" the woman whispered.

He shook his head from side to side. "Hard to see anything in this darkness but I don't think so. Look—see? The light is walking away from our little gateway."

That was almost as disturbing. "Then why the sentry?" she wondered. "They have never done this before. Not up here, anyway."

He considered the question. "Listen! What do you hear?" he asked her.

She was quiet for a moment, then shook her head in bewilderment. "Nothing. I hear nothing. What . . . ?"

"No wind," he told her. "Suddenly there is no wind. It is dying with the coming dawn. The sky is clear. And now a sentry even here."

She suddenly realized the import of those facts. "The test—they will do the test today!"

He nodded. "We had better be going. They could do it any time and if we are not in place all our efforts are wasted."

Quickly, yet silently, they moved off into the darkness.

A red phone buzzed and Colonel Houlton Withers grabbed it. Even he would disapprove of his appearance and bearing this predawn morning. He'd slept not at all in over forty-eight hours.

He picked up the phone. "Withers," he snapped.

"Captain Garnes, sir," a voice responded crisply. "All sentries now deployed, all systems green and in working order."

That reassured him, but only slightly. "Very well," he responded, trying to sound as crisp and military as the captain. "Report any abnormalities to me immediately."

He no sooner hung up the phone when a familiar face popped just inside his doorway. "Holly, you look like hell," General Bruse said sourly. "You going to stay buried here when she pops? Come on, man! Last chance for a ringside seat."

Withers winced at the nickname and vowed once more silently to banish its use forever when he got his first star. "I'm coming, General," he sighed tiredly. "Be with you in a minute."

He didn't really want to go; he was driven more by a sense of duty than of history. In fact, for all the time he'd been with the project, he really had no concept of just what it was they were going to do up there. A giant bomb, that was all. Just another giant bomb. What he *did* know was that nobody but authorized personnel were permitted to witness its test and that it would be his ass if any breach occurred.

"Wind velocity three miles per hour from the northeast," a loudspeaker snapped, echoing throughout the walls of the concrete blockhouse. "Thirty minutes to zero and counting."

The bunker was one of many and not the closest. The steel tower holding the test object was over ten miles away, out by itself in the white, sandy valley of central New Mexico. Still, it was very crowded by the time Withers reached the main viewing area. There were lots of people there with badges and photo IDs and lots of little cards, too. He saw that a large number of them were middle-aged civilians, some with foreign-sounding accents. He automatically disliked and distrusted them on both grounds, but he could not fight their presence—*he* did not make the list. He looked around uncomfortably. Hell—those two old geezers over there were speaking *German* to each other, for Christ's sake! German!

Less than ninety days after V-E Day, in the most top-secret military installation possibly in the world, it was enough to unnerve the most liberal of officers.

He spotted Bruse and, thankful for a familiar face and a kindred spirit, glided up to him.

The general nodded, smiled, and handed him a pair of what seemed to be welder's goggles. "Here, Holly. When the count comes down to a minute or so put these on. If this thing's anything like it's advertised it might blind you without 'em."

"Like a miniature sun, possibly," agreed an older civilian with a Dutch accent the paranoid Withers took to be pure German.

The colonel looked suspiciously at the goggles. "Well, maybe I just won't look until it's over," he said uncertainly.

Bruse found his chief aide's tone and manner amusing. "Hell, Holly, do you realize what we're going to see here?" he prodded. "Why, man, this could be the greatest weapon in the history of mankind. Right, Doctor?"

The Dutchman nodded. "That is true," he agreed. "Or it could be a big fizzle, a big dud." He made a sputtering sound that spit slightly. Withers turned away, more than a little uncomfortable.

"Or maybe ve can't stop it, eh, Karl?" another of the scientists called, sounding not a bit worried about the idea. "Maybe in the next few minutes ve destroy the vorld, heh? Some fizzle!"

Karl shrugged. "Not to be helped, Nils," he responded fatalistically. "It's going to go this morning, though."

Withers continued to look more and more upset, more from the company than the conversation. A young Army sergeant came over, dressed in medical whites, and pinned a funny-looking card on him. He started to protest, then realized that everybody else was wearing one and shut up.

"It's a monitor, detects radiation, Holly," Bruse explained. "Keep it. It could save your life. This thing might kill at a distance."

Withers looked around conspiratorially and lowered his voice to a whisper. "Can I speak to you privately for a minute?"

The general looked puzzled but nodded and they went to the rear of the observation area, apart from the others who were all jockeying for best view. "What's worrying you, Holly? This end-of-the-world talk?"

Withers shook his head. "No, no. I don't follow all that bullshit, you know that. A bomb's a bomb to me. It's *them!* Hell, they're all Krauts and Frogs! About the only thing we're missing are some Japs!"

Bruse chuckled. "But—Holly. They're on *our* side! In this room you have some of the world's greatest scientific brains, all those who aren't directly connected with the test."

"They're Krauts, Frogs, and Wops," Withers persisted. "They should be in camps someplace, not here. Especially not here."

The general sighed and shook his head. "But—Holly! They

invented the damned thing! That little fellow over there—he did a lot of the math, the Dane and the Dutchman and the little Italian fellow over there did most of the physics. This is *their* baby. About the only big brain that wasn't involved was Einstein."

"Krauts, Frogs, Wops—at least no Kikes, I see," Withers responded glumly. "Shit. I wonder why you even bother with security at all."

Bruse gave up and sighed. Withers was as dense as the concrete in the bunker and had about as much imagination. But his very hardheaded paranoid bigotry made him good at his work. He'd never failed to do any job assigned him, and security for a project like this was made for a mind like his. Still, Bruse couldn't resist a parting shot. "Well, Holly, under those rules you shouldn't be here, either. We fought two wars with the country your ancestors came from."

"Huh?"

"Your ancestors were English, weren't they?"

"Twenty minutes to zero and counting," said the loudspeaker. "The bomb is now armed. I repeat, the bomb is now armed."

Dawn was coming up slowly but steadily. Darkness was so absolute in the remote desert that the effect was of someone slowly turning up an electric light. The stars provide little illumination despite being displayed in a number and depth inconceivable to citybound folks; now they faded into a brightening twilight. The sentry was glad for that; there is nothing more discomforting than such dark isolation.

The fact that he was only a few feet from potentially lethal voltage didn't help, either. He'd stayed very near the outer fence since being dropped off; the light would give him a lot more confidence as he made his rounds.

It also produced funny sensations. As he walked back toward the center of his post he thought the fence sagged oddly in one spot. As he approached it he saw signs of some sort of disturbance in the hard ground there. At first he dismissed it, since it was close to where the Jeep had dropped him off, but now it looked a little too dug up for that. He approached it gingerly, nervously, as if it were a nest of snakes.

And then he saw it. Faint, yes, but there it was—a light print of a horse's hoof. He straightened up, puzzled. Did they use horses to patrol these remote sections sometimes? He wondered, but he didn't know.

Boredom sometimes makes geniuses of ordinary minds. He turned to the barbed-wire fence and went up close to it, peering studiously at the ground. There *did* seem to be disturbances on the other side, and he cursed under his breath his inability to get to the other side and take a closer look at them. He was a farmboy from Iowa. He'd love to see if the hoofprint inside the outer fence would match those that just might lie beyond the second.

He turned and examined the electrical fence, still too nervous to get really close to it. It sagged a little, yes, but it didn't really look out of place. He walked to within a couple feet of it, as close as his own caution would allow him.

There were some metal seams there, yes—but they appeared rust-covered. The fence had obviously been patched, any fool could tell that, but the question was when and by whom? Yes —he could see faint impressions on the other side where some work had gone on. The dry air and hard-packed soil would preserve such signs, he knew. They could have been made yesterday—or a month ago. Fences wear out, this kind even shorted out—often—and repairs were always needed at one point or another, he knew.

He felt oddly relieved and started to walk away, rifle on shoulder. It took about five minutes before it occurred to him that in a climate like this rust would be very unlikely on new work.

A phone buzzed and a staff sergeant picked it up, talked for a few seconds, then looked around.

"Colonel Withers?" he almost shouted over the conversation in the crowded area. "Is a Colonel Withers here?"

The security man barged through the mob without an apology and almost snatched the phone from the sergeant's hand. "Withers," he snapped.

"Colonel? Joe Kerrigan. One of the sentries thinks he has a breach of the fence up north of Trinity. Outer perimeter, middle of nowhere, but he says he's got a horseshoe print inside the outer-fence ring and signs of tampering with the electric fence."

Withers didn't like that at all. "You're sending a team out there?"

"No can do until H-Hour, Colonel," Kerrigan replied apologetically. "They've grounded us and everybody else. Too close to test time."

Withers' mind raced. "No sign of a voltage gap?"

"Nothing," Kerrigan admitted. *"That* we'd know, although even that wouldn't mean much. Sections up there short out all the time when a coyote gets curious. But the sentry says there's an obvious fence-section patch, some disturbances on all sides of the two fences, and rust on the patches. *Rust,* Colonel."

Withers understood the problem. Enough moisture to create any amount of rust in this climate would also have aided in obscuring the prints. They were either unrelated or something was terribly wrong. There *could* be a logical explanation, but still . . .

"Have you checked with maintenance? Any patches in that sector?"

"Dozens, Colonel," Kerrigan responded. "As I said, something's always going wrong. But I can't check on anything specific until after the test. Everybody's battened down. It'd take some time to rustle up somebody and go through all the records and we don't have the time."

"Make time," Withers growled. "And notify Cameron at FBI Command Post. He's not as restricted as we are. Call me back when you have something." He slammed the phone

down, looked around and spotted General Bruse, and stalked over to his superior.

"Something wrong?" Bruse asked, seeing Withers' expression.

"May be a breach of the perimeter up north," Withers replied ominously. "I think we ought to postpone until it's checked out."

The general was interested. "What've you got?"

Quickly, precisely, Withers gave him the information from the sentry and answered all the questions he himself had asked Kerrigan.

Bruse wasn't convinced. "Hell, all you got is the suspicion of some bored eighteen-year-old with a gun and a uniform, nothing more. We couldn't postpone on that, Holly. You should know better. Every delay costs enormously in time and money." He looked around. "Not to mention that we've got a lot of bigwigs here, including a lot of big political power and more brass than you can imagine. Bring me a confirmed breach and I'll back you. Otherwise—well, *you* want to call General Groves and tell him he's got to stop it?" Withers opened his mouth to reply but Bruse didn't let him. "Let it lie, Holly. I thought you were ambitious."

That got him. The colonel went back to the phone and called Major Kerrigan.

"Can't scrub," he told the other man. "Get a team out there as soon as possible after the blast. Let's assume that if anybody got in that way they'll try to get out that way. Let's just make sure they don't get out. You call Cameron?"

"Yeah. He's heading there now—but it's gonna take a hell of a long time. No roads. We'll probably still beat him there when we can go."

Withers thought furiously. "How about a small plane?"

"Nowhere to land it," he was told. "And, besides, there're planes up now for the test and even they don't want to get close to the bomb. Our pilots just aren't up to it. Nope, we're stuck."

Withers sighed and hung up. There was absolutely nothing that could be done until the test was over.

"Five minutes to zero and counting," said the loudspeaker.

The man and woman were set up now, still eleven miles from the blast site but as close as they dared come. The truth was, they hadn't the slightest idea how close was "safe" and it worried them, but they knew that some of the buildings on the proving grounds were closer than they and it reassured them a little. If the official observers, who knew what they were doing, felt safe, then they should be safe, too.

They were well hidden. A low-flying observer plane had passed by a couple of times but that was long ago. Everything was quiet now—almost too quiet. Unearthly still, like death.

The woman lit a cigarette nervously and wiped the perspiration from her forehead. Only a small bit of it was from the building heat. She looked at her watch. 6:28. "What do you think it'll be like?" she asked nervously.

He shrugged. "Who knows? Like a little sun, they said. I don't know just what that means." He leaned over and checked his cameras on their tripods, all with motor-driven film and linked together with a single activating cord, which he grasped in his hand.

They could not see the tower or the bomb; they didn't dare go over the last of the range for a clear view of the valley as much as they wanted to—there was no concealment, no protection there. They heard the noise of airplanes overhead, seemingly circling.

The man yawned. "Looks like we might have another wasted day baking in this forsaken hole," he grumped.

That almost relaxed her a bit. "Maybe it didn't work," she suggested hopefully.

"I don't know. I—" he started to reply and, suddenly, there it was.

It was so abrupt and unexpected that he was slow in triggering the cameras. It was a lousy view but they could see it all the same—an enormous flash of incredibly intense light turning the dawn to full daylight and beyond in an instant. It was so bright they both had to turn away from it. The cameras clicked on automatically.

In a small plane overhead Captain Parsons gasped, then stared awestruck at the immensity of the explosion.

In the bunkers everyone gasped as the fireball flared and grew. Many turned away; a few prayed, the rest stood transfixed watching the spectacle through their thick welder's goggles. Some were awestruck, some fascinated, others horrified.

"Oh, my God!" someone whispered. "What have we created?"

"There's the end of the war," another remarked pragmatically.

"Not until we drop one on Japan," the voice of General Groves responded.

And after the great light came the firestorm, sweeping out over their mock village and reaching the closest bunkers. The men there were well protected and well insulated, yet even they could feel the intense heat penetrate over ten feet of solid concrete and lead.

And now came the sound, a thundering roar greater than any had ever heard before, the cry of a process that seemed to make the very earth scream in pain and agony. The sound always came last, as if a slow runner was rushing to catch up with the pack.

The entire world seemed to shake. It was an earthquake; it was more than an earthquake. Things and people fell and shifted and the depth of the sound went right through them.

Moments later it reached the hidden and unauthorized observers on that rocky outcrop. Fascinated, almost spellbound by the visual pyrotechnics, they were totally unprepared for the massive shock wave and it knocked both of them off their feet. Rock shifted, the cameras toppled and rolled down the grade and were soon covered by rock and dirt. There would be no photographs.

The horses panicked and reared, trying to get away from their tethered position.

And, finally, there was a massive wind as air rushed to fill the hot vacuum in the center of the nuclear storm.

The woman recovered first and got shakily to her feet, then ran down to the terrified animals, tried to quiet and soothe them. The man pulled himself erect and looked first down the slope at his wrecked equipment. Buried, he thought sickly. Only then did he look up in the direction of the explosion.

There was a massive cloud rising there now, growing darker every moment, a giant magnification of the greatest man-made explosion known prior to that moment. Dirt, sand, everything around Ground Zero had been broken up into the finest component bits and thrown skyward an impossible distance.

It looked like a thunderstorm in the shape of some giant, hideous, misshapen mushroom. Its awesome hellishness made both of them shiver.

The shock wave, vastly diminished now, rolled past the perimeter. From the vantage point of the sentry the sky had simply grown suddenly bright, then dimmed back to normal. He was not prepared at all for the shock that followed, no longer with the force to knock him down but almost strong enough to make him lose his footing. The fences writhed like serpents and as he watched he saw the suspicious patches in the suspect section of fence give ever so slightly, then come apart at the top, leaving a very even tear. There were sparks flying.

The light was easily seen as far away as Albuquerque; the shock wave was still strong enough to rattle windows in faraway Las Vegas, Nevada. People awoke all over the Southwest, shaken, and there were thousands of calls to local police, newspapers, everybody who should know what it was. There were lots of questions and few answers.

The official explanations were glib and tailored for each area. It was an earthquake; it was a gas explosion; it was . . .

well, whatever seemed convincing. No need to be worried, nothing was harmed. Locals were glibly informed that it was a big new blockbuster under test; those close enough to know but who should not were told that it was an accidental explosion at the testing grounds, not to worry, nobody hurt.

But only those observers actually at Trinity knew what had really happened. A coded telegram was now going to Potsdam to inform the President and his closest advisers. Over at Hunter's Point Navy Yard in San Francisco they still knew nothing, would not until Furman and Nolan were safely on Tinian.

Only the select group knew. They and two others.

It was several minutes before Withers could reach the red phone. Not only was he still stunned by the atomic vista that had left even him affected, but also the blockhouse was now in pandemonium, with men shaking hands, slapping backs, cheering, and in some cases trying to get to their own communications systems to check with observer groups closer in, scientific-instrument stations, and all sorts of other things.

Almost as frustrating was discovering the red phone already in use by a brigadier general. Withers fumed and waited as best he could, getting jostled in the process. He considered trying to force his way back to his office but since the lines there were interconnected with the red phone here it might not offer any improvement.

Finally the general was finished and handed the phone back to the sergeant. There were lots of phones in use but only this one would connect Withers with post security. He idly wondered what the hell the general had to talk about, and to whom. For a second he had a chilling feeling that he was less autonomous than he believed. Who watched the watchers?

The thought passed quickly. He had nothing to worry about himself, he knew, and if he were higher up in Pentagon circles he'd have somebody watching the man in his position anyway. Fair was fair. He grabbed for the phone, told the special operator the number, and was quickly connected to Major Kerrigan's office.

The phone rang and rang, and it started to make Withers nervous. Where the hell *were* these people, anyway? It never once occurred to him that the reaction of the people in the blockhouse might be echoing throughout the hand-picked command structure.

Finally the phone was answered with a sharp, "Kerrigan." There was a lot of noise in the background, lots of people who knew a lot less about what was going on were still talking excitedly.

"Major? Colonel Withers. Have you dispatched anyone to that sentry post as yet?"

Kerrigan sounded almost apologetic. "No, sir. I'll radio a picket Jeep to get out there in a hurry. We *did* check, though, and there *was* a break and a patch at or near that point about six weeks ago, so it doesn't look like anything. We'll check it out anyway, though."

Withers was furious. "Yes, you do that, *Major*. You see to it *personally!* And you call me the moment there's word." He slammed down the phone in disgust.

The two Russians lost no time in getting out of the area. Any delay might bring some curious observer or onlooker, but they were in no immediate danger. The blast had been so strong that it had knocked out large sections of the fence and most of the power to the northern section. Nervous sentries, particularly in areas where the fence had shorted or actually broken patches and fallen in, had been more concerned for their own health and well-being than with any breaches. Just looking around the region made it an absurd notion that any foreign spies could be anywhere in the vicinity—and the Japs were now the only enemy, anyway. Nobody would let Japs within a thousand miles of this place.

By the time such men had calmed down and moved to cover themselves when their sergeants arrived, the unseen pair was long gone into the barren mountains. About eight miles from the perimeter they were able to relax and rest their horses.

Observer planes occasionally passed overhead, but nobody noticed and nobody sent out alarms. They even waved to some of the aircraft and at least one waggled its wings back in greeting.

Back at the original breach Harvey Cameron arrived first and saw very little out of order. More than a little shaken by the glare and tremendous tremors of the bomb himself, he found it easy in his own mind to justify the sentry's nerves as nothing more than that. The desert was a lonely place at night.

Even Withers, by the time he arrived up the Jeep road, was pretty well at ease about the whole thing. He'd seen the condition of the men and the fences farther back, and found, if anything, less out of the ordinary than at other places along the line. Still, he studied the enigmatic hoofprints and patches carefully before shaking his head, thanking the sentry for his vigilance, and getting back into his Jeep.

Harvey Cameron came over to him. "Well? What do you think?"

"There *could* have been a breach," Withers replied carefully, "but I'll be damned if we could ever be sure. It'd take somebody real professional, like the Krauts, to do it this good —and they're dead and plowed under now. I'd say we say the hell with it and go get some sleep."

Cameron nodded. "Yeah. Who would be spying on us now?"

"Don't matter anyway," Withers spat. "Damn! You oughta seen the enemy bastards they had right at the test site! They may as well have put it on the front page of the newspapers."

The FBI man chuckled, then yawned, made his apologies to Withers, and headed for his car. This little thing didn't bother him at all. His mind was far away now, thinking about that enormous explosion and a certain ship. He wondered how Jim Fargo was right now—and where.

Hunter's Point Navy Yard, San Francisco Monday, July 16, 1945

The ship's PA gave a low, piercing whistle at exactly 0300 and a cool, clear voice announced, "Now hear this. Now hear this. Heads of departments prepare to get under way. First Division work detail lay up to the hangar deck. Sea and anchor detail report to stations."

There was consternation all over the ship, consternation mixed with irritation at having been awakened. Although a few men both in officer country and down in the enlisted areas whose own work was not yet to come rolled over and tried to get back to sleep, for the most part the ship came suddenly alive. Having been called back, then given one day of sea trials, then moved to Hunter's Point on a weekend without liberty in enticing San Francisco, there was the general feeling that whatever had caused all their problems was now happening. The chiefs took charge of the milling, half-dressed mobs and managed to keep everything from coming unglued.

On the bridge a wide-awake Captain McVay assembled the senior officers, including Captain Edward L. Parke, head of the Marine detachment aboard and in overall direct charge of security for the ship and its cargo. Parke didn't look like a captain. In fact, he looked more like a drill instructor, which is exactly what he had been.

"Gentlemen," McVay began, "in about an hour we will be taking on top-secret cargo. Captain Parke has already been advised of this and, I assume, is at the ready." Parke nodded solemnly but said nothing. "I cannot tell you exactly what the cargo is," the captain continued, "but I can tell you that every hour we save will shorten the war. As such, total security is now imposed upòn us for the duration, including radio silence and full main and gun watches even in friendly waters. A twenty-four-hour Marine guard will be established both around the large package we will receive and secure amidships and the smaller package, which will be secured in Admiral Spruance's quarters below. Our job is simple—to get this cargo to the Forward Area as quickly and as safely as possible. Emergency procedures have been worked out to save the cargo even in the event of hostile action. The cargo comes first."

They all nodded, puzzled but not particularly worried. Like McVay, they had confidence in their ship. A few, however, had less confidence in their crew and voiced that reservation.

"We're going to have to break them in as we run," was all the captain could tell them. "Although this mission is vital it is no major challenge. Let's work the devil out of them. This ship was chosen for its speed, among other things—let's see just what the Navy Yard boys did with her. All out, gentlemen."

There were a few other preliminaries, then they were dismissed. Parke looked a little glum and McVay stopped him. "What's the trouble, Parke? Security not to your liking?"

"Oh no, sir, not that," Parke replied, still downcast. "Well—hell. I just got married, Captain—and I can't even say good-bye."

McVay laughed and put his arm around the burly six-footer. "She'll wait," he assured the newlywed. "It's a Navy tradition."

Parke just nodded and then walked out to brief his men, but as he did he grumbled, inaudibly, "Yeah, that's why I joined the Marines."

Only a very few on the ship were fully aware of what was about to go on.

Jim Fargo put out a cigarette and walked out into the commotion. The smoking lamp was long out but he'd been chain-smoking since early that evening when he'd gotten indications that they would sail shortly. Now he elbowed his way past hastily dressing and half-dressed officers and walked out onto the deck. The wharf was brightly lit and there were people all around, including a fair number of Marines on the dock setting up their own positions. They weren't part of the ship's company, though. These were the last of Withers' security people on shore. He wanted to light another cigarette but knew he couldn't here. It disturbed him, this urge; up until a few months before he'd been an occasional smoker hardly thinking about it and certainly not habituated. Nerves, he told himself. Just nerves.

He hadn't gotten any sleep; there was still too much going on inside him, very little of which had to do with the ship or its cargo. He'd checked in the day before with base supply, but there was still no ship then. And he'd had the whole previous evening to kill and decided to go into the city.

He'd been to San Francisco several times before, usually on business, but he really wasn't interested in seeing the sights or eating seafood or riding cable cars. He really wanted a nice, quiet bar without hordes of soldiers and sailors on leave. Just a nice, quiet place to drink and think, or maybe not think.

With the aid of a cabbie he found pretty much what he was looking for, a tiny little place occupied mostly by a few businessmen and artist types and without so much as a jukebox to its name. He took a small booth and ordered a Bourbon, but when it arrived he mostly stared at it and sipped indifferently, deep in his own thoughts.

"Hi, Admiral. Want some company?"

The woman's voice startled him and he looked up to see a woman in her midtwenties, no raving beauty particularly in that hairdo and print dress but not too bad either.

"Sure," he replied. "Feel free. Only it's Jim. Jim Fargo."

She smiled and sat opposite him. "I'm Sam. Short for Samantha but nobody dares call me that."

He laughed, relaxed a little more, and took a bigger drink. He wondered who or what she was. A local prostitute, maybe, or a bored housewife? For a few moments his mind toyed idly with the idea that she might be a spy for somebody or other but he dismissed the thought. If she *were* a spy she sure had picked the wrong man.

"What ship you with?" she asked, sensing the unease in his manner.

"No ship," he told her truthfully. "I work in the supply section at Hunter's Point. Pretty dull stuff, actually. How many beds on such-and-such a ship, how many oranges on another, that sort of thing. Not very romantic, I'm afraid."

She shrugged. "Everybody has to do his part, isn't that what they've always said?" Her drink came, he paid for it, and she raised her glass and said, mock-solemnly, "Loose lips sink ships!" and downed a healthy portion.

He laughed. "And what do *you* do for the war effort?" he asked her, still chuckling.

"Morale boost, I guess," she told him. "Rosie the Riveter I'm just not cut out to be. A few friends and I run an art store —'gallery' is too dignified a word for us—over in Sausalito. Used to be good before the war, I'm told, but now it's mostly selling a bunch of landscapes to hotels and such for five bucks a shot. It's a living, sort of. Maybe when the war's over we can make something of it."

"So what brings you over to San Francisco?" he asked cautiously. "An urge to seek out lonely naval officers in small bars?"

She laughed again. "Maybe. Something like that. No, actually I had to get out of there for a little while. I've been up the past three nights doing some phony seascapes for some Army club and I just decided to come into town and wander around a little. Some local artists hang out here once in a while, usually on Friday nights, and I thought I'd find somebody I knew, but nobody's in tonight."

"So you settled on me," he said lightly.

She shrugged and laughed. "I'm—I'm not usually this forward," she came back hesitantly, a slight trace of embarrassment creeping into her voice. "I—oh, I don't know, really." The lightness and playfulness seemed to fade for a moment and she added, very softly, "I guess I'm lonely, too."

And so they'd gone up to Grant Avenue and eaten Chinese food and gone downtown and seen a Fred Astaire movie and gone to a couple of other bars that managed to stay open despite the blackout and wartime austerity. Things were looser now in San Francisco. Nobody expected the Japs to steam under the Golden Gate Bridge any longer. Finally they took a street car down to the Ferry Building, the only survivor of the great earthquake and fire, and they kissed and she went back to Sausalito and he to Hunter's Point.

On Saturday he spent most of the day with the base supply officer familiarizing himself with what he'd have to do aboard ship, then called her, and this time she invited him over to Sausalito, since she couldn't leave the shop until eight.

The unnaturally cool air of San Francisco cut into him as the ferry went out from San Francisco Harbor, turned left, and passed near forbidding Alcatraz, the island's lonely beacon cutting through the gathering fog. There was something eerily beautiful about the scene. This was a city of dreams, of insubstantial promise somehow, and he could understand why so many had flocked here to live.

And then there was Sausalito, the little town that was

mostly an artist's and writer's colony on the northern peninsula just up from the Golden Gate. From this little town John C. Fremont had launched his attempt to take the Presidio, then a Mexican garrison, and proclaim the independence of California. A different war so very far away in time and dimension.

The store was a little thing sandwiched in some old row houses across from the dock. Sam closed for lack of business and they went to a little Italian restaurant near the ferry dock, then to a small upstairs bar across the street. They talked, but not about anything consequential, mostly about the beauty of the area and the fog and never about navies, wars, and bombs. It grew late, and he knew he was supposed to be back at Hunter's Point—the *Indianapolis* would be there now, getting its orders and provisions. He tried to put it out of his mind, although there was the little nagging question as to whether or not, even now, an FBI colleague or one of Withers' boys sat nearby watching and taking notes. His old suspicious nature and training, he decided.

Finally they wound up at her apartment, a little one-room affair filled with clutter. It looked like the back storeroom at an art-supply store, but around were a number of paintings and he looked at them appreciatively. They were damned good and he told her so.

She seemed pleased, and fixed a final drink from a couple of bottles under the sink. She was aware of the lateness of the hour and his concern over it. "Tomorrow, perhaps?" she said hopefully.

He looked sad and shook his head. "No, they're sending me out soon and this is my last free night," he told her. "Temporary duty, but I'll be away a few weeks at least."

She stiffened slightly, cleared her throat, then drained her drink. "Well, then . . . I . . . ah . . . oh, this damned war!" she snapped in frustration.

He pulled her to him and just held her for a long moment. She seemed to be fighting back tears, a reaction that caught him by surprise despite the fact that he felt much the same way. He held her tight and kissed her and she responded. He wanted her very, very much, he realized, wanted and needed her in the worst way—and he knew she felt the same.

"The hell with the clock," he murmured.

Later, she'd roused a friend who had a car and some gasoline and gotten him back to Hunter's Point. During the afternoon rigid security had been clamped on the whole Navy Yard; it took some doing just to get himself in, but his rank eased the way and also eased the explanations. Officers, particularly of a senior variety, seldom had to explain irregularities that would have landed an enlisted man in the brig.

He hadn't slept much since then. Everyone was restricted to base pending the sailing, everyone except the higher-ups, most of whom were leaving for someplace unknown.

He'd reported to the ship on Sunday afternoon, been put up with a maximum of grumbling from a crew that was already brass-heavy, and now, here he was, standing on the deck, waiting for the mother lode.

A strange week. For the first time he didn't want to sail at all and he still wasn't sure why.

"I don't believe it!"

Don Sobel heard the exclamation and turned, puzzled, as he came aboard the ship. He sought the source of the comment and squinted to make him out.

"Don! Don Sobel!" Johnny Coyle called and ran to the other man, grabbed his hand, and started pumping it vigorously.

Sobel looked at the other chief for a moment, then recognized him. "Coyle! Well I'll be damned!"

The gunnery chief stood back and shook his head in wonder. "Who'd ever have expected you on the *Indy?* Or, for that matter . . ." He suddenly stopped and decided to go no farther with the thought.

Sobel knew what he meant. "Or on any other ship, either,"

he finished. "Yeah, I know, Johnny. I been cooling my heels at the Fire and Salvage School up in Bremerton. No, this was a surprise to me, too. Can't say I'm sorry to get it, though."

Coyle nodded understandingly. "Well, we'll put that jinx stuff to rest this time. Ain't *nothin'* gonna sink *this* ship!"

"I can believe that," Sobel told him, looking around. "She's magnificent. I can see how she got her nickname, though."

Coyle frowned. "Nickname?"

"The *Swayback Maru*. Kinda weird to find two super-structures and the hangars in the middle."

"Don't ever say that name around here," Coyle warned. "Most men hear that and it's a fight."

"How's the skipper?" Sobel asked, changing the subject.

"A hell of a good one," the other assured him. "The crew worships him. You won't believe this—he once went fishing with a bunch of enlisted men!"

That was unusual and far away from Navy tradition. Sobel wasn't sure he liked it. "Sounds like too easy a man for this ship."

"Naw. Not like that at all. The Old Man's regular Navy all the way. When you got the Flag aboard you gotta run a spit-and-polish operation—that's where you and me come in. You never met Admiral Spruance." He made an unpleasant face. "Made outta iron, inside as well as out. Colder'n the South Pole. Pipes classical music through the ship to give us low-classers culture. Has shit fits if he sees a pinhead of rust on thirteen-year-old metal. Naw, it's a tight ship, all right—but run *right*. You run into trouble, get the runaround, just gotta see the captain—you see him. No special stuff, no permissions. He'll see the lowest deck swabber and listen to 'im and if he's got a case he'll do something. You sail twenty years to get a skipper like Captain McVay."

Sobel looked around at the mess on the decks. Paint peeling and worn, rust apparent, dirt, grease, coils of rope, and all sorts of junk all over the place and shook his head. "Don't look like any spit-and-polish ship to me."

Coyle looked to heaven. "That's what's crazy about all this. We needed another couple of weeks to clean the old girl up, then maybe a month of sea trials to get things in shape—about a quarter, give or take, of the crew is new—and then we'll be ready to bombard the Japs. But they pull us out, leaving everything the way it is, give us one day to see if she works right, then bring us over here and tell us to get ready to sail. It's crazy. If Spruance came aboard now he'd keel over and die of a heart attack."

Sobel nodded. "Well, I can see I'll have to learn as you go, too."

"At least you been on cruisers before. A lot of the new guys haven't even been to sea! Hell, we got two of 'em seasick just moving from Mare Island down to here!"

"Sounds like a good challenge," Sobel responded. "I like challenges. It's been too long, Johnny. Too long. I don't have a single pair of pants without a hole through the ass of 'em."

"Where you assigned?"

"The usual. Damage control. Don't know what division yet, though. If we ever get off the deck here I'm going to report and get my assignment and my billet. *Then* I'm gonna go around until I know this ship better than you know your gun crews."

"I'm in CIC now," Coyle told him. "No more out in the open." CIC was the combat nerve center of the ship; under attack it gave the orders—who shot, what to shoot, and when. "If we see any action this trip you'll take your orders from my people."

Sobel smiled. "Damage control—remember? I only work if you fuck up." He looked around at the massive twin superstructure, the deck longer than a football field, the solidness of the ship. A good ship, he told himself.

It was in his familiarization walks the next day that he began to get disturbed. The *Indianapolis* had been built in 1932 under the treaty limiting naval armaments. She was an anachronism, a peacetime ship built for peacetime duty.

They'd had to weld shut four rows of portholes, the bottom row close to the waterline, to even make a pretense of it being watertight.

Ventilation was also a problem. Here, in San Francisco, it wasn't at all bad, but in a tropical zone it'd be a hotbox below. The entire main deck was open inside the superstructure—no watertight doors, fire doors, anything. And because of the ventilation problem just about every door and hatch on the ship was open all the time. He just couldn't help worrying, as a damage-control man, about all that. She was top-heavy and open underneath. If any water were to get in it'd find no obstacle to the engine room. She'd fill with water and sink in a matter of minutes, probably capsizing first. It was not a pleasant thought. Like all cruisers she depended on her speed and her escorts for protection. Speed she supposedly had—faster than anything else her size afloat—but escorts? There was no sign of any in the harbor.

Still, escorts hadn't saved the *Juneau,* he reflected, putting the concern from his mind. From here to Hawaii would be a milk run, and from there they'd surely give the old girl escorts to wherever they were heading. Just drop this secret whatchamacallit off and then sail off to train, clean, and spruce up for the Flag. The Imperial Japanese Fleet was in shambles, the Jap air force reduced to isolated *kamikaze* raids near the home islands. No worry there, either. And flagships were always the best-protected ships in the whole damned fleet.

Ron Sarbic surveyed the huge ship apprehensively. Two physics degrees had assured him of four very comfortable and businesslike years in nice, safe Bremerton. The war was no more real to him for all that time than, say, an atom or some atomic particle. You knew the thing was there but it didn't really concern you, you couldn't see it, and it was useful mostly in theoretical work.

Stark reality was something else again. In all those years he'd never sailed in anything more formidable than the

Bremerton–Seattle ferry. Even sailboats made him nervous. Working out and testing physics problems in the labs was one thing—but those huge guns there, those were the end products of all that work. He'd helped perfect the new radar guidance system that directed them, but that was, as far as he was concerned, all that his duty and conscience required. To actually have to depend on them was asking a bit too much.

He also knew roughly what the cargo was to be. Not that anyone had told him, but when you're asked to bring radiological detection gear aboard and check over the ship after the cargo has been unloaded to see if there was any danger or leakage of radiation, and if you were well grounded in physics and had a reasonable imagination, you could guess what it might be.

He was less nervous about the cargo, though. That was more or less of a known quantity, something constructed by knowledgeable scientists, probably the best in the world, and under the most rigid controls. Scientific laws always held; they were reassuring, constant, something you could handle. Not like a screaming suicidal plane diving straight at you, or some torpedo lobbed from the depths into your midsection.

War, he reflected, was only useful because it spurred scientific research.

He sighed, arranged for his gear to be brought on board, and walked onto the ship.

Commander Flynn was less than thrilled to see him. "For Christ's sake! A lieutenant commander, yet! This will be the only ship in history with more officers than enlisted personnel!" Sarbic said nothing, knowing that the exec was venting his wrath more at the powers that be than at him.

Flynn looked again at the orders. "Well, it's just TDY anyway. O.K., Mr. Sarbic, glad to have you aboard." The executive officer now knew from the orders that Sarbic was here in connection with the mysterious cargo and the upcoming mission and decided not to press. Just find a place to put him until he got pulled, that was all. That was enough!

After getting settled, Sarbic, like Sobel, made a complete tour of the ship. It all looked huge and imposing to Sarbic, as safe as standing on solid cast iron. He thought of the torpedoes he'd tested and tried to imagine them hitting the ship. He simply couldn't imagine them doing anything more than slowing her down.

The Combat Intelligence Center fascinated him. The two seamen on duty there were eager to show their equipment off to an interested newcomer, officer or not. They showed him the radar, the master firing controls, everything. Sarbic was uneasy about only one thing and asked about it.

"Where's your sonar?" he wondered.

"There isn't any," one of the seamen explained, then, seeing the startled expression this caused on the face of the obviously deskbound officer hastily explained, "There never is on capital ships, sir, for a lot of reasons. But capital ships always have destroyers and other escorts to cover for us. I wouldn't worry about it, sir. We go too fast for a sub to hit us anyway."

Still, to a man who'd just spent a couple of years helping perfect better torpedoes, it was not very reassuring.

Staff Sergeant Bill Glass stood at attention before the desk of First Lieutenant Edward H. Stauffer, junior officer of the thirty-nine-man Marine detachment aboard the ship. He studied the new man's orders carefully and a little suspiciously. He didn't like surprises.

"You're assigned as an observer," he noted. "Just what does that mean?"

"Sir, it means just that. I'll take a turn with everybody else for duty, but my purpose here is to see how security for our cargo is handled and make a report on it."

Stauffer frowned. "A report to whom, Sergeant?" He naturally felt resentment that somebody had called his unit into question—it reflected on all of them, and he was pretty proud of his men. It hurt even worse that they'd sent a sergeant. Not even a senior NCO, but a staff sergeant. Too high for any

dirty details, too low for any real responsibility. He suspected
that this guy wasn't a staff sergeant at all. He'd heard of such
things. Security or CID would plant a corporal or a sergeant
someplace and he'd turn out later to be a major and a cop to
boot. Glass answered, "Ah, the Pentagon, sir."

"Where were you before this?" he asked suspiciously.

"My last assignment, sir? A—a bond tour." He looked genuinely embarrassed.

Stauffer was aghast. That was the last and most ridiculous
answer he could ever have expected. "A *bond tour?*"

"I was on Saipan, sir," Glass explained. "We got some high-
ranking Jap brass but I was the only one to come out alive."

The lieutenant frowned even more. That sort of cover story
made even less sense. This whole thing didn't make much
sense. Well, that would be at least partially Captain Parke's
problem. "O.K., Sergeant, I guess all is in order. Get one of
the men to show you a bunk space—we're kind of short on
space at the moment since we have far too many officers
aboard but I'm sure you'll find something suitable. Ever been
on this kind of duty before?"

"No, sir," Glass answered honestly. "Oh, I been on a number of rust buckets but not a warship, no, sir."

Stauffer nodded absently, then filed the orders in a basket
on his desk. "All right. Dismissed." After a perfunctory salute,
Glass did an about-face and walked out the door.

This much brass—all Navy, really, except for Stauffer and
this Captain Parke—made him nervous, but he dismissed any
anxieties he had and decided to relax and enjoy the trip.
Withers had promised him no more combat if all went well
and he wasn't going to rock any boats. He smiled slightly to
himself at the thought of the pompous little asshole. Just like
all the rest of them. If they only knew, he thought, and not for
the first time. But they never would. Maybe here, in this madhouse, the dreams would stop, the hauntings would stop.
Maybe here he could finally get some sleep.

John Coringa was like a man obsessed once on board. He prowled, poked, asked questions, and answered none, showing particular interest in the security procedures and personnel involved in the dual radio rooms. That startled him. *Two* radio rooms! One far forward, the main one aft, with a large antenna amidships. He concluded quickly that he didn't like the ship much and didn't trust the men. They were much too lax, much too casual about top-secret stuff. The radio rooms, for example, were just filled with people, almost all enlisted men. If there was the slightest thing wrong they'd probably break radio silence out of sheer panic.

He had his own ideas on things like that. Once they dropped the cargo these men would relax, not realizing that some Jap sub could trail them, find which island the stuff was dropped on, then bomb the hell out of it. Withers gave him most of the course. They'd head straight for Pearl, refuel and drop those passengers, then head straight for the secret drop point. After that—Guam, most likely, then Leyte for training. If anybody was following them and found them using the radio right after they'd left the drop point—why, hell, they'd know exactly where it was dropped off. Better to leave them guessing among three points. He resolved to take it up with the captain, to try to convince him that the mission didn't end with the drop-off.

It was very plain that this mission would determine Coringa's future. Glory or all the shit. No two ways about it. It wasn't going to be shit. He'd make sure of that. If the captain and others couldn't be convinced, well, he'd make sure things were tight in spite of them all. By God that whatever it was, was going to be dropped on the Japs or shot at them or whatever. He'd see to that. No breaches. Not if he had to sink the goddamn ship.

They were all there a little before 0400 as the strange cargo was hoisted aboard. Curious faces by the hundreds watched as two U. S. Army trucks rumbled up to the almost deserted dock and stopped amidships, where the big gap was in the super-structure. One held a huge crate on which all eyes were fastened. The other was empty except for a very small-looking metal cylinder. Most of the crewmen saw little else. Only those like Fargo and Coringa and Glass noticed that the shadows were alive with men, mostly in civilian clothes, just watching quietly in the dark. Now a huge gantry crane crept laboriously down the pier. Men of the ship's Fourth Division clustered around as the crane arrived, quickly attaching strong metal straps and chains to the large crate, which was then slowly and carefully hoisted aboard and placed on the hangar deck. Shipfitters waited in the dark and quickly fastened the crate to the deck so solidly that even if the ship capsized the crate would still be there. One of the shipfitters shouted something and suddenly there was the sound of running feet. Within seconds Marine guards from the ship's detachment took up their positions around the mysterious crate.

All of the onlookers now knew for sure that this was top-secret cargo. One mystery was now solved—the haste, the reason for all the secrecy, the mission of the *Indianapolis*. Another mystery began, though, as already they started whispered guesses as to what the huge crate contained.

Only five of the onlookers even noticed a couple of sailors slip a pole under the ring atop the small metal container, lift it onto their shoulders, and carry it aboard, then forward into officers' country. Behind walked two Army officers looking relaxed and a little sleepy but otherwise just like the additional passengers the crew took them to be. With the label went the assumption that the small case was their problem, unrelated in any way to the big crate, which was the mysterious cause of the mission.

McVay and Flynn decided to use the flag lieutenant's cabin since there'd be less of a problem should Spruance come aboard early and find his cabin messed up. The sailors with their strange burden entered, followed by Nolan and Furman, and were met by Lieutenant Commander Moore and a couple of shipfitters. Quickly they welded pad eyes to the deck in the middle of the cabin and attached metal-hinged straps to them. The strange cylinder was placed in this holder, secured, and then Major Furman removed a large, heavy-duty padlock and clicked it tight around the straps.

"That'll do nicely, thank you," Furman told the Navy men, who nodded and filed out.

"Call if you need anything further," Moore told them, "there'll be a Marine in the hall at all times ordered to admit the two of you and nobody else without your permission."

"I think that'll do nicely, Commander. Thanks," Furman replied, dismissing the officer. The door shut behind them.

Nolan's gear had been brought on earlier in the day and he removed some of it now and checked the cylinder and the surrounding area for radiation, also taking note of the residual radiation at this point. Satisfied, he put the stuff away and sat down in a chair.

"Say, Bob?" the doctor called hesitantly. "What's a lieutenant commander, anyway? Does he outrank me?"

"Just go by the insignia," Furman told him. "No difference there. Not on ship, anyway. I don't think." He seemed hesitant. "That would make him a major, I guess."

"Hmph. 'Lieutenant commander' sounds better and fancier."

Furman shrugged. "Remember, in the Navy you're just a lieutenant. The Army's made you a captain. Works both ways."

"I suppose," Nolan said absently, dismissing the line of thought. "I guess we ought to see Captain McVay now."

They went out and, with a lot of help from a lot of people, found the captain on the bridge. The captain had been expecting them and took them back to his emergency cabin just in back of the bridge area. Even in normal times he spent more time here than in his much more luxurious cabin below—he always liked to be near the bridge while the ship was under way

—and now it was doubly so, since this was a special mission. He closed the door behind them.

"Captain, I'm Major Furman and this is Captain Nolan," the major introduced. "We're the ones ultimately responsible for the cargo and its safe delivery. As you might have guessed, we're not artillery officers, although we *are* in the Army. I'm with the Engineers."

Nolan shifted. "Captain Parsons suggested I level with you, sir," he said uncomfortably. "I'm a doctor here to monitor the shipment." He saw McVay's face show alarm and quickly reassured him. "Sir, on my word as a doctor and an officer there is not a single thing in this cargo that could harm anyone on this ship in its present form. I want absolutely to assure you of that."

McVay just nodded, then said, "I didn't think we were going to use BW in this war."

Nolan started to reply, saw Furman's look, then closed his mouth again. Better the rumors than the truth.

"Gentlemen, we're sailing under some difficulties, as you might have heard," McVay told them. They nodded, remembering Flynn's memorandum. "You have the run of the ship, but please bear with us at least until we can dump the passengers at Pearl. We'll get you there as quickly and smoothly as possible, though, and you can have every confidence that Captain Parke's Marines are expert at what they do and entirely at your disposal. We leave at 0800 exactly."

The two Army men nodded, understanding the full meaning of McVay's statement. You stay out of our way and we'll stay out of yours.

They parted amicably, shook hands all around, and were told to get in touch with Flynn's office if they needed anything else. The ever-present Marines would direct them wherever necessary.

One thought struck the captain, though. "You know, we have an abnormal number of TDYs all the way to Leyte," he remarked. "I suspect you have more than just our Marines shepherding you."

Furman and Nolan just looked at each other. Truthfully that had never occurred to either of them. Such was the stuff of cloak and dagger, Nolan thought, not without a slight sense of excitement.

McVay went back onto the bridge and found Commander Glen DeGrave, the ship's engineering officer, waiting for him. He saw in the man's face that it was bad news. "Didn't get around it, huh?"

DeGrave's expression could have killed the Japanese Army. "They finally got me, Charlie. Beached! Beached, damn it all, when we get to Pearl! I tried to tell 'em the new kid's too green but I guess I pulled strings once too often."

McVay put his arm sympathetically on the other man's shoulder. Overage had caught up to the senior engineering officer at last. "Go out in style, Glen," he suggested. "Let's break the record to Pearl."

DeGrave gave a sour yet determined look and walked out. The captain and the others on the bridge looked after him a little sadly, all thinking the same thing. They wouldn't want to be in the engine crew for the next couple of days. Not on a bet.

At precisely 0800 on a gray morning with just a hint of sunlight in the east the great ship cast off all lines and moved slowly out into the main channel of San Francisco Bay. Few crew members had slept that night, some in anticipation of the voyage and others engaged in lengthy gossip about the nature of the cargo that kept everybody else awake.

Within six minutes the great ship passed under the Golden Gate Bridge and out into the open sea, still slowly, carefully, then almost due west, when, clear now of the harbor entrances, Captain McVay rang for flank speed. By the time they cleared the Farallon Islands, the last American territory they would see for a while, the ship was making close to twenty-nine knots, all four giant engines roaring and thrumming with full force and life.

Commander DeGrave was mad as hell and he was going to show them all a thing or two. He cursed and yelled at his foul luck and coaxed the engines on. He didn't see the Farallons, of course, but he'd see them again because of his foul luck.

For most of the men on the *Indianapolis* it was the last look at home they would ever get.

Between San Francisco
and Honolulu
Tuesday,
July 17, 1945

"I'm worried about our little package," Major Furman told his associate. "It's been pretty rough and I keep asking myself, What happens if she goes down?"

Nolan nodded uneasily. In truth, he was a little seasick. The rough weather they'd hit about the middle of the sixteenth wasn't much to seasoned hands—a few rain squalls and some winds and chop, routine stuff and typical for July but very unroutine to the unseasoned crew. Furman, who was no old salt himself, sympathized.

"Come on. Let's go up to the wardroom and see who's there," he suggested. "It'll break us out of this lousy cabin, anyway."

Although Nolan really didn't feel like company, he agreed. He yearned for his medical kit so he could have done a little self-prescribing but he dared not. As they made their way to the wardroom Furman suggested, "Why not go back to the dispensary and get something?"

Nolan stared at him a minute. "Are you kidding? You want me to keep being artillery or not? Get me in a modern ship's dispensary around a doctor who knows his stuff and I'll make some slip that'll give it away."

About a dozen officers were in the wardroom that afternoon, mostly just talking or playing cards over coffee. Furman spotted Casey Moore, the officer who'd supervised the fitting of the uranium to the cabin deck the night before, and they joined the lieutenant commander. The talk all around them was about the mysterious crate amidships. Some of the officers were guessing, some were trying to act unconcerned. One or two darkly hinted that they knew what it was but couldn't tell anybody. None paid any attention to the two Army men. Like the two civilians over in a corner, there, they were just a couple more passengers.

Furman, in low, casual tones, conveyed to Moore his worries over the cylinder. The Navy man was slightly amused by their concern but quickly perceived that the two men took this very seriously indeed.

"Tell you what," he said helpfully, "if it'll make you feel any better I'll have a life raft brought up and fastened to the bulkhead right outside your cabin. In an emergency you could lash it to the raft and toss it overboard."

Nolan nodded appreciatively. "That would be a help, at least."

Furman, however, wasn't so sure and before they knew it Moore had them and a couple of other trusted officers in his own office going over plans. They tried carrying it to the side with the idea of lowering it into a small boat alongside. They even did some dry runs, although at twenty-eight knots practice was out of the question.

Both Army men's paranoia seemed to know no bounds. Furman found a length of rope so long that it took three men to get it into the cabin. They tied one end to the cylinder and the other end to a flotation buoy. If the thing sank, at least the spot would be marked.

None of the naval personnel tried to dissuade them. If it made them sleep better, then O.K. The fact that the Pacific was over two miles deep in places they kept to themselves.

They spent the early evening back in the wardroom, Nolan feeling better as the weather moderated but trying hard to avoid Dr. Haynes, the chief surgeon. At one point one of the gunnery officers asked Nolan how large were the guns with which he normally worked and Nolan had made a circle with his hands and said, "About this big," as Furman nearly had a stroke. There was a sudden freeze in the wardroom and then everybody burst out into raucous laughter. Nolan, who wasn't aware he'd made a joke, joined in uncomfortably and they managed to change the subject after that. Finally when it came back to technical questions, Furman came back with, "You don't look so hot today, Captain. Why don't you go below and lie down for a while?" Nolan gratefully exited.

Wincing in the background but unable to help was Jim Fargo, who settled for almost choking on his coffee.

Still, all were mostly just starting to settle in, and the first day passed without further incident.

The dreams returned to him on shipboard, particularly late at night, particularly when all seemed quiet and still and the only thing you could hear was the distant noise of the ship's great engines and the hypnotic vibration they caused. It was always the same, back in the hotel rooms of the bond tour, back in the barracks, now, here on the ship, even when sleeping with thirty other guys. It didn't matter. When all was quiet and still his mind automatically went back to Saipan, no matter what tricks he tried not to think about it. . . . Saipan . . . Saipan . . . Saipan. Always Saipan . . .

You died on Saipan, the voice of Sergeant Murphy whispered to him as it always did. *You died with the rest of us, there, on a dirty hill overlooking a miserable cave.*

"Go away, Murphy!" he always shouted back. "I got you your fucking Bronze Star. You're a big hero, just like you wanted, and I'm back here, safe, waiting out the war just like I wanted."

Only your miserable carcass is alive, Murphy taunted. *Your mind's back here in the muck with the rest of us. It'll always be here, Glass, just like we'll always be here. You sold your soul on Saipan, Glass.*

A corner of his mind told him it was only a dream, that Murphy was long dead, they were all long dead, and it was only the fact that he remained in the military that kept the memory so very much alive. He tried to tell himself that, but, as usual, he wasn't entirely convincing. He saw them clearly now, although he'd barely known any of them. The faces, the dirt and sweat, they were all too real, all too near. Howitt, Guerney, Montrose, Saklad, all of them and the rest. Eight of them in all, led by Sergeant Murphy. Eight of them and him, just a buck sergeant same as Murphy.

Image, he'd decided, was everything. Even when they'd drafted him they told him he looked like a Marine. He'd been a football player, so the basic training hadn't been that bad, but he'd read up on all the regulations, played up to all the right people, and was too smart to get suckered by that hero shit they used to brainwash the farmboys. He even made all the required protests when they'd sent him to admin school, screaming for infantry. Image, yeah. They never gave you what you wanted if they *knew* you wanted it.

So it was file this, type that, while the rest of his comrades at Parris Island had gone to nameless rocks to get blown to bits. Not that he hadn't gone into action, in a way. He'd watched many a naval bombardment from the deck of a heavy cruiser or battlewagon, always on the office staff of some general or other, cutting the orders that sent all those ignorant plowboys over the side. The biggest worry was an occasional torpedo or Jap plane, but even that threat was exaggerated, he discov-

ered. Once a torpedo had ripped right through a cruiser he
was on and it had barely slowed down.

He also had prepared the casualty reports for those landings. He'd watch them through binoculars, hundreds upon
hundreds of landing craft heading for some booby-trapped
beach on some godforsaken coral island. Know to the man
how many went in, and know from the reports he correlated
how many never came back. But he was as distant from that
as he would be back home.

Until Saipan.

The landings had been routine, but the losses had been horrible. From this island the new B-29s could bomb Tokyo itself,
laying waste to Japan as they were doing to Germany half a
world away. The Japs knew it, too; thirty thousand combat-
hardened troops were determined that the island's two airfields
would never fall to the enemy.

A combined operation, Army to the south and Marines to
the north, with the Japs well dug in in the middle. The Army
boys weren't used to this, and when they tried to move into the
center of the island they were simply cut to pieces, with the
key mountain pass becoming known as "Death Valley" for
good reason. The Army's problems infuriated the Marines,
where impatience, pride, and service rivalry had overcome
General "Howlin' Mad" Smith and his Marine command.
They threw every "nonessential" Marine into the fight for the
middle of the deadly island, clerks, cooks, everything they
had, including Bill Glass, who, before he knew it, wound up
with a rifle and a canteen in the middle of a volcanic tropical
hell.

The problem was finding a way through the volcanic bush
and highlands in intolerable heat against a dug-in enemy. The
Marines were moving south, yes, but far too slowly and at far
too great a cost.

Glass found himself assigned to a squad whose job was to
go into that crap and find a way through. Nine men, led by
Sergeant Joseph X. Murphy, a tough veteran ex-DI who

looked something like Pat O'Brien but thought he was John Wayne. The veteran left no doubt of what he thought of "desk jockeys" and made it clear from the start who was in complete charge.

Glass had hated him from the moment he met the man. Glass realized that Murphy wanted and relished the hatred, nurtured and cultivated it. All of them kept thinking, "If that son-of-a-bitch can do it, I can, too."

They were two days out and Glass had been scared to death. Murphy never let up on him. They'd been shot at a few times, and shot back when it happened, but nobody could tell who, if anyone, was hurt or hit.

They came up the side of a high ridge and Murphy suddenly signaled for them to drop fast. "Japs up there," he whispered and pointed. They all strained to see and Glass finally made out what appeared to be a small cave with black smoke pouring from it.

"What do you think it is, Sarge?" a lance corporal named Desmond whispered nervously.

Murphy shrugged. "Could be anything. They're not makin' sukiyaki up there, that's for sure. Best guess is that we stumbled on some headquarters and they're burnin' their papers. I dunno. Only one way to find out." He glanced around. "Desmond! Glass! Belly up as close as you can and see what's cookin'!"

Glass was stunned, frozen with fear. He knew he showed it, knew Murphy and maybe the rest of them could smell it in him, and knew that Murphy had made certain he couldn't refuse.

Image. Appearance. That had been his whole life. Even if they let him live he'd be branded forever, Murphy would see to that. Glass looked at the sergeant and saw traces of an evil grin, then looked around at the others. Howitt, Guerney, Montrose, Saklad—even Desmond—and saw that same look in their faces, too. The sons-of-bitches. He hated them all.

Silently, burning with that hate, he and Desmond slipped into the underbrush.

The going was easy for a quarter mile or so, bringing them almost to the edge of the cliff, to a path that had to lead directly up to the cave, when, suddenly, they came face to face with a Jap major.

The major was almost as surprised as they were. Quickly, though, he pulled his pistol and fired directly into Desmond's face. It seemed to explode and a splatter of reddish goo fell near Glass, who was too frozen to do anything. Unaccountably, the major had made a run for it as he'd shot, leaving Glass alone now on the path leading up to the cave. Alone and scared.

He moved back down the hillside, back into the secure cover of the underbrush, and waited in the heat for what seemed like hours. Finally he recovered enough to crawl back down to Murphy.

"Where's Desmond?" he asked worriedly.

"Dead," Glass told him. "You were right about the cave. A bunch of dead officers in there and a lot of burning stink. Not much else. We ran into one Jap major, the one who got Desmond, on his way down. I guess he oversaw the *hari-kari* session and then decided not to join them or something. He ran off into the jungle before I could get a clear shot at him."

The sergeant nodded. "I *thought* that was a pistol shot." His eyes narrowed suspiciously. "You sure you went all the way to the cave? No live Japs left to surprise us?"

"I can't guarantee the back of the cave," he answered glibly, "but I made it to the front and there was nobody alive. I didn't want to meet a couple more Jap majors with no backup."

Murphy nodded. "O.K., Glass. Good job. O.K., everybody —let's see what that cave has to offer, then we go home. Glass, you take the rear just in case. Let's move out!"

Everything was fine until they reached the path and Desmond's body. Already some kinds of flies and crawling insects were into it, and it was a gruesome sight. They tried not to look at it as they passed on the way to the cave.

The path curved just ahead, and Glass hung back, letting the others get far ahead. He stopped still, unable to take another step. Even Desmond seemed preferable to going up there. There was a deathly quiet; the air seemed thick, like just before a thunderstorm would strike.

The storm was a sudden and terrible hail of rifle and machine-gun fire; men screamed and there was the sound of a grenade, which echoed across the ravine over and over again. Two bodies fell into view and bounced on the rocks below—American bodies.

And then there was silence. Deadly silence. He waited there, still frozen for what seemed like an eternity, then couldn't stand it anymore. He felt Japs coming down the trail, Japs coming back from the jungle. They were so real he *knew* they were there, and he took off, back, back into the jungle and bush, back toward his own kind as fast as his legs would carry him. He ran until he could run no more, then dropped, exhausted and worn, and passed out from shock and fatigue.

The next morning he awoke to the sounds of furious fighting to the south. It was far off, but it sounded tremendous. Later he learned it was the last gasp of the Imperial Japanese Army on Saipan, a costly, bloody suicidal charge. Within three hours he made contact with a Marine patrol and learned that Saipan was essentially secure.

He told his story to debriefers first, then to top officers in "Howlin' Mad" Smith's command that he knew. They were impressed with his tale of furious fighting, and congratulated him on his good luck at being the sole survivor. Later reports from the same patrol that had found him confirmed his story of a last-ditch battle and ambush on the cliffside, and, to their amazement and his, inside the cave were the bodies of Generals Saito and Igeta and Admiral Nagumo, the commanders of Saipan, their remains burned after ritual *hari-kari*. The press and PR men with the Naval Command drew the obvious conclusion that Murphy's squad had precipitated the final ritual suicides of these men and ended the threat on Saipan. Glass, as the sole survivor, was suddenly a very big hero. He made no effort to dissuade them, and heroes who lived through their deeds were more valuable back home than at the front.

There was no harm. The only man who might know the truth was a Jap major probably long dead in that *banzai* charge.

But Murphy knew different. Murphy whispered to him in his dreams, made him replay the entire scene over and over again, always when he was asleep, always when he couldn't control things. Murphy taunted him still, then, haunting him in the dark places of his mind, growing stronger, more real, as time went on.

Glass awoke sweating and almost banged his head on the upper bunk. He looked around, nervous and embarrassed, but there were only the snores and occasional rustles of thirty Marines of the ship's company trying to get some sleep.

That was long ago, he told himself, breathing hard but trying to relax. This is the here and now. I'm here, alive, on the U.S.S. *Indianapolis,* near the end of the war, on a craft so fast it couldn't be hit. I'm safe, safe! he told himself. But Murphy still laughed. . . .

Don Sobel was enjoying life again. There was nothing like a ship at sea; the feel of the great engines, the slow, monotonous slight rocking, the feeling of *community* as well—the ship was really a small town.

They'd given him greenies and no chance to whip them into shape. He liked them, though, and did what he could with small drills and a lot of routine work. He loved his boys already, though. They were closer to him than his own children, of whom he tried to think very little. A failure in his private family, he was a roaring success as boss, father figure, confessor, and adviser to this Navy one.

Among his youngsters the rumors about the cargo ran especially high. No mention had been made of the small container, which he'd correctly guessed was the whole ball game, and the more imaginative lads were thinking everything from some super kind of V-2s that would level Jap cities from a great distance to really crazy stuff like a kind of radar that would kill only Orientals. He neither knew nor cared if any were the truth. He dutifully noted them all.

His friendliness had already made him the center of these young boys' lives, though, and they constantly badgered him about the subject. "Come on, Chief, what's the dope on this thing?" "You know everything—you got to know what it is. Spill it."

Finally he just got sick of it and told them, "Look, I hear tell they didn't even tell the Old Man. What's the difference? If it's anything big we'll hear about it when it's used. If it isn't, well, better guess big than be disappointed, huh? I bet if we knew we'd be let down anyway."

That neither satisfied them nor stopped it but it helped a little.

Even the chief's wardroom wasn't immune and he thought he'd blow his stack seeing men as old and experienced as he acting just like the recruits.

Coyle, his old friend, commiserated with him. Luckily their duty hours coincided so they were able to keep in fairly constant contact. Coyle was not only a familiar face but also an introduction to the others. He was the veteran old pro they all wanted to show off to.

"What bothers me most," Coyle grumped, "is that the ship's so stuffed with passengers and shit that we haven't been able to so much as hold an abandon-ship drill, a battle-stations drill, anything."

Sobel was philosophical. "What can you do, Johnny? I hear tell we'll drop most of the stuff at Pearl and that'll help a little bit. When we get rid of this cargo it'll be smooth sailing."

Coyle was suddenly interested. "You mean you know we're gonna drop the cargo at Pearl?"

Sobel threw up his hands. "Not you, too!" he sighed. "Well, for your information I just happened to hear that it won't be dropped at Pearl but somewhere up in the Forward Area. Won't be long, though."

"You know what it is?" pressed Coyle.

"I do not. And I don't want to know," Sobel said flatly. "I just wish they'd made up some lie we could all believe. It'd be nice to talk about something else."

Sensing the chief's ire, the CIC man quickly shifted subjects. "Well, at least today the gun crews are getting a little practice. They're gonna have an artillery contest. Real shooting-gallery stuff. They invited those two Army officers to judge it."

"I can't go up there," Captain Nolan protested. "I only know the difference between a pistol and a machine gun because I saw a lot of war movies."

Furman chuckled. "I don't like it either. I'll tell 'em you're still under the weather and that'll get you off the hook but I'm afraid I'm stuck. I'll bluff it through somehow." He went out, leaving Nolan to take his hourly Geiger counter readings and check his other instruments around the cylinder.

He'd become obsessed with the idea that the thing might go critical and blow the ship to hell and him with it. The fact that they'd assured him it wasn't possible didn't help. He kept thinking that the *Titanic* was unsinkable, too.

Lieutenant Coringa had been prowling around, all over, and making a general pest of himself. He considered enlisted men little better than trained monkeys and made no attempt to hide his feelings. Consequently he was the butt of a lot of nasty practical jokes.

He was still obsessed with total security. The captain had listened to his concern, essentially patted him on the head, told

him he was a good sailor, and ushered him quickly out. It was
what you got for putting a vital mission in the hands of old
nuts-and-bolts men, he grumped.

Well, things had gone smoothly so far, he kept telling himself. Maybe they'd continue that way. The radio lingered in his
mind. That was the weak link, he felt certain, and something
would have to be done about it.

Sobel went to work just after 1600, prepared to do another
mock drill, but he'd no sooner looked over his clipboard and
decided what to do when alarm bells rang all over the ship and
he could hear men running all over the place.

"Fire! Fire!"

He checked the intercom and was told that there was a fire
in the forward hold. He and his men, with full equipment,
were off in an instant.

It looked bad. Smoke was billowing out of the engineering
passages forward around the main deck. Thick, black smoke
with no apparent flame. They moved fast. Their biggest problem was getting through the gathering crowd of jittery
onlookers.

He shouted to bring up masks, donned full fire-fighting
gear, and waded into the smoke. The trouble was quickly spotted and when realized what it was he almost exploded himself.

Suitcases. Dozens and dozens of suitcases, stacked here, in
the fire-control area, right against the forward stack which, at
twenty-nine knots, was hotter than pitch.

It took them only a few minutes to pull the suitcases away
and douse them with water but Sobel and a couple of supervising officers were furious. It was strictly against Navy regs
even to bring suitcases aboard a ship of war. It was against
common sense to stack them or *anything* against a main stack.
The area was a fire-control area. There would be a nasty hunt
for whoever decided to dump the stuff there, and a lot of passengers were going to have to find new wardrobes at Pearl

Harbor. By 1630 everything was under control and the crowd
started to disperse, talking anxiously about the excitement.

On the bridge Captain McVay was getting a report from his
fire-control officer and ordering a board of inquiry. McVay
was doubly irritated. Such a situation as this showed how
green the crew was and how desperately they needed training,
and it had also forced him to slow his pace to a crawl. He rang
angrily for flank speed once again, comforted only by the
knowledge that, at least, the fire brigade knew what it was
doing.

Sobel, too, was proud of his boys' reaction and irritated
mostly by the cause of the fire and the slowness with which the
alarm had reached him.

Of all aboard, only one, Lieutenant John Coringa, stared at
the forward hold and wondered if this might not be some sort
of subtle sabotage. The more impotent he found himself in security matters the more deeply paranoid he was becoming.

On Wednesday Jim Fargo was doing inventory in sick bay. He
had no trouble getting help here. The ship's only air-condi-
tioned area was this small but well-equipped hospital.

The ship shuddered from intermittent artillery practice.
Neither Fargo nor any of the others not accustomed to the
ship had gotten much sleep since they'd started. It was the one
kind of drill they could hold without causing problems, and
McVay, not alone among the officers, was particularly concerned that the gunnery crews be prepared for a Jap plane. He
hadn't forgotten Okinawa.

He was also snapping at people and irritated by it. It was
this damned tension, this pressure to deliver this cargo, he
knew. It was getting on everybody's nerves. He would be more
than happy when this was over and they could relax.

To break the tension, and because he wanted the Army men
to remember him as a gracious host, he arranged an inspection
tour of the ship for Nolan and Furman, which went very well,

the two officers for the first time seeing the ship in its entirety. Then they got to sick bay.

Lieutenant Commander Lewis L. Haynes showed off his new hospital. Furman was fascinated and also grateful for the air conditioning. He was reluctant to leave it for the hot and humid air outside. He failed to notice Nolan's increasing discomfort as the doctor didn't dare say a word for fear of betraying something of his medical background.

Fargo, still on inventory, watched with barely concealed amusement. He felt for the poor doctor and was ready to step in with an interruption, whatever, if things got sticky.

Finally the Army men left and Haynes went over to Fargo shaking his head. "That guy's no more artillery than *I* am," he noted. "The quiet one—the captain, I mean. Would you believe his artillery insignia had a broken clasp and wasn't even on right?"

Fargo just smiled. "What else could they be?" he asked innocently.

"Just remember that cargo crate down there," Haynes reminded the other man. "Top-secret stuff. I'll bet my bottom dollar that Nolan is FBI. They're a certain type, you know. I can spot 'em."

"That's very interesting," James Fargo responded and went back to checking his forms.

On Thursday, July 19, 1945, shortly after dawn, they spotted Diamond Head. While the preparations were being made for approach and docking, a lot of calculations were being made at Captain McVay's instigation. In a few minutes Commander Janney made it official. McVay put it on the horn immediately throughout the ship.

"Now hear this. Now hear this. Commander Janney has now verified that our crossing of seventy-four and a half hours for the official transpacific distance of two thousand ninety-one miles between Farallon Lightship and Diamond Head is a new world's record. We repeat, we have just set a new world's record for this crossing."

The entire ship went wild. There were cheers from bow to stern and toasts of coffee in the wardrooms. Down in the engine room the black gang was even wilder and they raised three cheers for Commander DeGrave. And, while no one could swear to it, it seemed that the crusty old engineering officer was wiping away tears.

Carriers, battlewagons, ships of all types got out of the way as the *Indianapolis* steamed through the narrow channel and into Pearl Harbor, directly for Ten-Ten Dock and a quick turn-around. Orders had arrived. For the time she would be there, the *Indy* was the king of the hill, the preferred customer. Everything stopped if it got in her way.

Dr. Haynes prepared to disembark a man recovering from a delicate operation and notified Commander Flynn, requesting an ambulance at the dock. Flynn was down in sick bay in an instant.

"How critical is he?" he asked. "The truth, now. Would it hurt him to stay here? Would it kill him?"

Haynes frowned. "Well, no, but he'd be a lot better off in a hospital than here."

"Sorry," Flynn told him. "Nobody—and I mean nobody—from the regular crew leaves this ship without specific orders. We're under top security, Doc."

Damned FBI men, Haynes thought sourly.

McVay walked off with Commander DeGrave, the one man who wanted desperately to stay aboard but was specifically ordered off. It was an emotional and personal farewell and De-Grave could hardly stand it. He cursed the regulations, the Navy, the unfairness of the system, and, most of all, the rotten luck that wouldn't even allow him to complete this mission and break in the new man properly.

Lucky, lucky Commander DeGrave.

Traffic Control was impressed by the new record. "You're ahead of schedule," McVay was told. "Some of the people flying to meet you when you arrive haven't come close to taking off from the States yet. Head straight for Tinian, but knock her down a bit—say, twenty-four knots or so." He grinned. "You're showing up all these brand spanking new cruisers."

McVay accepted the compliment. "She's a fine ship. But I'll still be glad when this assignment's over, I'll tell you."

The traffic-control officer at Pearl checked his charts. "At a steady rate of twenty-four knots you should reach Tinian on, uh, let's see, twenty-six July. I'll notify Hunter's Point and other interested parties. "Good luck and a quiet journey," he wished the captain.

By late afternoon fuel and provisions had been loaded, the last of the passengers except for Furman and Nolan had disembarked, and the big ship pulled out of her slip and was again sailing through the narrow harbor mouth. Once in deep water she turned almost due west and set sail into the giant sun.

The new engineering officer, twenty-seven-year-old Lieutenant (j.g.) Richard Redmayne, more than a little nervous at becoming the engine boss of the Fifth Fleet flagship, expertly deployed his crew. They were making a steady twenty-four knots in minutes, sailing westward into history.

Tinian Harbor
Thursday,
July 26, 1945

The absence of the passengers gave the crew more room to maneuver and there were drills, drills, drills all the way from Pearl Harbor to Tinian. Pulling into the tiny harbor at Tinian was the end of the great odyssey for them. It was a picture-postcard scene: a small tropical island with a dead-calm sea and a bright tropical sun overhead. The crew was anticipating this moment. Now, they hoped, the secret of the mystery cargo would be revealed.

The *Indianapolis* pulled to within a thousand yards of shore, as close in as McVay dared take her, and dropped anchor. Within minutes the place erupted with people.

Boats by the score approached the great cruiser and soon there was a flood of top brass of both services. Never, most of the crew thought, were so many generals and admirals on one ship, in one spot. This was really big.

An LCT pulled alongside the ship. It was a long, flat barge, and *Indy* shipfitters quickly cut away the large crate. The men of the Fourth Division manned the aviation crane, used to pick the ship's aircraft out of the sea. They attached the big crate to it and then lifting it up, gently over the side, put it lightly down on the deck of the barge.

Brass clustered around the two Army officers who saw just in the expression and manner of several important officers that Alamogordo had been a success and Trinity had been born. It made it all worthwhile.

More shipfitters freed the cylinder from the cabin deck and it was carried out and attached to a large winch, which was to lower it to the LCT. It went down, shakily, and stopped six feet short of the barge deck—the line was just too short.

There were so many people around that the *Indianapolis* crew had to endure a lot of jeers and catcalls, which infuriated them. They all felt they'd done their job well.

Furman and Nolan watched the dangling canister, and the doctor shook his head. "And to think we were going to lower it over the side into a boat if we started to sink," he muttered. Furman only smiled and nodded.

By midafternoon it was all over; the bomb parts, the Army men, the brass, all gone. It was an enormous letdown for the crew; they now knew exactly what they knew before—nothing at all. Still, they knew from the reception that this had been something special. They had made history and were proud of it. They only hoped that, someday, somebody would tell them just what history they'd made.

Captain McVay, along with his entire crew, relaxed. It was as if a huge black cloud had been lifted from the ship and now the sun was shining and the birds were singing.

A petty officer brought the captain a dispatch from CINC-PAC, the office of Commander-in-Chief, Pacific—Admiral Nimitz. CINCPAC ordered him to proceed immediately to Guam for refueling then proceed to Leyte, undergo seventeen days' training and refresher courses, then report to the Commander, Task Force 95. Copies went to that commander, Vice

Admiral Jesse B. Oldendorf, and to Rear Admiral Lynde D.
McCormick, who was to be the ship's training officer and
schedule those seventeen days. It was a simple dispatch. Quite
routine.

Admiral Oldendorf received the dispatch at sea. It was one of
countless others and was sent to him mainly to tell him that he
could expect the addition of the ship at a future date. It said
nothing about when the ship was to report to him and it didn't
ask him to do anything, so he initialed it, handed it back to his
administrative clerk. It was duly filed and forgotten.

The dispatch caught up with Admiral McCormick and was
sent to cryptography for decoding. A junior cryptographer,
new at the job, started on it and immediately started coming
up with gibberish. The three-line address was hopelessly garbled. It had reached McCormick's offices only because of its
being placed in the correct routing box. The clerk didn't
bother to go any farther—if the first couple of lines were fouled
up probably the whole thing was unreadable. He wouldn't
press it. He was due to go off duty in a few minutes, so he left
it in the "garbled" basket and went on. A few minutes later his
replacement arrived, sat down, and started work. He hardly
glanced at the "garbled" basket—he simply assumed that his
predecessor had shot back a request for a better version of the
dispatch and that it would come in in due time. At the end of
his watch, as per procedures, the man came around, dumped
the garbled box into his incinerator can, and went on his
rounds.

    The message hadn't been addressed to anyone else, so no
one else knew about it. From the viewpoint of higher command the *Indianapolis* had just vanished.

That night the *Indianapolis* pulled out of Tinian and made the
short trip south to Guam. Once safely in Apra Harbor, taking
on fuel, provisions, and ammunition, McVay and some of the

other senior officers left to confer with CINCPAC. On a pretext, a Naval Intelligence officer came aboard and sought out Fargo.

Fargo gave his report briefly. There wasn't much to say. "It's been tight as a drum. Wild rumors all over, of course, with the prevailing idea that it's some kind of deadly germs—I hear even the captain thinks that. Nobody else is even that close. Uh-uh. I'll check with the others if you want, but I bet there's nothing else."

The ONI man nodded. "About what we suspected. I'll see the others briefly but you're the man I wanted to see, since you're now the only man aboard who knows what was *really* carried. I don't know why they needed any more than you anyway. Five covert shadows on a ship of the line at sea under maximum security? Somebody's either very scared or crazy as a loon."

"Crazy's the word, all right," Fargo agreed. "Obviously you've never run into Colonel Houlton Withers. He's so nuts I bet he bugs his bedroom to find out if his wife heard him say anything in his sleep."

The other nodded glumly. "I know the type."

"So when am I getting out of here?" Fargo wanted to know. "It all sounded so nicely romantic but it's been the biggest bore of my life—and I got somebody I want to get back to."

The ONI man nodded understandingly. "Well, good news and bad. We thought we were to take you all off here but no orders came through to that effect. I'll collect your reports here, then you'll have to sail with the *Indy* to Leyte until we get proper disposition instructions. Frankly, I think you're such a minor cog in all this you've been largely forgotten by your Colonel Withers. I'll get you off when you get to the Philippines."

"I was afraid of that," Fargo muttered, as much to himself as to the other man. "Well, at least one of the men will be happy. Chief Sobel's having a ball here. You're going to have to pry him off with dynamite, I think."

CINCPAC headquarters was in a large building overlooking
the harbor, an almost picture-book view. Captain McVay
marveled at the transformation the place had undergone in so
short a time. He remembered helping retake this place from
the Japs. But that was some time ago, and his main concern in
calling on Commodore James B. Carter was to refamiliarize
himself with the Forward Area. Beyond his sailing orders and
departure date, he wanted to know just what local conditions
would be like. The Japanese were still very much around.

Carter wasn't helpful. "You won't be routed by us," he told
the captain. "That's handled by Naval Operating Base, Guam.
We're anxious to get you out for training, though, so you can
embark the Flag as soon as possible."

McVay nodded. "Do you want me to leave immediately or
can I wait until tomorrow morning?" he asked. "I'd like to
complete reprovisioning and refueling."

"No rush," Carter told him, "except to get that training.
The admiral wants you in shape fast and all the training's now
handled out of McCormick on Leyte. We have nothing whatever to do with it."

It seemed pretty simple. McVay now went over to the
officers' mess and met with Admiral Spruance and his staff
over lunch. The admiral wasn't in such a hurry as Carter had
implied. "Nothing big's in the wind," he told McVay. "In fact,
after you finish the refresher I'll probably bring you around to
Manila so we can use the ship before things start popping in
the fall."

That pleased the captain. He'd have little pressure now and
plenty of time to whip the crew and ship into shape. After that
he could offer them liberty in a liberated Manila as a reward.
Things were working out perfectly. He'd never felt better
about the future than now.

Later in the afternoon he went down to the Naval Operating Base near the harbor, still trying to get his sailing orders.
Lieutenant Joseph Waldron, the convoy and routing officer,
quickly turned him over to his aides, Lieutenant Northover

and Ensign Renoe, who handled most of the routine assignments. Northover asked McVay when he wanted to leave and what speed he'd like to make.

The captain was startled. "I'm a little surprised at the questions, frankly. I haven't been to the Forward Area in more than three months and I figured you people would know more about conditions here than I. The sixteen-knot speed limit's still in effect, isn't it?"

Northover looked questioningly at Renoe, who shrugged. "I don't know—we'll find out, though," he assured the captain.

It was. Every gallon of fuel had to be tanked from the U.S. mainland and it was found that sixteen knots was the most fuel-efficient speed. It was slow and would make something the size of the *Indianapolis* vulnerable without escort.

"I'll ask for one for you but I doubt if one's available," Lieutenant Waldron told him, then called the office of Vice Admiral George Murray, Commander Marianas, about it. It went to a junior aide, of course, who was irritated at being bothered by such a question. "No escort is necessary," he told Waldron irritably. "She's only going to Leyte for training."

Waldron was irritated at the manner as well as the reply. He knew an escort wasn't "necessary"—but if other ships were heading in that direction it would be easy to arrange them in escort fashion. He started to point this out, but the aide, who felt he'd already given the answer and was upset at being bothered again, snapped, "You know very well an escort's not necessary!" and hung up on the lieutenant.

Waldron sighed. How quickly some people forgot there was a war on when it'd passed them by, he reflected. Still, there was nothing he could do. An escort *wasn't* required this far from the battle lines and most ships were far to the north, arranged to pick up downed B-29 crews in a joint Navy–Air Force exercise. The *Indianapolis* would surely be safe.

With McVay gone, it was Commander Janney's turn. The navigator arrived to discuss course and speed with the same team. He was to use the most direct route, Code Route Peddie, between Guam and Leyte, leaving Apra Harbor at 0900 on Saturday, July 28, proceed at 15.7 knots along the course, and arrive off Homonhon Island off the Leyte coast at 1100 on Tuesday, July 31. The distance would be 1,171 miles. While the waters were considered safe there was always the chance of a lone-wolf Jap sub, so the orders instructed the *Indianapolis* to zigzag at the discretion of the commanding officer.

The Intelligence report showed no islands in Japanese hands within hundreds of miles of the course—in fact, there was just about no land along the course at all—and while there'd been reports of some Jap sub activity in the area it was all old stuff and mostly unconfirmed anyway. Every skipper saw a hundred subs on every trip. Now, if something had been reported sunk, that might have been different. This was just the usual jitters.

Back on the ship it was mail call and sheer bedlam. Jim Fargo found three letters—one from Carol, one from Harvey Cameron, and the third had a return address in Sausalito. He went back to his cabin, pulled the curtain, and sat down looking at all three. Harvey's would surely be the least wrenching, so he picked up that one first. It was generally full of local stuff, reports of local agents married, new kids, that kind of thing, and mention of a huge baby being born to some old Alamogordo friends. They were going to name her Trinity.

He grinned. Good old Harvey! He wondered what it'd taken to get *that* past the censors. Still, it was satisfying to read that the routine work had gone well and that the bomb had worked. There was also a reference to Uncle Houlton being a real pain, but that was all.

He picked up the one from Carol next. It wasn't much, really—more of the same. She was going to night school, she missed him, she wanted him back, she'd had no other man since That Day, all the usual. He could read between the lines. A divorce would kill her parents, maybe tarnish her. A divorce with her pregnant might result in a particularly messy attempt to prove or disprove paternity. Back home it would make the papers. Messy. Scandal.

He tossed it aside. It was funny—it didn't mean much to him anymore. Somehow it just didn't matter.

The third, of course, was from Sam. It wasn't much—some chitchat about the store, about her crazy friends, that kind of thing. Nothing terribly romantic. Sam herself wasn't really important, he knew that. Maybe she would be, maybe not, but that wasn't the point. What he owed her was reminding him that he was a human being with a life to live and a future. He realized now that it had been his pride and manhood that Carol had wounded—his vanity, really, nothing more.

He put the letters away and walked out onto the deck. The wind was light and warm, the temperature getting comfortable. They were setting up a movie on the quarterdeck—first-run, too. Only the best for CINCPAC headquarters and they'd had their pick.

Back in his cabin, Lieutenant John Coringa was hard at work scanning diagrams and notes. He was angry that they all considered the mission over. Particularly out here, with these islands still crawling with Orientals, some of whom had to be Jap spies—even here, on Guam. You couldn't tell. Confusion, that was the key to confounding spies.

There'd be no security broken because of him. No, sir.

It was 0910 on the morning of July 28 when the *Indianapolis* steamed out of Apra Harbor, Guam, bound straight west again for Leyte. The crew was confident, if not exactly looking forward to the training period—which also meant cleaning up the mess, chipping, painting, and all the rest. Captain McVay was also confident; the three days would allow additional drill on the way and the seventeen days off in Leyte should be just right to get the old girl in the spotless shape the Flag would demand.

Before she was even out of sight of CINCPAC headquarters

on the hill overlooking the harbor the port director's office sent the following message to all these people: the shipping-control officer for the Marianas; the port director at Tacloban, Leyte; Admirals McCormick, Spruance, Murray, Oldendorf, Commodore Gillette of the Philippine Sea Frontier, and just about every other commander in the central Pacific. Even Admiral Nimitz was sent a copy. It said, "U.S.S. *Indianapolis* (CA 35) departed Guam 2300Z 28 July, SOA 15.7 knots. Route Peddie then Leyte. ETA position Peter George 2300Z 30 July. ETA Leyte 0200Z 31 July. Chop 30 July." There it was—the routine dispatch telling just about everyone in command in the area of a thousand miles that the ship had left, where it was going, on what course and speed, and where it should be both at the halfway (chop) point and when it should arrive at the other end—and where. A simple, foolproof, routine system the Navy had used all during the war. The crew worked hard and without much complaint. They were very proud of their ship right about now and wanted it to shine. Besides, as the chiefs kept telling them, they'd gotten off pretty lightly so far with this secret-mission business.

The sea was clear, the air hot and humid, and there was nothing in sight from one edge of the horizon to the other.

Code Route "Peddie"
Sunday,
July 29, 1945

Sunday dawned overcast and choppy but nobody really minded. The wind gave a little relief from the oppressive heat but even with all the doors open below and all the air vents open as well there was little to be done if you wanted to sleep without frying. Most just hauled something out on the main decks and slept under the stars. Lieutenant T. M. Conway, the ship's chaplain, prepared for morning services. He was pleased; there seemed to be a few more people than usual.

An hour after his Catholic service ended Doc Haynes assisted him in setting up and performing the Protestant service. A strong Catholic from a totally Catholic Buffalo neighborhood, he was uncomfortable handling that second service, particularly when some of the Protestant advisers, like Haynes, would suggest a hymn by someone like Martin Luther.

By noon it was all over, the smoking lamp was lit, and almost immediately lookouts and surface radar reported a ship

far off and heading north. It turned out to be an LST off to do
some target practice outside the shipping lanes. The communications officer, Lieutenant Commander Stout, talked
briefly with her and exchanged pleasantries.

Coringa happened to be in the wardroom when somebody
came back from Radio I with the details of the exchange.
Coringa almost had a fit. If any Jap sub were stalking them it
would now know that they were no longer under radio silence
or other restrictions. It would be clear that they had dropped
off the cargo. It confirmed all his worst fears about the crew.
He had a vision of Japanese bombs raining down on Tinian.

That afternoon, too, Doc Haynes decided the time had
come to give a new set of shots. There were some outbreaks of
cholera in China and nobody could be sure the *Indianapolis*
wouldn't have to go there at some point—or meet someone who
had. His medics were more than a little pissed; they were due
to take their rating exams in another couple of days and had
wanted the time for study. But by early evening they'd administered almost eleven hundred shots. Some of the officers
and a few enlisted men temporarily beat the rap.

The weather was getting nasty. The sea was getting rough
and you could see the bow lower into the troughs, only to surface once more and repeat the pattern. The ship rolled and
tossed and creaked a little. Visibility was getting poorer as
well but that didn't bother anyone. There didn't seem to be a
damned thing out there. The ship's boilers, only half on line,
kept the 15.7-knot speed steady through it all. They even operated the four screws at different rates, which would confuse
the hell out of enemy listening gear. The slight difference in
rpm's would produce an intermittent sound on hydrophones. It
would make them tough to locate and even if they were pin-
pointed, they might be taken for more than one ship.

Lieutenant (j.g.) Charles McKissick took the watch at 1800
hours and, after a routine stop at CIC, went to the bridge.
There was a message there from a merchant marine freighter
named the *Wild Hunter* that said it'd spotted a periscope at

1620 the previous afternoon at a position some seventy-five miles south of the *Indianapolis* route and just a bit ahead. At 1648 hours *Wild Hunter* again reported sighting and firing on a periscope, probably the same sub. No result, but he'd put stern to the thing and poured on the coal.

It was routine. Dozens of these reports came in every day and most could be easily dismissed. The odds of even being found by a sub in this great expanse were very slim indeed. If you were the captain of a merchantman with only a puny little armed guard and one or two small howitzers aboard you'd probably be seeing periscopes everywhere. Nobody put much credence in the report. Even if it had been a sub, any commander who could track a merchant ship for half an hour and not get off a good shot wasn't anyone to worry about.

Like Mr. McKissick, the captain and crew of the *Wild Hunter* had never even conceived of something like the *kaitens*, the torpedoes steered by a human strapped to them. Nor had the men around the bridge table in the officers' wardroom that evening. Jokes about the ineptitude of this alleged Jap sub were all over, and even Commander Janney jokingly said over his cards, "You know, we're going to pass a Jap sub around midnight."

"Don't worry," someone cracked. "Our destroyers will get him." Everybody laughed.

Jim Fargo spotted Ron Sarbic in the wardroom and went over to him with a nod. He'd seen little of Sarbic during the voyage, a fact that wasn't surprising given the size of the ship and the fact that Sarbic had only left his cabin to carry out his duties. He was depressed and lonely. On top of that he now knew he was a lousy sailor.

Sarbic cocked his head toward the bridge game. "You really think we'll be near a sub around then?" he asked nervously.

Fargo shrugged. "I don't worry about what hasn't happened," he responded. "If I did I'd never drive a car, hell, never even leave the house. I'd say forget it. Those guys have been at this a lot longer than us and *they're* not worried. Why the worry? Can't swim?"

Sarbic smiled sourly and changed the subject. "Well, a couple more days and it'll all be over."

"For us," Fargo noted. "Not for these guys. They've got Japan to crack yet."

"You really think it'll come to that?" Sarbic said, surprised. "I think they'll surrender after our little package is delivered."

It was Fargo's turn to be surprised. "You know what it was?"

"I figured it out long ago," Sarbic told him. "Hell, Withers asked me to take radiation readings in the cabin after the cargo was off-loaded to make sure there was nothing residual."

Jim Fargo sighed. "That man has the brains of Mount Whitney," he said sourly. "I wonder how people like him get to be where they are anyway?"

"Powerful men always like to have someone around to take the blame for them," Sarbic replied. "That way you hate the man who enforces the order, who's powerless, and forget the man who ordered it. The services are full of Withers. The world's full of them. They have an almost animal sense of self-preservation. If this had gone wrong he already had the man picked out to be crucified for it. I used to have an old chief working for me at the Navy Yard and every time he'd come across a Withers type he'd just mutter, 'There's a million kinds of sharks in the world but some of them ain't human.'"

Fargo laughed and felt easier, as did Sarbic, talk of the sub forgotten.

Captain McVay was seldom in his cabin when the ship was at sea, preferring a small auxiliary room just in back of the bridge where he was available on twenty-four-hour call. He couldn't use his cabin now, anyway—while on Guam he'd offered it to an old Annapolis classmate who needed transportation westward.

Now McVay walked onto the bridge, checked conditions,

talked briefly with the men on duty, then peered out into the gathering darkness. It was a nasty afternoon and looked to be a dark and cloudy night. They had been zigzagging during daylight as a precautionary measure to confuse enemy subs. But it was a wasteful and time-consuming procedure. "You may secure from zigzagging after twilight," he told McKissick.

"Aye, aye, sir," the lieutenant replied. A little later, when darkness fell, he gave the order and the ship straightened to Course 262° True.

The watch changed at 2000 hours and McKissick was replaced by Commander Lipski. Unknown to everyone, Lipski was the logical man to have been in charge of security during the earlier secret mission. He'd been a top Naval Intelligence man who'd become bored with routine and pulled every string to get a ship. Commander Janney came up a little later with the routine night orders. He also informed them that a hunter-killer team was searching for a sub about 120 miles west. Again, nobody was much concerned.

Visibility was poor for the first couple of hours. The bridge could see practically nothing. Around 2200 it started to clear a bit and a few stars even peeked through the clouds.

Ensign John Woolston had the watch in damage control. Woolston had gotten along well with Sobel from the start. Sobel had just come from Bremerton, and Woolston was a native of Seattle, just a ferry ride across Puget Sound. Sobel liked the kid. He had the bug all right, and the pride in the ship.

He'd been at sea all of two weeks. He was two weeks shy of his twenty-first birthday.

He related well to big Don Sobel, and was thankful for the veteran's experience. In fact, Woolston had been surprised to discover that Sobel had spent the last couple of years on land. He was obviously made for a ship like this.

"Somebody said you were on the *Arizona*," he said to Sobel.

Sobel nodded. "Good old Johnny's been talkin' again. Yes, sir, I was with her four and a half years. I got off lucky at

Pearl—I was in a Honolulu flophouse sleepin' off a big drunk. I got off because it was my birthday—the sixth, that is."

Woolston considered it. "And they stuck you on shore duty just because of that?"

"Oh no, sir!" the chief responded quickly. "Hell, they couldn't keep me off the sea. I got lucky at Pearl, but I had eleven hundred young lads go down with her and I owed 'em somethin'. The Good Lord didn't want me to go with 'em, so I figured he had somethin' else in mind for me. No, they dry-docked me for a while, but eventually I found a berth on the *Juneau.* That's what got me nailed to the dock."

Woolston looked puzzled. "How's that?"

"You remember the *Juneau,* sir. The Sullivans were on it—I knew 'em. Fine bunch of boys. All gone. She went down like a stone in seconds. I was on deck at the time and got blown clear into the water before I knew what happened. Only eleven of us survived."

The ensign thought he understood. "They think you're a Jonah."

Sobel nodded. "Oh, the Navy don't officially believe it, of course, but it's like accident insurance. You don't pay much as long as you don't have an accident. Have one and they sock on the rates. Have a bunch and you can't get that insurance. They call you accident prone or somethin' like that. They don't believe in jinxes, no, sir, but they figure it don't cost them much for a little insurance, like keepin' me off ships. And, besides, they had a job for me that didn't make 'em hav'ta ship me out."

Woolston just shook his head. "Well, I don't believe in jinxes, Chief. I'm happy to have you here. I need you in this job."

Sobel grinned. "Don't worry, sir. They won't get *this* ship from me without a fight. No, sir, I'd wrestle the devil himself for this beautiful baby."

The young ensign smiled back. "O.K., Chief. Carry on. I

think it's time to make my rounds." And, with that, he went topside and out onto the deck, into the hot night air.

Woolston loved night duty and he loved prowling the ship in the late hours. Every once in a while he'd come across a crap game somewhere below. Now and then he'd stroll down the deck and see the stars and smell the salt spray, all the time trying not to trip over the hundreds of enlisted men who had lugged mattresses up on deck to sleep in the fresh air. There were a lot of such tonight. The sea was calming and the weather definitely was clearing.

As for Sobel he was in heaven, sipping coffee and reading an old magazine from the ship's library. It was full of bad detective stories but he didn't care. It was a problem concentrating anyway, since Woolston was always calling in and making sure that all five damage-control stations reported in regularly.

He didn't mind. Ever since he'd been a seaman he'd tried for night duty. Most chiefs were early-to-bed types who felt sorry for anyone who had to stay up after dark and so night-duty personnel tended to be left alone in their own little worlds.

About 2300 Johnny Coyle dropped by, having been relieved at 2000 in CIC and having watched the movies on the hangar deck. He didn't feel sleepy and stopped by to chat. Within a few minutes the mystery magazine was forgotten as he started playing Coyle a little gin rummy.

Captain McVay had been on the bridge most of the late evening but decided to call it a day around 2300. He checked final orders, then went back to his small cabin just a few yards from the bridge and stripped naked, lying down on his cot. The ship's roll was comforting to him and he was asleep in a matter of minutes, not a care in the world.

Midnight approached; the watches started changing, and you could now see a hint of moon and stars overhead. Forward visibility remained poor.

Most of the 1,199 men on board slept peacefully.

Jim Fargo just stood at the rail looking out at the calm, silent
sea. The ship's rhythmic *thrum, thrum, thrum,* the vibrations
from its powerful engines, was a calming, almost hypnotic ca-
ress from this great creature of armored metal. She was no
longer a thing at all but a person, a friend. She was not a machine. She was, instead, a great, motherly, comforting creature
of the beautiful sea.

The sea was eerie. Phosphorus and algae atop the waters
gave off a weird luminescence, like some scene out of a fairyland. The sound of the water being pushed back by the ship's
mighty lunges pushed any lingering uneasiness he might have
had about enemies and sinkings far back into his mind. The
jewel-like twinkling of the sea and the solidity of the ship were
an enchanted setting that was to be enjoyed. For a moment the
fear disappeared.

It was not a time for thought, only a time for being, for
your soul to shout to the world, "I'm alive!"

The real world—there was thinking enough there, all right.
The bomb had been dropped off on Tinian, the mission was
accomplished. The responsibility was now on others' shoulders.

But as he stared at the fantasyland of the glowing Pacific,
thoughts did come. They poked and probed the outer reaches
of his mind and found ways to slip through no matter how he
tried to push them back.

He thought of Carol. That was the real world, too, he knew
—more real to him than any superbombs or *kamikaze* planes.
He wondered if she felt the peace and solitude he now felt.
Here, alone at the rail. Probably not, he decided, more sad
than angry at that conclusion. She'd complain about the vibration and noise and worry about the Japs and complain that it
was damned stupid to be standing on a rusty deck so late at
night just doing nothing at all. The sea would be a terrifying
place to her. She never saw the beauty in things.

She was right, of course. The ocean was placid only on the surface. There was a jungle below as savage as any in darkest Africa, predator feeding on prey in a battle for survival. It wasn't that she was wrong in such things, no. Just that she could see no romance, no beauty in common things. His poetry was the oneness he felt with everything around him. He loved the desert and mountains back in New Mexico, too. She hated them for their remoteness. In fact, hadn't that been her very defense of what she'd done?

Sam was different. You could see it in the way she reacted to things. He hardly knew her, and on the surface they had little in common. He wondered what her reaction would be if she knew he was an FBI man and not just another naval reservist. It was on a basic, romantic level that they'd clicked—the emotional, the natural, not the real world at all.

Most people were like Carol, not Sam, he thought sadly. You couldn't explain it to them, show them the beauty of a sunrise or the glory of stars from a ship at sea. You couldn't tell them that there had been enough killing, enough marching feet, and enough superbombs. You could never make such people understand that life had to be worth living.

Living. He rolled the word over in his mind. He hadn't really wanted to do much of that anymore, had he? A dangerous mission, uncharted seas, voyages into the enemy's backyard— why not? Millions had died and their deaths had meant *something,* surely. Hitler was dead, Germany was smashed, all because of their blood.

He remembered reading a fantasy story a few years back—a lifetime back, perhaps—that theorized that this world of ours was hell, and that it worked by always giving you what you didn't want and taking from you all that you did want. How many deskbound servicemen back in the States yearned to get into the war while everybody rooting Japs out of caves on countless atolls would sell their souls to be back at Great Lakes. Like the crew of the *Indianapolis,* much as they loved her. Most of them still griped when told to report early and would gladly trade all they had for a ticket home.

He had decided he might as well die; therefore, the mission had been accomplished without so much as a hangnail. He would never trust or get really involved with a woman again, and there Sam had been. Now, here, on the deck of the ship, in his own private and soothing world, he couldn't quite bring himself to ask if he were still so eager to face death. The thought was unsettling, as if it demanded a ghostly answer. He pushed it away, frantically, almost desperately, lest he think the unthinkable, that to live is now what he wanted desperately to do, and, somehow, by that admission to die suddenly and horribly.

He had to stop reading stories like that, he told himself.

And still the ship sang as it pushed itself through the moon-lit seas: *Thrum! Thrum! Thrum!* Quivering, surging forward as if shouting to the world that it, too, lived and took joy in the fact.

The sea's deadliest predator raises an eyestalk high until it breaks the surface. It turns first this way, then that way, and the glass over it reflects ever so slightly the phosphorescence of the waters and the feeble rays of a quarter moon. Now, behind it, it puts up a second stalk whose little flag atop starts twirling, scanning the skies for the deadly flying enemy. It sees nothing and, slowly, carefully, it rises out of the water, a great black thing.

Suddenly a voice calls within it. "Bearing red nine-zero degrees, a possible enemy ship," it calls.

Now the predator stops, almost quizzically, and its many eyes of many types stare intently out toward the horizon, straining to see. A glimmer? Something's coming! Something's coming! it seems to say in an odd mixture of suspicion and anticipation.

Atop the thing a man stares through binoculars, sees something in the dark, and says, "Dive!" Men scramble back down

*hatches and they are quickly closed. In moments the predator
has vanished once more beneath the waves.*

*The eyestalk rises once more and deep within the preda-
tor's bowels, a man stares hard into the oddly illuminated
night. For the barest of seconds, he pauses to reflect on the
ocean's fairyland beauty.*

*"Ship in sight," the man calls out. "All tubes to the ready.
Kaitens stand by."*

In Japanese he calls.

Lieutenant John Coringa lay on his bunk staring up into the
dark. He couldn't sleep; he always had trouble sleeping, and
now there was so much to think about.

They'd done it! *He'd* done it! The security had not been
breached, the cargo had been delivered and signed for, and he
was about to go home—home to full restoration, to honors,
perhaps, to a career, certainly. Withers—Withers was his kind.
Withers would reward excellence as surely as he would mete
out doom to failures. It would be all gone—the stain, the memories, the blows to career and pride. He'd shown them! He'd
shown them all that they hadn't misplaced their trust in John
Coringa.

He frowned slightly. But nothing must go wrong even in the
final stages. Particularly not now. And it still wasn't over yet,
not until Leyte. The enemy might have seen them loading
something but not yet know they'd unloaded it at Tinian.
Maybe Guam—or maybe Leyte. It wouldn't be wise to slip
now, not when victory was in his grasp. Confuse the bastards.

The fears were creeping back. Suppose Tinian was bombed
just by accident? Suppose it would be just a freak thing and
they still didn't know it was a breach? Would they blame him,
take it out on him?

He sat bolt upright in the darkness. You bet your ass they
would. They would need somebody to blame. He was *it*. He
was the one on the spot.

"You are responsible!" Withers' voice seemed to come, ac-

cusatory, out of the air around him, so real that he jumped at
the sound that he knew was in his mind alone.

Responsible. You. Me. I.

Suddenly he was wide awake and frantic. The Congressional Medal of Honor, a ship command, all the dreams
seemed to shatter and fade to nothingness where but a moment
before they'd danced before his eyes. His mind raced. The island, the bombs, the planes he could do nothing about. Nothing. It was frustrating but that was the way it was. He would
have to trust to God and blind luck on that. But here—aboard
this ship. That *he* could control. That *he* could do something
about.

He jumped up and pulled on his pants and shirt. One more
check, he told himself. It never hurt to do one more check.
The idiots couldn't be trusted to do it right, couldn't *ever* be
trusted to do it right. The officers couldn't either—not after
that LST call.

Radios I and II continued to be obsessions. He'd taken all
the preliminary steps but hadn't made the final decision yet.
Not yet. Now he realized he'd been wrong. They could be
transmitting even now. . . .

Idly, as he dressed, he snapped on the small bedstand light
and glanced at his watch. It was a minute or so before midnight. . . .

*Deep within the ocean predator, just below the surface, the
captain stares at a shape closing in on him, a tiny black trian-
gle, a ghostly, unreal shape in the darkness. He worries. The
speed with which it's approaching and the straight line toward
his position make him fear it is a destroyer already on to him.
He curses his broken-down hydrophones.*

*Not long ago he'd been sound asleep but the last of that is
gone now, replaced by excitement mixed with worry. He is
cautious; he is one of only four submarine captains left at this
point in the war.*

He peers again through the periscope. The shape keeps

coming on resolutely, growing impossibly large as it does so. At this rate the ship will run right over him. He can't make much out of it, can't see the height of the mast. He needs range, course, and speed before firing and he can't get them this way. Briefly he considers radar, but radar can be heard by others as well. If this ship is bearing down on him it would tell them exactly where he is. Too many variables, too great a speed at night with limited visibility—but he doesn't want to let this one go.

"Range: fifteen hundred meters," he tells the kaitens *waiting. "Bearing green forty-five degrees." Both pilots acknowledge the orders and beg to be launched immediately.*

"Launch No. 5," the captain orders. The ship shudders. He is anxious. The kaitens *might be his only protection from destroyers. "Launch No. 6," he orders.*

At that moment the kaiten *pilot shouts, "We will meet again at Yasukuni Shrine!" and the ship shudders again as he is off.*

The moment they are launched the captain regrets his actions. The ship is clearly in two parts now and will miss by two thousand yards or more. A big ship. The mast looked to be thirty meters high! A battleship! Probably the Idaho, *reputed to be off Guam.*

He orders the ship brought on a course parallel with the enemy and all six tubes at the ready. He waits almost half a mile away, eyes on that big ship, every minute passing like eternity. If the kaitens *did not strike soon he is determined to get this great monster ship himself.*

Ron Sarbic finished off the small bottle of whiskey he'd carefully secreted aboard and reflected with a rosy glow that there were distinct advantages to being a technical expert with a lot of top-secret gear.

That was the worst part of it, too. The loneliness. Here I am on a ship with twelve hundred young men and I'm alone. That talk with Fargo had been an attempt to help that but it only increased Sarbic's sense of isolation. That had started it, and hadn't gone that far away from him despite the whiskey.

He looked around at the tiny cabin. Metal walls, rivets, constant vibration, a tiny little light, and that was that. A prison, he thought sourly, or a monk's cell.

Not any different, he told himself. Not really. Smaller, more graphic, but absolutely appropriate for his life. The whole goddamned world was his prison, his monk's cell. He burned with desire, burned within himself at his frustration and rage, and knew that he would probably burn just as surely in New York or San Francisco.

Not for the first time he cursed himself, the way he was, the way he would always be. His parents had such high hopes for him, and he'd lived up to some of them. The shy, introverted, bookish son who hadn't much luck with athletics had a great deal of luck in the academic subjects. A physicist. His father had been particularly pleased that his son had become an egghead in a field he couldn't even spell, let alone understand. But the other dream, that of his becoming a professor and settling down with a wife and a bunch of grandchildren—well, the war had provided enough of an excuse for not doing that. After the war he'd find something else.

Not that he hadn't tried. He wanted desperately to have at least that normalcy, that sense of contact with the human race. It just wasn't possible, wasn't in him. He knew it and hated himself all the more for it. He wouldn't ever settle down with a woman. Not with a woman, damn it all.

Well, here he was and here was the *Indianapolis* and there was the atomic bomb safely on Tinian, being checked and assembled while a crew drilled on how to drop it safely on the Japs. Pearl Harbor would be avenged. If Japan didn't quit then, well, there'd be no more Japan.

There was some satisfaction in that. And in the fact that he'd had a part, however small, in making it happen. Not that his presence here had really mattered, but it was, well, like being present at the Gettysburg Address or something like that. Just being there made you feel a part of the event, an event you knew would change the history of man forever.

The bomb would end the war, that was for sure. Nobody could have such a thing turned against him without realizing surrender was the only alternative to total annihilation, not even fanatics like the Japs. But afterward . . .

He considered that again. Not the military, surely. Maybe a nice, quiet lab job away from people, away from pressures. That was one thing he was born to do, his one true element— the lab, research. There he wasn't different, wasn't "queer" or out of place at all.

But not nuclear, oh no. Not anything that would require a government security clearance. He had one now, sure, but this was wartime and nobody looked very closely. He'd been cloistering himself all his life, suppressing any emotions that might betray him, but it was a losing battle. Sooner or later he would succumb, sooner or later the secret would be out.

And the next war—it would be fought entirely with those kind of bombs. With those bombs, or with better and bigger models of those bombs, so they could wipe out the whole damn human race, maybe even set the atmosphere on fire. He felt suddenly that his life was much shorter than it had looked even a few weeks ago. . . .

He carefully hid the whiskey bottle and popped a couple of Sen-Sen into his mouth just in case, then lay back in his bunk and flipped off the light. He ran his hands over his naked body and tried to get a little relief from the burning, burning Ronnie Sarbic, there, alone, in the cell, in the dark, alone. . . .

The captain frowns impatiently. There is no noise anywhere in the sub except for the clatter of rats back in the galley. Where were those kaitens? *Did nothing work? If he did not act soon, or if the* kaitens *did not strike soon, then he would lose a battleship, by the gods! A battleship! He can never face his ancestors, he knows, if he lets this one get away.*

"Green sixty degrees!" he calls. "Range five hundred me-

*ters! Stand by to fire all tubes! Angle on the bow three de-
grees!"*

*The ship comes about; all is in readiness for a launch. Six
white buttons glow ominously before the torpedo officer's
hand, waiting only the final command.*

"Bow tubes ready!" the captain snaps.

"Bow tubes ready," the torpedo officer responds.

"Stern tubes ready!" comes the command.

"Stern tubes ready," the torpedo officer assures him.

"Bearing! Mark!"

*"Speed 15.7 knots, heading due west, bearing still green
sixty degrees."*

*We've got him now, the captain thinks smugly. Six tor-
pedoes will be fired, fanlike, at an object so large and tempting
that it would be like shooting carp in a fish tank with a
cannon.*

"I'll see your two bits and raise you another quarter," Glass
said confidently.

Private Phil Lanier and four other Marines of the ship's detachment stared hard. The single naked bulb hung over the
makeshift poker table, barely giving enough light for the
game. Cigarette smoke hung thickly in the storage room aft,
near the brig.

The game was seven-card stud and there were already over
twenty dollars in the pot. Glass chewed on his cigar and
waited, an amused twinkle in his eyes. The four exposed cards
were a trey, a six, a nine, and a king, but they were all diamonds.

"I think you got it, you lucky son-of-a-bitch," grumbled the
man next to him, folding. "So do I," moaned the next and also
turned his cards over.

"I'll call," Lanier said confidently, tossing in a quarter.

Glass shifted nervously and looked a little closer at Lanier's
cards. A pair of fours, an eight, and a queen. Big deal.

The final man also folded, leaving just those two. Glass's

smile turned into a wide grin as he flipped over his three down cards—two were low-rank clubs, but one was the ace of diamonds. "Fair enough?" he asked in evident satisfaction.

Lanier nodded. "I thought you had it," he told the sergeant and turned over his own cards. One was a jack, but the other two were both fours.

"Son-of-a-bitch!" Glass swore. "Four fours! Don't that beat all! I ain't seen luck like this since Saipan!"

The others all froze at that. They knew a little of his history —people talk aboard ship.

"You mean you lost the night before that patrol?" one of the other Marines said uneasily.

Glass nodded. "Couldn't win for nothin'. I'd have a full house, tens and jacks, and the next bastard would have a boat with queens and kings!" There was a curious silence for a moment that made even Glass uncomfortable.

"Sarge—nobody in that game lived through the next day, did they?" Lanier almost whispered. "Nobody but you."

Either it didn't penetrate or it didn't bother Glass much. "Yeah, that's right, I suppose. Guess you can only have so much luck."

The others stirred uncomfortably. "It's gettin' to be after midnight," one noted. "I think it's about time I turned in."

"Yeah, me, too," another said nervously. "I got duty at 0800." One by one, like dominoes lined up in a row and triggered by the push of the first, they made their excuses and got up to leave. Glass finally realized what had happened.

"Hey! Guys! Wait a minute! You ain't gonna be scared by a little thing like—oh shit! Big, rough, tough Marines! Hey—if anything happens, I'll protect you!" He laughed at that and kept on laughing as the others filed out without looking back at him or making any sort of a reply. He was still laughing when he discovered that most of them had left all or part of their winnings on the table. He started scooping them up.

Even the ghostly laughter seemed more robust than usual— or was it just his own echoing off metal walls?

"Six torpedoes, in series," the captain orders. "Fire bow tubes one and two."

Torpedo Officer Tanaka presses the large white studs and as he presses them the lights wink out. There is a shudder through the ship.

"Fire three and four," orders Captain Hashimoto.

"Three and four fired, sir," Tanaka replies.

"Fire five and six."

"Five and six fired, sir," Tanaka responds, pressing the large white firing buttons. Again the ship shudders.

Dr. Modisher walked through the sick-bay waiting room and shook his head from side to side. It was crammed, mostly with his own medics but also others. He had given them permission to use the light and air conditioning to help them study for the rating exams coming up on Tuesday. He wished them well, but wondered how much ship efficiency would suffer because of their lack of sleep over the next couple of days.

"Running time two minutes, forty-five seconds," Tanaka tells the captain.

"Take her down?" the engineering officer asks nervously.

Hashimoto shakes his head. "No, I still have no sight of escorts. We'll wait from here to confirm the kill. The explosions will bring the escorts—then we go down. Stand by and time."

Tanaka looks at the sweep second hand of the submarine's master clock. "Two minutes," he announces, switching on the ship's intercom so all can hear.

Jim Fargo sighed, still at the rail, and took one last look at the beautiful, glittering ocean now suddenly illuminated by moonlight.

"One minute, thirty seconds," Tanaka announces.

John Coringa walked toward Radio II, reached it, saw five

men inside monitoring routine transmissions. He didn't care. He scrambled up to where the antenna connector emerged in a small pipe from the radio room to carry the signals to the main antenna. Kneeling down, he removed a small hacksaw from his belt and continued to saw where he had in the darkness the past two nights. It was almost cut through now.

"One minute and running true," Tanaka announces.

In his bunk up in officers' country Ron Sarbic found relief but no satisfaction and buried his head in his hands.

"Thirty seconds," Tanaka announces. You can cut the tension with a knife.
  Six hydrogen-propelled torpedoes, leaving no wake, speed toward the dark shape at a speed of over forty-eight knots. Each warhead carries more than twelve hundred pounds of explosives.

Don Sobel laid down his cards. "Gin," he announced, and Johnny Coyle could only sigh disgustedly. From nearby was the sound of intense snoring and he said, "I think I might turn in as well. I can't concentrate between all the snoring just forward and all those damned check-in calls."
  Sobel chuckled. "Any old excuse, huh?" he kidded the other. "Face it: You're just a bum card player."

"Fifteen seconds," Tanaka says, and everyone's heart seems to stop.

On the bridge, Lieutenant Commander Casey Moore turned to Ensign Marple, and said, "Well, it's been an easy one this trip."
  Marple looked surprised. "Were you expecting anything?"
  "Naw," Moore shook his head. "But we've been through the mill in this damned war. We were due an easy one. I don't

know what was in that box we delivered but I had the feeling from those who did know that this might just be the end of the war. That wouldn't be so hard to take, would it?"

"No, *sir*," Marple agreed.

"Ten seconds!"

Bill Glass started forward toward his bunk. Down the hall Chief Sobel walked into the chamber filled with sleeping men just to make sure all was O.K. His boss, Ensign Woolston, reached the wardroom and started to pour himself a cup of coffee.

Seamen Ray Sinclair and Clarke Seabert, both just out of boot camp, took their chairs on the starboard side of the bridge and started scanning the sea with binoculars. They were looking at nothing at all. Despite the moon, visibility was still pretty poor, a periscope was almost an impossible thing to spot in this sort of real-life situation. Torpedoes speeding toward you at forty-eight knots wouldn't be visible in time to do anything even in broad daylight. They didn't think about it much; a cool breeze had sprung up and they relaxed and enjoyed the relief it brought.

Tanaka's voice breaks with the tension. "Five seconds!" he calls out.

Jim Fargo's eyes suddenly bulged as he saw a dark shape seem to disturb his fairyland very close to the ship. For a moment he thought it was a whale; only at the last second did his mind scream, "Oh, my God! It's a torpedo!"

"Four! Three! Two! One!"

A tremendous explosion seemed to blow off the bow of the ship; men were knocked down and thrown against bulkheads and out of bunks. Before they could recover, a second torpedo exploded amidships, right below the hangar deck.

Fargo was thrown first against the rail, which, mercifully, held, then back against the bulkhead. He was bruised and shocked but picked himself up quickly. He started heading aft but had no idea why.

Coringa was blow right off his perch outside Radio II and fell more than ten feet to the deck. He got up, bruised and shaken, fearing his left shoulder might be broken.

The lights flickered in Radio II and there was a lot of yelling and screaming in there. Carefully he approached the doorway. "No messages!" he screamed. "This ship is under top security!"

Captain McVay came awake with the first explosion, which almost threw him to the deck. He thought first that a *kamikaze* had again found the *Indianapolis,* but before he could put that theory to the test the second explosion tossed him around on the deck. He picked himself up and stalked out onto the bridge, stark naked. This was no suicide plane. It was torpedoes.

He spotted Lieutenant John Orr. "What happened?" McVay called out.

"I think we took a couple of fish, sir," Orr responded.

"Do you have any reports?"

"No, sir," Orr responded. "I've lost all communications. I've tried to stop the engines, tried to get through to anybody. It's dead, sir."

"Well, do the best you can," McVay told him. "Get off a distress message." And with that he walked back to his cabin and picked up his clothes, dressing as he made his way quickly back to the bridge. He was still fairly unconcerned; the ship had been hit before and survived. The list was hardly there at all—the idea that she couldn't be saved hadn't yet entered his head.

Casey Moore came back from a preliminary inspection tour

and spotted McVay. "We're hit bad in the bow," he reported.
"Most of the forward compartments are flooding fast and we
haven't got anybody up there working on it. You want to
abandon ship?"

McVay shook his head. "No. Our list's still slight. Go below
and get me a more comprehensive damage estimate. I think we
have plenty of time yet."

"Aye aye, sir," Moore responded and was off. No one ever
saw him again.

Below decks Sobel had been tossed against the iron rail of a
bed and then straight on top of a sleeping sailor with the first
blast. With the second the ship seemed almost to rise out of the
water, then settle again with a hard smack that was worse than
the first.

His whole left side hurt like hell and he knew that something was broken somewhere. But he got up, grabbed onto the
bunk, and tried to gain control of bedlam. From down below
there came horrible groaning and shrieking, as if a gigantic
beast were in agony. The ship was crying out in pain and no
one knew what that meant more than Don Sobel.

"Don't panic!" he bellowed at the top of his lungs. "Follow
me out! Don't stop to take anything! Just move your asses in
time with mine! As soon as you're on deck get immediately to
your damage-control stations!" He almost said their abandon-
ship stations but caught himself in time for two reasons. No
reason to utter those most feared of all words yet. They hadn't
had much in the way of abandon-ship drills.

It took a lot of yelling, screaming, and cursing to get them
collected off the floor and it took a lot of running up and
down, hauling people up and kicking butts, to get them out
without trampling each other. Some of the metal bunks had
snapped loose from the force of the explosion. The lights went
on, flickered, then went out again. They scrambled for the
doorway and air and light, barely able to stand as the ship

shuddered, trembling now although there was still surprisingly little list.

Sobel saw one young sailor tugging at some lockers, trying to pry them off somebody. He ran over to the boy—for that was all he was—and stooped down. An arm protruded from beneath the locker and he grabbed it and felt the wrist.

"No good, son! He's gone! Save yourself!" the old chief told him.

The boy just froze there, looking so young in the near darkness and so helpless wearing only boxer shorts.

Sobel grabbed his arm and yanked him away.

Bill Glass found Lieutenant Stauffer mustering what Marines he had been able to find on the fantail. The officer seemed calm and confident. The brig guard arrived, two prisoners in tow, and Stauffer ordered him topside to get some life jackets for the prisoners. Glass looked around and saw a dozen Marines, including Lanier and one or two others he'd gotten chummy with. The first torpedo had struck near the bow, right under officers' country. That was also where the Marines were billeted.

Hordes of sailors were pouring onto the fantail, making it look like a panicked Grand Central Station at rush hour. Stauffer and some of the petty officers started trying to establish order and make certain everybody had life jackets but it was chaos. They could do little to control the mob. Many of the men were shouting to abandon ship. The Marine officer screamed against the tide. "No one is to abandon ship, damn it! Not unless we get the signal from the bridge!" He rushed over and tried to pull one seaman from the rail but was shoved back. The man jumped and some of the others followed. The bulk of the mob, though, just stood, milling around, waiting for somebody to tell them what to do.

The second torpedo had effectively sliced the connections between the forward and aft sections of the ship. Radio I was

dead; it was mostly a receiving station anyway, and the intercom to Radio II, where the big transmitters were, was dead.

A petty officer ran into Radio I and shouted, "The captain
wants SOS on five hundred!"

"Can't do! I'm dead!" the radioman replied. "I'm sending a
runner back to Radio II now."

"I'll do it!" the petty officer told him and took off again
down the deck.

"Any word yet on whether or not we got out a distress call?"
McVay asked Lieutenant Orr.

"No, sir. No word yet. We've sent runners back but nobody's returned."

At that moment Commander Janney appeared and McVay
called to him, "Go back to Radio and make sure we get a distress signal out with our position!"

Janney nodded, turned, and went down the ladder.

Joe Flynn arrived only seconds later on the bridge. "We've
been hit bad, Charlie," he said. "We're taking water fast, the
bow's way down, she's listing three degrees to starboard, we're
slowing down—and we got no power or communications. I
think we're finished. I'd recommend we abandon ship while we
still got the chance."

And that was it, the captain realized sadly. He knew the
signs, heard the noises, but he couldn't bring himself to order
it until Flynn had pushed him. It was the toughest order any
captain had to give.

"All right, pass the word to abandon ship," he called out in
his steadiest tone.

There was nothing more he could do except be damn sure a
message had been sent that they were going down. He turned
and headed down the ladder toward Radio I.

The petty officer ran right into John Coringa, knocking both
of them down. "Sorry, sir," the PO apologized, "but I gotta

get back to the radio room and make sure a distress signal is sent."

Coringa was up in a moment. "You'll do nothing of the kind!" he shouted. "Don't you realize we're under radio silence?"

The petty officer stared at the lieutenant a moment as if he couldn't believe his ears. "Sir! We're going down! If we don't get a message off soon nobody will even know we're missing!" He moved to pass Coringa.

The lieutenant leaped on the man and came down hard with both hands on the back of the neck. There was a cracking sound and the petty officer cried out and was still.

Coringa got up slowly, gasping for breath. "Fucking enlisted bastards!" he snarled.

Radio II didn't wait for any instructions. Radio Technician Second Class Herb Miner, after some initial power problems, got the things warmed up enough and started to send. The needle jumped, showing that some power was getting to the antenna, and he broadcast the SOS on 500kc, the international distress frequency. He got it off three times before the ship abruptly listed as if starting to capsize and most of his equipment came crashing down around him. He and his three other technicians got out—fast. They were sure that they had gotten *something* off.

Jim Fargo was running, running along the rapidly slanting deck. At first he wasn't sure where he was running to, or why, but finally he'd settled on the radio room aft. From the explosions he was certain that the bow had been blown clear off and that nothing up there was any good anymore anyway. Before he got into the water he wanted at least a rough idea of how long it would take air-sea rescue to find them and send ships to pick them up. It shouldn't be long, he told himself. The night was rapidly clearing.

Men were already going over the side and a number of

rubber rafts were being launched but he and everybody else knew that there were very few rafts aboard. As he passed a hatch a burly petty officer shoved a life jacket at him, almost bowling him over. He took it and continued on back to Radio II while tying it on. It wasn't one of the inflatable kind, which he'd prefer, but he didn't have time to blow one up, anyway.

Suddenly he was stunned by the sight of Coringa apparently committing murder near the radio room. The ship listed sharply, there were bangs in the radio room, and then four men cleared out fast.

Holding on, Fargo rushed up to Coringa. "My God, you maniac! Just what the hell do you think you're doing?"

Coringa looked genuinely confused by the question. "What do you mean? We are under radio silence. Maximum security. You know that. This man was about to order a distress signal sent. A traitor. That's what I give to traitors."

Fargo stared, unbelieving, at the man. "Good lord! What kind of an animal *are* you, anyway?"

Coringa seemed not to hear the comment. There was a strange, almost contorted look on his face and those eyes! They *burned!* He looked down at the dead man. "Wouldn't have done the bastard any good, anyway. I sawed off the antenna leads outside the radio room" anyway."

"You *what!*" Fargo screamed, anger welling up in him. "That means no SOS got out! Coringa, there are twelve hundred men on this ship and you just might have murdered us all, you included! Who the hell were you so nervous about? The Japs? They know, Coringa! They sank us!"

Coringa seemed startled. "Murder? No, no. My ship—my record. Colonel Withers would never—"

"What the bloody hell good is Withers if you're dead?" Fargo screamed and launched himself at the other man.

The two were locked in a death grip. Fargo was slightly larger but Coringa had the strength of a madman. They grappled on the rail as the list grew so great it threatened to toss them both into the sea at any moment.

Commander Janney came along the deck, hand over hand on the rail. He saw the fighters and screamed, *"What the hell are you men doing?"*

Coringa, who could see who it was, released Fargo so suddenly that the FBI man almost tumbled into the sea. Fargo rolled, felt his neck, and thanked God that that petty officer had given him the life jacket that had protected his neck from those madman's hands.

"No SOS was sent," he gasped to Janney. "That son-of-a-bitch cut the antenna wires."

Janney looked shocked. "All right, both of you," he said evenly without a trace of the anger and desperation he felt. "I want you to swear to me, both of you, that you'll tell no one of this. *No one,* understand? If they know they'll give up and we'll lose them in the water. I want your words on this!"

Coringa nodded limply. Fargo hesitated, then realized that the navigator was right. "O.K.," he breathed. "But if we live this is going to be known."

"Worry about one thing at a time," Janney cautioned, and they all just stood there for a split second. Then Coringa whirled and leaped into the sea.

The word to abandon ship never got past the hangar deck. The stern of the ship was largely untouched by the damage and for quite some time the officers and chiefs back there had been organizing men into damage-control parties and waiting for orders. Even when the ship started to list badly and the bow began to sink many of them screamed for the men to remain as they were. They didn't believe that this ship could go down. But now, as the list approached sixty degrees and the stern was rising almost out of the water, the fact could be denied no longer. The men in the stern started going over the side.

Chief Sobel gave up any attempts at damage control as soon as he saw the extent of the damage. There was simply nothing more to be done. He spotted Johnny Coyle, who headed for him.

"I was just up in CIC," Coyle told him. "No power. It's dead as a doornail. They finally said to abandon ship."

"How many we lose, Johnny?" Sobel asked. "You been on this ship a long time. You saw the damage. How many?"

Coyle shrugged. "Three, four hundred tops, but that's only a guess. That's if the rest of us get off this can and clear in the next two minutes. She's going down fast, Don. Real fast."

Sobel whistled and looked back out at the moonlit sea full of swimmers and debris. "That means eight hundred men or more in the water. My God!"

"The stern's rising fast," Coyle noted calmly. "We better get off the old girl, Don, or we're going down with her."

The water was coming up to meet them; it was as if the ship were doing a slow corkscrew turn as she sank, bow first. Both chiefs wore life jackets. Sobel spotted some debris—a big wooden crate top. "There's our lifeboat, Johnny!" he shouted, pointing to the wooden slab. "Let's go!"

"After you," Coyle responded and they both went over the side and slipped into the water. In a matter of seconds they were both at the piece of wood, which seemed to be a pallet of some kind. There was oil all over the water; it stank and burned.

"Let's get clear so she doesn't suck us back in when she goes!" Sobel called. The other man nodded, and they moved away into the water, pushing their makeshift wooden liferaft before them.

They had gone perhaps a hundred yards when Coyle shouted, "Slow up!"

"What's the matter, Johnny? Getting too old for this?"

There was no humor on the other man's face. He lifted an arm and pointed off to one side. "Out there—just beyond this oil slick. I saw fins, Don. Lots of fins."

For a second Sobel didn't comprehend. "What the hell you talking about?"

"Look out there," the other man urged, pointing. Sobel peered in the direction indicated, almost directly at the moon, and saw—something. A trick of the light? The phosphorus and the oil? A chop? Or—dorsal fins? It had to be a trick of his oil-scorched eyes, he told himself. There weren't that many sharks in the world.

As he stared and tried to bring the shapes into sharper focus he heard, over the yelling and shouting of hundreds of men in the water, a calm, almost detached voice say, in total shock, "My God in heaven! We were dead as soon as we hit the water!"

The sharks, if that's what they were, seemed to be staying clear of the growing oil slick—but the oil was so acrid that it burned and choked and poisoned those it touched. It was a hell of a choice to have to make. Sobel and Coyle knew it.

"Being eaten's quicker than slow death from this scum," he called to Coyle, who was already retching. The other man got hold of himself, gasped, and nodded, and they struck out again away from the ship.

Captain McVay was barely down the ladder from the bridge when he ran into his old classmate and passenger, Captain Crouch.

"Charlie? You got a spare life preserver?" Crouch asked calmly.

McVay nodded and went back to his cabin, coming out with a pneumatic type that needed blowing up. A seaman walked by at that point and McVay tossed it to the enlisted man. "Blow this up for the captain," he ordered, then turned and started back down from the bridge once again. At that point the big list came and a huge wave knocked him gently off the ladder and into the sea.

The ship was rising now, rising up in the water, looming so huge over the captain that he feared for a moment that it was going to fall on him.

From the eight hundred or more men in the water, many of

whom had been yelling and screaming, there came a sort of collective cry from those near the ship. "There she goes!" somebody screamed, and now those near the ship were yelling much the same.

The ship's massive, mortal wound amidships was clear down to her bottom now and her four giant screws stood out, silent now. Then, in an instant, with a rushing sound and a great circular wave, she went quickly to the bottom as if on a slide or chute, in water that was over ten thousand feet deep. Tremendous bubbles of air continued to break the surface for a minute or so, causing a few more waves.

A few men, including some in one of the few rubber rafts, were still too near when the ship went down, and the suction of her burial carried them down with her. Most of the men were in the clear. She had continued forward motion almost to the end and her crew was strung out over more than two miles.

What they all had in common was a sense of shock and a terrible ache as the ship vanished majestically. It remained for Chief Sobel to say it, in a tone of mixed shock, fear, and disbelief.

"Now it's just us and the goddamned sharks," he whispered, more to himself than to anyone else—but it voiced what eight hundred or more were thinking in common, from the captain to the lowest enlisted man, at that moment.

Jim Fargo was thinking that as well. He'd shed his shoes and now floated in the water, staring at the blank, still moonlit sea where only moments before a great ship had been. He, like most of the others, had already seen the great black dorsals of the sharks and knew that they would quickly exhaust the bleeding dead in their insatiable, insane hunger for flesh and blood. They'd stay around as long as there was food—and there was lots of shark food in the water.

Don't tell the men there was no SOS, the commander had ordered, or they'll lose all hope and give up.

But what of *me?* Fargo thought miserably. I *know.* How am *I* to keep going? We're a banquet, he kept thinking, all laid out and ready to go. One by one we'll stay alive until it's our turn to get eaten—hundreds of miles from the nearest land and with no help on the way. It was—what? Monday morning. They weren't even due in until around noon tomorrow. Wouldn't be missed until then. Twelve hours until we're even missed, he thought. Another six or more to find us—in daylight, anyway, thank God. Eighteen hours, minimum, in the water. How many of these men could survive eighteen hours?

He looked nervously around. How long would it take two dozen sharks to eat eight hundred men, he wondered idly, thinking of it as a high school math problem, still too much in shock to allow the full force of his bottled-up terror through.

Depending on his position on the menu, he realized, he had a good chance of finding out the answer to that problem.

Damn that Coringa!

The I-58 had sighted the Indianapolis *at 2138. She had launched* kaitens *at 2150, then, when that failed, launched conventional torpedoes at 2159, plus or minus a little. The ship had been struck at two minutes after midnight by the I-58's clock, either two or three times. After confirming the kill, to the joyous shouts of the crew and cries of "Banzai!" and other enthusiastic sentiments, the ever-cautious Hashimoto had crash-dived and ordered his torpedo tubes reloaded. He was certain that the escorts would be on them in a moment, but, after fifteen minutes, there were no sounds, not even garbled ones on the barely functioning hydrophones. He decided to go up and take a look at fifteen minutes after midnight.*

There is nothing. Nothing in the periscope, nothing at all. No destroyers, no big ship in its death throes, not even any evidence of lifeboats or major debris. He is puzzled and for a moment it crosses his mind that somehow the big ship got away. No, he tells himself, the hits were too solidly placed. She must have already gone down, he realizes. What was such a ship doing without an escort? It was crazy. The hand of heaven was surely visible in this, he decides, and he leads the crew in a little prayer, then orders the ship to continue on course. He is certain that rescue vessels will be in the area within hours and he has no wish to get caught in this moment of victory.

He doesn't know that there are no rescue vessels coming, no planes searching, that nobody even knows the ship is missing. He could not believe it if he had been told. He is correct about one thing, though: The ship was struck at two minutes past midnight. It sank in a little more than twelve minutes.

Six Hundred Miles
West of Guam
Monday,
July 30, 1945

Captain McVay had been one of the few aboard ship to re-member abandon-ship drill. Everyone else was too busy, too confused, too panicky, or simply too inexperienced to do so. Many men had gone into the water wearing little or nothing at all. That was all to the good tonight, but the next day, with the sun beating down on them, they'd have no protection at all from the elements, neither from the sun nor from the abrasive salt water and acidic oil.

McVay was lucky from the start. Almost immediately after the ship sank he'd run into a crate of potatoes—my new com-mand, he thought sourly—and used it to keep afloat. After a while a desk came floating by and he transferred to that since it had better buoyancy and a larger surface. That he was not physically hurt in any way was a miracle. Of all the officers and men on the bridge he would be the only officer, and one of only four men, to survive. His only immediate problem was

with the damned engine oil. It was everywhere. He regretted
now that he had insisted on a complete refueling at Guam. It
seemed impossible that any ship, even one as big as the *Indianapolis,* could hold this much oil. In an early wave he'd
gotten some oil in his left eye and now it wouldn't open properly. It burned like fire. He tested the water around the desk to
see if there wasn't some clear water he could use to wash the
stuff out, but his hand kept coming up a gritty black.

Keeping the bad eye closed, he looked around. It seemed
like the whole world was empty save for him. For a moment
he entertained the thought that he was the only man left alive.
That would be some kind of irony, he knew. He could see the
court-martial right now. They'd throw away the key—1,199
men and only the *captain* survived? He recalled someone saying that Jap skippers still went down with their ships and wondered for a moment if that wasn't such a good idea after all.
If he got out of this alive they'd nail his hide to the Pentagon
door anyway.

Suddenly he heard voices and peered around. A raft! Only
twenty, twenty-five feet from him! "Hey!" he called out. "Over
here!" No, not one raft—two! He decided not to wait any
longer and plunged into the water, swimming quickly to the
nearest one and hauling himself in. It was empty.

But no sooner was he in the liferaft than he heard cries for
help. "Over here! To me! To me!" he shouted, over and over.
Soon he was joined by Quartermaster Vincent Allard towing
two limp forms. He looked up at the familiar face and almost
dropped his two charges. "I'll be damned if it isn't the captain!" he murmured.

Quickly he and McVay hauled the other two aboard. They
looked more dead than alive and soon were retching all over
the place but they were safe on the raft—at least for now.
Allard got the other raft and they tied the two together to form
a small chain, then looked them over. The rafts hadn't been
launched. They'd been attached to the side of some floater nets
and had floated off when the ship went down. Floated off up-

side down, it seemed, with all the survival gear, even the oars, lashed to the bottom and now certainly covered with fuel oil.

They could do nothing else until daylight, anyway, except watch for more survivors. For the rest of the night they saw or heard none. Both Allard and McVay began to have the horrible feeling that the four of them in the two rafts were all who remained of the crew of the U.S.S. *Indianapolis*.

Jim Fargo thought he would be sick forever. The fuel oil was just impossible, miserable, beyond any imagining. He was not alone in his misery, although it was hard to tell how many men were in the water. The seas ran from four- to six-foot swells, the oil damaged vision, and there simply wasn't much to be seen, anyway. Currents and winds were separating the men even more as the hours passed.

Almost without realizing it Fargo was suddenly among a large group of men—a hundred or more, it sounded like. They were crying and moaning, mostly, a lot of them screaming for a doctor or a medic.

Lieutenant Commander Haynes was in nominal charge of this group and by his forceful personality and strong, clear voice he'd been able to do at least some minimal organizing. But he could do little good for the injured and dying in the water. He had no instruments to work with and, in escaping the ship, had badly burned his hands.

Still his command and presence of mind were impressive. "O.K., all you men without life jackets you grab that floater net over there!" he yelled. "You men with jackets stick together. Rally around here. Keep an arm or something on the person closest to you! The ones who live through this are the ones who'll stick together. Drift away from the group and you're lost! Understand?"

A man paddled past Fargo using an odd-looking life preserver; most were orange or yellow but this one looked bright white. It was a few seconds before he realized that the man was clinging to a toilet seat.

Fargo was in the middle of the crowd now, his stomach feeling awful but calmer in the knowledge that there wasn't a damned thing left to throw up. He saw some men caring for others hung on some floater nets and drifted near them. Half of the men looked like they wouldn't last the night.

"Doc! Doc! Over here!" somebody called and Fargo saw Haynes swim over to where the voice came from. A man lay there, limp, in a life jacket. Haynes checked eyes, pulse, other vital signs, then shook his head. "Remove his life jacket and let him go, son," he said kindly to the man who had called.

The jacket was immediately passed along to the nearest sailor lacking one. The only thing Haynes could still do, medically, was pronounce someone dead—and make certain that his gear went to someone else.

"Remember, everybody—keep any clothing you've got on. You'll need it for protection," Haynes called out. "If anyone dies, remove any life jackets and articles of clothing and give them to those who need them. Pass it on!"

Fargo felt miserable physically yet somewhat better mentally. This group was well organized. Haynes was doing an incredible job and it looked as if these men, the whole ones, had a crack at surviving the eighteen hours he'd calculated they'd be in the water.

He stopped almost dead in the water. Not eighteen, he realized suddenly. They were due on Tuesday. This was only the wee hours of Monday.

His spirits started plunging down again as he realized that it wasn't eighteen, but thirty-six hours until they were overdue. Could a human being take that long under conditions like this? he wondered. Not many of these men, certainly. Perhaps not Jim Fargo, either.

He'd been in the water maybe an hour or two. No more.

Chiefs Sobel and Coyle had blundered into a smaller group and gathered them around. Among the more than thirty men was not one they knew and not a single officer. Worse, six didn't have life jackets of any sort, another six or seven had the inflatable type that wasn't worth beans. All were sick from the oil. There were no rafts or floater nets anywhere in sight, nor any other men, either. Some debris had floated by and was snagged—some ammo crates, of all things, and some welcome cans of lard that might sustain them for a little while.

Sobel organized as best he could. "All right! I want everybody to get into a circle, anybody without a life jacket between two men with jackets on!" he called and they were only too happy to have somebody in charge. "We'll take turns if you gotta sleep—and everybody's gotta sooner or later. If you feel a man's grip slacken, you grab on with all you can, you hear? I been in the water like this before so you listen to me and you'll stay alive like I did!"

They accepted that, not even questioning his experience. It was true—he'd been blown off the deck of the *Juneau* without so much as a life jacket, but then he'd been in the middle of a fleet. He'd been picked up within an hour or two. This would be a longer, lonelier haul—but there was no use in telling these boys. One night, two days, three days, a week—whatever it took they'd have to stick it out.

The only thing Coyle couldn't figure out right away was where the sharks were. He thought about it a moment, then decided on two possible explanations. One was that the oil in the water was keeping them away—it was bad enough being touched by the stuff but to have to *breathe* it would finish any shark. They'd keep away as long as the oil was in the water— perhaps a day or less before it dissipated into the vast Pacific. The second, equally believable, explanation was that they were finding more than enough food among the stragglers out there, the ones who hadn't linked up and formed groups, the dead and dying and bleeding to death. When they were exhausted, well, then it would be *their* turn.

Both theories were correct.

The forward torpedo had slammed in just behind the bow of

the *Indianapolis* right under officer country. It had knocked
Ron Sarbic for a loop and crashed him onto the deck abruptly.
He immediately knew what had happened—after all, he'd become a torpedo expert as a result of this war. He braced himself for the additional hits he knew were inevitable. The second one did him little harm because of this but, after half a
minute and no more reports, he got up quickly and dressed
and rushed out on deck. He had no thought of the ship actually going down.

There was a twisted tangle of metal and hot steam jets everywhere; it was clear that a number of officers had been badly
injured or killed in the first hit and that he'd been very lucky.

He had no real station on the ship so he decided to make for
the bridge.

He made barely thirty feet in that direction when the ship
gave a sudden lurch and he found himself falling, falling right
off the ship and into the sea.

A couple of seamen saw him go and one of them yelled
something at him from the lower deck and threw down an orange shape, which landed twenty or more yards away. Sarbic
swam for it, reached it, saw that it was a life preserver, and put
it on gratefully.

To his dismay he watched the ship continue on, obviously
out of control, two gaping holes in her side and smoking
furiously. *She's going down,* he told himself.

Others were in the water, too, he realized now. He wasn't
alone after all.

"Hey! Anybody! Over here!" he called, and, getting no response, decided that there was only one thing to do. Despite
the futility of it, he started swimming slowly after the ship.
Maybe, just maybe, he told himself, I'll be in a line to link up
with some more men in the water.

He was right. The first man he found looked half dead and
scared to death and also about twelve years old to Ron Sarbic.
My God, so young, he thought sadly.

"Take it easy, son," he soothed gently. "I'm Mr. Sarbic. Are you hurt?"

The kid shook his head hesitantly in the negative. "I—I don't think so, sir."

He smiled and nodded. "All right, son. We're the lucky ones, you and I. We have to find some others while we still can. The more people we find, the better off we'll be until rescue arrives. You understand?"

The kid nodded.

"What's your name, sailor?" he asked pleasantly.

"Marriott, sir. Electrician's Mate Third Class."

"You have a first name?"

"Yes, sir. Ron."

"Well, that's my name, too, Ron," Sarbic responded soothingly. "I guess we're in charge of getting this act together. You a good swimmer?"

"I did some in high school," the boy replied.

"Good! Good! All right, we're going to go off that way because that's the way the ship went. I just want you to follow me. I figure we'll run into more people going that way."

"Right behind you, sir," the boy said, a little less nervous now.

"Where you from, Ron?" Sarbic asked as they swam slowly after the ship.

"Green Bay, Wisconsin, sir," young Marriott replied. Suddenly he called out, "Mr. Sarbic! I don't see the ship anymore!" His panic was coming back.

Sarbic stared after the ship. Nothing. Nothing all the way to the moonlit horizon. For a moment he was stumped—he was sure he could see farther than the ship could possibly have traveled, particularly with a couple of hits like those in her. The awful truth sank in.

"I think she's gone under, Ron," he told the boy.

"Oh, Jesus!" he heard Marriott say behind him. "Oh, Jesus, Mary, and Joseph!"

"Just you stay calm," Sarbic soothed once more, somewhat

amazed at his own confidence and manner. "You stick with
me and help me out and do what has to be done and I'll get
you home to Green Bay."

And he meant every word of it.

Murphy was laughing at him again, this time with good reason. *"You're in the drink, Glass, six hundred miles from nowhere. You're gonna die, Glass, and we're waitin' for ya."*

They'd been standing there on the fantail when the ship
gave its final huge list and nobody had waited anymore for orders. They'd gone over the side in droves and swum away from
the ship just barely in time. Only the fact that there was less
than normal suction had saved him then. He was certain that,
having gotten off the ship in such a miraculous manner, it
wasn't his time to die just yet.

Within minutes he was startled to see a strange shape coming near him in the water. Suddenly he realized what it was
and laughed out loud. A raft! "Hey! Over here!" he called, but
there was no response. He frowned. Maybe the men in it were
dead. He swam for the raft, grabbed hold of the side, and
pulled himself over the side into it, trying hard not to capsize
it.

He was stunned. There was nobody in it. Nobody. It
must've floated loose when the ship sank—they were hung in a
way that they were supposed to float off when the ship went
down—and been drifting here waiting for him ever since. He
looked around for the emergency stores but found the small
compartment open and most of the stuff gone. Some of the
medical stuff was still there, though. He didn't need it but
somebody might. Hell, if he saved a couple of important
officers he could wind up with the Congressional Medal this
time out, he thought optimistically. Even if nobody else
showed up, he could hold out a day or two, maybe longer, in
the raft—and even get some sleep. A lot better off than those
poor bastards who *had* to be out there, not too far from him.
He strained his eyes and decided to stay alert awhile on the off

chance that somebody might be going by. Often he thought he saw or heard something but couldn't find anything or anybody. There were cries and shouts of men all around, too, but they seemed to be far off and coming from all directions. There wasn't much he could do but drift and wait, he decided, and lay back down to relax while he could.

Murphy's ghost was curiously silent.

Dawn broke clear and sunny, with only wisps of clouds in the sky. The sight of the sun seemed to cheer most of the men in the water who'd spent their first chilly night adrift at sea. As the sun began to climb, however, it began to look more like a mixed blessing as the increasing heat and the salt in the water started the insidious process of dehydration in the middle of the world's largest body of water.

The night had also spread them out a bit. The badly injured were gone now, and while you could still see the oil slick you could also see that it was dissipating, a welcome thing to all except Johnny Coyle, who still looked nervously for the fins of the previous evening.

As Coyle had theorized, they remained at the edge of the slick, picking off the straggler and the dead who floated clear. The shark is not descended from any prehistoric creature of the age of dinosaurs. He *is* that creature, the same one, unchanged during those millions of years. He never sleeps, for his lungs are so primitive that if he doesn't keep moving constantly water will not be forced through his system and he will suffocate. He swims, he eats, and he breeds—but the millennia have also taught him survival characteristics. He knows what creatures to avoid. He is a coward; he'll take the easy food first and the dangerous stuff later. He's easily panicked and easily startled—but not easily dissuaded. Eating is his favorite pastime.

Few men in the water had actually seen any sharks by midmorning; many of the bodies from the *Indianapolis* were about, and during that first night another fifty or more died and were not seen again.

Perhaps the only indication that something was out there, lurking, was the absence of dead bodies floating by. But if many men thought of it they quickly dismissed it from their minds. There were more pressing concerns in staying alive right now.

Captain McVay's party had stayed alert all night scavenging and they'd come up with a pretty good catch. They'd gotten the paddles from the underside and had snared some cans of Spam, malted-milk tablets, and five cartons of Camels, which were met with real enthusiasm until it was discovered that absolutely no one had any matches, lighters, or anything else to light them. It drove the smokers crazy and it was finally decided, by vote, to throw the cartons back to the sea so at least they wouldn't think about them.

McVay surveyed the haul and nodded appreciatively. "All the comforts of home," he cracked, but deep down he was less than overjoyed by the knowledge that there was no water at all. A man can go without food an awfully long time—but water is lost constantly and must be replaced.

There was a fishing rig, too, and they put the lines overboard trailing lures. They didn't catch anything that first day but it gave them some indication of their drift.

Their first shark showed up then as well, an incongruous white dorsal followed by the small top of his tail fin showing him to be a little more than four feet in length. He cruised in and out and all around, even going in between the lashed-together rafts, and they'd tried to beat him away with paddles but he wouldn't go. All he did was make certain that no fish would come near their lines and make a general nuisance of himself. He was also a psychological problem, a topsy-turvy buzzard circling, waiting for someone to die. There was little they could do, though; even if somebody had nerve enough to take him on, there wasn't a knife or other sharp instrument anywhere on the rafts.

Overall, though, the men in the rafts had it pretty good. They could sleep comfortably, sleep being what was needed even more than water at this point, and they had some provisions and leadership. It was out there in the water that things were getting bad.

"I—I can't see!" the boy screamed. Ron Sarbic moved to comfort him as best he could, although he was pretty well blinded himself. So were the others, the dozen or so they'd picked up during the night. The only difference between them and him in this situation was that he knew what the problem was.

Photophobia. The sunlight reflecting off the water and the oil slick created a sort of snow blindness somewhat like having a flashbulb pop directly in your eyes. The retinas were slowly scorched and so showed two blazing orange masses and little else.

"Just a little sun blindness," he soothed. "Keep your eyes closed and relax and it'll fade. You can't fight it so live with it and if you have to open your eyes make sure it's toward me, low, and away from the sun. Understand? All of you!"

That seemed to calm them down and he felt a little more satisfied. He'd been shocked at the ages of the enlisted men he'd picked up in the dark. Was anybody except the officers on that tub past puberty? he wondered.

"I'm afraid to shut my eyes," one of them complained fearfully. "I'm afraid I'll go to sleep."

"Just grab hold of the men on either side of you," he instructed. "And you men—take turns dozing. If anybody slips out of your grip you get 'em back, you hear me?"

There was a chorus of "Yes, sirs," from the assembled group.

There were long periods of silence now, broken occasionally by somebody moaning or complaining or Sarbic calling the roll to make sure everybody was still alive. He cursed the sun blindness. Not only did it hurt but also it made his own job all that much more difficult.

"God! I'm thirsty!" somebody muttered. "All this damned water and we're dying of thirst. May as well be in a desert someplace."

"Don't drink the seawater!" Sarbic shot back commandingly. "The salt in there will just soak up whatever moisture is left inside you and kill you in a nasty death. You hear?"

They murmured assent. As the sun got hotter and hotter temptation would arise.

At about 1300 they heard a plane. It was a beautiful, sweet sound that broke them out of their depression and they all started splashing around in the water and even yelling although they knew that their voices would never carry to any plane.

Sarbic's vision had come back a little and he was able to make it out, just a silvery speck in the blue sky obviously too far up to see them. A bomber, most likely, on its way to Japan.

The several hundred men in Doc Haynes' group also saw and heard the plane and started the same kind of commotion. As the largest group, a group which included a couple of rafts, floater nets, and the like, they raised the biggest racket and had the greatest odds of being spotted. But the plane, flying almost two miles up, could not see them. The sun was just too bright and the distance too great.

It was evident after a few minutes that the plane hadn't seen them and had vanished off to the north, but for some time there was a lot of optimistic talk among the group.

"Hell, even if he saw us, what could he do—land?" one older sailor pointed out. "He'll send back help by radio or when he's through plastering the Japs."

Jim Fargo, like Doc Haynes, was far more realistic about that but he kept it to himself. What these men needed more than food, more than medicine, more than water or sleep was hope. Without hope they were all dead men.

They had salvaged some canned food, mostly carrots and

beans, and Fargo helped pass it out to the men. It was precious little but there was no need yet to ration anything—many of the men's stomachs were so upset from ingesting and vomiting oil that they couldn't take food; others refused because they feared it would only increase their thirst.

Water was very much on their minds.

"Now, we're in a million square miles of water, right?" one seaman was saying to an interested junior petty officer. "So the big problem with all this stuff is the salt. The way I see it, we get some of them cans and we evaporate the stuff out."

Others joined the discussion. "Yeah? And what do you use for a fire?" somebody sneered.

"The sun's hot as hell as you know," the seaman explained. "We got enough shiny things here. We can rig something, Boy Scout style, that'll start a fire from the sun."

"I ain't never been in the Boy Scouts," another grumped. "But it's worth a try, hell."

Fargo decided it was time to step in. "Hate to be a wet blanket, men, but it won't work," he told them.

The originator was not dissuaded by this. "Why not? You think we can't rig a spot of heat?"

"I'm pretty sure you can," Fargo admitted. "So it comes down on your bucket of seawater and does what?"

"Evaporates out the salt," the man replied in a manner of one explaining the obvious to an idiot.

"Salt doesn't evaporate," Fargo pointed out. "Water does. What you'd have would be a bucket of salt, and who needs that?"

It struck the others like a thunderbolt and they spent considerable time trying to recover their honor by blowing holes in his comment.

This led to ideas of straining the water, maybe through a handkerchief or something, and several attempts were made, but cooler heads prevailed. "That stuff'll still kill you," they pronounced.

By midday a few men, driven to their limits, tried it anyway.

It was awful to watch them as they went through choking spasms, as their tongues swelled, cutting off their air. That stopped further experiments for a while.

"Jesus! I once saw a guy hung and he looked like that," somebody said.

"About the same," somebody else agreed. "And about as quick and messy, too, from the looks of it."

Others, farther out in the group and on the nets, sought some sort of reassurance, feeling they could hold out if only they knew help was on the way. Every officer, Fargo included, was being constantly deluged with questions.

"An SOS was sent, wasn't it, sir? I mean, they're on their way," one sailor pressed.

Fargo was polished by now. "I'm sure there was," he told the man. "One of the radiomen's over there and he swears he got it out at least three times. Don't worry about it. Even if it didn't get picked up we're due for target practice tomorrow at eleven or so. When we don't show in an hour or two they'll send out search parties all along our route. If you can hold out through tomorrow I'm positive somebody will be here."

He only wished he felt as confident.

A man off a little by himself from Sobel's group was spotted. "Hey! Come on and join us! You're safer with a group!" he called out.

The man seemed to hear and turned to come toward them.

"Yeah! Come on in! The water's fine!" cracked one confident seaman. Nobody laughed.

The man was only a few yards from them when he suddenly seemed to stand up straight in the water, an odd, shocked expression on his face, and he cried out.

They watched in stunned silence as he thrashed and then seemed to be pulled under by some horrible, invisible force. Blood churned all around the spot where he'd been only moments before.

Somebody saw it first. "Jesus God! It's a shark!"

"Yeah! I see him! Over there!"

"No! He's over here!"

"No! Over *here!*"

"Oh, my God! It's a whole fucking pack of 'em!"

The one kill had attracted others, bringing them up from below following the blood scent. It looked like a frenzy.

Chief Coyle, who'd been paranoid about sharks from the moment they'd hit the water, was the first to recover. "Band together!" he screamed. "Hit the water with the palms of your hands—*hard!* Make a hell of a lot of noise!"

Suddenly they were in a panic, banging the water and yelling at the top of their lungs for good measure. After a few minutes they stopped, not all at once but a few at a time, and looked around. There wasn't a sign of fins.

Sobel let out his breath. "Hey! Johnny! Where'd you learn that trick?" he called.

"Them bastards is cowards!" the little CPO shouted back. "Give 'em a good scare and they scoot first and see what's the problem after. I read it in a book once. Not a Navy book," he added. Everybody knew what Navy survival manuals were worth.

"Wha—what'll we do if they come back?" somebody asked worriedly.

"If one comes for you, punch him in the nose," Coyle told him. They all stared at the little chief to see if he was joking but he was dead serious. "Yeah. Punch him. Them fish got tiny brains right behind their snouts. It'll shock the hell out of him and he'll run. Just make sure you punch the nose and not into the mouth, though, or you ain't gonna have no arm."

Across the more than five miles now separating the men in their various groups the new terror was coming on. True to Coyle's prediction the sharks generally didn't try for any of the large groups but concentrated on the lone wolves, the swimmers who either hadn't found a group yet or who refused, for one reason or another, to join or stay.

Up and down that ragged line of survivors, though, through

the hot afternoon, they all spotted dorsal fins, calculated the size of some of the sharks by the distance from fin to tail—a few were more than fifteen feet long, they saw—and saw or heard an occasional cry and saw a man pulled under in a pool of frothy sea and blood. It was inconceivable and horrifying.

At 1500 another plane passed over, as high as the first and with the same result. What had been initially greeted as a sign of imminent rescue was now beginning to be a source of despair. Still, nobody expected to be rescued by plane, not really. They were in a busy shipping channel and it would be that way, most felt, that they'd finally be discovered and picked up.

The watchword for everyone was to hold on until Tuesday, that rescue would start when they failed to appear at target practice. Just one more day and all would be all right.

Just one more day . . .

"Here comes Whitey again, blast his hide," Allard snorted.

Captain McVay turned and saw the now-familiar fin of the shark glide by to his left. He wondered what on earth could be keeping that shark around the rafts. Not fish, certainly. They ran when a shark was about, and nothing was more frustrating than barren fishing lines all day while schools of mackerel could be seen barely below the surface fifteen yards away.

It was getting dark, and McVay's little navy had held together extremely well. They had food, fishing line, medical kits. The worst of it was the realization that they were drifting north, away from the main body of men they were sure were out there someplace, men who could use what they had.

As the sun set in the west like some sort of tropical vision, McVay stood in the raft and called them all together. "Please pray with me," he called out. All of them bowed their heads and several repeated the words with him.

"Our father, who art in heaven, hallowed be thy name. . . ."

At about 2100 another plane came over, lower, it seemed,

than the others, and showing its running lights. McVay's group had found Very pistols and flares and they shot them off into the sky.

Almost at the same instant the sky to the southwest erupted in still more fireworks. The McVay group was stunned. It was the first real evidence that a large number of the crew were, in fact, out there and alive, and it made them feel a lot better no matter what happened with the plane.

As before nothing *did* happen; the plane continued on and soon vanished, leaving them alone again in the endless sea.

Hold out until Tuesday, they'd said. On Tuesday we'll be missed and they'll come looking. . . . Hold out till Tuesday. . . .

At the port office in Tacloban, Leyte, Lieutenant Stuart B. Gibson looked over the sailing orders for the *Indianapolis* with some surprise.

"Hey! Morrisey! Come in here!" he called and his chief clerk appeared. "Sir?"

"I got sailing orders for the cruiser *Indianapolis* here," he told the other. "Isn't there some kind of reg against that sort of thing? I don't remember ever getting a combat ship's orders before."

The petty officer thought a moment. "Yes, sir. CINCPAC 10-CL-45 and Seventh Fleet 2-CL-45 are pretty clear: 'Arrival reports shall not be made for combatant ships.' If we had to worry about them as well as all this transport and convoy stuff we'd be swamped. Nobody ever tells us anything about combatant ships anyway—why broadcast to the world where they are? Their own people know. The *Indy*'s Fifth Fleet, isn't she?"

Gibson nodded. "Reporting to McCormick, I think."

"Well, then, Fifth Fleet's got the worry."

"What do we do with this, then?"

The petty officer shrugged. "I'll send a copy for Commander Sancho and one for Commodore Gillette and file this one here."

"O.K. Do it," Gibson ordered, and that was that. He really couldn't imagine why they'd sent that thing. It wasn't his responsibility.

Tuesday, July 31, 1945

On the big shipping maps at the port director's office in Guam, and also at the routing offices on Leyte, a plot was made along a giant map grid. It had started when the *Indianapolis* left Guam, and each day the little symbol representing her was pushed a little farther along "Course Peddie" from Guam to Leyte as computed by her filed 15.7-knot speed. Shortly before noon on Tuesday, July 31, the ship symbol reached Leyte on both master maps and was promptly erased. The boards were for higher-command information only. The *Indianapolis* was due to arrive off Leyte for target practice. She was assumed now to have arrived and to be on Fifth Fleet training's board.

Nobody looked out the window in Leyte to see if the ship was really there. It didn't matter in any event; if she was, well and good. If not, there was obviously a good reason for it. Neither the Marianas Command nor the Seventh Fleet on

Leyte had any command over the cruiser. Orders could well have been changed at sea and they would never have been informed.

It was somebody else's responsibility.

It had been a night of terror for the men in the water. Not only were their physical problems getting worse, but also every once in a while a man would simply slip into the water, dead of shock or exposure. And then there were the screams and a lone swimmer pulled beneath the waves. Several groups faced the horror of severed limbs floating past.

The oil had dissipated pretty much by now. The sharks were moving in. There were a lot of them out there—most from three to four feet long, some twelve, fifteen feet or more and weighing close to a ton.

A number of planes flew over during the day, including a whole flight of B-29s, contrails flaring majestically from twenty thousand feet, but with each pass morale sank lower and lower. This was supposed to be the day they were rescued. Where were the rescuers?

"Them damn officers—they're hoarding all the food," somebody muttered and other voices took up the angry whispering. Fargo started getting nervous. The men were beginning to have the look of a mob, a lynch mob, maybe, and being an officer was a distinct disadvantage now.

He'd helped the exhausted Doc Haynes as much as possible but now Fargo, too, was beginning to feel the worst of it. His kapok rubbed against him and had caused some saltwater ulcers to form. He was not the only one afflicted—everybody who wore one of the stiff, canvas-covered life jackets was coming down with them and they hurt like hell. They formed not only from the rubbing, but everywhere you had any kind of cut, and around lips cracking from dehydration.

There were few officers left. They'd lost Commander Lipski during the night. He'd died in Doc Haynes' arms. It had been a mercy and no surprise. They'd fished him out of the water badly burned and beyond medical help. It'd been slow torture to see him sink by degrees into oblivion, conscious to the end.

In the middle of the night, with only the ocean sounds around, his voice had cried out to Doc Haynes. "I'm going now, Lew. Tell my wife I love her, and I want her to marry again." The chaplain, too, was going, weakened by exhaustion, having worked all the previous day and night to keep the men together, in line, and giving them hope. He had burned himself out.

Now there were barely half a dozen officers remaining, including Fargo and Haynes, now the two senior men. The others were j.g.s and ensigns in no better shape than the enlisted men. Only the fact that several of the toughest chiefs had survived and were now using up their own energies trying to control the mob saved them at all.

Fargo floated there and thought mostly of home. There wasn't much to do at this stage until a fight broke out or the mob came for him.

What would happen when he was gone? Somebody would live, of course. They'd send a telegram to Carol—maybe already had. He could see her getting that telegram and reading it with an expression of joyous relief she'd be hard pressed to hide. No messy divorce, no scandal, no problems at all. A war widow. Another heroine.

Oh, she'd make a good widow, really. Beautiful in basic black, pretending to hold back tears, receiving the flag at a memorial service, salute and all. Maybe a Bureau citation, too.

Then she'd be free. The kid would have all the VA benefits, maybe even an appointment to Annapolis if it was a boy. He probably would go that way, he thought sourly. Orphan of a war hero and all that.

The more he thought about it the more furious he got. Uh-uh, Carol. Oh no. Imagine your place when I come back—come back one of the survivors. We'll be celebrities, all of the survivors, once the bomb is dropped. Big heroes. Try that on your family and friends. He returned from the grave just to have the satisfaction of divorcing you.

He was going to live, he told himself. He was going to live just for that very moment.

He had something else to live for, too. Coringa. That bastard had jumped well ahead of him—without a life jacket, true, but he had no doubt that psychopath would kill for one. Psychos like him never died from normal causes. They walked away from things that would kill anybody else. He actually thought they were going to decorate him for that job on the antenna! His will to live would be overpowering no matter what. Unless a shark got him, he was out there somewhere.

Jim Fargo would give anything to find him now, out here in the open sea. Anything.

There were fights up and down the line now, almost too many for the few officers and chiefs to handle. Men were accused of hoarding rations, of hogging their turn on the few rafts. It was getting ugly and the best men in the group were killing themselves keeping the weaker ones alive. Old friends and shipmates, their faces distorted by ulcers, salt water, and exposure to the sun, blind from photophobia, were striking out at each other, accusing each other of just about everything. It was a powder keg, growing worse as the day grew on and the sun rose higher, then started to dip in the west. No help arrived.

They'd held out through Tuesday, damn it. Now where was that promised rescue? Somebody had to be blamed.

Worse, if rescue was on the way, no man wanted to be the last man to die. Let it be the other guy.

They waited, waited for rescue or explosion. It had to be one or the other. Fargo knew it, Haynes knew it, they all did. Even the men growing ugly and insane in the water knew it, deep down.

"It just ain't fair," the young seaman complained. The group, arranged in a wide circle, numbered more than twenty now, with Ron Sarbic swimming around, pulling in stragglers, giving pep talks as needed. He was tiring and he knew it, but he didn't think about that, didn't really think about anything but keeping these men going.

"What ain't fair?" somebody croaked.

"I been in the Navy for ten weeks. I been at sea for two. And here I am, gonna die out in the middle of nowhere."

"You aren't going to die!" Sarbic snapped at him. Was that terrible hoarse croaking really his voice? He tried to soften it a bit. "How old are you, son?"

The boy hesitated. "Seventeen—almost eighteen," he added.

"Well, I'm over thirty," he came back. "And I'm going to get picked up and sent home. You know why? Because I *want* to. If you give up, then you're dead. Only if you give up."

The boy was about to respond but somebody else called, "Hey! Mr. Sarbic! C'mere! Quick!"

In a flash he pushed off and was around to the others. The ulcers stung all over and he was as blinded and swollen as they but somehow he managed to keep moving. He almost had to pry his eyelids open to see anything now.

The cause of the concern was clear. "He—he just sorta went limp and let go o' my hand," the sailor said, unbelieving. "I reached out for him but he was all limp and funny."

Using his swollen and wrinkled hands as best he could, Sarbic checked the man in question, painfully keeping his eyes open. There was no doubt now—the man in question was dead. He looked to be no older than the boy he was just arguing with.

He sighed. "Help me get his life jacket off," he said quietly. The boy had died from simple exposure. Like a lot of the lower enlisted men he'd been sleeping nearly naked on deck and thus his whole body was exposed to the elements.

They got the jacket off—it was becoming tougher now, though, both for them in their increasingly bad condition and because the jackets were waterlogged and almost welded to the skin. "Pass it around the circle until it gets to somebody who needs it," he told the boy.

The dead man's body was allowed to float now, and he pushed it in the direction of the current. He saw the upturned face of the boy illuminated by the orange rays of the sun.

The body continued to float on its own, five yards, ten, twenty or more from the circle of men, and then something from below seemed to bump into it, jostle it a bit. Again there was calm, again the bumping. Finally a huge shape surfaced, great fin and tail making it fifteen feet or more in length, and then it seemed to go away from the body. Then it turned around and made straight for it. A great mouth filled with rows and rows of teeth opened and grabbed the dead man's legs, then pulled the entire body down beneath the waves.

There were no screams, no thrashing. The men in the circle never even knew about it. Sarbic kept it to himself.

Bill Glass wasn't in the best shape, but like all the men in rafts he was a lot better off than those in the water. He continued to pass into and out of a half sleep. Several times during the day he'd passed men in the water but they all looked too far gone for him to have done them any good. There had been some who'd seen him and pleaded with him to take them aboard, but they were so weak and blinded that he'd been able to get away from them without trouble.

A few times he sighted other rafts, only a few and mostly alone, all with no more than four people in them, usually less. He couldn't get near enough to them really to do anything anyway—the paddles were still lashed to the underside of the raft, and since seeing the sharks all around he'd decided he would not dive into the water.

Bloody parts of bodies had floated by, too, occasionally, sickening him and terrifying him at one and the same time. He wondered whether anyone not in a raft would fail to be eaten before any sort of help arrived. Even in a raft, a flimsy, rubber structure, he didn't feel all that secure. One bite by a shark and he'd be in the water.

He searched the waters and found, finally, a large wooden slat that must have been at one time part of a crate or packing case, and after a little work he had a reasonably balanced hardwood club with a rusty nail at the top. It was a vicious-looking weapon, but it was mostly a comforter. He wasn't sure whether it would do anything to a shark.

"No sharks," Murphy's voice came to him in mock reassurance. *"That's too quick. Oh no, you're gonna lie in that raft and dry out, dying by little inches. Even that is more than you deserve—but wait. After that lingering death you'll come to us. To us, Glass. We're waiting. . . ."*

The sun was set now on the day of hope. Tuesday had passed without so much as a hint of a search party. Under these conditions it was amazing they had held out as well as they had; salt water, dehydration, saltwater ulcers, little or no food, no real sleep, and the sharks, the damnable sharks, swimming around, circling the larger groups warily, gobbling up the dead and the stragglers, coming from all around as well as underneath, where you couldn't see or hear them until it was too late. The men held out mostly because it was Tuesday, the day they'd be missed, the day they'd finally be rescued. Hold out until Tuesday. . . . But the sun was gone now, darkness was creeping over the desolate deep, and they were no nearer rescue and a lot nearer death.

It was no good now for the few surviving officers and chiefs to tell them to hold out through Wednesday. Men were giving up now, giving up hope, sustained only by the inner will to live that was strongest in only a few. Over eight hundred men had gone into the water and, despite all the horrors, most had clung to life if they were able, clung to the hope of Tuesday.

But it was night now, the cold, terrible night once again, and they had been in the water almost two full days. A mind without hope reacts in various ways. That night the fears that had been suppressed in many would come out in strange ways. Those who got through this, in many cases, might do so at the cost of their reason.

"I see Rover's coming 'round again," a man noted tiredly.

Don Sobel peered into the gathering darkness. It was getting harder and harder to see. All day they'd scared off the sharks by pounding on the water, yelling, screaming, and all day it'd worked although the same sharks, five of them, seemed to stick with them patiently. They'd go away for a couple of hours but they'd come back, always come back. The shape and size of the dorsals made them recognizable, and they'd given them names. Rover was the big one, a huge black fin in the water who circled their own human circle about twenty feet out over and over again, working on their nerves but never coming closer. French Fry had been the worst. He was a small one, maybe only five or six feet, but he was brave. They knew him because one of his fellow sharks or something had taken a nasty bite out of his fin. He'd make fake runs at them, but always backed off at the last minute due to the pounding. They were getting bolder now, though; they didn't scare like before. Sooner or later, they all knew, the sharks would lose patience and attack.

And there was nothing to do but float there and wait for it.

"There's running lights over there!"

"Where?" a chorus comes back anxiously.

"There! Over there! See?"

"Naw, I don't see nothin'."

"Yeah! I see 'em. Funny-lookin', though. Not like a ship's lights at all."

"Where?" "Where?" "Yeah, I see 'em!" "There's nothin' there!"

"It—it looks like a conning tower! Like a sub!"

"Yer crazy. Ain't no subs around here."

"Oh no? I suppose we got here because we hit a snag."

"Oh, God! Suppose it's the Jap sub?"

"Japs?"

"Japs!"

"Japs! It's a Jap sub! He's come back to machine-gun the survivors!"

Riot. Hundreds of voices all over the place screaming out in terror, knocking people out of the few rafts, slugging each other, screaming in blind terror. It goes on for hours in the dark, spreading infectiously.

Tricks of phosphorescent waves. Tricks of moonlight playing on the waves against swollen faces and salt-seared eyes. Venus becomes a plane's lights; a small cloud making a dark patch on the otherwise bright sea becomes a ship, possibly an enemy.

Fargo worked his way over to Haynes. "They're going mad, poor devils," he muttered, trying to keep out of their way.

"Lucky devils, you mean," the doctor replied grimly. "By morning they may still be here in body but mentally they'll be in some better place. It's tempting, isn't it, to go that way?"

Fargo felt a chill run up and down his spine. "How long before we join them?" he wondered aloud.

"Not long," Haynes replied. "It's easier to join them than to try and be keepers of a madhouse without walls."

They were silent a moment. Finally Fargo said, almost in a whisper, "You know, I saw those running lights, too."

Haynes' head nodded slightly as he bobbed in the water. "So did I. And I bet we weren't even looking in the same direction."

Fargo was definitely frightened now more by this than by any terror of the water. "What'll we do?"

"If morning comes and we're still sane," the doctor told him, "we stay out of the way and survive. We just survive."

Wednesday,
August 1, 1945

Orders directing the *Indianapolis* to Leyte had been sent to just about every command but they had not been specific about to whom the ship was to report. All of the offices and officers who received those orders glanced at them, filed them, and did nothing else. Combatant ships were never reported; they showed up when they showed up. With so many commands involved any one of them could put in an order to the ship at sea and redirect it elsewhere. This was done so frequently that there was often more surprise that a ship arrived where and when it was supposed to than when it did not. Every port director in the Pacific was used to hordes of ships, from destroyer escorts to battleships, showing up any old time when they were thought to be hundreds or even thousands of miles distant.

Thus the only man *expecting* the *Indianapolis* was the Fifth Fleet training officer, Admiral McCormick—or he should have

been. But he wasn't. Because of a garbled address the order
was never decoded; because it was around shift change it was
never shot back for a clarifying repeat. So, at 1145 hours
Tuesday morning, McCormick had put to sea for training maneuvers with the ships he *did* have with no expectation that the
Indianapolis was due, let alone overdue. He was aware that
she'd sailed on some sort of secret mission and that she would
show up one of these days for training but nothing was in the
wind; it could be anytime. Until she *did* show up there was no
way to find out where she was if he wanted to, thanks to security, and he had enough ships to worry about as it was. Until
the ship showed it just wasn't his responsibility. . . .

It was the day of the madhouse and somebody had forgotten
to lock the asylum.

Fargo was on the floater nets taking a rest when he heard a
cluster of men babbling excitedly and decided to see what was
up. He slid off the netting and over to them.

"I'm telling you the ship didn't sink!" one man was saying.
"I went down and I saw her! Must've been an air bubble or
something! She's only a couple fathoms down and the scuttlebutts are open! Pure water! By God, I'm going down for a
drink!"

A number of other men murmured excitedly and the group
was attracting more and more interested parties. Fargo was
worried; he considered getting Haynes, now taking a well-
deserved nap in one of the three small rafts, but decided that
nothing short of a major catastrophe would excuse waking
him up. Haynes had been the lifeline of these men. Fargo
looked around for some other support, the chaplain, all-in as
he was, or maybe Lieutenant McKissick or Captain Parke, but
found no one. Fargo felt helpless.

There was no stopping them, either. Sick, weak, and ema-
ciated as he was, he watched with horrified amazement as a
delusion of a single sailor spread rapidly to several dozen.

With relief he saw a couple of chiefs responding to the excited mob, trying to wade in and calm things down.

"No, Chief! I'm tellin' ya! I been down to her! She's there! Water! Fresh water!"

"I'm for a long, cold drink!"

"Yeah! Let's go!"

The first two or three men dived beneath the waves. The chiefs and Fargo managed to bully some of the others but one or two men punched and thrashed and broke free and also dived.

The first men went down, down into the ocean, and when they got a couple fathoms down they saw her, sitting there pretty as she'd been, the *Indianapolis,* their ship, just floating there like it was some kind of ghost ship, her scuttlebutts open, gushing forth streams of beautiful, clear, fresh water. You could see the water, tell it was different, clearer. They went up to the stream, felt the cold chill of fresh icewater, and drank deeply, deeply, deeply. . . .

A minute or so later the sea in the middle of the crowd of men erupted with the swimmers, smiling wondrously, one chubby seaman saying rapturously, "It's true! It's true!"

Some others dived under, too quickly to see the smiles of the men suddenly become contorted with agony. They started choking and retching, screaming in horrible, twisted pain. It was all Fargo and the chiefs could do to hold them down, but there was little they could do. The massive quantities of salt water they'd ingested was working its hell on their systems. They thrashed in their torture. Their screaming stopped only when their tongues swelled so large they choked on them. Convulsions ripped through them and, one by one, they died.

And still the rumor was spreading! The chiefs were swimming about, yelling to all who could hear that it wasn't so, there was nothing there, but not even the convulsions of the early ones and the bodies now accumulating up and down the line could dissuade others from trying. Here and there throughout the large group, throughout the whole day, men would dive to drink deep or, as it got worse, to go to the gedunk aboard, which was dishing out ice cream in twelve delicious flavors. . . .

By midday the delusion had finally run its course, but others in the group were finding still other amazing facts. One sailor insisted he was in a general store in Kansas and to go away and not bother him while he picked the best and juiciest watermelon to buy. . . .

Several men worked out elaborate routing and set off swimming, some east, some west, depending on whether or not they thought Guam or Leyte was a closer swim. . . .

A sailor lay on a wooden crate, leaning over the side, pulling at something only he could see, pulling, pulling all over again. He drew some quizzical stares, which he finally noticed, and explained that he was trying to start the outboard motor on the damned speedboat but it wouldn't start. Wouldn't you know? Big, fancy speedboat just pops up out of nowhere in this damned ocean and it's out of gas. . . .

Two Marines came by on another crate and they had better luck. They had a sailboat, which they figured would put them in Leyte in a day or so with a decent wind. . . .

But the biggest stir was the report of the Island. Nobody had noticed it before, just over there a few thousand yards, but there it was. See it? Big, fancy hotel, airstrip, everything. . . . Several men headed for it and finally almost vanished in the distance, written off by the remaining sane ones in the group, but such was not to be. They returned in an hour or so with disgusted expressions. The damned hotel was full.

This infuriated a larger number of men, who swam off to make damned sure that they were allowed on the Island no matter what bigwigs and tourists were in that hotel. After a while, they returned as well, saying the damned Chink who owned the place had called out the Seabees to keep them off the beach.

The convincing, matter-of-fact way in which not one or two but a large number of men came back with these reports convinced others and half convinced still more. Soon large numbers of men were off to the Island and, once there, were in furious fights with Seabees only they could see. One fellow stayed back in the water, moaning to everybody about the unfairness of it all. The Chink was only the manager; his own *mother* owned that hotel and she wouldn't even let *him* come up!

Not everyone got to that point of frustration. Lieutenant McKissick, for example, and a few others got all the way out there and found that they'd arrived at the wrong time—the Island was underwater right now and they'd have to come back later.

Another group was kept from landing by vicious guard dogs but they didn't mind. The airstrip was sufficient. They could hold out.

At that point a large and very real flight of B-29s roared over on their way to Tokyo, causing many of the men on and around the Island to start yelling, screaming, and pounding the water, pointing to the Island and the airstrip.

"What the hell's the matter with those bastard flyboys?" somebody sneered. "Don't they see the airstrip?"

"Maybe they just don't want to pick up Navy men, the sons-of-bitches," somebody else suggested angrily.

"Yeah, the sons-of-bitches," another agreed.

The big problems with all the delusions were more than the few fatalities and the wasting of precious energy. They were splitting up the large group into dozens of smaller, fragmented groups over a much wider area. The strength in numbers was gone. The sharks could sense it.

Fargo could relax against the floater net, bring his head up a bit, and see some of the terrible damage. Unwilling to attack a large group, now the sharks were clearly in evidence—dozens of them, it seemed. He watched as isolated swimmer after isolated swimmer cried out and was dragged beneath the waves. In some cases the larger sharks would almost come out of the water and you could see their huge, gaping jaws around a screaming man's torso as they came up, great gray behemoths of the deep, visible in all their horror for an instant, then plunged back beneath the waves.

It finally became too much to bear; he prayed for sun blindness so that he would not have to see the carnage anymore.

The sharks were getting bolder now. A small group on its way to the Island, four or five men, were attacked by one huge shark. The screams and thrashing and blood from its first victim attracted the other sharks in a frenzy of bloodlust. In a matter of three minutes the entire group had been eaten or chewed to pieces.

All this was going on in the midst of the insanity around them. It was terrible to see a man grabbed and chewed to pieces next to another man who was so delirious that he didn't even know what happened to his companion. One young seaman, fresh out of boot camp, remained sane by just lying calm, floating with little or no motion, and saying the rosary over and over again. All around him thrashing men were being attacked, chewed, and eaten by sharks, yet he stayed calm and nearly motionless.

Not a single one of the sea giants touched him. Not one. It was just like the training manual had said at Great Lakes—sharks are attracted to motion, to the movement of the legs underwater, like a fish lure. If you just stayed still and calm and floated they might bump right into you but they'd never eat you.

This wasn't quite true, for they'd certainly eaten the bodies of many men who'd died in the struggle against the elements, but it held as long as someone else *was* providing that lure—and a great many men were.

Out at the Island the boy whose mother owned the hotel called the place to see if he couldn't soften some hearts but all he got was a steward from the *Indianapolis* who told him that enough was enough, he'd take no more calls and refer no more people to anybody. He looked up at the other men, waiting expectantly in the water, and finally Lieutenant McKissick said, "Let me talk to him!"

The boy looked blank. "He hung up on me! The bastard hung up on me. . . ."

Men were singing, men were dancing at USO clubs, men were babbling out of their heads about everything, nothing, and anything at all. Men were totally past the boundaries of sanity and they were in a better world. . . .

Fargo heard frantic splashing near him and turned anxiously, afraid that one of the sharks had gotten bold enough to invade the main body, but all he saw was a lieutenant diving down again and again in determined effort to do something. Finally, when he came up for air at one point, Fargo called, "Hey! Jimmy! What'cha doing?"

"I dropped my damned car keys!" he gasped. "I can't drive to the dairy in New Hampshire without my damned car keys!"

Fargo had to agree with the truth of that statement.

The worst part of it was that he felt so damned *helpless*. He couldn't accept Haynes' calm assessment that these men were perhaps better off than they because they no longer suffered despite the logic he saw in that argument. It was a logic borne of the absolute futility of helping, of stopping what was going on. King Canute might have ordered the sea not to come in just as they wanted to save these men but, like the King, whose authority never extended to tides, and who drowned in the attempt to roll back that other cruel ocean, that would be their fate if they even tried to stem the lunacy.

Life jackets were at a premium now. Although the kapoks rubbed and caused ulcers, they were more reliable than the inflatable ones. Most of them would hold up, particularly if they were hard enough and sealed enough to keep from becoming totally saturated. Some of that saturation was occurring—the kapoks were only guaranteed for forty-eight hours—sinking men like stones but, for the most part, they held up very well indeed. Until then it was the inflatable type that was

causing the biggest problem. They had never been intended
for long periods in the water. Valves leaked after a while with
all that weight and pressure on them, nor were they built to
hold a firm load of air for very long periods of time. There
were leaks, bad seams, all of that.

By now, Wednesday, they were all but useless and the
wearers knew it. Those who remained even slightly sane realized that they had no chance, no chance at all, without a
kapok, but the sharks weren't always leaving the life jackets—
at least not in usable condition—and others were dying now
more and more spread out.

As the sun passed to the west and started its dip for yet another day a pattern developed as desperate men without life
jackets went out to places like the Island and treaded water,
waiting, waiting for the lone swimmer or looney to come
along. Waited, then attacked those swimmers, taking the life
jacket in any way they could.

Cold, premeditated murder was being committed in isolated
pockets out there. Most of the men who did the killing ration-
alized their deeds by telling themselves that the loonies were
going off to die anyway. As good as dead might as well be
dead, they reasoned, if by this action one life, at least, could
be preserved.

In late afternoon Captain Parke, the leader of the Marine
detachment, swam up to the floater net and rafts that were
Doc Haynes' headquarters. For three days now Parke had
been a dynamo, going here and there with almost no sleep at
all, refusing his turn in the rafts or the nets, hauling men back,
physically if need be, from their own lunacy. He looked near
dead now to Fargo.

The Marine looked over at the FBI man and said with a
strange, empty look in his eyes, "That's it. I just can't do any
more."

Before Fargo could so much as respond the light faded
from the captain's eyes. It was eerie, as if something inside of

him had simply flipped a switch from "on" to "off." Fargo knew that the captain was dead.

He did what he could, but he could not breathe life into a body that had burned itself out. Haynes was contacted and made his way over, checking the captain out, but all he could do was shake his head sadly.

Fargo felt tears welling up inside him, tears he knew couldn't be there for sheer lack of water. "Oh, God, what incredible, brave men are we losing today," he breathed, his voice choking.

They were silent for a moment. Then Haynes said, "I'm sorry I couldn't get over sooner. I found Chaplain Conway over there, about thirty yards down. The same thing." He sighed mournfully. "He died in my arms," he whispered, his voice cracking, too.

"Agh!" Fargo cried out. "How much more of this can any man stand?"

"I'm afraid we'll find out," the doctor responded. "I'm very much afraid we will find out."

For Don Sobel's group, the worst part was that there was absolutely nothing to do.

For the first day he and Johnny Coyle had calmed them by asking them about themselves, about their families, birthplaces, hopes for the future, anything, until they'd gotten to know them all pretty well. Tuesday they'd been able to calm them by singing really filthy songs of the past thirty years, telling the worst puns and most outrageous Navy stories in the history of the service. They'd lost four men to the elements but none yet to the sharks, ever-present and circling though they were. Overall the group was in good shape with confident spirits. Thanks to a circle-and-watchdog system they'd all even managed a little sleep—not much, but some.

Johnny Coyle was sleeping now, so quiet you'd almost think he was dead. Sobel was grateful for Coyle. Alone Sobel wasn't sure he could have managed it, but the two of them together with their strong wills had kept these men organized. True, they were awful to look at, half blind, swollen, a lot closer to death than they had ever been, but they were alive in numbers larger than he'd hoped for at the start. He gave them another twenty-four hours if nothing else happened. It might not be enough, but it was all he could give them or himself. He was realistic about it all. They might be spotted, they might not—but he'd done all he could for as long as he could.

They were more than his responsibility—they were his children, all of them. By God, no other child would suffer because of him, no other mother would grieve and hate and blame because of something he did. *This* time, he was determined, their mothers, wives, sweethearts would point to Don Sobel and say, "See him? He's the man who saved my boy!"

The more he thought about it, the more confident he was of eventual rescue. Twice he should have died in this dirty war and twice he'd been miraculously spared. The *Arizona* had gone down with almost every crewman aboard, yet he had survived by a fluke. Now he wasn't sure it *was* a fluke. Not when you considered that the *Juneau* had gone down so fast and so violently that it, too, took almost everybody with it. By sheer chance he'd been on that particular deck near that particular rail on that particular side of the ship. . . .

The hand of God, he realized now. This was not punishment for his poor, dear daughter, no, this was atonement. The more he thought of it the more certain he became. God had saved him for this. For this ordeal. For these young lads. Not jinx, not here by a terrible turn of fate—here because here was where he'd be needed, where the Lord in His omnipotence wanted him to be, where he could save these lives.

"Better wake Chief Coyle," he suggested. The young man to Coyle's left nodded and shook the sleeping chief and got no response.

"Chief? Chief? Wake up!" the boy almost shouted.

In shock both men on either side of Coyle let go of him and

he fell forward, face splashing into the water, his lower torso exposed abruptly.

Those closest to him screamed and screamed and screamed.

Somehow, while they were holding onto him, without him ever even waking up, Johnny Coyle's lower half had been eaten away. . . .

The loonies were coming from everywhere. Bill Glass couldn't believe what he was seeing, the men going by single-mindedly shouting that they were swimming to Leyte. One gunner's mate even announced that he was swimming on ahead to make sure they set up the targets properly for the ship's gunnery practice.

Some tried to get on the raft, of course. Terrified for days now and with the elements also telling on him, Glass was horrified at the prospect of these maniacs climbing into his haven of safety. He pushed them off, fought them off, then started taking his makeshift club to them.

One was particularly insistent. "You are the devil incarnate!" he roared at Glass with the fury of a prophet newly down from the mountain. "I am the avenging angel of the Lord sent to punish thee!"

The words did something in Bill Glass's mind. "Oh no, Murphy! You don't get on this boat!" The club came up, then smacked down with full force on the man's head. Glass pulled it away, and the struck man looked slightly puzzled, then rolled his eyes and sank back into the water. The rusty nail had gone clean through his skull.

"Hey! Look! It's a raft!" somebody yelled and soon others were swimming over to him, grabbing the sides, rocking the raft.

Glass stared at them a moment. Oh, my God! he thought, fear shooting through him. It's them! Murphy! Desmond! Gonzales! Benson! All of them! They're coming up from the ocean! They're coming for me! Oh, God, look at them, look at how the flesh is peeling away from their dead and rotting bodies.

"No!" he screamed and started beating at them frenziedly with his nail-spiked club.

Men yelled and screamed, others came at him from all directions. Some were as mad as he, others just desperate.

He was like a madman with his club and kicking at them, hitting them, flailing at them with all he had. "No!" he kept screaming. "You're all dead and I'm still alive! I killed you all once! Stay dead! Stay dead! Do I have to kill you all again?"

Hit, slash, club, kick. . . .

And suddenly they stopped coming. They stopped coming and backed off, either hurt, dead, or because something scared them off. He didn't know nor did he realize they were gone. He continued to swing his club frantically, battling fifteen Marines long dead on Saipan, battling, battling ghosts, dead men who continued to rise up and clutch at him.

He must have looked strange from just beneath the water, a moving, wiggling figure swaying this way and that, swinging his club, frothing the water around the raft with his movements. Two huge, black, expressionless eyes saw the frantic movement and it attracted the creature, already pulled there by the smell of blood in the water. The huge fin circled the raft twice to get its measure, ignoring the few men remaining near it in the water, still as death, and then turned abruptly and came straight for the raft at breakneck speed.

A few feet before the raft the huge gray-and-white body leaped out of the water, gaping mouth open, fifteen feet of it, a ton and a half or more, leaping effortlessly over the edge of the raft, eyes only on the rapidly moving creature fighting ghostly invaders. It struck Glass and bowled him over, out of the raft, and landed itself on the other side.

Glass felt as if he were suddenly hit with a pile driver. He was flung fifteen feet or more out of the raft and entered the water with a tremendous splash. The blow broke several bones and he screamed and thrashed about in agony.

The great white shark, attracted again by the tremendous movement, closed in on him, mouth agape, and grabbed onto his legs, chewing, pulling him into massive jaws, slowly chewing him up and forcing him back farther down the massive gullet.

Glass didn't quite know what was happening but just before the end he screamed, "Murpheeeeee . . ." and then sank in a pool of blood beneath the waves.

The more cautious men about stayed away from the now empty raft for some time, until the giant dorsal finally vanished off to the south. Only then did other men carefully approach the raft and pull themselves aboard.

For Captain McVay and most of the others in rafts and raft trains it was a good day. They couldn't know of the agonies of the swimmers and could have done little had they known. McVay figured they had enough rations to last another ten days if they were careful. Some of the canned stuff contained just enough moisture to sustain them. It looked as if a squall was approaching, anyway. The seas were picking up, the wind was rising, and some ominous clouds were approaching from the west. He didn't fear the approaching storm. It would provide needed water for everyone.

But the storm didn't hit. It passed off to the north and was quickly gone.

Night fell without any further incident and they settled down to wait it out once more. Nobody was optimistic about imminent rescue anymore, but they were alive, they were all right, and morale was high in the rafts.

Still, a dispirited McVay started figuring how to make the rations last twenty days rather than the existing ten. . . .

Planes flew over all evening, and all evening they shot their flares and fired their Very pistols up and down the increasingly spread-out line. McVay was not optimistic that they'd been seen, either, but he was more concerned by how far off the other flares looked. It appeared either he was drifting north while the rest of the survivors were headed south, or else one or the other was caught in some kind of opposing current. He took some of the flares to be over eight miles to the south of his position. . . .

Along the floater nets around Doc Haynes' position the night was proving more horrible than the day. Harmless delusions like the Island were fading, and even delusions like the conviction that the ship was just below. With the night came the darker delusions and sheer, unreasoned, maniacal terror. The man next to you wasn't a shipmate anymore, nor even a fellow shipwrecked sailor.

It started much the same way the other delusions had started, innocently, when one swollen, exhausted man reached out to grab onto the floater net and instead grabbed another man he could hardly see.

The grabbed man, jolted out of a stupor, screamed, "A Jap! A Jap! The Japs are crawling all over!"

The cry was picked up back and forth along the line in the dark. "Japs! Japs!"

"There's Japs on this line!" someone else took it up.

Men started flailing out at other men, punching everyone near, throwing cans, garroting with line. There were screams as men pulled the few knives they had and plunged them into the backs of other men nearest them.

It was a wild, riotous, insane, and murderous fight, compounded by shouts of encouragement from those too weak to fight and the battle for life jackets whenever some poor devil was drowned, strangled, or knifed to death.

"Japs! Japs! They're all over us!"

The madness spread to everyone within earshot. Doc Haynes leaped in to try to stop it and two men jumped him and pulled him beneath the water. Fargo leaped in after them, down into the dark waters, and when they came up again it was two against two with one huge sailor trying to choke the doctor with his bare hands. Fargo managed to pull the other, smaller sailor off and knock him cold, then brought both hands together into a ball and came down hard on the back of the big man's neck. He cried out and let go and Haynes slid back into the water, choking and only semiconscious.

With what felt like his last breath Fargo plunged back and retrieved the doctor, pulling him back up and supporting him on the float. A few others of the very few still sane individuals on the line came over, horror in their faces, and together with Fargo and the doctor made a sort of defense line against any future attacks. The grim, still line of sane men did not attract attention, not the kind that the moving, swinging men down the line did, and they managed to pass the night without any further harm to themselves.

But they could hear, out there in the darkness, the frantic, lunatic cries of pure terror and hear the screams as madmen fought madmen in their own private hell that endured almost to the dawn.

Thursday,
August 2, 1945

The death toll had been horrible. All around the sharks feasted on the remains, and on the netting hung limp, torn bodies from the night before. And yet, with the new sun, the madmen passed from lunacy to near catatonia. They had given up. Wednesday's insanity had used up the last of their strength, the last bit of energy and fight any of them had. The barely sane were burned out and approaching the fate of Captain Parke and Chaplain Conway. Those already across the border into their own dream worlds were far beyond now, moving entirely in a mental miasma that made them incapable of action.

Haynes, Fargo, and a couple of chiefs along with two or three seamen who had, together, stood off the terror of the night, pushed off the bodies nearest them and tried to clear any blood from their immediate vicinity. They didn't want the sharks to consider it an open invitation to finish them off.

The sharks, however, were already coming in. More terrible for a still sane man to watch than even the madness of Wednesday was to see a tall, sinister dorsal approach a man drifting in the water and pull him down without the victim uttering a scream or making any kind of struggle at all.

Incidents like this were few, though, since almost all were still now, providing less of a lure for the great, prehistoric monsters that roamed all around and just beneath them.

Doc Haynes looked around and said, matter-of-factly, "Well, this is it. They've got no more left in them. Rescue comes today or we're all goners."

Fargo could only nod in agreement. He was all in and, while he still retained his grip on sanity, he was beginning to appreciate Doc Haynes' point about the men who'd gone around the bend being the lucky ones.

Haynes was sustained, it seemed, by his sense of being needed. He simply would not permit himself to die and leave his patients without what little services he could provide. As for Fargo—what had kept him going, he wondered, over all this time?

It was hate, he realized now. Not the fiendish, maniacal hatred of the psychopath but the sense that the world had somehow wronged him and that he could get even. The thought of Carol, for one, with the knowledge that she'd profit by his death; Coringa, too, of course, not only for what he'd done but also because of what he'd been allowed to do. Withers had placed him on that ship. There was no question he was Withers' man.

Fargo looked out at the catatonic band of men up and down the floater line. Were they, in fact, any more insane than a Withers? It could not be, it should not be. He would survive if at all possible, he'd survive to get even at least.

But rescue had to come today. It had to be today. There was no way they could stand another day in the water.

How long have we been in the water? he wondered. A couple of days? A week? How many nights and days have passed?

He tried to reconstruct it and could not. A week at least, he guessed. A week.

Score another one to get even with. Whoever was responsible for reporting missing ships and sending out search parties was going to pay for this, too. What survivors there were of the *Indianapolis* would guarantee that. The United States was still a nation of laws and someone had committed cold-blooded murder here.

Ron Sarbic's group, too, was almost gone, all hope fled. They'd been in the water without even benefit of a single raft or floater net since the sinking, over eighty-four hours. By his own force of will, his kindliness and seemingly endless reserves of energy that had calmed and kept together his band of stragglers, they'd gotten this far. But this was the end of it. Everybody felt it now, felt that nobody was going to come looking for them, that even if there'd been a search they had somehow drifted too far from course to be found and been abandoned as lost with all hands.

They'd been lucky with the sharks. Rover had continued to circle the pack off and on. But there had been no attacks. There didn't have to be, really. Despite Sarbic's best efforts, of the thirty-one men he'd wound up with he'd lost eight to the elements and would surely lose another dozen or more in the next few hours. That was how far gone they were, how beaten they were. Even he was coming to the end of his limits and he knew it. He could feel himself slipping away. He was so swollen and numb now that there was little pain. That was a help, the only help.

Somehow, too, they'd made two cans of lard snatched from the floating debris last until now but it was gone and there was no hope for any more.

Another young man—it was Marriott, he thought although it was hard to tell from these bloated, misshapen faces—sank into the depths, dead, finally running out of the spark that had kept him going. They were too listless even to do much about him, although, finally, somebody pushed the body away from the group, out to the waiting sharks.

Sarbic felt the loss personally every time he lost one. Somehow, to lose even one, even under these conditions, was a black mark against him personally, a failure who stood out, accusingly. Not their failure, for they'd done all they could, but his.

His hands went down to the small pocketknife they'd taken off a dead sailor. It'd been used and reused cutting away life jackets from the dead. And, not for the first time, he considered the easy way out, how simple, a few stabs in the right places and either you died or the sharks came and got you. Easy.

But he couldn't do it, much as he cried out for such a release. He had his responsibility to these young men who'd trusted him, believed in him, stayed alive for him, and he was going to save as many as he could.

He looked around for Rover, conscious that something was wrong, something was different. He couldn't put his finger on it, but everything had been so boring, so routine, all along that anything out of the ordinary set him on edge. The large, menacing dorsal was no longer sailing around the group; it was moving off in a funny kind of zigzag pattern, moving off, then turning.

Oh, God! he realized suddenly. The old bastard's finally tired of waiting us out!

Most of the others did not or could not see it; only his own sense of duty and watchfulness had sensed it as if, after all these long days and nights in the water, he was as much a creature of the sea as this thing that had stalked them.

The sea was choppy; for a few moments he lost sight of the fin, but no! There it was! Coming for them! Coming straight on like a sleek, gray express train! So close to the surface that between some of the wave chops you could see the great body itself.

There was no way to stop him! he thought, panicked. No

way at all! "Rover's coming in!" he croaked hoarsely, and that
stirred them a little, moved them back, turned heads.

Without thinking at all, without any plan or consideration,
he pushed off from the group and pulled out the penknife,
placing himself between the oncoming shark and the group of
half-dead men.

The shark was almost to him now, and he suddenly and
quickly moved aside, knowing in a corner of his brain that the
creature could not change direction at that speed and angle of
attack. It was a living torpedo and he had experience with torpedoes.

As it passed him, so close he felt the clamminess of its skin
and saw the huge, black eyes and open mouth with its thousands of teeth gleaming and ready, he brought the knife up
and plunged it into the gray-white expanse of the shark,
brought it down again and again and again and again!

Blood spurted and the shark jerked spasmodically and
seemed to twist out of the water, looking back to see its at-
tacker.

Sarbic dropped below the water, somehow actually coming
under the shark. He could see its white underbelly as it
thrashed and see, too, the wisps of blood from his first wounds.

He couldn't stay under long with the life jacket on and so he
kicked and rose right at the confused shark, plunging the knife
now into its soft abdomen, again drawing blood. The shark
rolled and twisted, and he grabbed onto it, trying to mount it
as he would a horse, continuing the jabbing, jabbing, jabbing
with the penknife.

But the sea was the shark's element after all, not his, and
the penknife was too small to go deeply enough to cause real
injury. Worse, the shark was tasting its own blood now, and
this drove it into a frenzy. Still Sarbic hung on, plunging over
and over in furious desperation at the shark that symbolized
all that was hateful about the last few days.

Awakening from their stupor, the men remaining in his
group watched in horrid fascination as the struggle went on

only ten feet or so from the nearest of them. They could do nothing to help. They could only watch and wait.

Both shark and man vanished now beneath the waves for a moment, and burned and swollen eyes strained to see. Incredibly, the shark leaped out of the water, the man still clinging to it, still stabbing and seemingly screaming and yelling something nobody could make out. It wasn't in pain, though; it was almost a joyous, primitive bloodlust the man had, matching that of the shark's, as all the hate, fury, and frustration of four and a half days in the water was coming out in one final spree.

The shark leaped up again, twisting incredibly in the air, this time forcing the man off with a violent twist and he plunged back into the water throwing up a plume. The shark, too, belly-whopped back and sank, writhing, beneath the waves, and, suddenly, there was silence.

They strained to see, to find out what was to happen, but there was nothing, nothing at all except the wave chops and the silence of midocean. No dorsal, no man, no thrashing or blood, nothing.

Both Lieutenant Commander Ron Sarbic and the shark they'd named Rover were, seemingly, gone, vanished off the face of the earth.

"Might as well try to round up the strays if we can," Doc Haynes said wearily and with no trace of enthusiasm. "You feel up to it?"

"Frankly, no," Fargo replied. "But I think we can make do. How are some of our fair-haired boys?"

"Zimmerman's dead, and Kowalski," the doctor replied. "But I think we can round up four or five if we can talk 'em into it. I don't think any of the ones out there are going to give you any trouble."

"Or any help, either," Fargo sighed and slid off fully into the water.

That much was true, and it was also hard talking anybody into helping out at this stage of the game. The few left with any grains of sanity could only shake their head and say, "But what's the use?" and then they went and helped out anyway. There was simply nothing better to do.

It took a couple of hours at that, although most of the men were already at the borderline between life and death. Occasionally he'd reach out for an apparently comatose individual and have an arm come off in his hands or find only an upper torso or not much more. The sharks were having their banquets.

He didn't care about the sharks anymore. He was beginning not to care about anything anymore, not even Carol or getting even.

A lone swimmer off fifteen yards or so from the base of the floater nets caught his eye, primarily because, as he approached, Fargo saw that the uniform was an officer's and there were damn few of those left.

The man's face was so swollen and his exposed body areas so full of sores it was hard to tell who he'd been or what he'd looked like. Two silver bars, though, said he was a lieutenant. Like most of the stragglers, and even most of the men on the line, the man looked dead.

A funny thought crossed Jim Fargo's mind. Wouldn't it be some sort of ironic justice if . . .

He floated cautiously up to the man. "Coringa?" he called out hoarsely. "Lieutenant Coringa?"

The man stirred; puffy eyes tried to open, barely made it. The officer muttered something but he couldn't catch it.

All the horror, revulsion, and anger welled up inside Jim Fargo. "It *is* you! God has delivered you into my hands!"

The man stirred slightly. "Whozzat?" he managed through terribly cracked and swollen lips.

"It's Fargo, Coringa. You remember me." He wondered what man the bastard had killed for that kapok.

"Fa—Fahgo?" the man managed, as if trying to remember something from deep in his mind.

For four days Jim Fargo had lived with a dream, to find

John Coringa and strangle him with his bare hands. To squeeze out his life as the little weasel begged for a mercy he neither deserved nor would get.

This pitiful hulk wasn't what he'd had in mind. So easy to do, so effortless. With one hand he could probably hold the lieutenant down under long enough to drown him—but not this. Not this shell, this vegetative horror.

"Give me your hand, Coringa," he said softly.

"No. Don' wanna," came the reply.

"Come on. We'll get you into a raft and have Doc take a look at you."

Coringa suddenly showed a burst of energy and moved away from Fargo. "No!" he screamed.

The hate was still there, though. The hate and the bitter fruits of justice. "What's the matter, Coringa? Aren't you proud of yourself? You did this to yourself," Fargo taunted. "You did this to you and me and all the other men. What good's your bomb and your Colonel Withers now, huh, Coringa? Tell me. Tell me *why*. Tell *them* why. I want to know, Coringa. I want to understand. They want to understand. The dead ones and the living dead like you and me. What did you prove, Coringa? What did you accomplish?" He reached out, closing now, and actually touched the man.

Coringa shrank back. "No! Go 'way! Don' wanna!" Puffy eyes forced themselves open, looking at Fargo although not really seeing him. "You gotta understan'. I—I—I can' go wi' *them*. Not wi' *them!* You can' make me! Go 'way! Go! *Leave me 'lone!*" he shouted.

And with that, stunning Fargo with a burst of energy, John Coringa turned and started swimming furiously, swimming away from the nets, away from the rafts, away from Fargo, occasionally yelling, screaming, or babbling something or other.

He was gone from Fargo's view in an instant and the FBI man did not pursue. John Coringa, he knew, didn't have to die to go to hell. He was already there.

Fargo sighed and turned, feeling somehow empty and cheated, and headed back to the others for one last day.

There was the sound of a plane engine overhead but it neither excited nor interested him. All up and down the line, all over the more than eight miles now of Pacific littered with the scattered remnants of the *Indianapolis* crew, nobody paid the slightest attention.

And then he heard somebody shout. "He—he's turning! Oh, Jesus! He's turning! He saw us!" And the sea erupted at that point with the pitiful shouts and thrashings of men along the eight-mile perimeter.

They were a long way from being rescued, and the worst psychological ordeal was to come as men were wrenched by a small plane back to the real world, but while the plane did not represent rescue it did represent the one thing they had lost entirely.

Hope.

Fifth Fleet training was getting a little curious about where the *Indianapolis* could possibly be. Admiral Spruance had sent the port director a deadline by which the ship had to be in Manila, and suddenly realized that she was overdue. It didn't concern him overmuch. There were a thousand reasons why she could be overdue, the most likely being, at her age, something had broken down. He sent out an inquiry to all sea commands in the Philippine region asking whether or not they'd seen the ship and, if so, where she was. Purely routine. After all, he was currently stuck with a couple of battleships he hadn't expected that had just steamed in and set up shop.

The routine inquiry went, among other places, to Rear Admiral Elliott Buckmaster, Commander, Western Carolines Sub-Area, on the island of Peleliu. Admiral Buckmaster's area had once been a place of bitter fighting but now it was one of the most boring front-line areas in the history of the war. Oh yes, there were lots of Japs around on the various islands of the Carolines—forty thousand around Babelthuap, largest of

the Palaus, cut off from home—but it was his job mainly to see
that they stayed cut off and didn't interrupt shipping and
things like that. In addition, there was air-sea rescue of pilots
downed in the damndest places, things like that. Nothing happened anymore in the Carolines and the men often joked that
a rainstorm would get headlines in the local newspaper as a
break in the routine.

One of his units was VPB-52, which flew the small, light,
but heavily armed PV-1 Venturas on routine triangular patrols
over the stretch of sea between the Carolines and the Philippines. They were looking mainly for any attempt, even by submarine, either to resupply the isolated Japanese garrisons or to
evacuate them.

The Ventura was a fine plane to fly, quiet, comfortable, and
modern, and so sophisticated that it used a fancy new kind of
air-sea radar scan for its surveillance. In fact, the pilots
couldn't even see the water from the cockpit, nor did they have
any wish to. It would just blind them anyway, and, anyhow,
everybody knew you couldn't see anything short of a battleship with the naked eye from a plane.

Lieutenant (j.g.) Wilbur Gwinn took off at 0815 for his
routine patrol. He was late getting off; they had a new kind of
radio antenna they wanted checked out, one with a long, thin
trailing wire off the back of the plane that was so unwieldy it
required a weight to keep it straight and in place. That had
been the aggravation; this new weight, which was supposed to
stabilize the antenna better, had snapped off on takeoff and
they'd had to return to get a new one fitted. At 0815 they tried
again and, at least, the thing stayed on.

At about 1100 they reached the northern point of their triangular patrol, munched sandwiches, and tried to keep awake.
Mostly to break the monotony, Gwinn suggested to Ord-
nanceman Hickman that they test out the new antenna weight
again. Gwinn dropped down to 5,000 feet to give the optimum
conditions for the super long-range radio. The air was
smoother there, and the antenna itself, which was like a cross

between a steel cable and a bullwhip, was more effective there. As Chief Radioman Hartman watched, Hickman reeled out the line.

It was no sooner fully extended than the weight dropped off again and the cable started whipping around nastily, threatening the tail assembly of the plane itself.

There was a frantic call to Gwinn and he turned over control of the aircraft to Lieutenant (j.g.) Colwell, his copilot, and quickly scrambled aft to the tail gunner's blister, where the two enlisted men were wrestling with the wildly whiplashing cable.

It took two of them to reel the thing back in while a third cautiously guided it since it had the same potential to snag as a fishing reel—and if it snagged it would be out there as long as they were in the air, potentially whipping parts of the tail and rudder right off.

"Get me a piece of rubber hose or something," Gwinn ordered Hartman. "We'll try to weight it down with our own kind of weight and see if we can make the damned thing work." Hartman went forward to see what he could find to fit the bill, and, as he did, Gwinn's gaze wandered out to the calm ocean less than a mile below him. He frowned and rubbed his eyes. It looked odd down there. Not natural. "Hey! Look at this! What do you make of it?"

Hartman and Hickman peered down and saw it, too. "It's an oil slick," Hickman replied. "Hey—that could be a Jap sub down there!"

Gwinn excitedly scrambled out of the blister and went forward, filling in Colwell and turning the Ventura away from the sun so the men aft could get the best view, not from the blister but through the bomb-bay doors, looking straight down.

"What do you think it is, Will?" Colwell asked, grateful for a little excitement.

"A sub! A sub for sure!" Gwinn responded, matching the

cheery enthusiasm of the men aft. "Johnson! Open the bomb bay!" he called.

Mechanic J. K. Johnson eagerly opened the doors and Hartman and Hickman crowded around excitedly. Gwinn took the plane down to only a thousand feet and made a run straight over the slick. Nose slightly down, he could see it himself from the cockpit now that the angle and direction were right.

"Hey! There's somebody floating in that gunk!" one of the men shouted. Soon they were all peering expectantly. One life jacket—two—three. "There's a half dozen more!" somebody else called.

"Oh, my God!" Gwinn swore. "There's at least thirty men down there!" He turned to Colwell. "You remember anything about any ships in distress at this morning's briefing?"

Colwell shook his head. "I can't figure this one."

"Shut bomb-bay doors," Gwinn ordered over the intercom. He turned and made another, even lower pass over the giant slick. Down in the water the men who were able to do so shouted, thrashed, whistled, and cheered as he did so. He was telling them they weren't alone anymore.

Johnson opened the side door and Hartman and Hickman tossed out the Ventura's life jackets, liferaft, and two sono-buoys, small floating transceivers, in the hope they could establish some contact.

Now Gwinn climbed until he reached five thousand feet, the minimum needed for long-range radio transmission. He suddenly had a horrible thought. The trailing antenna was his long-range transmitter and it was makeshift now and only partway out. What if he couldn't get a message through? Well, he had to try, he decided.

At 1125 hours he radioed, "Sighted thirty men in water, position 11-30N, 133-30E." He cursed the antenna and circled, trying to gain altitude and increase the odds without panicking the men below into the thought that he was deserting them.

"Better change the message, Mr. Gwinn," Johnson's voice

came to him over the intercom. "You won't believe this but we just counted at least seventy-five heads down there."

By the time he had enough altitude for a third try the count was up over a hundred and fifty. The entire crew knew that they had blundered by mere chance into a major disaster, and the sense of being a part of a great event got to them.

Back in Peleliu, Gwinn's first message came through so garbled that the radioman on duty heard what he expected to hear—"Am circling liferaft." So what else was new? Some flyboy would be getting picked out of the drink as usual.

As Gwinn gained altitude, though, the messages came through better. The radioman heard seventy-five men in the water and sat bolt upright, stunned. He turned to call his supervisor, and as he did the third message more than doubling the second figure came through. He flipped on the speaker so they could all hear.

His supervisor, an ensign, listened, jaw dropping. "Jesus Christ! What have they found out there?" He rushed to the phone and called Admiral Buckmaster's office, getting Commander Anderson, the operations officer, almost immediately.

"Sir, I thought you should know immediately that one of our planes has just reported a hundred and fifty men in the water at about"—he glanced at the radioman's report sheet—"11-30N, 133-30E."

The commander, too, was stunned: A hundred and fifty men! He wasted no time, issuing orders to put every plane in the air to that position as quickly as possible and then calling Admiral Buckmaster and Captain Oates, his exec, as quickly as possible.

The admiral wasted no time at all. He and Oates sped down to the operations building and ran in with the speed of firemen going to a fire. People were accustomed to the admiral and exec coming by now and then, but nobody was prepared for the tornadoes that blasted through the door.

"You! Get me all the charts in the area of Vector nineteen!" Buckmaster snapped at one startled petty officer. Buckmaster turned on an ensign. "I want the name and position of every ship and plane within five hundred miles of the position of those men in the water!" he roared.

The staff scrambled to comply, many not even knowing yet what it was all about or what position it was the admiral was talking about.

Buckmaster cleared off the operations officer's desk with a quick sweep of a pile of papers and even the photos of Commander Anderson's family onto the floor. He started laying out the charts on the desk.

"I wonder what ship it is?" Captain Oates mused aloud as they tried to pinpoint the position.

"Got to be at least a destroyer escort," the admiral replied. "Lord! Look at that! What a hell of a place to get sunk! There's nothing around closer than we are to cling to!" He looked up at Anderson. "Any ships reported missing or overdue?"

Anderson shook his head, thoroughly puzzled. "The only thing I have even close to it is a routine inquiry from Leyte about the cruiser *Indianapolis*."

Admiral Buckmaster and Captain Oates both suddenly froze and the admiral's face went white. "Oh, my God in heaven!" he breathed.

Down at the airstrip it was pandemonium as mechanics rushed to top off the tanks of every plane available and crews got very quick briefings. There wasn't much other than the weather conditions they could be told. Nobody really knew anything yet. Lieutenant Adrian Marks, on standby duty with a PBY squadron, checked to see that his huge seaplane was loaded with every ounce of survival gear it could carry, then got his crew aboard and rolled—"waddled" was a better term—out onto the runway, taking off as soon as he got clearance from the tower.

Right behind him was Lieutenant Commander George Atteberry, squadron commander of VPB-152 in his Ventura.

Gwinn's gas would be running low and he'd need relief in a hurry. Atteberry was determined that he would be the one to relieve his pilot. Besides, he wanted to find out just what the hell was going on.

The commander roared by Lieutenant Marks in his PBY as if it were standing still. "Gambler Leader to Playmate Two," Atteberry called. "Gambler Leader to Playmate Two. Pardon my dust but we've got business up north."

Marks looked sardonically at his copilot. "Next time we're in the showroom, let's take a coupe instead of a sedan, O.K.?"

Atteberry pushed his Ventura to the limit and was on the scene by 1415 that afternoon. Gwinn was glad to see him but reluctant to leave the scene. Still, the gas gauge told him he'd just about overstayed his welcome as it was. All he could think about were those men down there in the water.

A little earlier a routine patrol plane from Guam heading for Leyte had passed nearby, caught Gwinn's messages, and dropped its own liferafts and other survival gear while radioing the story to Guam. It couldn't stay, though, and now Atteberry, sending Gwinn away, was alone. He reported back to Peleliu and an anxious Admiral Buckmaster that there were definitely at least one hundred fifty, "repeat, one-five-oh," men in the water, "no rafts in sight. I repeat, no rafts in sight." That increased the urgency enormously.

Still lumbering far behind, Lieutenant Marks picked up the message and shook his head. "I must be going crazy. Got to have my ears checked," he muttered. "I could swear he said one hundred fifty men in the water."

"Musta been fifteen," his copilot responded reassuringly.

Lieutenant Commander W. Graham Claytor was sitting in a deck chair near the bridge of his ship, the destroyer escort *Cecil J. Doyle*. Aside from shooting a few rounds now and then into the Jap-held islands just to feel like he was in a war someplace, he'd mostly been sailing up and down, back and forth, on a very boring tropical cruise to nowhere. He was steaming slowly south at about 1430 when he saw a large plane come overhead and decided to call him. Hell, it would break the monotony. He headed back to the radio room and soon had the plane tuned in.

It was Lieutenant Marks. Claytor was mildly surprised. He knew Marks, had played cards with him a couple of times on Peleliu.

"Graham, we got a ship down out there," Marks told him, giving the coordinates. "I dunno what it is but unless my radio's out of whack there's at least a hundred and fifty men in the water. I'm heading there now to do what I can. I guess you'll be getting orders to go on up there sooner or later. I think you're the closest ship."

Claytor frowned. "What was the position of the wreck again?"

Marks gave it to him.

The captain pulled out his chart and frowned deeper. It was more than two hundred miles from him—and he was the closest ship!

"Oh, what the heck," he muttered. "It might be hours before they remember we're here. What else are we doing on a fine summer's day like this?" He walked quickly back to the bridge.

"Bring the ship about, one-eighty degrees, and give me flank speed as soon as you're able," he ordered the bridge officers. Quickly the small, fast ship came about, although not without some quizzical looks from the officers and men.

"Have the navigator plot a course for 11-30N, 133-30E," he ordered. "Flank speed."

Within minutes they were on their way at a speed that quickly reached twenty-two knots.

His orders to proceed to the area didn't come through until almost 1600. By that time he was already well on his way. Still, it would be past midnight by the time they reached the area. He hoped those men hadn't been in the water too long.

Thanks to the messages to Guam and now Leyte and Admiral
Buckmaster's insistent pushing, starting a little after 1400
other ships started getting orders to proceed at flank speed to
the position. From all around the position ships of various
types were turning about, pouring on the coal, converging on
the area. From the west the destroyer *Bassett* and the destroyer
escort *Dufilho;* just behind them the destroyers *Register* and
Ringness. From the south steamed the destroyers *Madison* and
Talbot. Not a single one was less than two hundred miles from
the desolate oil slick.

Lieutenant Marks arrived at roughly 1625 that afternoon. He
surveyed the scene and was appalled. Between one hundred
and two hundred men were in the water, it was clear, and, it
was also clear, they'd been there an awfully long time. There
were some rafts here and there but not many. Most of the men
in the water were in waterlogged kapoks. He decided to concentrate on the smaller groups first, the more isolated ones.
The larger groups would stand a better chance of holding out
now, and the rafts would be the least concern. He made several north–south passes over the slick, almost ten miles long at
this point, his crew dropping what they could to those who
seemed to need it most.

As Marks flew low over the lines of men in their tight
groups he was first cheered, then cursed as he dropped material far away from them—ignoring Doc Haynes' group, for example, in favor of somebody indefinable thousands of yards
away.

Chief Sobel saw the huge, lumbering plane approach and
knew he'd won. He'd done it! Kept these men alive and kicking. Help was here now, pickup couldn't be far behind.

"You listen to your old chief," he croaked out hoarsely but
in the best of spirits now. "You see? They're coming. Just take
it easy, do nothing you don't have to do, relax, and wait." He
closed his swollen eyes and prayed silently. Thank you, Lord,
for giving me this chance, for causing mothers and wives great

joy instead of heartbreak. You are good, Lord, and merciful.

Some stuff dropped near them, but it wasn't much help. They were too weak to chase it.

Jim Fargo relaxed and watched the big plane approach, then fly over without dropping anything. Several of the men who'd cheered the PBY's approach now yelled out, "Hey! Don't we get nothin'?"

Fargo and Haynes had to agree. It was unimaginable that any group of survivors was worse off than they were. Nobody could have endured any more than they and lived. Nobody.

But they had.

Just seeing the planes and seeing something fall out of them was the morale booster the men in the water needed, but little of it was useful. They were too tired, too weak, too sick or too far gone to get it. Marks, who was flying almost at the tips of the wave chops, could see that for himself. He was worried now. His conversation with the *Doyle* and the dispatches since had confirmed his worst fears—there was no ship that could reach this spot before well into the night. He was so close he could see the faces of some of the men in the water and he could feel only tremendous pity for them. They had obviously been in a long, long time and might not last until the ships arrived.

"Between one hundred and two hundred survivors at position reported," he radioed back to Peleliu. "Need all available survival equipment while daylight holds. Many survivors without rafts."

Suddenly he heard somebody aft say, "Jesus! What's that?"

"My God! It's a shark!" somebody else came back.

That was enough for Marks. He turned over control to his copilot and walked back to the open cargo doors. The copilot brought the plane around again and, after a moment, he saw it. A huge monster, light gray, just beneath the surface. It made up his mind in an instant.

Getting back to the cockpit he sat thoughtfully for a moment, then got on the radio.

"Will attempt open-sea landing," he told Peleliu. "PV circling area."

Marks's commanding officer, Lieutenant Commander Max Ricketts, was just checking in from his own patrol when he heard Marks's comment over the loudspeaker. He looked up angrily. "Who's that?" he snapped.

"Lieutenant Marks, sir," replied the radioman.

"Tell him he can't do that! Stop him!" Ricketts ordered. "That's a pretty damned expensive plane he's got there. He can't endanger it to save one or two men!" He pushed the radioman aside and thumbed on the push-to-talk bar. "Marks! This is Commander Ricketts. You will *not*, repeat, *not* make a landing at sea. That is a direct order."

He straightened up and whirled around, looking dangerous. "As soon as he gets back I want his whole crew held and I want Marks in my office thirty seconds after he's off the plane! By God, I started in the Navy as an able seaman and Marks will end his days as one before I'm through."

He walked into his office and slammed the door so hard it rattled. He was so mad that nobody there dared go in and tell him what was going on.

It was more than an hour later, when his air-combat intelligence officer was summoned to see if Marks had yet returned, that Ricketts finally was told of the magnitude of the tragedy at sea and received orders to throw his whole squadron into the rescue effort.

Lieutenant Marks either didn't hear his commander or chose to ignore him. He brought his plane about and began to pick an area where he could land without killing somebody and come to rest where he'd do the most good. To him that meant where there were single survivors and only small groups of men.

It was a big risk, which was why Ricketts was so upset.

PBYs weren't designed to land on the open ocean with eight-knot winds and swells exceeding twelve feet at times. Still, he felt he had to try; those men simply wouldn't be there when the *Doyle* got there.

He brought the huge airplane into the wind, picked what appeared to be a clear spot, and put it into a stall. The big seaplane sank slowly toward the water to the total amazement of the men in the water.

One of the men in Don Sobel's group yelled, "He's going to land! My God! He's coming in!"

Sobel watched as the huge plane touched down, then bounced on the water more than fifteen feet in the air, came crashing down again, rose up about five feet this time, and then banged down again. The men inside the PBY were badly shaken up and almost immediately rivets started popping, causing small leaks.

Quickly men rushed to plug the holes with whatever was available—surgical cotton, gauze, pens and pencils, anything.

The great plane creaked and groaned in the swells and seemed to go over on its side; for a moment the *Indianapolis* survivors were sure she was going to sink. Gasoline poured out of one wing tank. But the huge, ugly plane settled on its side and on one float and seemed to stabilize.

Crewmen in the belly of the plane started the pumps; amidships seams had cracked and there was a steady seepage. Marks came back and found them ankle-deep in water. "Will she float?"

"She's good for a long, long time," the chief mechanic assured him. "We'll keep her up until help arrives, sir." But the unstated message was clear: She was at best a temporary refuge, and she would never fly again.

Using Atteberry as his eyes, since he was listing and riding too high in the water, Marks taxied the PBY over to the nearest small cluster of men. Ensign Morgan Hensley, one of the copilots, stood at the open hatch door and started pulling the men out of the water. A huge wrestler, it was nothing to him. The men didn't seem to weigh anything at all.

The first man in lay gasping on the floor of the aircraft a few moments as concerned airmen looked to him. "What ship?" the mechanic asked.

The other man gasped for breath. He was offered a canteen of water and was held to only a mouthful at the start. Finally he wheezed, "The U.S.S. *Indianapolis*."

Even Hensley stopped his rescue for a moment and stood there in stunned silence. Finally he said, "Better tell Mr. Marks."

The aircraft commander was even more stunned. The *Indianapolis*. Spruance's flagship! "Holy smoke!" he exclaimed in wonder. "How many men on a cruiser. Anybody know?"

They shook their heads. One said, "Got to be a thousand, sir."

He sighed. A thousand. At least. A thousand men.

"How long they been in the water?" he asked.

They shrugged. One went aft to check and returned in a minute. "They don't know how long they been in the water," a radioman told him. "But one said they went down on the twenty-ninth of July about midnight."

Marks couldn't believe it. Five days. Five days these men had been in the water—and nobody had even known the ship was missing.

The story of the century, he thought, at least as far as the Navy goes. I should report it—but how? He had no secret codes of any use aboard and there were strict regulations against reporting which ship was lost in the clear. Tokyo Rose would have a field day.

Aft of him, Hensley was hauling in the last of the Don Sobel group survivors. Hensley reached down for the chief, pulled him up, looked at him carefully, then let him drop back into the water.

"Hey! Whatcha do that for?" one survivor yelled. "That was the chief! That's the guy who pulled us through!"

"It cost him too much to pull you through, sailor," Hensley replied as gently as he could. "Your chief's dead and we got to tend to the living first."

"What're you talkin' about, dead?" the sailor croaked. "He just now pushed me up to the plane!"

"I reckon a man's only got so much to give," the ensign said sadly. "I think he gave it."

"C'mon! Let's try for the plane!" somebody shouted and there were murmurs of agreement from men who only a little while earlier were close to death.

"Hey! You! Wait a minute, all of you!" Doc Haynes yelled with incredible energy, considering. "Listen to me!"

They quieted down a little now.

"That plane's a good mile or more away," he told them. "Most of you would never make it. I know *I* wouldn't. You want to sink below or maybe wind up feeding a shark in the chance you'll make it when you can stay here and wait for the next plane? Not me! I stayed alive all this time. I sure as hell don't want to die this close to the end right now. Do you?"

It sobered them. There was dead quiet for a moment up and down the line. Finally somebody said, "Yeah, but that's the worst part, Doc. This waiting. I don't want to be the last man to die."

That sentiment was running through all the men up and down the line, in the water as well as on the nets and rafts. Nothing had changed, nothing would change until the ships got here, and who knew how long that would be? In the meantime they faced another night, another terrible night, alone with the elements and the sharks, made if anything even more unendurable by the knowledge now that rescue was on the way.

Everybody was terrified that he'd be the last man to die.

The ships were on the way with orders but without clear authority. Admiral Buckmaster, once he knew that these men weren't, as first thought, survivors of a Jap sub but Navy men, had not waited to write orders, clear with other commanders, or do anything about getting authority. He simply issued the orders and to hell with the red tape.

The original theory that it might have been Japs in the water was based on the knowledge that a sub was in fact operating in that area and in the belief that, had one of the U.S. ships gone down, they would have known about it. As they realized that a major U.S. ship had gone down, the truth dawned all around the western Pacific.

Orders, reports, everything they had on combatant-ship movements for the past week were being hauled out of offices on Guam and Leyte. Each and every commander wanted to know, each and every command wanted to find out what the hell was going on.

The answer was obvious to anyone who put all this information together. It was the only answer. There was only one combatant ship that couldn't be accounted for at one point or the other. Only one.

It was so obvious. . . .

Now.

Less than three hundred miles from the disaster site the submarine *I-58* surfaced for the evening to take in air, but Commander Hashimoto was nervous. The radio intercepts were telling him that the area was now crawling with ships and planes heading to some sinking site. It was a certainty that some large ship had gone down.

He wondered if another Japanese submarine was operating in the same area without his knowledge. He couldn't think of any other reason for a big ship going down in that desolate area.

The position seemed to indicate it was close to where they'd sunk that big ship on Sunday night. Could it be . . . ? No, Hashimoto decided. A ship that big could never go unnoticed for almost a week.

At about that same time, in naval headquarters all over the western Pacific, many high-ranking and lesser figures in the U. S. Navy were thinking exactly the same thoughts.

Army Lieutenant Richard C. Alcorn was flying his PBY south of Peleliu when he received orders by radio to divert from his essentially routine patrol and join the rescuers far to the north. Alcorn was not at all connected with Admiral Buckmaster and had never even heard of the Navy commander but he was the victim of Buckmaster's "damn the red tape, full speed ahead" string-pulling. Alcorn headed north, set down at Peleliu for gas, survival gear, and a short briefing, which told him only the weather conditions and that a major ship had gone down in the middle of nowhere. Then he was airborne again by 1500. He reached the disaster area just at sunset, with enough light to see the extent of the disaster but not enough really to do him any good. He dropped what he could to those who looked most in need, spotted Marks's downed PBY, and got in contact with him.

"We've got real headaches," Marks told him. "I got men all over inside, I got men clinging to the wings and strut supports, and everywhere I taxi I find more and more. I'm off-balance, half blind now from dusk, and I'm taking on water." He warned the PBY that he'd had a rough landing in choppy seas and it was doubtful that he would take off again.

"How far off are the ships?" Alcorn asked.

"Hours yet," Marks responded in frustration. "They're still dying like flies here, too. I'm afraid we may lose half of them as it is. It's why I sat down. Even worse, there are sharks bigger than the last known world record out there."

That did it. "I'm coming in," Alcorn told him. "Give me information on the swells and a good place to land."

The wind had slowed to five knots but the swells were still eight to ten feet, not much lower than what Marks had had to contend with.

For a moment Alcorn had second thoughts. Not about his

plane—he was sure that what a Navy pilot could do he could do—but about where these men were in the darkness. He was terrified that he might run over somebody in the gathering darkness. He had no choice, he decided, but to go in. Still—the chance of death from him was against the odds, and the fact that these men were in desperate straits was clear.

He said, lightly, "Now I want you Navy men to witness this —this Army pilot's going to set down in one piece and take off again later."

And he did just that. There were some bad bangs but nothing cracked or popped. He was down, whole, and taking on no water at all.

He was afraid to taxi too far; he could still run over somebody. After a while the tail gunner dangled a rope on a line out the rear blister and had a strike—a lone seaman grabbed it and was pulled up and into the flying boat.

Alcorn cut his engines in the darkness, not daring to move farther, and now, in the distance, all around him, it seemed, he could hear men crying out for aid and rescue. It was frustrating but there wasn't a thing he or his crew could do but holler and hope somebody found them. Nobody did.

There was the sound of great engines in the semidarkness. It was so strange and so unreal a sound that, for several minutes, they didn't react. Suddenly, however, Lieutenant Marks and his PBY taxied into view.

The men up and down the line cheered as Marks cut the engines to their minimum and taxied past. The burly wrestling ensign and a couple of equally burly enlisted men were ready.

"The worst only!" they called. "Only those who can't stay a little longer on the line!"

It did very little good. Men were moving in a wave toward the plane and Marks finally had to kill the engines entirely to keep them from harm.

The PBY crew had to be strict. They were seemingly merciless enforcers, taking no one from the line or rafts and only lone swimmers who looked to be at death's door. Men, refused admittance or passed by, yelled, screamed, and cursed their rescuers, but Fargo realized that this unknown pilot was doing the right thing. Fargo used the opportunity to get into a recently vacated raft and lay down to wait for rescue.

When darkness set in two enlisted men on Marks's plane got out a raft of their own and went hunting beyond the line, looking for more lonely stragglers. They returned in about an hour with two more. Their water—a sixteen-gallon tank—was now completely dry from the dehydrated survivors, and fifty-six men in varying conditions clung all over the plane, some kicking in wings and supports. It was beginning to resemble an ambulance made out of swiss cheese.

Off by himself and feeling pretty useless, Lieutenant Alcorn flipped on his wing lights to guide men to him. Suddenly the sky started raining survival gear, crates, buoys, just about everything, and he quickly doused the lights. A flight of B-17s stocked with survival gear from Leyte had been flying over trying to spot the disaster site and had homed in on his plane. Another minute of that and they'd have sunk him, Alcorn thought nervously.

At 2130 the *Cecil J. Doyle,* captained by Graham Claytor, arrived in the disaster area. She had made twenty-four knots, faster than her manual said she could ever do, and now Claytor faced the same problem as Alcorn. Claytor couldn't see a damned thing in any direction and he was afraid he was going to run down some poor devil in the dark. He tried to imagine himself out there, alone, in the dark. Well, he was never much by the book anyway, he thought.

"Starboard searchlight on, aim ahead. All available men on lookout for survivors," he ordered. The light went on and men strained to see ahead in the darkness. "Port searchlight—aim straight up. Even if we can't get to 'em ourselves it'll tell the poor devils out there someplace that we're here."

The beacon rose like a fountain of light to the clouds, visible for sixty miles around, and it had its effect. Every survivor

of the sunken ship now had a sign, a tangible sign, that someone was out there. For the lone swimmers in particular, and
the ones in isolated rafts and tiny groups, it was the thing that
kept them alive.

The *Bassett* and the *Dufilho* arrived now, and closed in on
the *Doyle*'s searchlights. The commanders of both vessels
thought Claytor was nuts to do what he was doing and they
had no intention of following his lead. One skipper was still
certain that these were really Japs from a sub out there, trying
to lure in rescue ships so the sub could torpedo them, and he
said so on the radio. He'd heard tell of such things, and he
wasn't going to be suckered like it seemed half the Navy had
been.

The other captain agreed with the caution. He was sure at
this point that those were their men out there, not Japs, probably a squadron of B-29s that had missed their landing fields
and ditched as a group in the sea, but it would still be very
tempting for a Jap sub to use them to knock off several destroyers.

The *Dufilho*, however, saw no problems in coming up at an
angle and to the rear of the alit *Doyle;* they could use Claytor's lights while keeping out of them themselves, about eight
thousand yards or so.

"Survivor off the port bow!" one of the lookouts of the
Dufilho cried, and very soon the motorized whaleboat was off
for him. He proved to be the best off of all the lone swimmers,
having somehow concocted a raft out of life jackets that had
protected him from sharks, the worst of the sea, and even
offered a little sleep.

But before the whaleboat could even come about and return
to the *Dufilho* the destroyer escort's sonar reported, "Possible
sub contact! Nine hundred yards north-northeast of the ship!"

"I knew it!" the captain growled. He considered his course
for a moment, thinking that he might inadvertently blow up
some of the survivors, but finally decided his ship was more
important and, besides, there was Claytor over there all lit up

like Times Square on New Year's Eve. He got on the radio to
Claytor.

"I'm going to make a depth-charge run. Now will you put
out those damned lights?"

Claytor didn't try to dissuade him, although the action
worried him a great deal. But there were proven Americans
out there in bad shape.

"Make your run," he told the *Dufilho*. "But I'm staying lit."

Doc Haynes, Jim Fargo, and the others had watched the lights
of the *Doyle* approaching. Now, rescue confidently in sight,
they were all content to wait until the ship eased in.

Suddenly the sea erupted a few thousand yards from them.
They all looked unbelievingly in the direction of the explosions. "What the hell . . . ?" was all any could muster.

"That idiot's running a depth-charge pattern!" one of the
chiefs exclaimed disbelievingly. "I don't believe it!"

The *Doyle* came to a dead stop in the water while this was
going on and Claytor was waiting impatiently for the jumpy
Dufilho to finish her attack. He was fairly confident that there
was no sub out there. He'd found it hard to believe that, after
all this time, it wouldn't have been spotted by the Venturas, at
least, who were geared to look for such things. Still, the
Dufilho continued to lay her patterns for almost twenty minutes, terrifying the remaining survivors in the water, not to
mention Marks and Alcorn. Even the circling Venturas
couldn't believe what they were seeing. But they could do
nothing.

Finally it stopped and the sound man reported no contacts.

"The asshole probably got a contact on a great shark a few
hundred yards from him and took it to be a sub at greater
range," the chief with Haynes's party guessed. "They've scared
hell out of everybody and maybe killed a couple of good men
because that captain's never seen sharks as big as these," he
guessed.

"Don't judge him too harshly," someone else put in. "After

all, he probably doesn't know what he has here and his first job is to guard his ship."

"Yeah, look on the bright side," somebody else chipped in. "There sure as hell ain't no sharks within five miles of us by now."

Lieutenant Commander Claytor relaxed a little when the attack subsided, but his confidence was slightly shaken. What if there *were* a sub out there? He called the *Dufilho* and requested that it run a sound screen around him to give him some measure of protection, then headed on, slow, looking for survivors, lights still blazing.

"Radar contact—large—dead ahead!" came a shout. Claytor ordered full stop and put his own boat over the side. "Looks like we were right after all," he muttered. "Looks more like a plane than a ship from the blip."

He was right. It was a plane but not the B-29 they expected. It was Lieutenant Marks's PBY up against the floater nets.

The boat loaded as many as they could and took them quickly to the *Doyle*. A lonely, thin figure, looking swollen, browned, and almost wizened, climbed wearily aboard and, unlike the others, didn't head for sick bay but for the bridge.

Claytor turned and saw the grim figure. The man saluted and said, "Lieutenant Commander Haynes, sir, formerly chief surgeon of the U.S.S. *Indianapolis,* commanding officer of this survival brigade, reporting, sir!"

The men on the bridge all stood still in stunned silence for a moment.

"The—the *Indianapolis?*" Claytor managed, the full horror of the situation finally hitting home.

"This is all that's left of her," Haynes reported. "We've been in the water at least four days."

They rushed around him, helped him to a chair, which he accepted gratefully and sank down into with a feeling of indescribable relief.

"My cousin's married to Captain McVay," Claytor told the doctor. "Have you seen him?"

The doctor shook his head wearily. He looked and felt like a zombie. "No. I think I saw him briefly in the water just after the sinking but I haven't seen him since."

Like Marks before him, Claytor was instantly aware of the import and dimension of the tragedy he was now in the midst of. A heavy cruiser, twelve hundred men, more than four days in the water . . .

He summoned his communications officer. "Send this at once to Vice Admiral Murray, Commander, Marianas: We are picking up survivors of U.S.S. *Indianapolis* torpedoed and sunk Sunday night. Urgently request surface and air assistance. And make it secret and top priority," he added.

A few minutes passed and then the communications officer rang him back. "Sir, Guam says it'll be about an hour and a half on the Top-Priority waiting list before we can send. What shall I do?"

Cursing red tape and bureaucrats, Claytor replied, "Make it urgent." The slightly higher classification was used only in the most extreme cases, and if higher-ups, reviewing those messages later, thought the category had been abused, they could have a skipper's head. He wasn't worried about that one bit, not sitting out here with all these survivors all lit up like this. Not one bit.

He was going to shock every brass-hat bureaucrat in the Navy with this message and he knew it. That part he liked. Before the war, Graham Claytor had been an attorney in Washington, D.C.

The destroyer *Bassett* didn't reach the scene until 0130 the next morning. Unlike all of the other ships ordered to the scene this wasn't from CINCPAC, under Admiral Nimitz, but instead from Seventh Fleet—MacArthur's Navy, out of Leyte, a fleet so independent that the rest of the Navy considered it a third force in the Pacific, like themselves and the Japanese.

It was this total hostility between commands that left this

vital crossroads of two of the most heavily traveled shipping routes in the western Pacific totally unguarded and the nearest ships so far away. Neither navy talked much to the other one and this no-man's-land where the two commands met at the "chop" line was considered by each commander to be the other's responsibility.

The *Bassett*, under Lieutenant Commander Harold J. Theriault, was Commodore Gillette's representative to the proceedings. Back on Leyte there had been the growing suspicion that what was out here was a major ship but they wanted confirmation. Theriault knew none of this, of course, only that he was to radio Gillette personally no matter what the hour with the name of the ship that went down.

Like Claytor, Theriault was not very worried about enemy submarines, not with this much traffic around in particular, but he was very worried he'd miss or even run down shipwrecked men in the dark. He ordered both searchlights turned on and was stunned almost immediately to be awash in men crying out in the water for help. He had come up right in the middle of the surviving members of Lieutenant Commander Sarbic's party, minus the commander, of course.

Ensign Jack Broser, in charge of the rescue boat for the *Bassett*, was a lot more worried about those figures in the dark water than his skipper, and Broser meant to take no chances. They didn't look right and their voices had odd traces of a mushy accent. As the boat pulled close to Sarbic's remaining band, the ensign pulled his pistol and took aim at the nearest of the men. Burned brown by the merciless sun, swollen by the salt water and wind, the men looked like no other human beings he'd seen up to that time.

"Who are you?" Broser shouted suspiciously.

"We're from the *Indianapolis*," someone managed in reply.

Broser wasn't going to be taken in like that. They still sounded like Japs to him. Besides, they'd have known if something as big as the *Indy* had gone down. "C'mon! Quit your kidding!" he shouted back, raising the pistol for emphasis. "Who are you really?"

"The *Indianapolis! Indianapolis!*" the men called back insistently. "We were torpedoed Sunday night!"

The ensign was close enough now to see that they were in fact not Orientals and were in pitiful shape. He put his pistol away and he and his men started hauling the first of them aboard. He still didn't believe this stuff about the *Indianapolis,* though. Hell, if a heavy cruiser could go down and not be missed for almost five days, then what would happen to a destroyer?

The *Bassett* worked through the night, though, picking up men by the score as she moved slowly southward. The first sailors to reach her deck were all ambulance cases and Theriault went down to see them and to interrogate them personally. They were from the *Indianapolis,* all right; he understood and believed that at once and got an immediate message off to Gillette on Leyte. He listened for a while as the men were placed on cots, their terrible sores treated, glucose administered where necessary, and fresh water provided, all the time talking about their terrible ordeal. He noticed one man with what looked like gaping wounds and asked what they were.

"Fish bites," he was told by the corpsmen. "Shark, barracuda, you name it. They were so numb they never even felt them."

One young sailor put his hand up. "We never would have pulled through without Mr. Sarbic," he gasped. "He pushed us, bullied us, rallied us, kept us together and alive. We all owe everything to him."

"Where's Sarbic now?" the captain asked.

The young man shook his head sadly. "Just today—a big shark. A huge shark. He took it on with a penknife when it attacked. He—he saved us. But he didn't come up. Neither did the shark. By God, what a man he was, though! What a man . . ."

The *Doyle* and other ships continued to work through the night from the south while the *Bassett* worked the north. It was a monstrous, massive job. The dead were piled high on the decks, many of them horrible to look at. Occasionally they'd find only skeletal remains, or parts of bodies eaten away by sharks; it was grim, gruesome work.

But there were survivors, too. Amazingly, there were survivors amid this carnage. Tales of horror and heroism were the order of the day.

At the northernmost extremity of the oil slick was Captain McVay and his line of rafts. Throughout the evening they'd seen the planes, knew discovery was at hand, and had at first been content to wait for the inevitable pickup. They saw the great spotlight to the south go on, indicating that at least one surface ship was also in the area. It cheered them for a while until McVay noticed that the great spotlight and the circling planes seemed to be heading ever southward, away from his position.

Finally he and his men hauled up a 40mm ammo can and set it up in the rearmost raft. McVay fired his Very pistol into a mass of garbage and debris in the bottom of the can, starting a blaring smudge pot they were certain could be seen for miles and most particularly from the air. They kept it going into the early hours of the new day without result, though; the ships and planes seemed to be going farther and farther away, and a sense of gloom settled over all of them.

They became terrified that the searchers were going to miss them.

The *Bassett* was having all sorts of problems with some of the survivors. One fellow sat atop a mountain of piled-up floats and life preservers and refused to come aboard because he was waiting for a friend. Another apparently whole sailor refused to walk on deck because "a shark got my leg." He had to be convinced that nothing of the sort had occurred, finally sighing and saying, "Oh, all right," and walking down to sick bay.

Some of these men would recover completely; some would have physical disabilities the rest of their lives. For a few their minds would never again be quite right. It was a miracle that it was only a few.

By morning when everybody could see what they were doing it became a much easier matter to pick up the rest. All the ships were there, now, and there was a great deal of swapping of medical personnel and supplies as the grim job continued. Lieutenant Commander Meyer, captain of the *Ringness,* had been picking up survivors right and left since it arrived on the scene from almost due north. At 1020 hours on Friday, August 3, the lookouts sighted a string of four rafts, and the ship put about to go after them.

Meyer hadn't actually known what he was going after until he was almost on the rafts, though, and he might have missed them in the rising sea but his radar operator had reported a small blip in this direction and he'd set out to find it.

Nobody had seen McVay's smudge pot, but his big can had reflected radar beams and saved him anyway.

The nineteen men on the raft cheered when they saw the destroyer bearing down on them. In minutes they were aboard and Captain McVay was warmly shaking hands with Meyer and got on the radio himself to talk to the other ships.

It was bad; not as bad as he'd first feared but certainly bad enough to qualify as the worst sea disaster in American naval history.

By the time the destroyers had picked up the last of the survivors, cleared away or sunk the last of the debris, and, sadly, watched as the *Doyle* fired on and scuttled the now abandoned PBY of Lieutenant Marks, it was late afternoon and they put about, some for Guam, most for Peleliu, and the obstinately independent *Bassett* for Leyte. For the survivors the horror was over, except the scars they would carry both on their bodies and on their souls.

Captain Oates met McVay on the beach at Peleliu and put

his arm around the surviving commander affectionately. They had known each other a long, long time.

Finally McVay asked, quietly, "What's the total?"

Oates paused and sighed. "We've lost a couple since the pickup, and one or two more are almost sure goners," he said honestly. "Charlie, I'd say you'll have three hundred sixteen survivors, give or take one or two, when it's all said and done."

McVay stopped and seemed a bit stooped, for the first time seeming to be in worse shape than he appeared. "Three hundred sixteen," he repeated softly. Three hundred and sixteen out of eleven hundred and ninety-nine.

"How many officers?" he asked his old friend. McVay knew almost all his officers well, the senior ones for many, many years. He knew their wives, their kids. They were like family.

Oates hesitated. "The truth?" he asked hesitantly.

"The truth," McVay told him.

"You remember that little mimeographed sheet they tacked up all over the ship showing the chain of command?" Oates began hesitantly.

McVay nodded.

"Well, between you and the next surviving officer there are thirty dead men, Charlie. I'm sorry."

McVay shook his head in wonderment. Joe Flynn, Janney, Casey Moore—their faces flashed in his mind. Gone. All gone.

Together the two captains walked up the beach toward the operations building.

On Sunday, August 5, Captain McVay met the press. After telling his own tale of survival and giving credit to his ship and men somebody asked the key question.

"Captain, how was it nobody knew you were missing? What would be the normal time before you'd be reported overdue?"

"That's a question I'd like to ask someone," McVay responded. "We were to be thirty miles off Homonhon at 0600 Tuesday morning. We'd asked for plane services so we could

have gunnery practice. If the plane didn't intercept, that probably wouldn't have caused suspicion, since they might have
thought they missed us, but we were due at anchorage at
1100. I should think that by noon or 1300 they would have
started to worry. A ship that size practically runs on a train
schedule.

"I should think by noon they would have started to call by
radio to find out where we were, or if something was wrong.
So far as I know, nothing was started until Thursday. This is
something I want to ask somebody myself. Why didn't this get
out sooner? Maybe it did. I don't know. I don't believe Rear
Admiral Buckmaster knew we were missing until Thursday."

A check showed that the *Indianapolis* hadn't radioed about
planes—at least it was never received at Leyte. Jim Fargo, who
was in the base hospital and moving between sleep and coma
and back again, could have told him why messages didn't get
out from the ship, but he didn't know about the interview.

In fact, no one did. The grip of total secrecy came down on
the entire *Indianapolis* affair. No news stories that went in got
printed. War censorship was invoked. The orders routing the
survivors were classified Top Secret, every one. Over on Leyte,
when the big hospital proved not secure enough for Naval Security personnel, the survivors were moved unless there was an
imminent threat to life to a smaller, more obscure, and more
easily secured hospital.

August continued. The men were moved to a hospital ship
and it was arranged for all survivors who needed medical help
to be consolidated on that one vessel for transport home.

A couple of days out and they were in Guam to consolidate
the Leyte survivors with the others. At that time a young, hard-
looking Navy commander came aboard and sought out Jim
Fargo.

"I'm Nelson, ONI," he introduced himself. "Some Army
bigwig named Withers wants to know why you haven't filed
your report yet."

Aftermath

As the *Indianapolis* survivors, Fargo included, were being prepared for embarkation on the hospital ship *Tranquility* for Guam, two planes had already taken off from Tinian airstrip heading north to Japan. A third plane had preceded them to their destination and was now starting back to Tinian with weather and flak information.

Captain William Parsons, in one of the B-29s, was the same man who had supervised the *Indianapolis* loading at Hunter's Point, then taken off for an aircraft observation of the Trinity bomb. Now he had the trickiest part of all: The bomb the *Indianapolis* had brought to Tinian was beneath his fingers. In the air over the Pacific the mysterious canister's contents was lowered into the contents of the mysterious crate and the atomic bomb was armed.

Clocks all over Hiroshima, Japan, the beautiful city on the Inland Sea from which the Imperial Japanese Fleet had sailed almost five years earlier for Pearl Harbor, and the same port from which Lieutenant Commander Mochitsura Hashimoto had sailed twenty days before for his fatal encounter with the heavy cruiser, was to have all its clocks stopped at 0815 on 6 August 1945.

The next day, panicked into premature action by the fear that they would have no voice in ending the war in the Pacific if they did not immediately get in it, the Soviet Union declared war on Japan.

On 9 August 1945 a second bomb was dropped on Nagasaki, the "insurance" bomb sent by other means.

Newspapers were full of the news of the atomic bomb. Word reached the *Tranquility,* where the survivors of the *Indianapolis* finally found out what the mysterious cargo was and how it'd been used. Most were very proud that the old girl had gone out in glory, her final mission instrumental in the end of the war. There were some, though, who wondered aloud whether or not the security that had been placed on the bomb was the reason nobody knew they were missing.

Jim Fargo knew that it was at least partially at fault. He suspected it was entirely at fault. He was wrong.

In papers and radio broadcasts filled with atomic-bomb stories and tales of the Russians moving in Manchuria, Korea, and elsewhere, there was not one word about the sinking of the U.S.S. *Indianapolis,* not one word that 883 lives had been lost in the worst sea disaster in history.

But Admiral Spruance, who toured the hospital ship, talked emotionally to the men he knew. The few chiefs and junior officers who'd served on her when he'd been aboard were warmly embraced and a tearful admiral left determined to know why the hell this had happened.

He was a fighting admiral with an emotional stake in the case. Like Buckmaster, it never occurred to him that the Navy wasn't really as concerned about why it had happened as it was determined to defuse the bomb that ticked slowly beneath the highest levels of naval command. They could keep it quiet for a while, even start issuing orders and directives to fill the obvious holes in naval regulations, but the war was coming to too swift an end, and with the end of the war would come the end of censorship. Then the families of 883 men would join the 316 survivors in demanding an accounting.

Naval Security and Intelligence did the best they could. They released the story on V-J Day, hoping that it would be buried on the inside pages or overlooked. The effort failed. On a day filled with end-of-the-war headlines, the *Indianapolis* news was there.

A Naval Board of Inquiry was quickly established and all commands in the western Pacific area were summoned and told to be sure to bring the officer in each command who had been responsible for keeping track of combatant ships. This confused most of the innocent commands, many of whom were already consolidating, moving, or disbanding with the end of the war. Hell, everybody knew that it was against U. S. Navy policy to keep track of combatant ships, always had been. So the operations officer was sent at least to tell them what they already knew. It did not seem to have occurred to any of the commands that the order for such nonexistent officers was deliberate and that the admirals on the Board knew that no such position existed. Hell, they, the men who sat on the Board, had drafted those very regulations.

The orders should have read, "Pick a scapegoat."

Testimony went on and on, all top secret. It was classified in such a way that it would never become public. Never. Not even the men called knew what was being discussed or what any of the others had said. None of the operations officers were even notified that, in a sense, they were on trial. The healthiest of the *Indianapolis* survivors, from McVay to Haynes to Fargo to loadmaster "Big Ed" Brown, were called.

The newspapers demanded explanations. The families of the dead demanded explanations, particularly when visited by survivors who told them their sons or husbands might have

lived had rescue come on Tuesday or even Wednesday. Public
pressure was building.

The Board charged Captain McVay with dereliction of duty
leading to the sinking of a ship in wartime and decided to
court-martial him. Letters of reprimand and censure were
placed in the files of all the operations officers and even Commodore Gillette.

To try McVay they chose Captain Thomas J. Ryan, Jr.,
Congressional Medal of Honor winner, nationally known
hero, and ambitious would-be politician. There was to be a
public court-martial, in November, at the Washington Navy
Yard.

Preparation was precise. Ryan had no stomach for this trial
and knew exactly why McVay was to be the only skipper to
lose a ship in World War II to be so tried. Ryan went over the
case again and again, feeling foolish but knowing he had to go
through with it, knowing what higher-ups in powerful positions wanted and had to have. Alienating those kinds of people
would kill a political career fast. Doing them a favor would
help enormously. Still, he had every hope and conviction that,
with a public trial, McVay would be acquitted. He need only
do the best prosecuting he could on these trumped-up charges
and watch, convinced that no Navy court-martial board would
convict one of their own after going through what McVay did.

But in order to avoid a charge of slacking, he had to be 100
percent thorough. He had to make sure that, if he lost, it could
not be said that he hadn't done his best.

"Jim?"

"Yes, sir?"

"I want you to have somebody take a deposition from Hashimoto."

The commander's eyebrows shot up. *"Hashimoto?* Why, for
God's sake?"

"Weather, mostly," Ryan told him. "I want the man who
sank the ship to tell us in a formal deposition that he saw the
ship at a distance of two miles or more, as he must have if

these records are right. If he could see the ship that far away clearly enough to shoot, that would mean that visibility was good, not poor, as McVay says, and weather overall nearly perfect—and that means the *Indianapolis* should have been zigzagging. See?"

Commander James Bronson was skeptical. "I don't know. Oh sure, the reason's O.K., but there'll be all hell breaking loose if we have a Jap commander testifying against one of our own. Hell, the parents and wives of those 883 dead would string up the little son-of-a-bitch.

"Sure is a hell of a way to treat a man who's gone through hell and done a damn fine job for his country, though. I'm glad I'm getting out of this chicken-shit service in March."

Ryan nodded sadly. "Me too, Jim. Me too. . . ."

Mochitsura Hashimoto had been forgotten in the peace that followed the surrender and that was the way he wanted it. He'd done his job to the best of his ability, he was sure, and his ship and crew had done nothing dishonorable either to themselves or to the Emperor. He was bitter about the outcome, particularly the malfunctioning *kaitens,* which had killed so many fine young men with so little result, and at Combined Fleet stupidity, which had ill used their superior submarines from the start. But he'd done his best, brought his ship and crew home, and now he had a wife and two wonderful children suffering because of the economic collapse. His duty and honor now required him to devote himself entirely to them. The Emperor no longer required his services.

The arrival of the young American naval officer came as a complete surprise. More Occupation nonsense, more red tape, Hashimoto grumbled to himself as he went to the door.

"Commander Hashimoto?" the man asked pleasantly. His Japanese was flawless.

"No longer a commander," he replied a little sadly. "Haven't you heard? There is no Imperial Japanese Navy anymore."

There was the faintest trace of a smile on the American's face as he appreciated the irony of the other's tones. "I've been requested to escort you down to the local Occupation commander's office," he told the Japanese.

Hashimoto was surprised. "Why? What is this all about?"

"Please just come with me. This shouldn't take very long," the other responded without telling him anything.

Hashimoto shrugged resignedly. "Very well. Just let me inform my wife and change into something more presentable."

The officer waited while the former sub commander did so. In truth, the American had no more idea of the reason for all this than did Hashimoto. He certainly looked neither dangerous nor sinister. If he was even suspected of anything criminal he'd have been arrested by a squad of Marines.

They drove in silence, Hashimoto realizing that there would be no answers to this until they reached their destination, a former Japanese Army barracks now under the control of the United States. He was ushered past some secretaries and clerks and into a small but comfortable office and instructed to sit and wait.

Finally a Navy man entered with a small briefcase under his arm and took a seat opposite Hashimoto. A full commander, the Japanese noted. A few moments later the lieutenant who'd picked him up also entered, probably as translator, and the Japanese decided not to tell them that he knew and understood English quite well. Less chance of anything being mistranslated—and he might hear more than they wanted.

The newcomer took out a pack of cigarettes and offered Hashimoto one. He declined, growing more than a little impatient with all this.

Finally the new man said, "You are Mochitsura Hashimoto, formerly lieutenant commander, I.J.N., commander of the submarine *I-58?*"

Hashimoto waited for the translation, then simply nodded and said, *"Hai,"* almost under his breath. What the devil was all this?

"In that capacity," the commander continued, "you sank on or about 30 July 1945 the heavy cruiser U.S.S. *Indianapolis?*"

His surprise was obvious but he nodded. It was his proudest accomplishment in a career that went all the way back to Pearl Harbor, although he was sorry in hindsight to have cost so many lives when the war was already lost. Still, he had been at war and it was a legitimate act of war. He said as much to his inquisitor.

Commander Bronson leaned back in his chair. "Commander, what was the weather like on that date?"

The questions went on like that, on and on and on. They had his logbook but still they checked and double-checked. All of the questions concerned details. Was the ship zigzagging?

"No."

"Would it have made any difference if it had been?"

"Not a bit." Like most sub commanders he was convinced that zigzagging was the stupidest tactic in the book. It never had saved a vessel, since the turning radius of any capital ship was too slow and wide to matter, and in a number of cases, including Japanese ones, ships that had been outdistancing pursuing subs had zigzagged and therefore slowed just enough to be hit.

Finally Bronson was just about through. He sighed, signed the provisional transcript, had the translator and Hashimoto sign, then sent it off to be typed formally outside. They only had to wait, now, for the formal, typed copies to come in, sign them, and that would be that. Bronson was thinking only of the trip home to a much colder Washington and dreading all of it. What a waste, he thought, even though McVay was charged with failing to zigzag and his defense of bad weather had been mostly contradicted. Here was hard evidence, yes, but it was kind of like having a murder committed in a busy intersection and only charging the victim with jaywalking.

Still, as they waited for the hard copy, Bronson decided to ask the commander about a couple of things that puzzled him.

"Just out of curiosity," he said, "there's been something

puzzling me about this sinking and maybe you can clear it up."

Hashimoto nodded politely.

"The Japanese Navy," Bronson continued, "never did much with its submarines. Never. We did—we even snuck into Tokyo Bay and tried to nab not only your big warships but also sink your freighters, break your supply lines. It was our use of subs against supply lines and your lack of a convoy system that was the most telling against Japan."

"I agree with you on that," Hashimoto responded. "There was no glory in sinking a freighter." And that's just why we lost, he thought. We went for glory and they went for guns, ammo, and food.

"Now, at your stage of the war, there were only four of the big long-range I-class subs left, right? With an obvious show-down coming up in the impending invasion of the home islands where a sub might do some real damage, and with big military ships of the line just sitting out there south of the home islands on picket duty ready for the torpedoing, you are sent out, with another of the four subs, and directed to a point far south of the real Forward Area, a backwater of the war, as it were, to wait on the off chance you'd run into something. Why? Why not go for the sure targets up north that were hurting your country? It doesn't make sense."

It was Hashimoto's turn to look surprised. "Why, I was told to make for that route not only because it was the point where two main routes converged but also because I was specifically told to look for a large capital ship that was to be heading west to Leyte carrying some sort of monster secret weapon to use against Japan. We were told to find that ship and sink it at all costs."

Bronson blanched, and even the translator seemed momentarily stunned as he managed the English version.

"You mean," Bronson almost gasped, "that you *knew* the Indianapolis was carrying the atomic bomb?"

It was the Japanese's turn to look thunderstruck. "So *that* is what it was!" He shook his head in wonder. "And I got it just *after* it dropped the thing off! Of course! I see it now! It had been assumed that any such weapon would be placed in General MacArthur's hands, not Admiral Nimitz's! Incredible! How history might have been changed had I been told to intercept *east* of Guam!" His voice trailed off in deep thought at the possibilities.

Bronson recovered sufficiently to dip back into his briefcase and thumb through the old transcripts and records once again. Something was nagging at him and at last he knew what it was.

"You didn't know it was the *Indianapolis*," he noted accusingly. "You reported sinking a battleship of the *Idaho* class."

"That is true," Hashimoto acknowledged. "You see, the *Idaho* was known to be off Guam—it had been for a while. No one told me which ship to look for, only that it would be a major ship of the line, and, at night, of course, and with that odd silhouette, I made the obvious but wrong assumption."

Unfortunately, that sounded logical to Bronson. "Who gave you this information and when?" he pressed.

Hashimoto shrugged. "I received very nebulous sailing orders from command. We had some trouble in the trials and I had to return to the *kaiten* base to get them straightened out and it was there the commanding officer told me this. What you tell me now explains much, as I had the same doubts and questions as you."

Bronson whistled softly. He didn't have to spell out what this meant—the Japanese had known in advance that the atomic bomb was on the way, down to the logical ships and probable routes it would take. They were sure enough to gamble two of their four remaining subs to nail her. They'd made only the very logical mistake of which command was to get it.

The security had been tight, so much so that even Truman had been President over a week before they told him about the bomb. The Japanese had no real spies in the United States. Hell, they'd even locked up the American-born Japs in camps.

The Germans were even worse spies than the Japs after the war started.

And yet, somehow, Hashimoto was telling him that there had been a leak, a leak so specific that it told the sub commander just where to be to catch that specific ship. It smelled of treason, nasty treason, by someone within either the Manhattan Project or the Navy. By someone probably still in place.

Bronson made a snap decision. This was too much for him to handle alone. He'd do what all good officers do in moments of extreme doubt and indecision—pass the buck.

"Commander," he said, "I want you to come with me to Washington and tell that story again."

Hashimoto was startled. "Washington! But I cannot! The war has already cost me much and kept me too long away from my family. I have responsibilities!"

Bronson cut him short. "We'll see that your family is well taken care of while you're away. Mr. Singer, here, will take you home to pack and collect your things. You'll not be under arrest but you will be well protected."

It might not be an arrest, the Japanese thought sourly, but it sure looked and felt like one.

Captain Ryan put down the phone and shook his head in wonder. An aide saw his face, and, fearing that some family tragedy had struck, asked, concerned, "Trouble, sir?"

Ryan shook his head more in wonder than in reply. "That stupid son-of-a-bitch," he swore. He looked straight at the aide. "That was Bronson. He's got Hashimoto *here*—in Washington!"

The aide, a young ensign so new he'd missed the war, saw the problem immediately. "There'll be holy hell to pay when this hits the fan," he noted needlessly. "The papers'll love it. Why did he *do* it?"

Ryan shrugged. "I have no idea. He said he couldn't talk about it on the phone. We'll know sooner or later. I expect he'll be around as soon as he checks Hashimoto in at the Navy

Yard." He looked longingly, questioningly at heaven. "Why me? Why me? Particularly now?"

But Commander Bronson didn't make it to Ryan that evening. As Bronson entered the base they were waiting for him—and "they" included a lot of people he recognized from the front pages and some he didn't know at all. These included four Army officers, the lowest-ranking of which was a full colonel; two civilians with FBI written all over their nice white shirts; and a two-star rear admiral.

Hashimoto, too, was impressed by this array, although he still didn't understand just why he was here.

The interviewing started comfortably in a private conference room near the SP barracks; everything was relaxed and fairly friendly, even to some catered small sandwiches and pastries. Only one man, one of the civilians, stared at him as if he were a horrible demon.

Although junior to most of the others in rank, it was Houlton Withers who took charge of the questioning. "Commander, you understand that we are not particularly interested in your nationality, your career, or anything else about you. We are only interested in your information on the *Indianapolis*."

Carefully, completely, he asked the same questions as Bronson and got the same replies. The conclusion was inescapable—there had been a breach, and every man there knew it.

"When was your ship ordered out of its base?" Withers pressed.

"July 16," was the reply.

"And when were you told of this big ship with a super weapon?"

"July 18. As I said, we'd been forced to return for repairs."

And there it was. Hashimoto had sailed the very day the ship had sailed from Hunter's Point, the very day the bomb had been tested near Alamogordo, without specific orders. But two days later his instructions had been very specific indeed. This totally eliminated the possibility of a leak aboard the *In-*

dianapolis, perhaps from some of the passengers put off at Pearl. The leak was prior to Hawaii.

That got a very thin, old-looking Jim Fargo off the hook and he relaxed a bit more as the inquisition continued. He kept staring at the little man in the chair and thinking, "This is the man who sent me to hell."

Hashimoto named the officer, they checked dispatches to Hirao, checked officer lists, and there was considerable muttering. The *kaiten* commander had taken his own life on the day of the surrender. The signatories on the dispatch to him from Imperial Headquarters were also dead.

"Commander, nothing you or we have said must ever leave this room," Withers told him. "From this point on you received no such information, you had no foreknowledge, it was just a freak chance thing you ran into the *Indianapolis.* And I don't mean just for the next few days, weeks, months, or even years. I mean *period.* Your name is already popping up all over the place here, and I can tell you you're not very well liked in this country. Newsmen may try to get to see you, and while we'll try to shield you from them they are often very resourceful. You will say nothing. Even if you write your bloody memoirs you will say nothing of this."

Hashimoto started feeling real fear for the first time since this began. He understood now that he held what the Americans called a "hot potato" in his hands. These men—high-ranking officers all, still on the way up—had obviously had the bomb's security entrusted to them. No matter that it would start a witch-hunt for the hidden spies and, he well knew from experience in his own armed forces, a lot of careers would be ruined. The fact that they were actually court-martialing the captain of the ill-fated ship showed the level of scapegoating and cover-up being done here. Were this to get out it would spread far beyond this captain and some other officers. There would be a purge, perhaps, in which all those charged with security might well wind up in a dock with McVay—*these* men, he realized uneasily. These very men in this room.

He felt acutely uncomfortable. You're not a prisoner, they'd told him, yet those guards were there to protect him from the American people. The war might be over but anti-Japanese feeling was still running high. All these men had to do to kill him was hand him a plane ticket, announce it to the papers, and tell him to get out of here. He knew it and didn't like it one bit. Clearly the politics of the American armed services were as intense and nasty as they'd been in his homeland.

"You have my word on it," he assured them sincerely. "You are currently occupying my country. It is a defeated nation. I have a wife, children, a strong set of reasons for not wishing to become involved in anything controversial."

That satisfied most of them but not Withers, whose brigadier's star was pending. He had a big, bright future in which nothing was beyond his grasp, but the fall could be quick and severe. Look at McVay.

"Commander," he said hesitantly, trying to get the words just right, "Occupation won't be forever and we're not old or stupid men. Just bringing you here has made front-page news. You will have to testify at McVay's court-martial now. You'll be a celebrity—the man who sunk the *Indianapolis*. Americans will hate your guts; your own countrymen will push you up a notch in the pantheon of military heroes. You'll be a public figure, not forgotten. In time they'll come to your house to interview you, there'll be offers to do a book—I've already seen this sort of thing not only here but in your own country as well. Pardon my bluntness, but your nation is defeated, disillusioned, demoralized, and cynical at this point and they'll need heroes—something to believe in—and your leaders will create them." He smiled grimly. "You used *kaitens* on the *Indianapolis,* didn't you?"

The abrupt change startled the Japanese. "Well, yes, I launched them but they didn't do any good. I finally had to use conventional torpedoes. That whole *kaiten* program was a mistake. They never worked right."

Withers nodded satisfactorily. "You are aware of the impending war-crimes trials?"

Hashimoto felt a little indignant. "What would that have to do with me? I committed no such acts!"

"General Homma had no knowledge of the Bataan Death March," Withers pointed out, "and tried to stop it when he learned of it. Yet he will be tried for it, convicted for it, and hanged for it. The same with Yamashita and the Manila massacres." He paused a moment. "Do you understand why Captain McVay is being tried? A major ship was lost. Eight hundred and eighty-three men were lost, and even the survivors will suffer. One, Mr. Fargo over there, is in this room right now."

Hashimoto glanced over at the gaunt figure in mixed sorrow and amazement.

"Parents, wives, children hold others responsible for that. The public requires that someone take the responsibility for that loss," Withers pointed out.

Hashimoto just nodded. He understood now. In the Imperial Navy a captain went down with his ship—or, if there was a good reason why he didn't, he was expected to apologize to the Emperor as soon as possible by committing *seppuku*. Good generals had died in such a manner on long-forgotten islands, taking their lives even though they'd fought as well as any man could. Somebody had to take the responsibility for a loss; it was a Japanese tradition. The Americans were following the same principle here. They were doing it less bloodily but, in a sense, causing more shame and suffering. The Japanese way was best, he decided. Better death than what Captain McVay and his family must be suffering now.

"Commander," Withers went on, "in the waning days of the war the *kamikaze* took a great many lives. These young men were literally anxious to die for their cause and country. You know this well, for the *kaiten* is an outgrowth of the *kamikaze* idea. You know that these programs were opposed when first proposed even in Japan. To die in battle, yes; to take your

chances, yes. But not even in Japan was there any tradition
that said men must kill themselves in this manner. And all of
those involved in setting up the *kaiten* program have now died
or committed suicide themselves. There's no one to try for it,
Commander. No one except the four surviving sub commanders who used them."

Hashimoto thought only of his wife and children and his
homeland so far away. "So you will try me, and silence me in
this way?"

"You misunderstand, Commander," the rear admiral put in.
"That would not be in our best interest, either. Too much
could come out at such a trial. The colonel is not threatening,
he is bargaining."

"There's no statute of limitations on war crimes," Withers
pointed out. "A lot of Germans we badly wanted have slipped
away, for example. But the agreements cover Japan as well.
You could be charged a year from now, ten, twenty. Say, if
certain information should ever come out on a certain matter."

Now he understood clearly and it was all he could do to re-
tain his composure. There was something funny, in an ironic
sort of way, about all this. Here they were, the winners in a
long and bitter struggle whose commands now controlled his
country and plotted his people's lives and futures—all of them
nervously bargaining with a minor and insignificant former
officer of the defeated nation. His face remained impassive but
inwardly he was grinning from ear to ear. Despite the threats it
was now clear that these were frightened men, and he was not
the blackmailed but the blackmailer.

"I did not record the *kaiten* attack on the *Indianapolis* in
my log," he told them. "Instead I claimed that we'd sunk a
couple of ships with them a few days later. It seemed better to
tell families their pilots had died meaningfully instead of being
blown up in an empty sea. All right, sirs. No foreknowledge,
no responsibility."

Most of the men smiled.

Withers glanced at Bronson. "I'll talk to you about this

later. In the meantime, neither you nor the commander, here, will discuss this with Captain Ryan. This meeting never existed. I'll talk to him myself—tell him that Hashimoto was brought here to discuss a classified matter and that, since the investigation is still pending on it, we'll need a cover story, which will be Hashimoto's testimony."

Bronson nodded. He was leaving the service shortly to set up a law practice and he fully understood the business he could expect if he kept his mouth shut. Making waves wasn't worth it. He wanted to be rich and successful and you didn't get that way by breaking confidences.

"We'll talk about the weather that night," he suggested. "And the zigzagging. And that'll be that."

Even Hashimoto smiled at that one and hardly anybody noticed he hadn't waited for a translation.

Jim Fargo and Harvey Cameron walked out of the building and into the crisp night air. After almost four months Fargo still had nightmares, and would off and on for the rest of his life. He had nasty lesions from the saltwater ulcers, permanent scars that would forever remind him of the ordeal. His handsome youthfulness was gone, too. He looked old and very tired.

"I think I'm going to be sick," he said to Cameron.

"What could you do, Jim?" the other man asked fatalistically. "Do you blow the whistle on them? It won't stop it, just transfer it to a different set of little men in high places."

Fargo nodded glumly. "I know, I know. I had that explained to me in explicit detail. Keep quiet and, sure, they'll convict McVay, but of something minor and with no real sentence. A year or two from now, when things have quieted down, they'll quietly overturn it, send him the Bronze Star he deserves, then allow him to retire as a rear admiral. But they could crucify him, too, with the same verdict. Put him in jail for years, strip him of rank, ruin him. So just keep quiet and be a good boy," he added mockingly, then spit.

"They've called a nationwide press conference, you know," Cameron told him. "NBC, CBS, Mutual—everybody. They're going to read the names of all the commanders the Board of Inquiry reprimanded."

"The sons-of-bitches," the younger man muttered.

"You better believe it. How'd you like to be retired from the service, puttering around in your yard or something and suddenly get the blame for eight hundred eighty-three deaths?"

They were silent for a while. Finally, Fargo said, "What gets me is that we can't even blow the whistle. There's no way we can do anything without making it worse for the innocents. Nothing."

"That's why they're where they are," Cameron replied philosophically. "And that's the true history of the world, Jimmy my boy. What bothers me is not that they're doing this but that they're the ones who have inherited the Earth."

"Maybe they've always owned it," Fargo responded sadly. "How would we ever know?"

The two men walked out into the waiting night. "Chilly, isn't it?" one said.

The other nodded. "Yeah, as soon as my divorce comes through I'm heading out of here. They've given me my choice of assignments, you know."

"Oh? Where you going?"

"Well, I kind of took a liking to San Francisco. . . ."

Viktor Lemotov was met at the plane when it touched down in Moscow. He knew the look of such men; the same kind of look he once had. His old friend Bukovsky was with them. Lemotov stepped down the last few stairs from the plane and shook hands with his old comrade warmly.

Bukovsky's face was anything but reassuring. "Viktor, I come on this dark night with a sad mission," he said hesitantly.

Lemotov suddenly felt the Russian winter grow deeper and his smile faded from his face.

"The Secretary blew his top when the Americans an-

nounced the atom bomb," the old comrade explained. "He
wanted to know how the hell a project the size of Manhattan
could have gone on without him knowing about it. He blames
you."

Lemotov was stunned. "But—Nicolai! I *sent* all that information! He refused to listen to it, refused to believe it—but I
sent him facts, figures, names, places, dates, and confirmation
earlier this year. I even tried to stop its delivery—damn near
succeeded, too. If the Old Man doesn't know this it is hardly
my fault!"

Bukovsky smiled grimly and there was an air of apology in
his tone. "Yes, your reports arrived, Viktor. They went to
Beria, who you must know has his eye on replacing our be-
loved leader when he should pass on. Beria was the one who
broached the subject with Stalin first—and got a tirade in
reply. He made a terrible error, it is true—but Stalin convinced
Beria not to pass on any more reports. You see, he can't admit
his mistake to anyone, even himself. You know how he is,
Viktor. How they both are. They want heads. It can't be Uncle
Joe's, of course, for he's the leader. It can't be Beria, for he
has too high a position. And that leaves you. You're the only
logical choice, Viktor. I'm sorry."

Lemotov nodded sadly and patted his old friend on the
back. It was starting to snow now, harder and harder. "I understand, old friend. I really do." He looked across the tarmac
and saw a grim black limousine. Four nasty-looking men in
overcoats lounged against it. He sighed. "Yes, somebody has
to take the responsibility."

They walked off slowly into the dark, toward the sinister
black car.

Historical Note

On November 29, 1945, Captain Charles McVay was formally charged with negligence. There were two counts: first, that he failed to zigzag in clear weather, and, second, that he failed to order "abandon ship" when he should have in order to allow a proper evacuation. An early ruling from the chief trials judge specifically limited all testimony to these two questions and no other. Absolutely none of the heroism nor the question of why nobody missed them was allowed to intrude. Several of the survivors were less than generous to the captain, covering their own backs. Oddly, it was Hashimoto's testimony that proved most important to the defense. When asked whether or not it would have made a bit of difference if McVay had been zigzagging under those conditions, he responded that it would not. His appearance, which was never explained, outraged press and public and even most naval officers, many of whom suddenly became unsure as to which side had won the war.

Not only Captain Ryan but the press as well believed that there could be no verdict but innocent. All were stunned when, on December 19, 1945, the court-martial found McVay innocent of the abandon-ship charge but guilty of failing to zigzag and therefore causing his vessel to be sunk. All testimony was to the contrary, but it was clear at this point that there was a railroad process going on that exceeded anyone's imagination. McVay thus became the only skipper of a U.S. combat vessel in the whole of World War II to be tried, let alone convicted, for being sunk.

The public and press outcry was tremendous. The con job was simply too blatant, too transparent. Survivors, talking to the kin of those who'd been lost in those four terrible days as well as to the press, made it clear that McVay was more hero than anything else. But he was lowered to the bottom of the promotion list, and his career was effectively ended. All members of the court, the judges and Ryan included, also appended a clemency plea. They were ashamed of themselves.

McVay's old commanders, starting with Spruance, also urged that the verdict be overturned during the Navy's automatic appeal process. McVay himself did not fight it, although he understood what had gone into it. He knew he'd never get another cruiser, never become an admiral, and decided that, if they wanted one man to take the blame, it was in the best interest of all concerned. He had nothing personally to regret or be ashamed of.

The Navy, however, was very uneasy. The weakness was that the top rungs in the appeals ladder were occupied by the very admirals who had created the situation with their standing orders. If McVay wasn't guilty, then they most assuredly were—and with the families of over eight hundred dead servicemen and an anxious press and public wanting to know the truth, that was not permissible. It *was* decided, however, that McVay should not be penalized so heavily, and they remitted his sentence, which would allow him to retire, at least, with the rank of rear admiral. They also awarded him the Bronze Star for Valor. McVay retired in 1949, and refused all offers to write his own memoirs, a loyal Navy man to the day he died.

This action mollified the public, who saw the captain as a scapegoat, but left a problem. If McVay couldn't be blamed, and if the commanders whose own mistakes had created the gaping hole into which the *Indianapolis* had sailed and sunk couldn't be blamed—then who would be fed to the public and press as the men who really killed their loved ones?

The inspector general's office continued its own inquiry, increasingly under pressure since they wanted to forestall a threatened Congressional probe that might show the wrong people to blame. Somebody had to be trotted out, and fast. They held large numbers of "off the record" interviews with all sorts of people involved, no matter how peripherally, in the incident. The men talked freely; they hadn't been charged with anything, and most were now out of the service anyway.

On Saturday, February 23, 1946, the U. S. Navy held a public press conference to which the entire Washington press corps was invited. A long statement was read that officially put the Navy's version on record.

Stuart Gibson, no longer in the Navy, was puttering in his garden outside his Richmond, Virginia, home, the radio playing in the background, when suddenly the news came on and he heard, to his amazement, his own name. Over the radio networks, and in every newspaper in the country, the U. S. Navy said that the entire fault for the *Indianapolis* disaster was that of Jules Sancho, port director at Tacloban in the Philippines, where the *Indianapolis* was due, and his aide, Stuart B. Gibson, for not noticing that the ship did not appear on schedule, and Commodore Norman C. Gillette and his chief of staff, Alfred N. Granum, in command of the Philippine Sea Frontier at that time, for failing to issue procedural orders that would have made the loss impossible!

Nothing further was offered, and since this press conference did not come out of a normal legal proceeding and was, in fact, just a press conference, there was no way to check out the Navy version or question it. All decisions leading up to it were verbal, or by memo later carefully destroyed, as had been the records of initial inquiry hearings shortly after the rescue. With all documentation destroyed or sanitized, these four men, very minor cogs, were publicly branded without prior warning to the entire American public as the men who were responsible for all the misery and deaths.

All four men were furious. Even their friends and neighbors believed the Navy, and there was absolutely no way to fight it. Except for letters of reprimand in their files there had been no legal proceedings whatsoever. They had been accused, tried, and convicted by press conference—and no court recognized that as grounds for appeal. But appeal they did, fighting the reprimands, and, when all had blown over, the Navy very quietly, on direct orders of Secretary of the Navy Forrestal, on December 9, 1946, sent each man a letter stating that their letters of reprimand had been pulled and all allegations dropped. The Navy did not hold a press conference, and none except the four men and the Secretary of the Navy knew the action had taken place.

Lieutenant Commander Hashimoto wrote his memoirs, *Sunk*, which became a best seller in Japan, parts of Europe, and enjoyed great success in the United States. His account of the sinking of the *Indianapolis*, which doesn't make sense to submarine officers, began the chain of logic that led to the ideas proposed in the plot of this book.

Acknowledgments

This book is the product of a lot of people's hard work and time. Certainly it wouldn't have come about if Hugh O'Neill at Doubleday hadn't liked the idea and been extremely helpful and cooperative throughout, demonstrating more patience than could be reasonably expected. Also, of course, thanks should go to Eleanor Wood for talking him into handing me the assignment. I found it fascinating and rewarding to do. Special thanks must go to Frank Olynyk, naval historian *par excellence*, who, when told of this project in a conversation, immediately loaded me down with every book, magazine, and historical writing on this tragedy and to boot gave me the names and addresses of just about everybody in the Navy, past and present, who could fill in the blanks. Since little on the *Indianapolis* is available through normal channels (something I hope will change if this book meets with any success), I can literally say that it would have been nearly impossible to do without him. My thanks, too, to my wife, Eva, for patience in the writing of the thing and for being my first-line editor and copy reader and chief constructive critic. As for the rest—the list is too long to thank everyone individually, but let this be a collective thanks from a writer who felt privileged to get this project and fascinated by its history and implications.

Manchester, Maryland
January 12, 1980
JACK L. CHALKER